The Good Neighbors

WHAT HAS COME BEFORE

When **Rue Silver** was a little girl, she saw daffodils bowing their flowered heads to her ethereal and strange mother, **Nia**. As she got older, Rue decided that even if she couldn't stop *being* crazy, she could stop *seeming* crazy like Nia. If Rue sees vines growing over buildings in a single night or people with animal faces, she simply ignores them.

When Rue's mother disappears after a loud argument with Rue's father, **Thaddeus**, Rue tries to ignore that, too. But then **Sarasa**, a girl at the university where Thaddeus teaches, is found dead. The police become convinced that Thaddeus murdered both his wife and Sarasa.

As Rue tries to figure out what actually happened, her grandfather, **Aubrey**, shows up. Not only does he seem not to have aged since her parents' wedding, but neither does his young servant, **Tam**. Rue comes to realize that Aubrey is one of the "good neighbors," faeries, and that he means to take over the city by encasing it in vines.

Rue also uncovers the fact that Thaddeus won Nia for his bride after passing a test. As with all faery bargains, there was a price: If Thaddeus was ever unfaithful, Nia would have to leave him. The night she disappeared, he'd had an affair with his friend **Amanda**.

Aubrey sends a changeling to pose as Nia. She is meant to sicken and die, so that no one will look for Nia anymore, but Rue sees through the trick. She and her friends dig up the body . . . and find a creature made of sticks.

Rue's mother has disappeared again. . . .

the Good Neighbors

BY

HOLLY BLACK
& TED NAIFEH

book two
KITH

New York Toronto London Auckland Sydney Mexico City New Delhi Hong Kong

This book was originally published in hardcover by Graphix in 2009.

ISBN 978-0-439-85566-2

10 9 8 7 6 5 4 3 2 1   10 11 12 13 14

First Scholastic paperback printing, October 2010
"Good Neighbors" title lettering by Jessica Hische
Lettering by John Green
Edited by David Levithan
Book design by Phil Falco
Creative Director: David Saylor
Printed in the U.S.A.   23

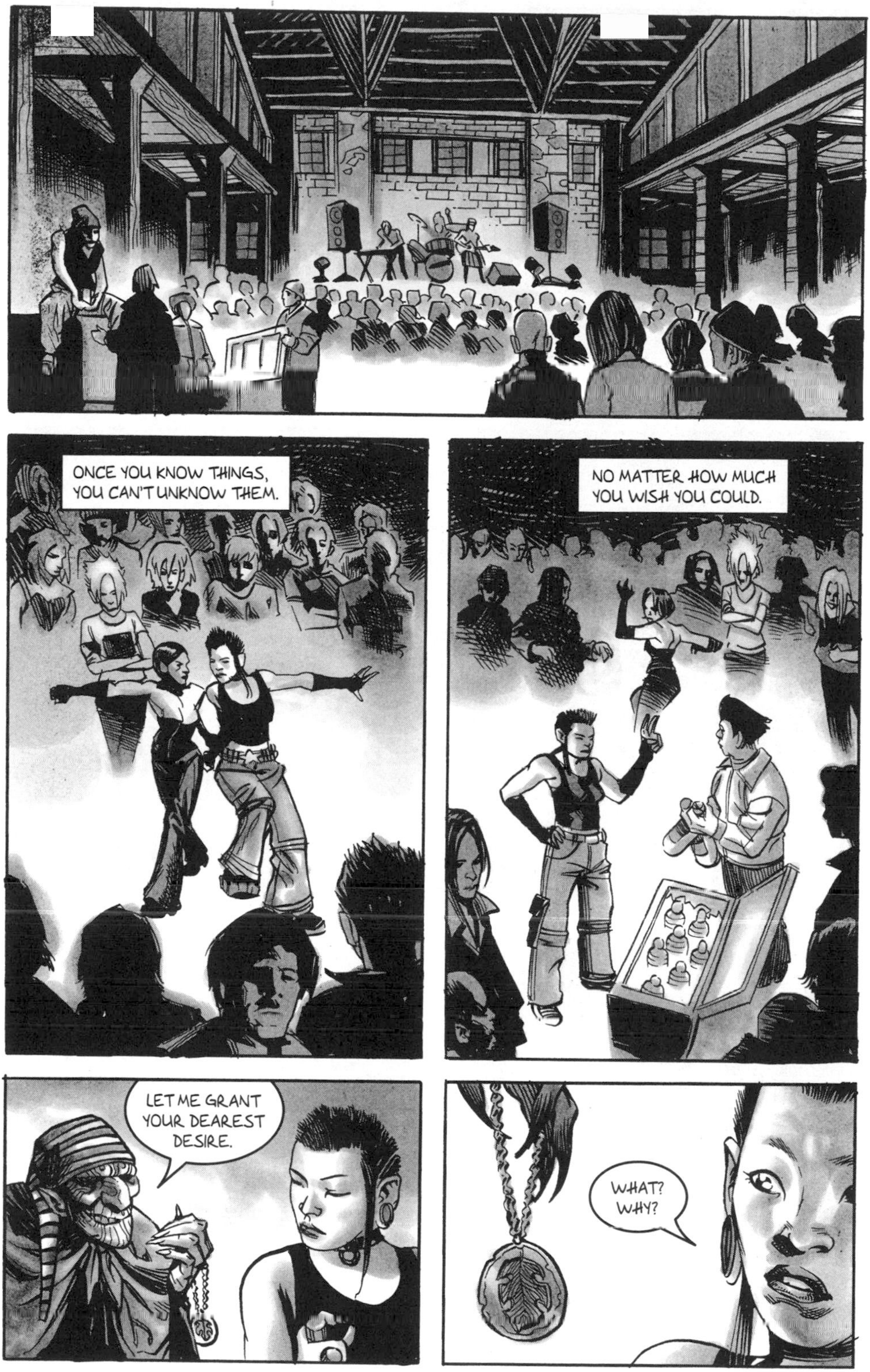
ONCE YOU KNOW THINGS, YOU CAN'T UNKNOW THEM.
NO MATTER HOW MUCH YOU WISH YOU COULD.
LET ME GRANT YOUR DEAREST DESIRE.
WHAT? WHY?

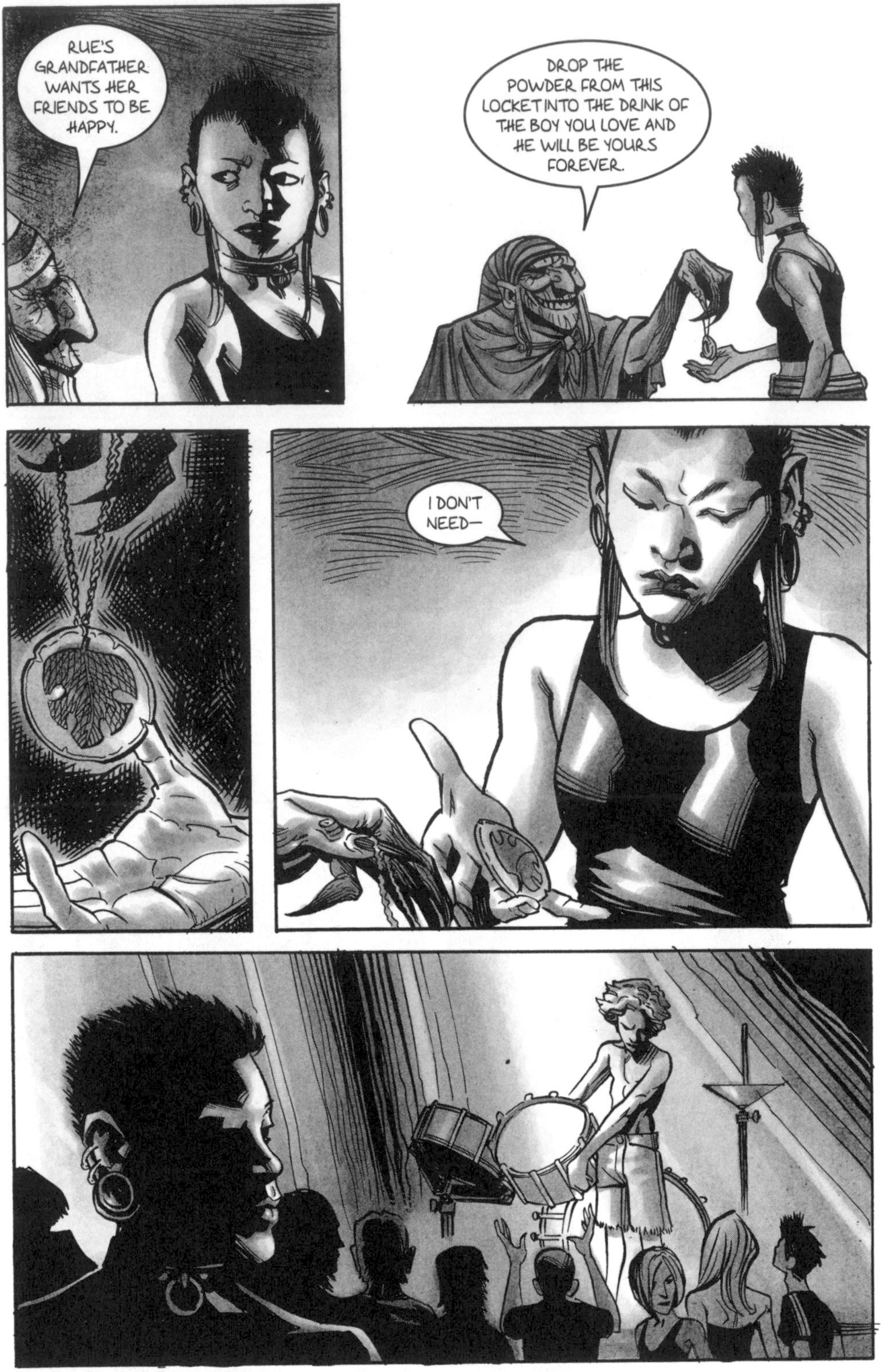
RUE'S GRANDFATHER WANTS HER FRIENDS TO BE HAPPY.
DROP THE POWDER FROM THIS LOCKET INTO THE DRINK OF THE BOY YOU LOVE AND HE WILL BE YOURS FOREVER.
I DON'T NEED—

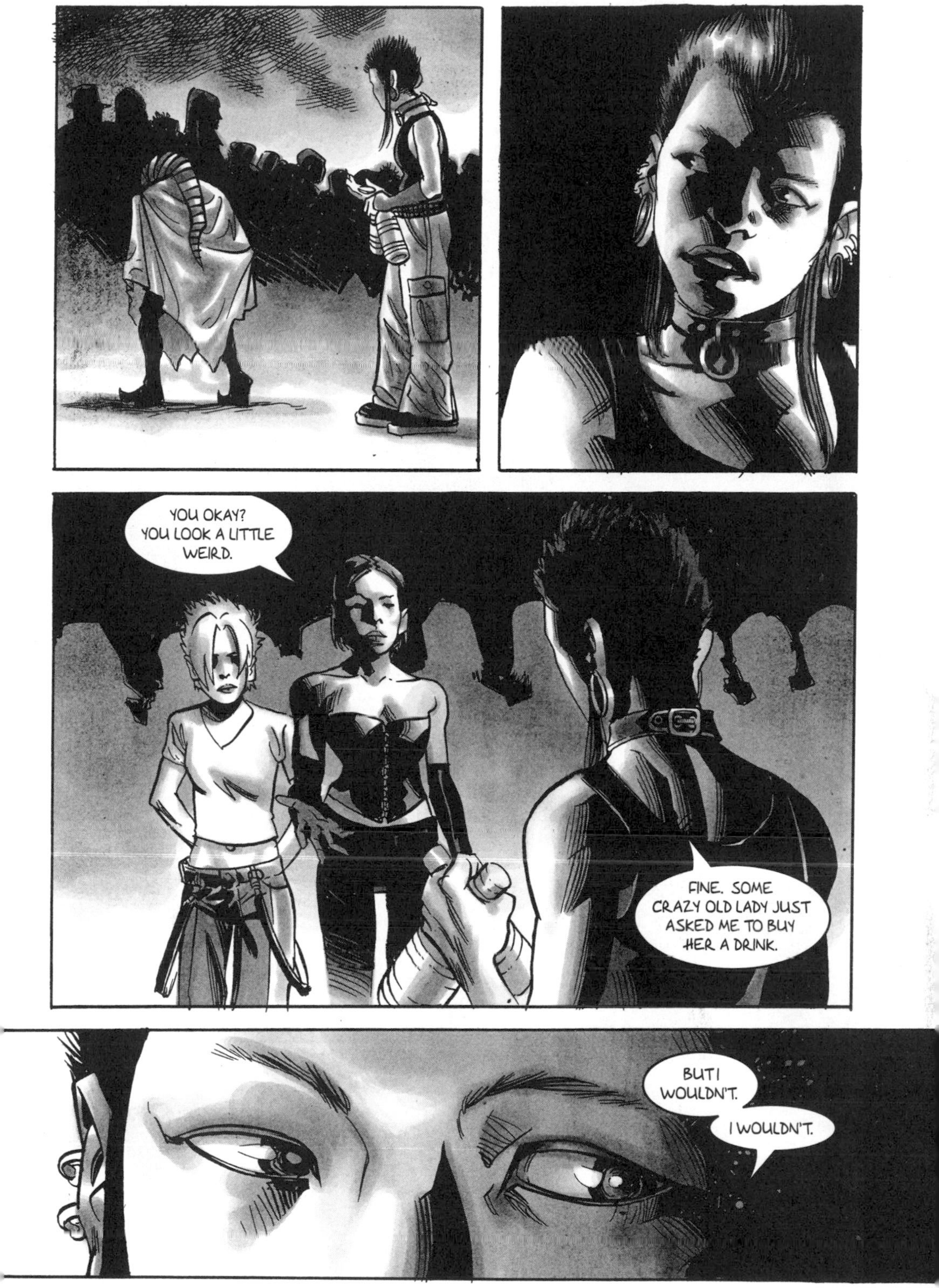
YOU OKAY? YOU LOOK A LITTLE WEIRD.
FINE. SOME CRAZY OLD LADY JUST ASKED ME TO BUY HER A DRINK.
BUT I WOULDN'T.
I WOULDN'T.

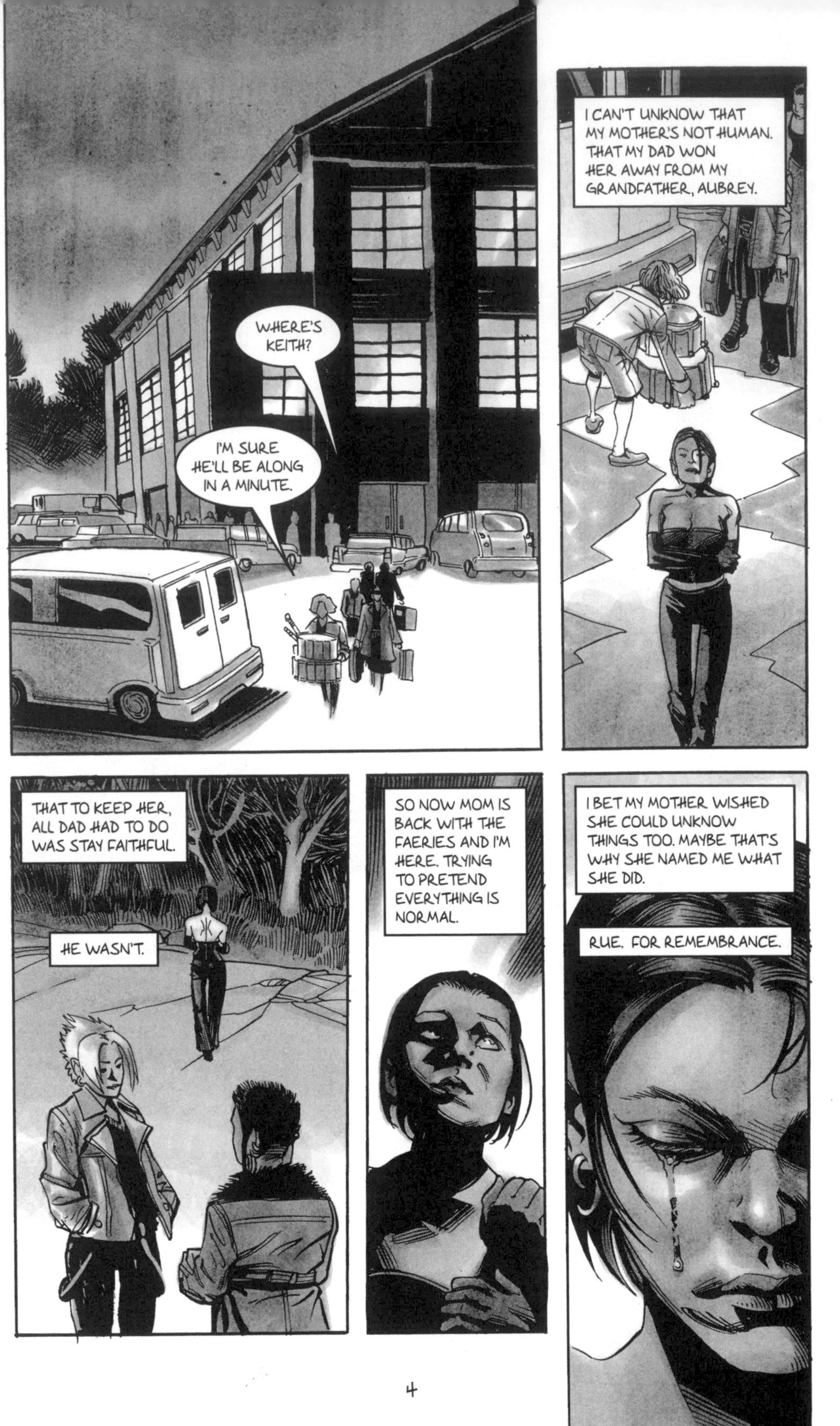
WHERE'S KEITH?
I'M SURE HE'LL BE ALONG IN A MINUTE.
I CAN'T UNKNOW THAT MY MOTHER'S NOT HUMAN. THAT MY DAD WON HER AWAY FROM MY GRANDFATHER, AUBREY.
THAT TO KEEP HER, ALL DAD HAD TO DO WAS STAY FAITHFUL.
HE WASN'T.
SO NOW MOM IS BACK WITH THE FAERIES AND I'M HERE. TRYING TO PRETEND EVERYTHING IS NORMAL.
I BET MY MOTHER WISHED SHE COULD UNKNOW THINGS TOO. MAYBE THAT'S WHY SHE NAMED ME WHAT SHE DID.
RUE. FOR REMEMBRANCE.

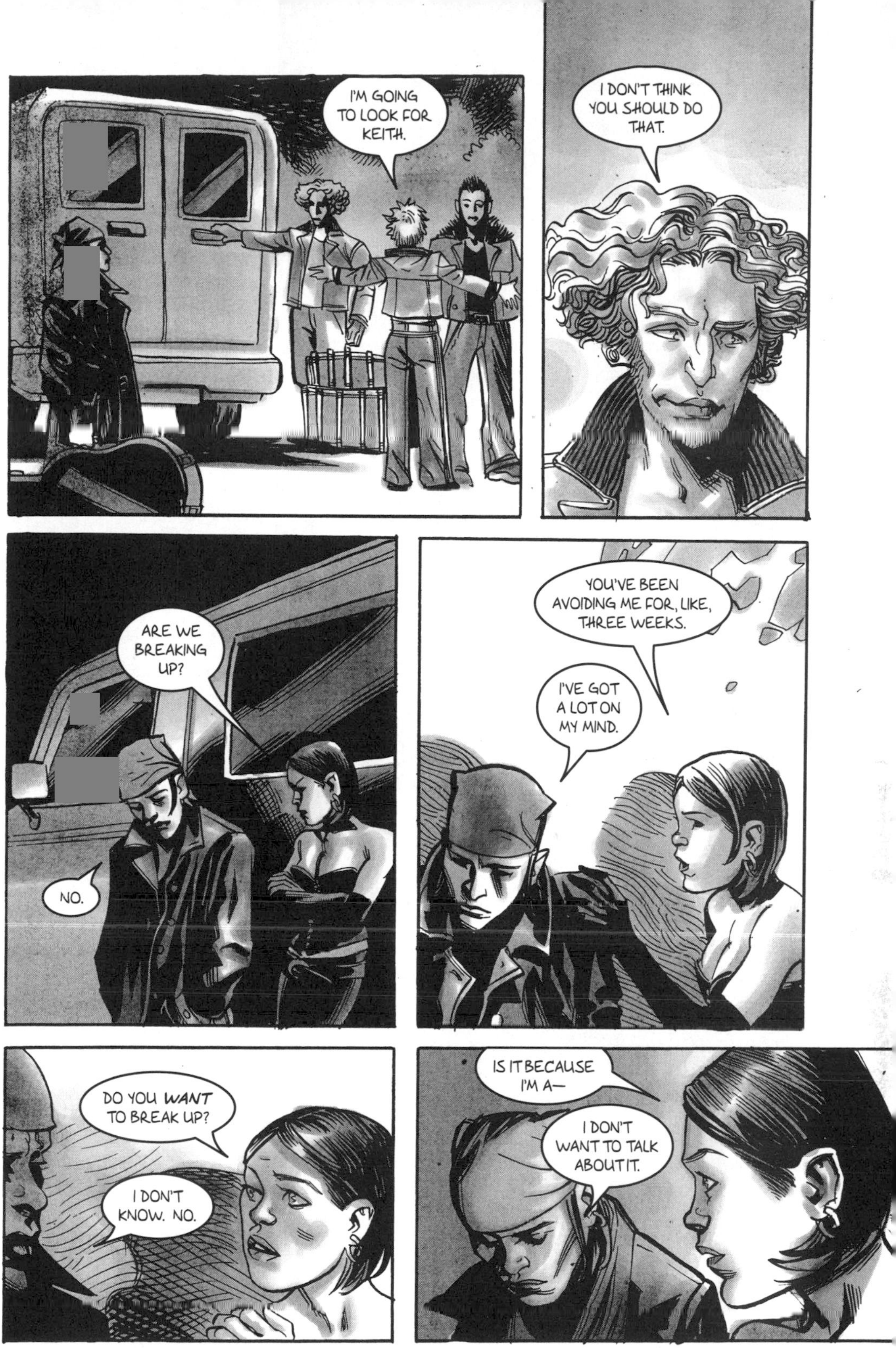

I'M GOING TO LOOK FOR KEITH.
I DON'T THINK YOU SHOULD DO THAT.
ARE WE BREAKING UP?
NO.
YOU'VE BEEN AVOIDING ME FOR, LIKE, THREE WEEKS.
I'VE GOT A LOT ON MY MIND.
DO YOU *WANT* TO BREAK UP?
I DON'T KNOW. NO.
IS IT BECAUSE I'M A—
I DON'T WANT TO TALK ABOUT IT.

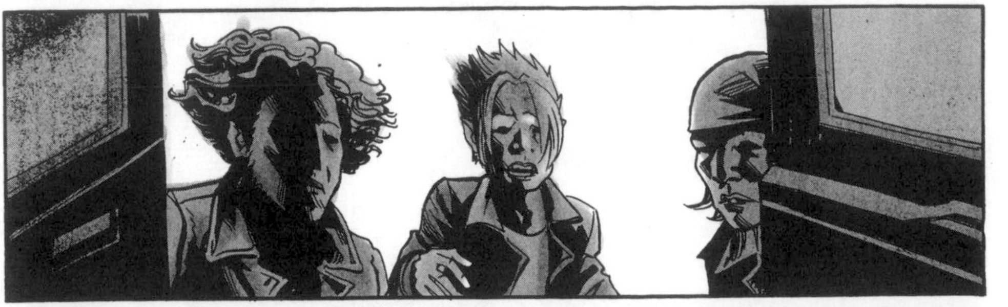

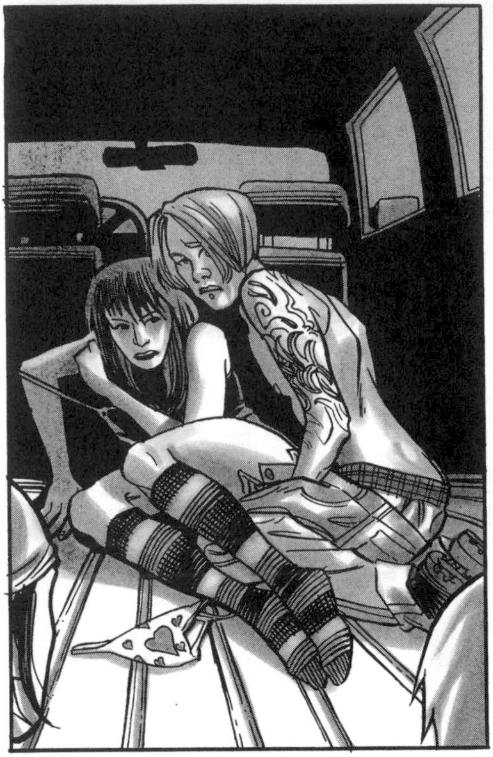

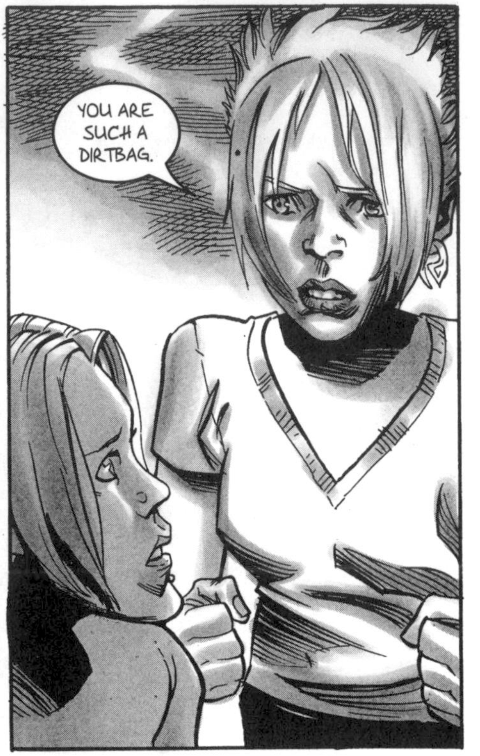
YOU ARE SUCH A DIRTBAG.

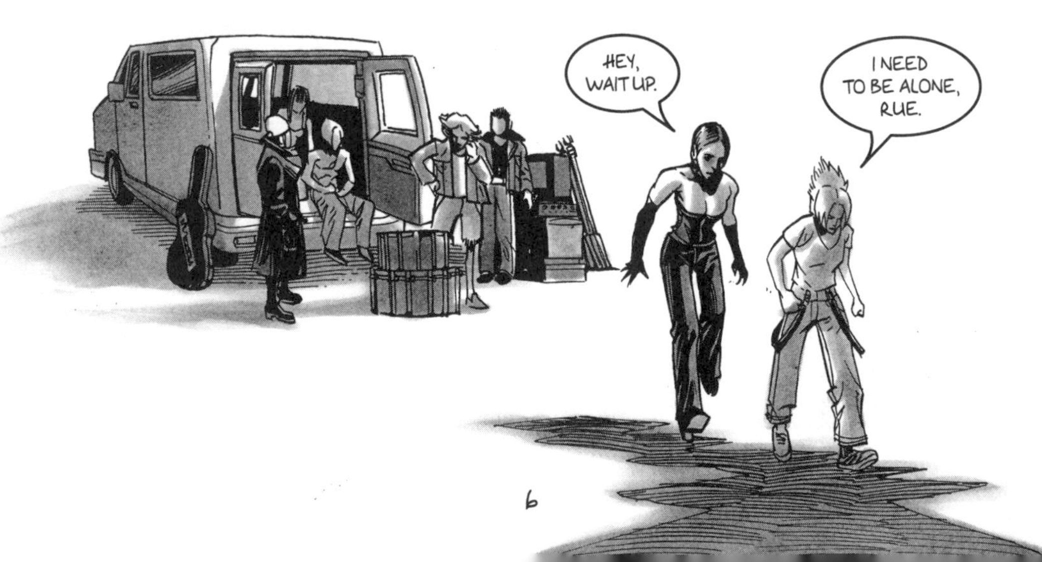
HEY, WAIT UP.
I NEED TO BE ALONE, RUE.

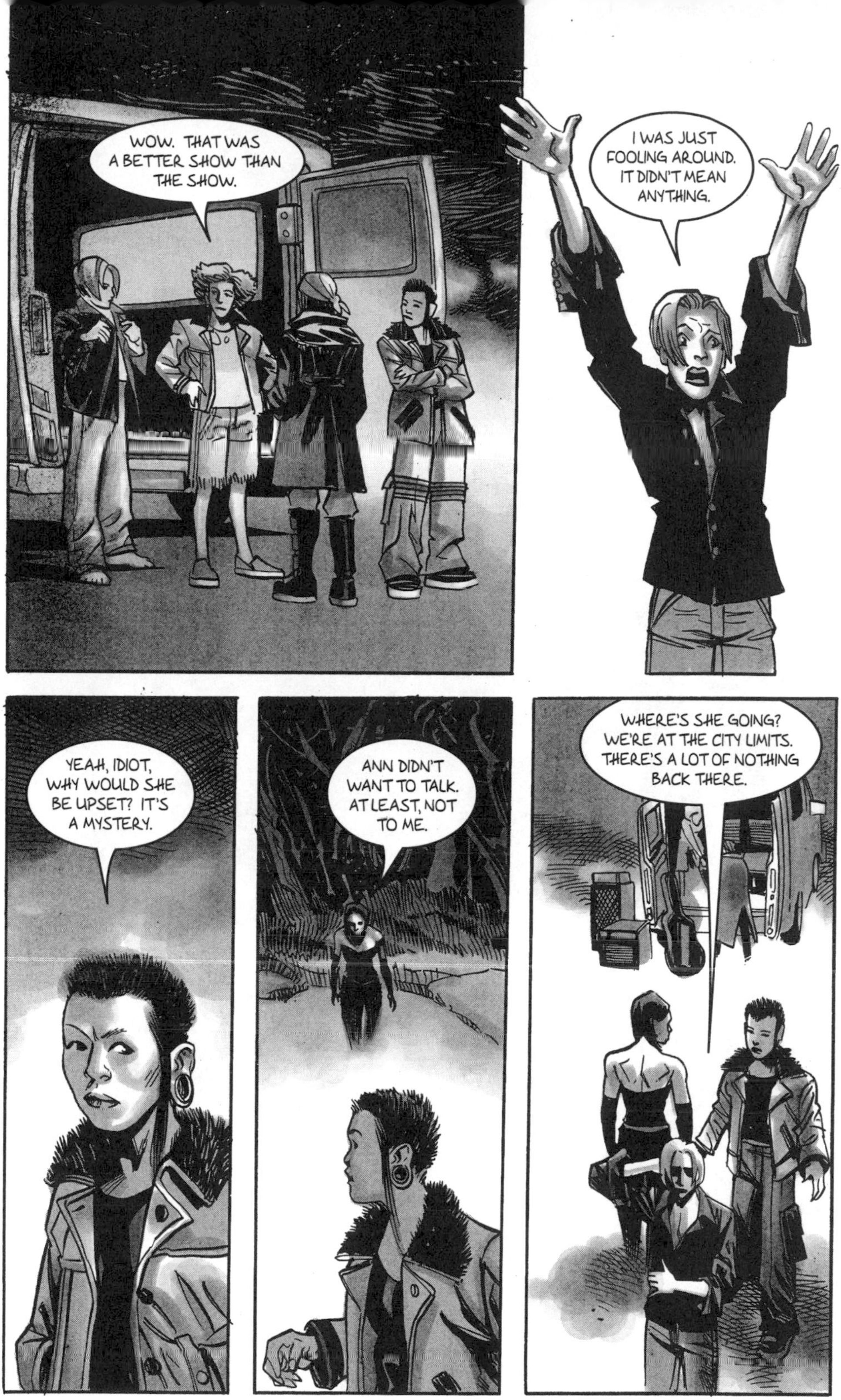
WOW. THAT WAS A BETTER SHOW THAN THE SHOW.
I WAS JUST FOOLING AROUND. IT DIDN'T MEAN ANYTHING.
YEAH, IDIOT, WHY WOULD SHE BE UPSET? IT'S A MYSTERY.
ANN DIDN'T WANT TO TALK. AT LEAST, NOT TO ME.
WHERE'S SHE GOING? WE'RE AT THE CITY LIMITS. THERE'S A LOT OF NOTHING BACK THERE.

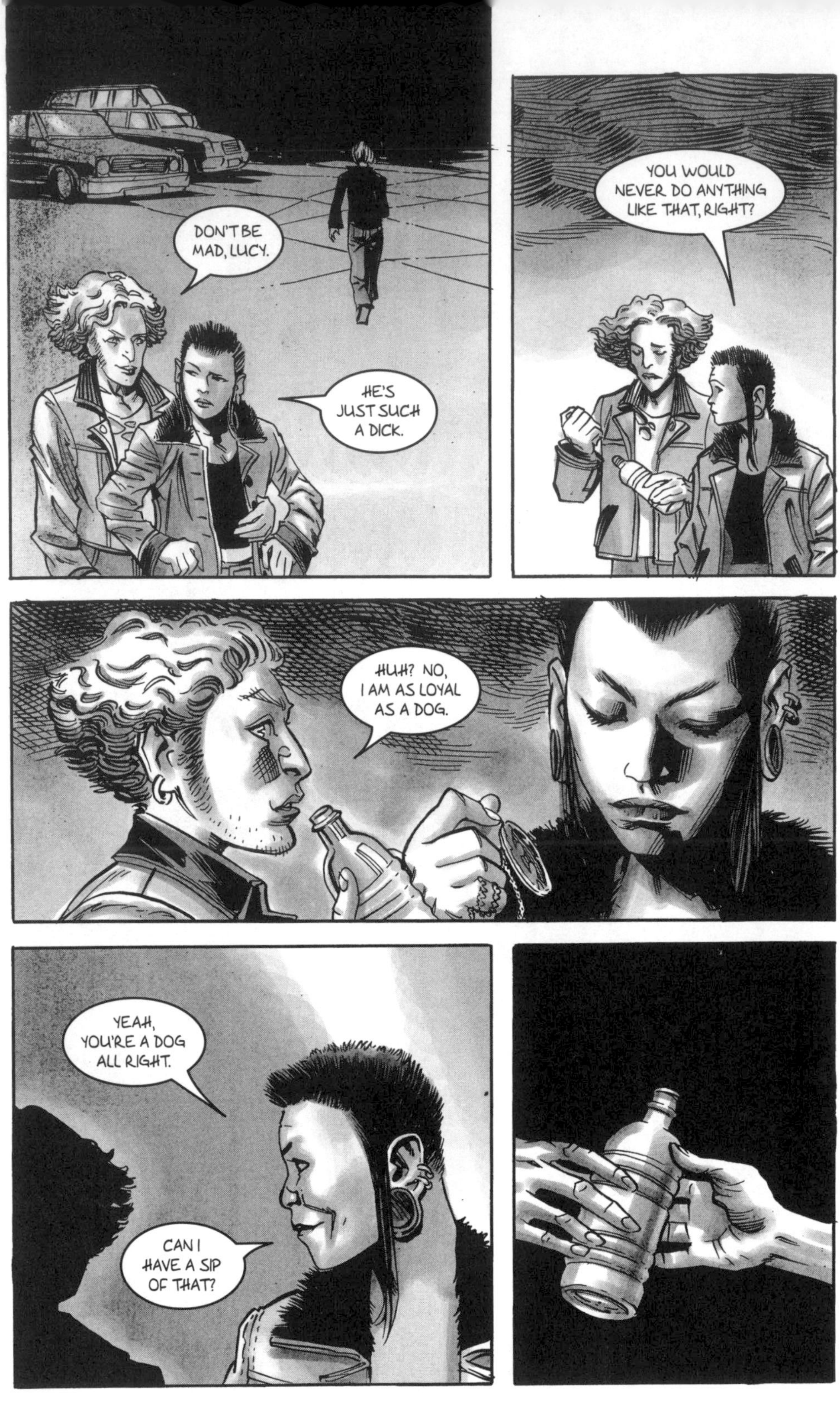
DON'T BE MAD, LUCY.
HE'S JUST SUCH A DICK.
YOU WOULD NEVER DO ANYTHING LIKE THAT, RIGHT?
HUH? NO, I AM AS LOYAL AS A DOG.
YEAH, YOU'RE A DOG ALL RIGHT.
CAN I HAVE A SIP OF THAT?

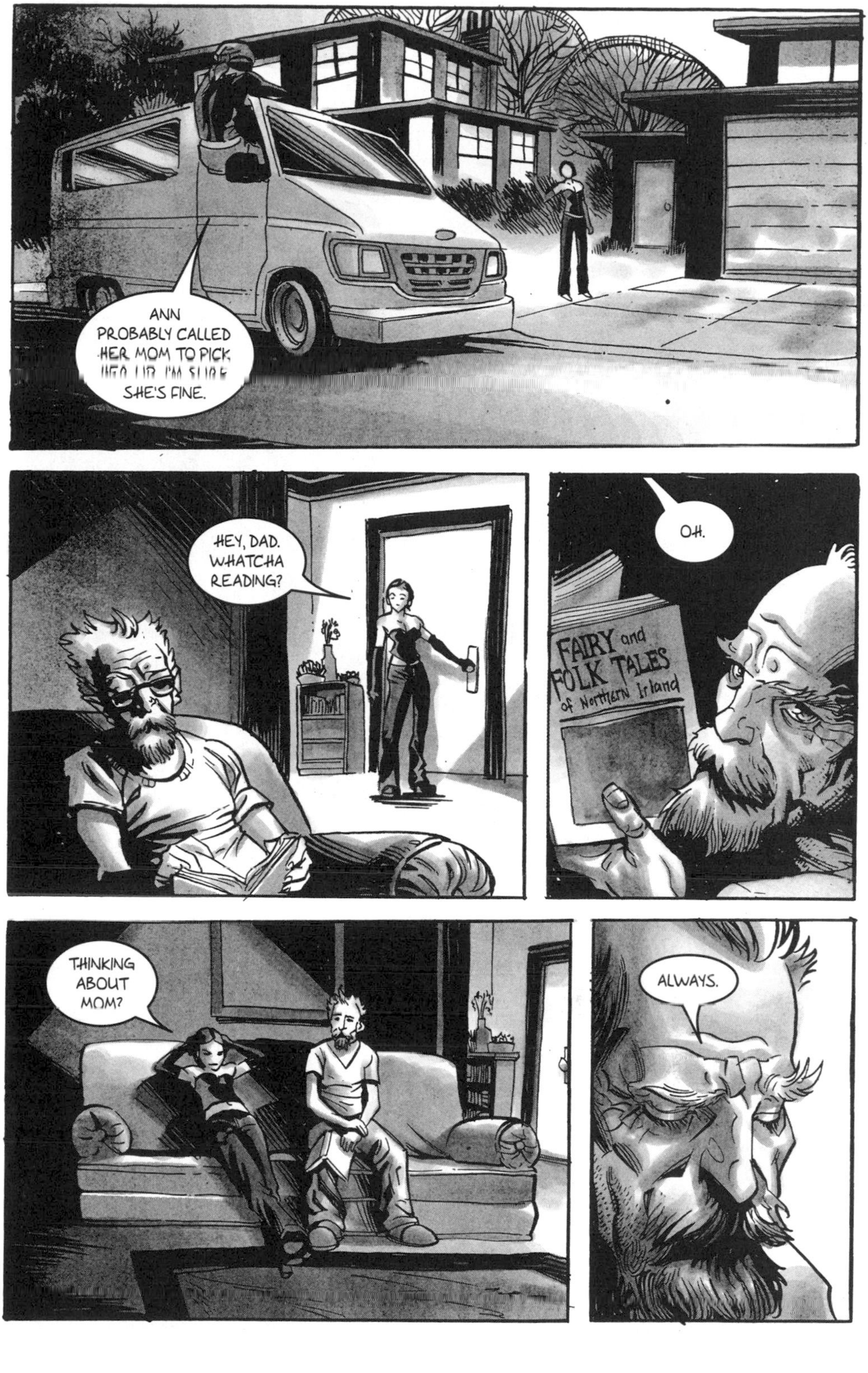
ANN PROBABLY CALLED HER MOM TO PICK HER UP. I'M SURE SHE'S FINE.
HEY, DAD. WHATCHA READING?
OH.
FAIRY and FOLK TALES of Northern Irland
THINKING ABOUT MOM?
ALWAYS.

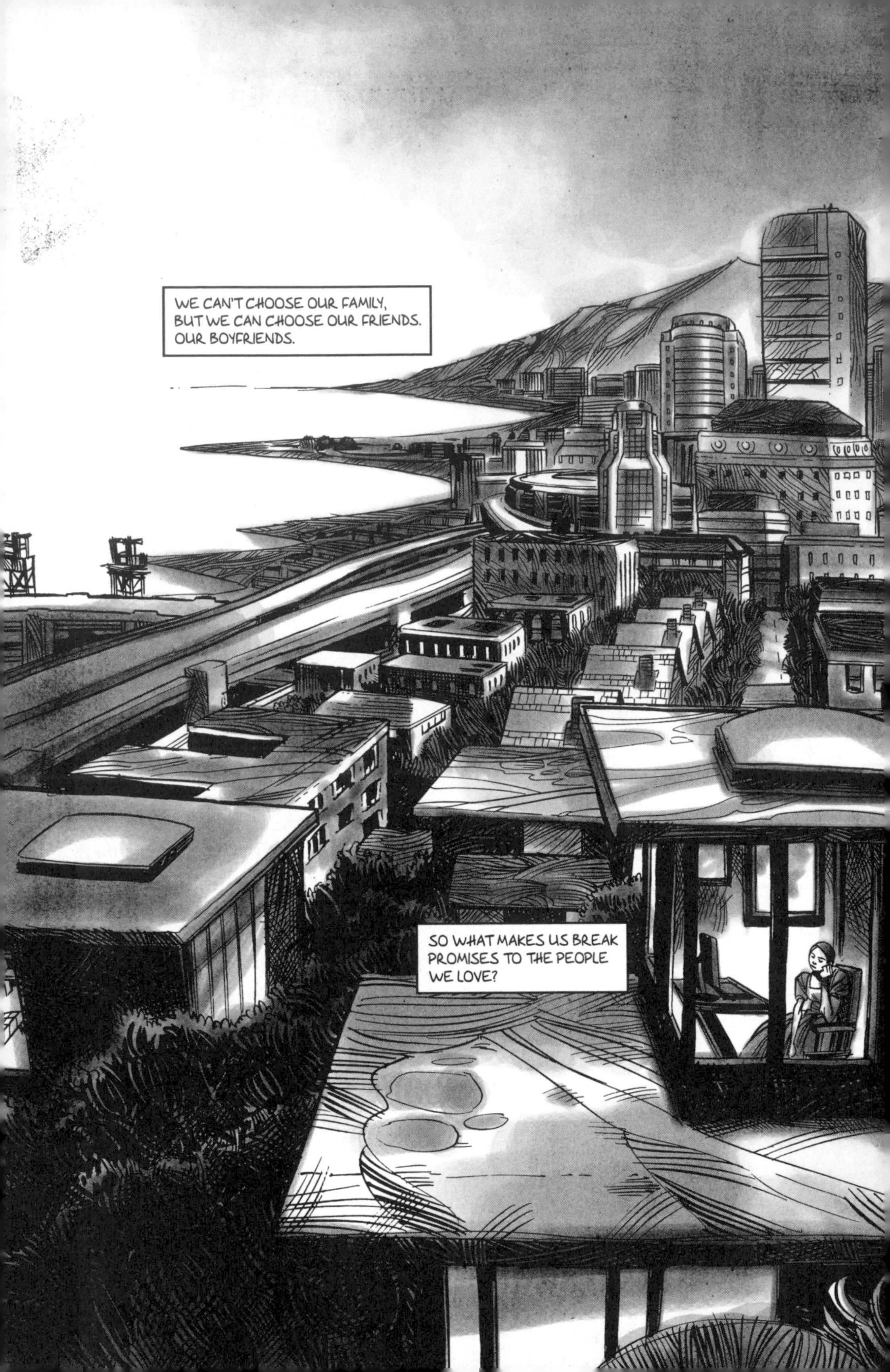
WE CAN'T CHOOSE OUR FAMILY, BUT WE CAN CHOOSE OUR FRIENDS. OUR BOYFRIENDS.
SO WHAT MAKES US BREAK PROMISES TO THE PEOPLE WE LOVE?

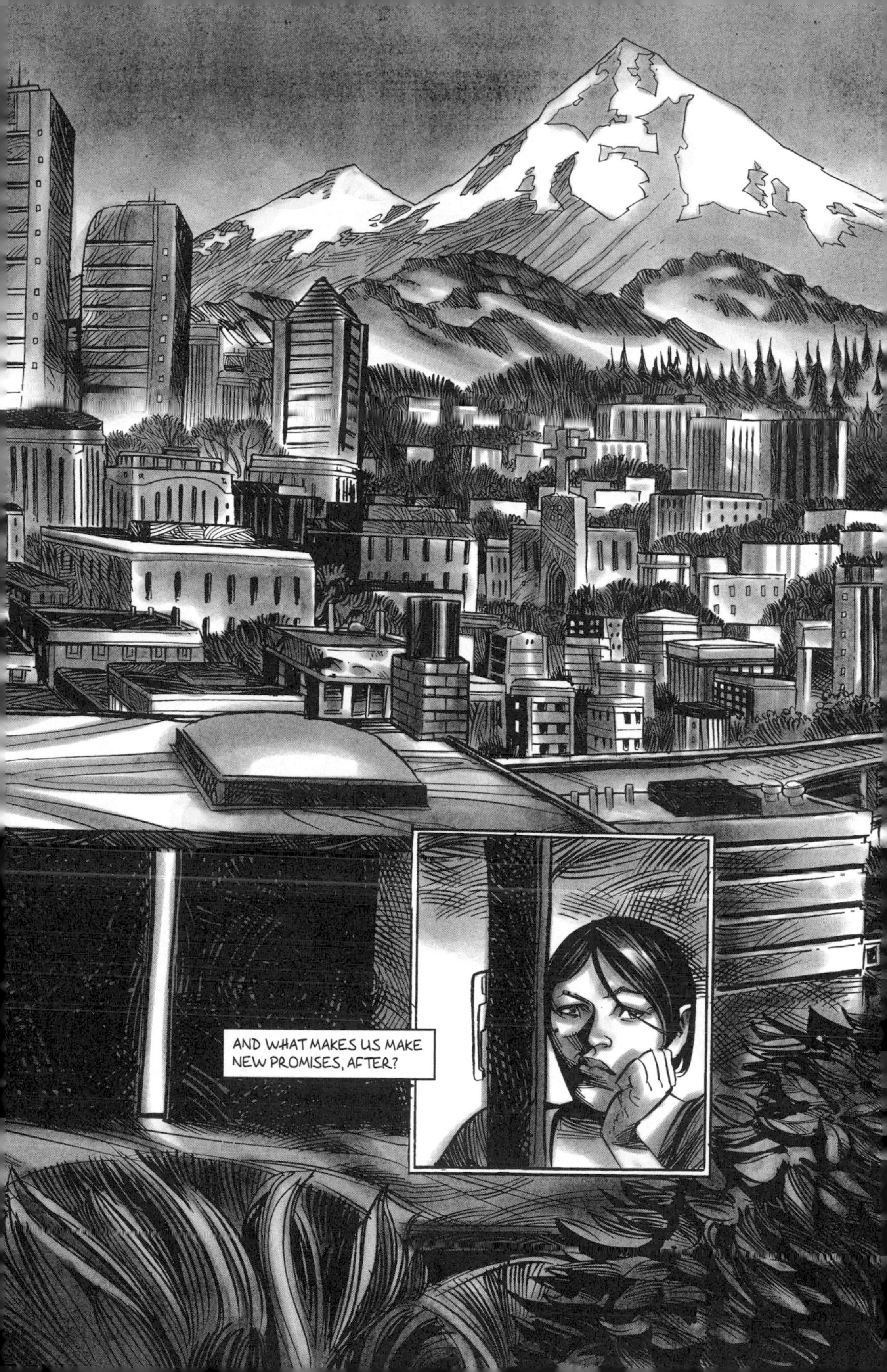
AND WHAT MAKES US MAKE NEW PROMISES, AFTER?

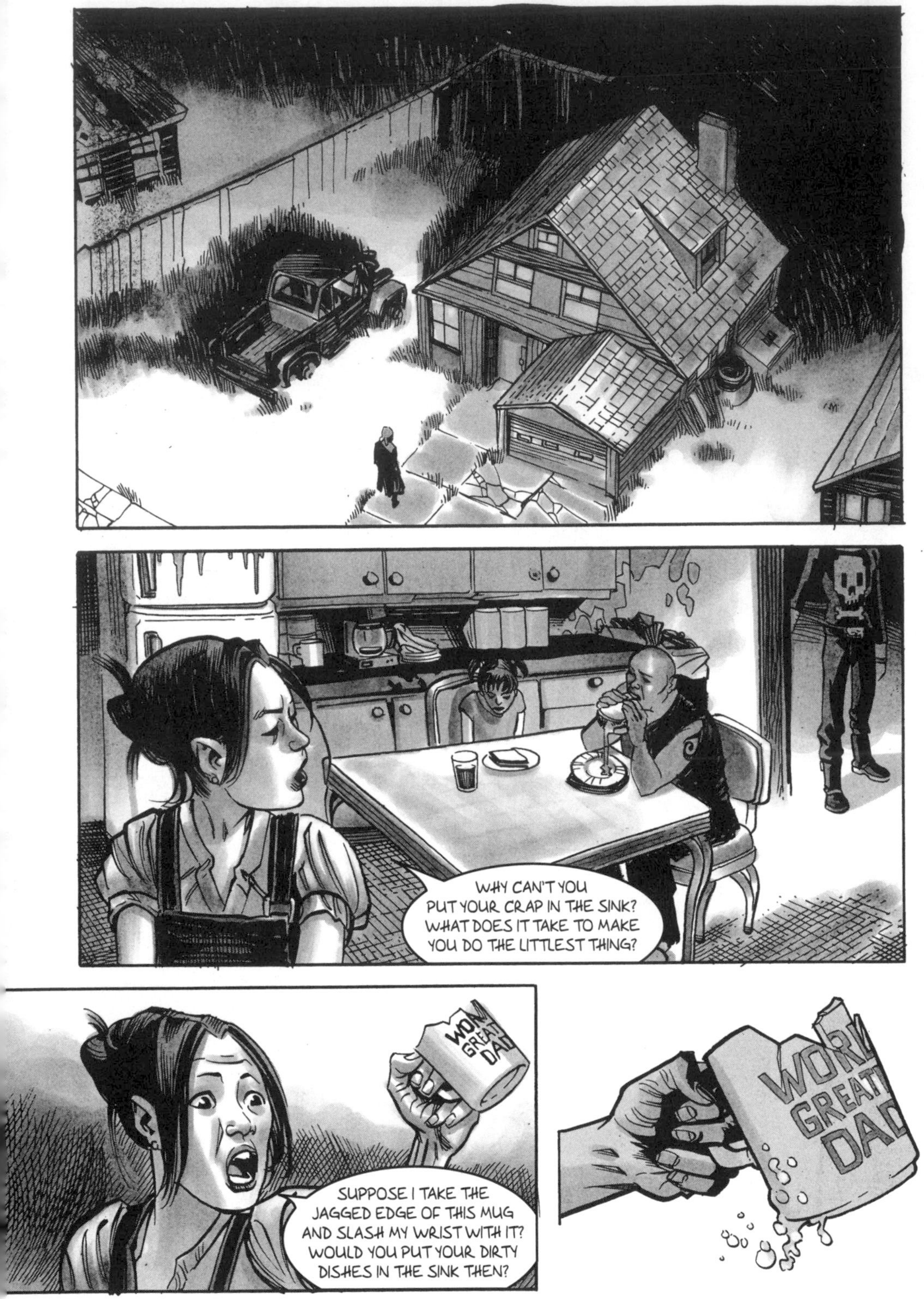
WHY CAN'T YOU PUT YOUR CRAP IN THE SINK? WHAT DOES IT TAKE TO MAKE YOU DO THE LITTLEST THING?
SUPPOSE I TAKE THE JAGGED EDGE OF THIS MUG AND SLASH MY WRIST WITH IT? WOULD YOU PUT YOUR DIRTY DISHES IN THE SINK THEN?

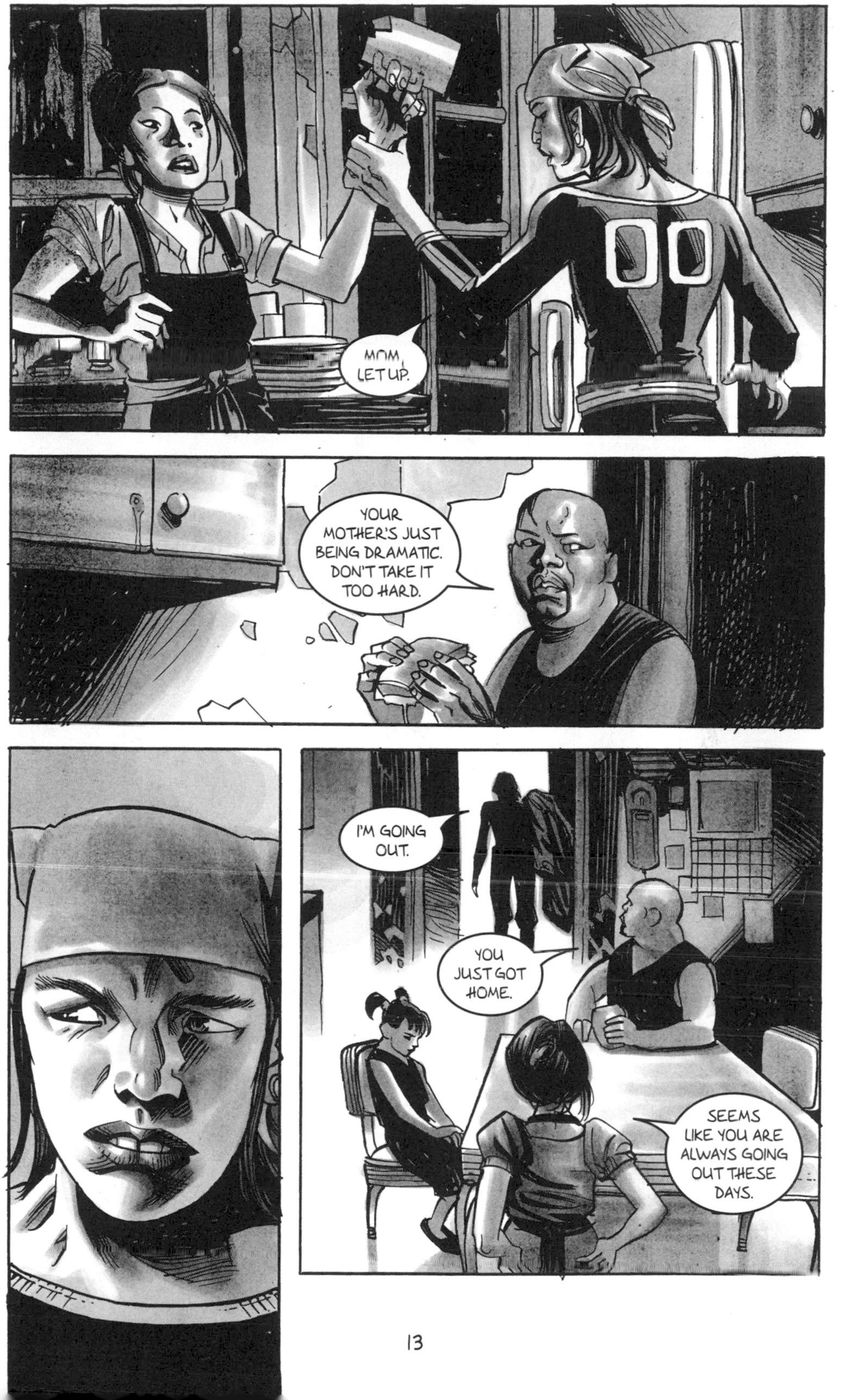
MOM, LET UP.
YOUR MOTHER'S JUST BEING DRAMATIC. DON'T TAKE IT TOO HARD.
I'M GOING OUT.
YOU JUST GOT HOME.
SEEMS LIKE YOU ARE ALWAYS GOING OUT THESE DAYS.

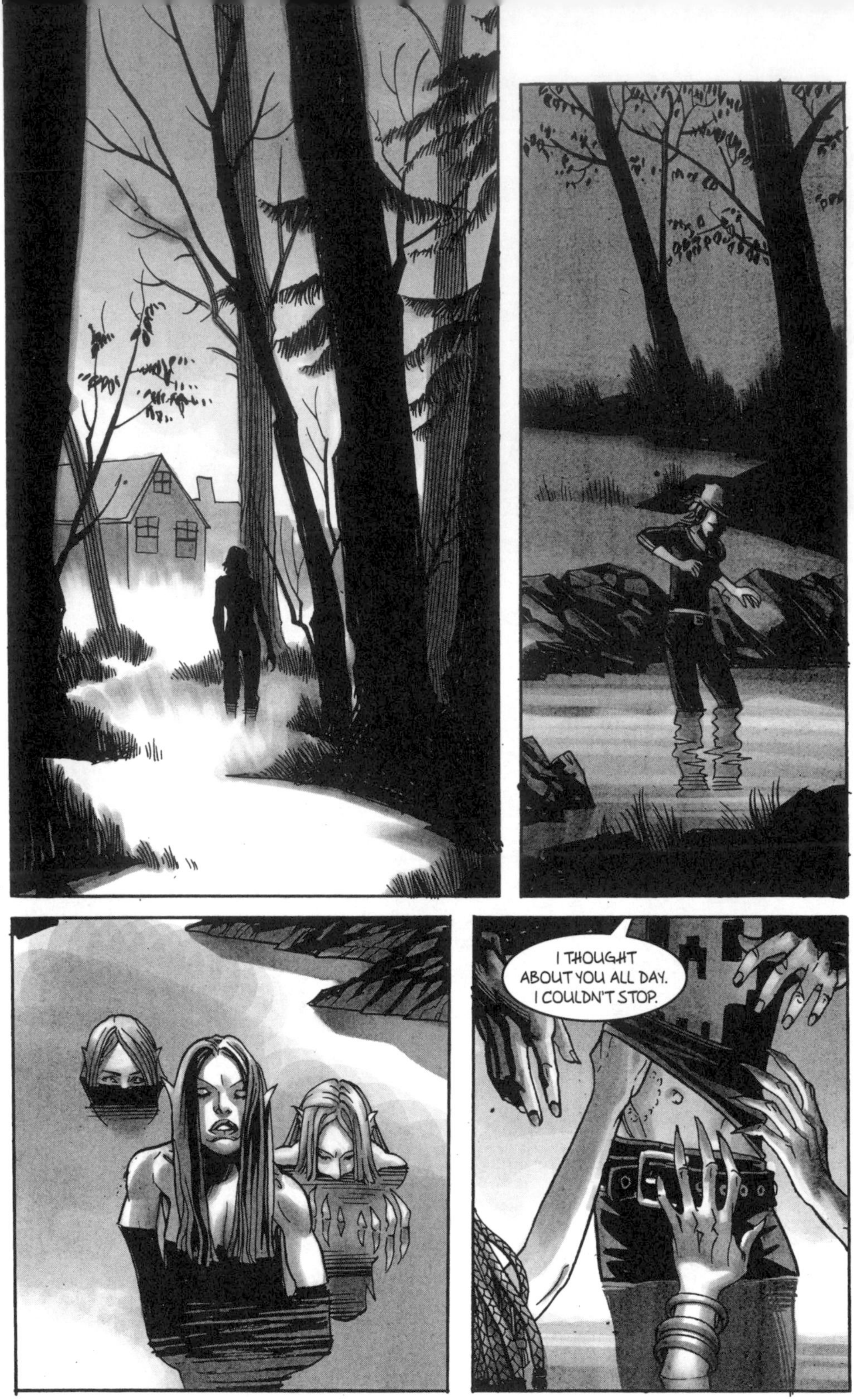
I THOUGHT ABOUT YOU ALL DAY. I COULDN'T STOP.

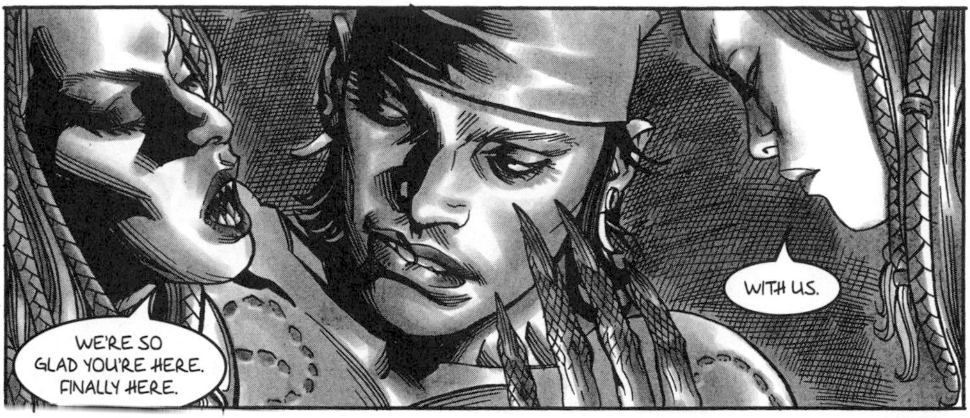
WE'RE SO
GLAD YOU'RE HERE.
FINALLY HERE.
WITH US.

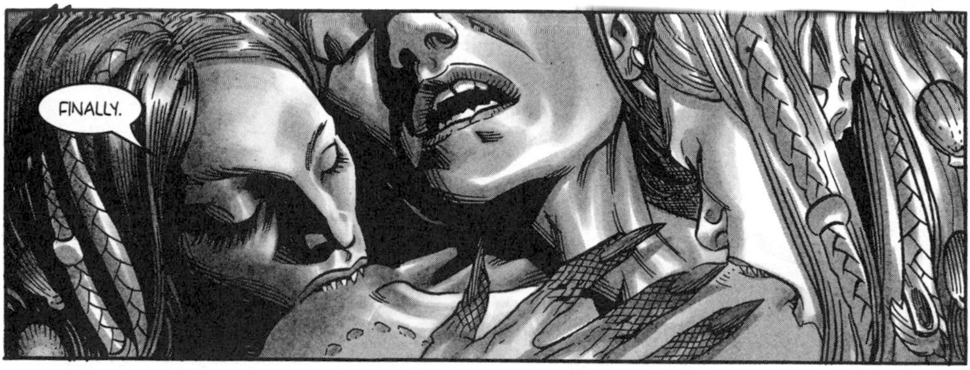
FINALLY.

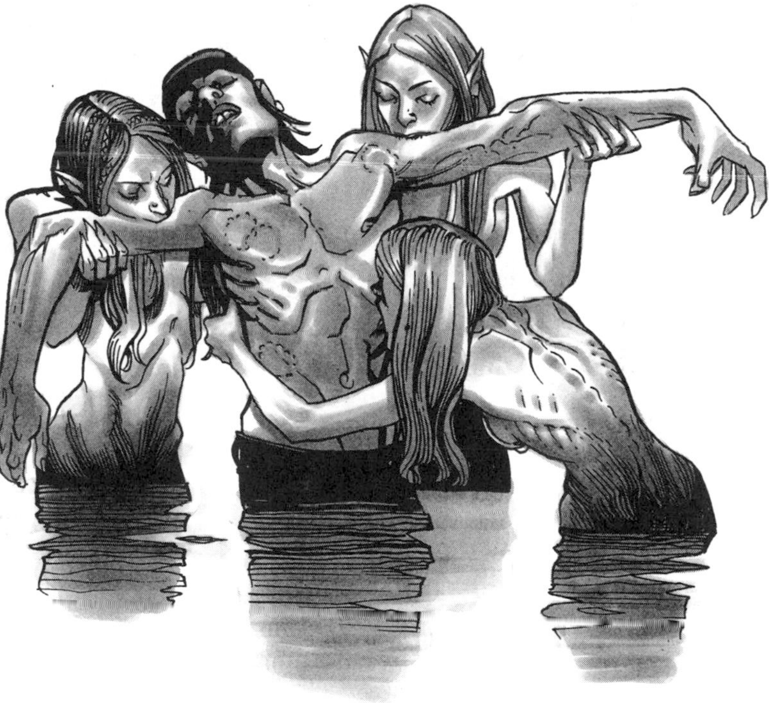

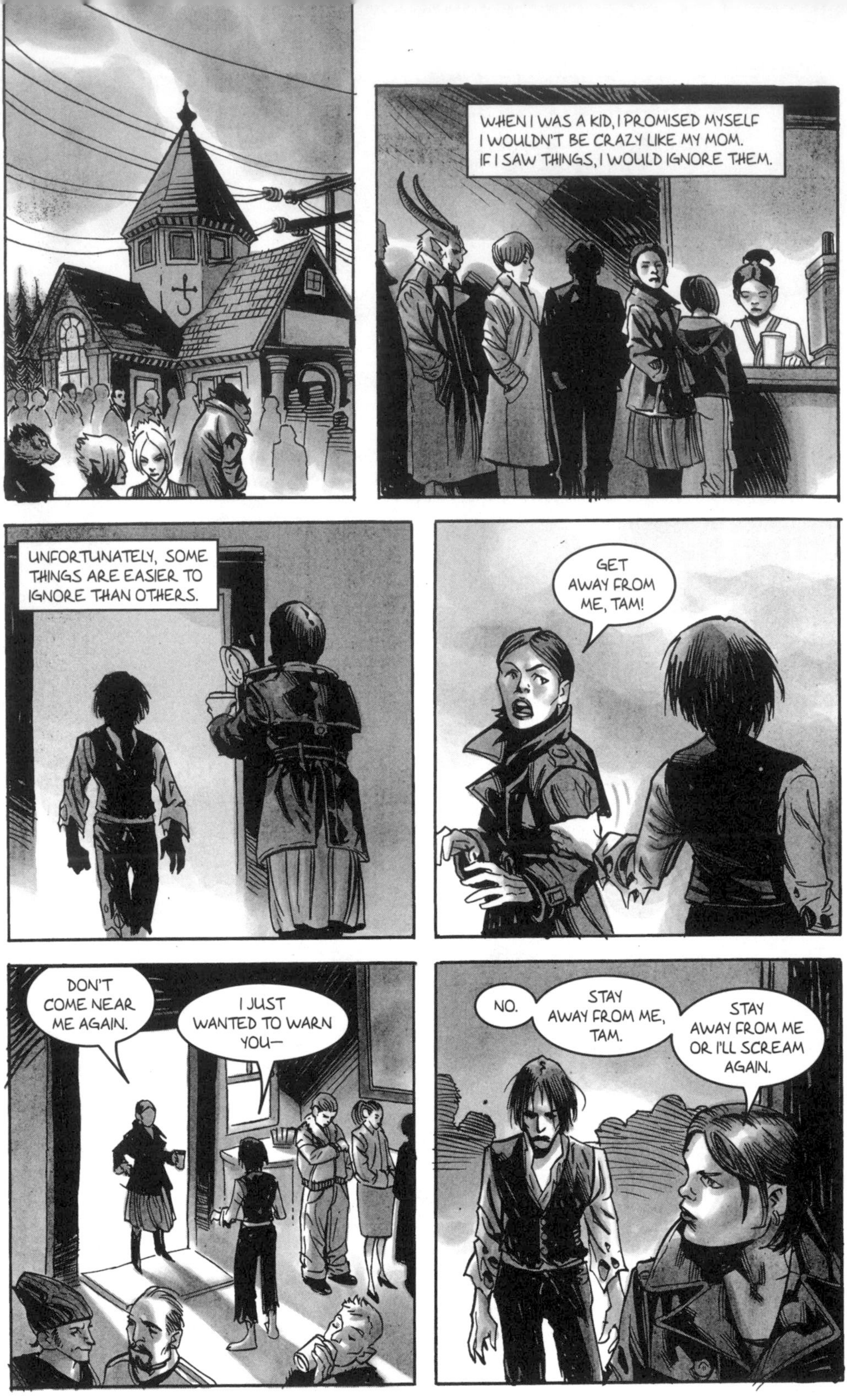
WHEN I WAS A KID, I PROMISED MYSELF I WOULDN'T BE CRAZY LIKE MY MOM. IF I SAW THINGS, I WOULD IGNORE THEM.
UNFORTUNATELY, SOME THINGS ARE EASIER TO IGNORE THAN OTHERS.
GET AWAY FROM ME, TAM!
DON'T COME NEAR ME AGAIN.
I JUST WANTED TO WARN YOU—
NO.
STAY AWAY FROM ME, TAM.
STAY AWAY FROM ME OR I'LL SCREAM AGAIN.

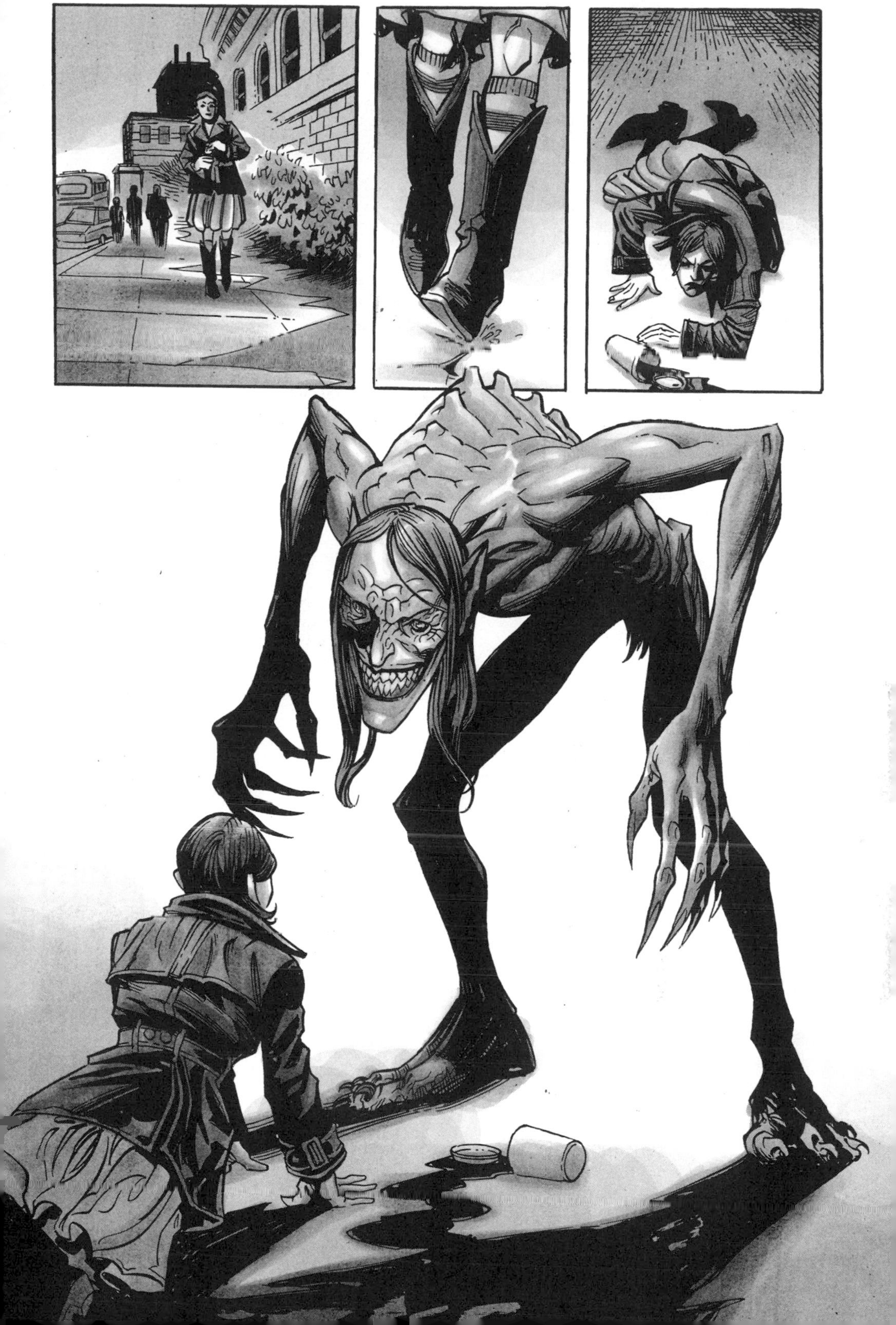

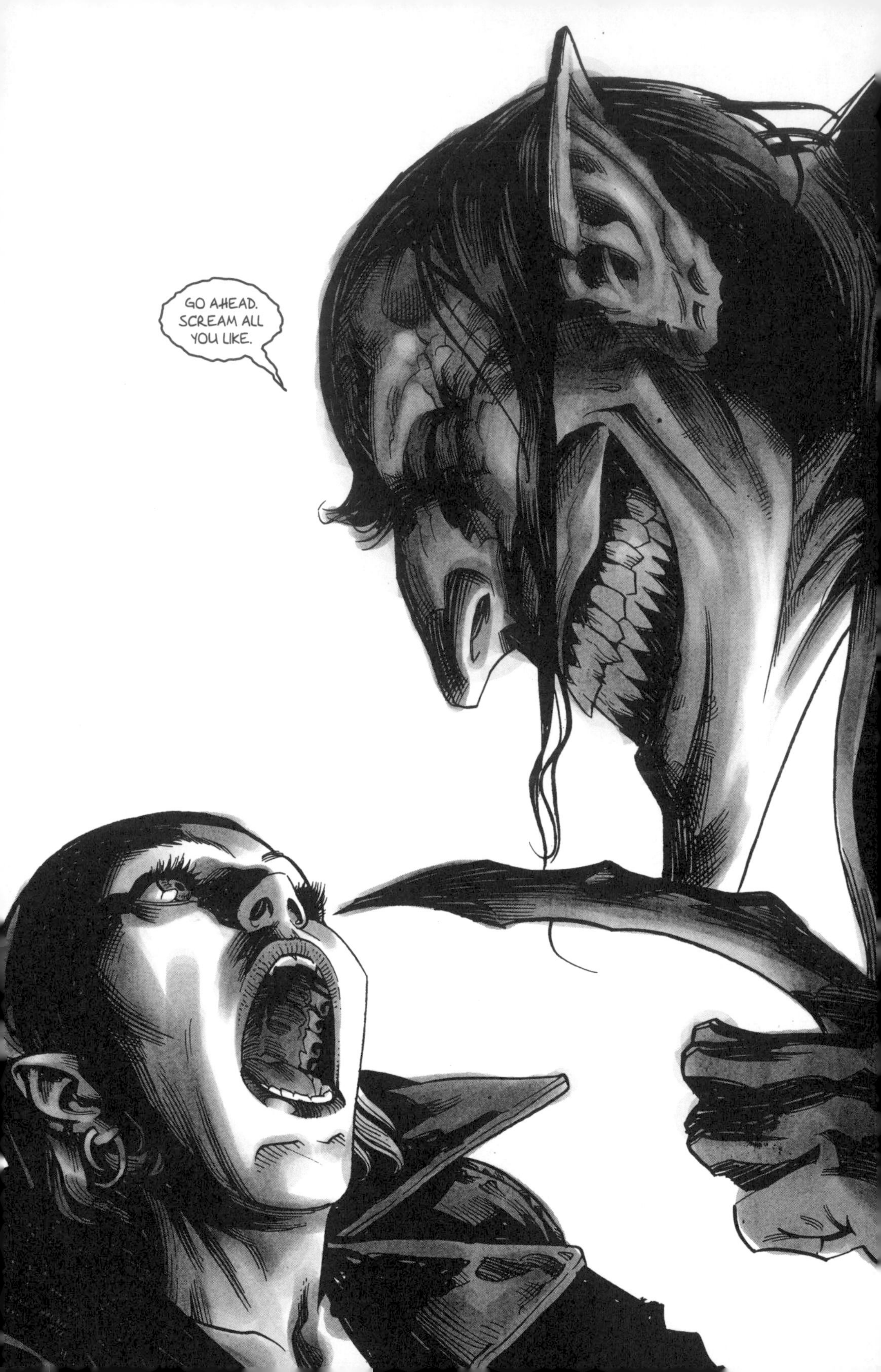
GO AHEAD. SCREAM ALL YOU LIKE.

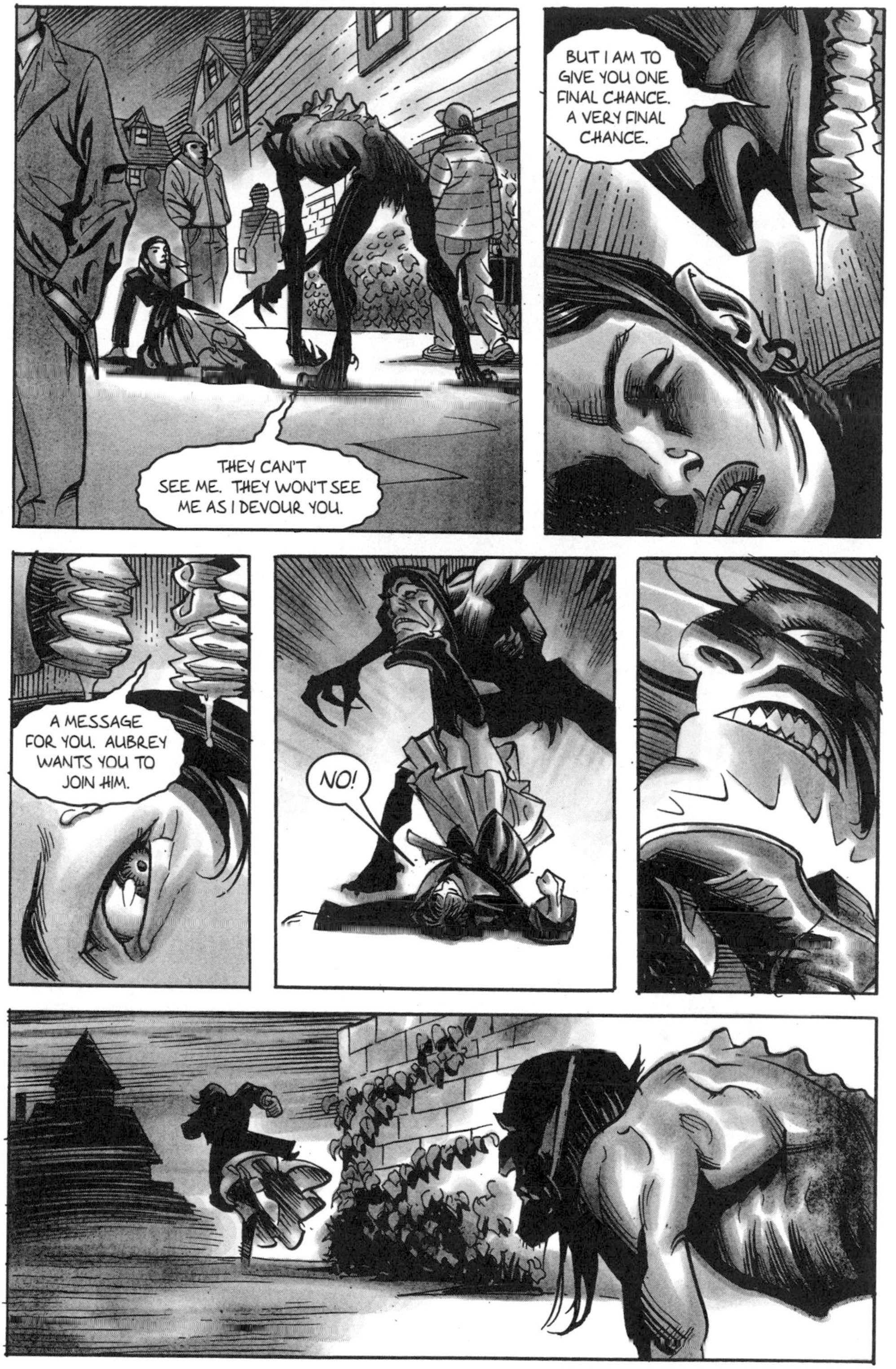
THEY CAN'T SEE ME. THEY WON'T SEE ME AS I DEVOUR YOU.
BUT I AM TO GIVE YOU ONE FINAL CHANCE. A VERY FINAL CHANCE.
A MESSAGE FOR YOU. AUBREY WANTS YOU TO JOIN HIM.
NO!

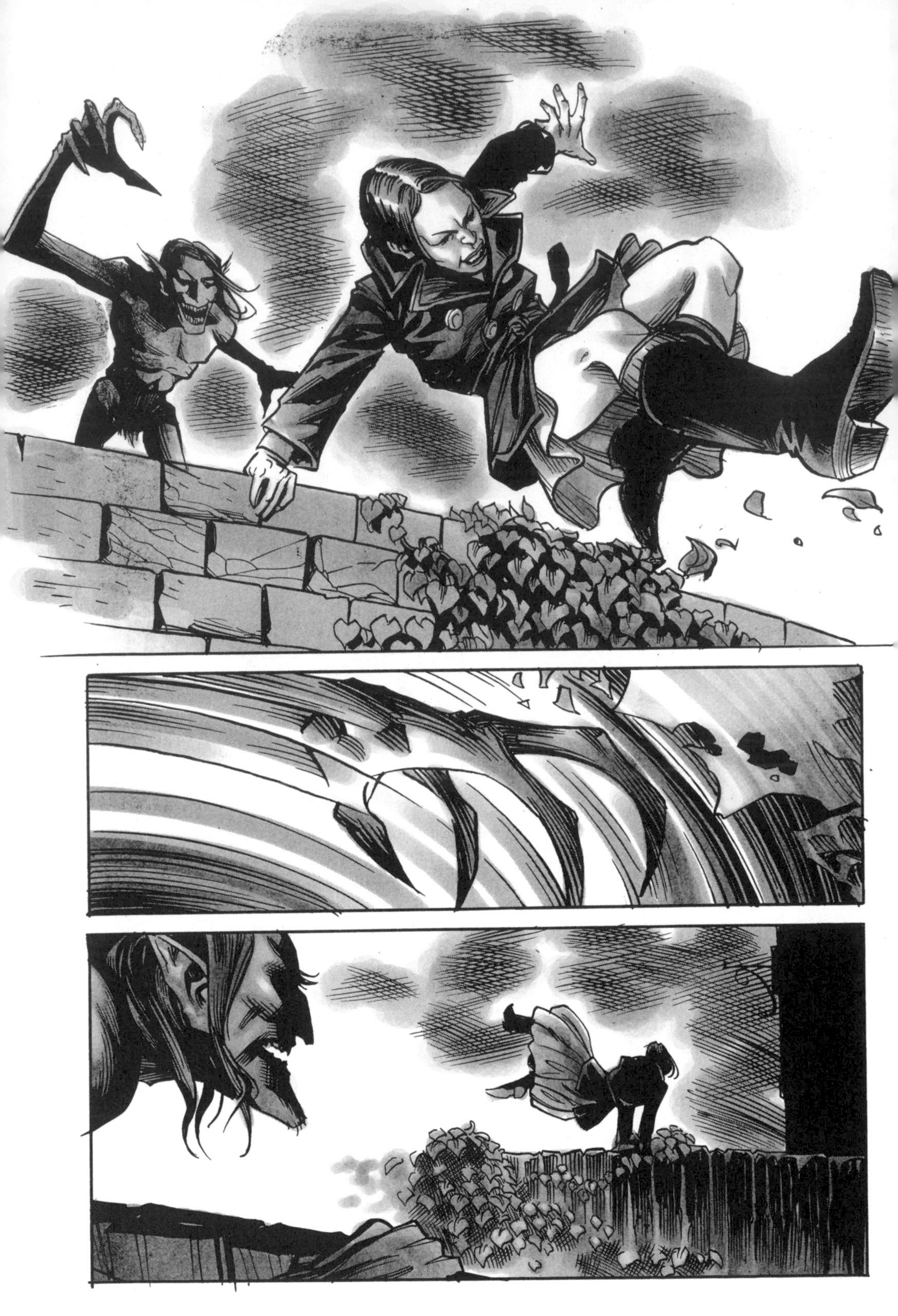

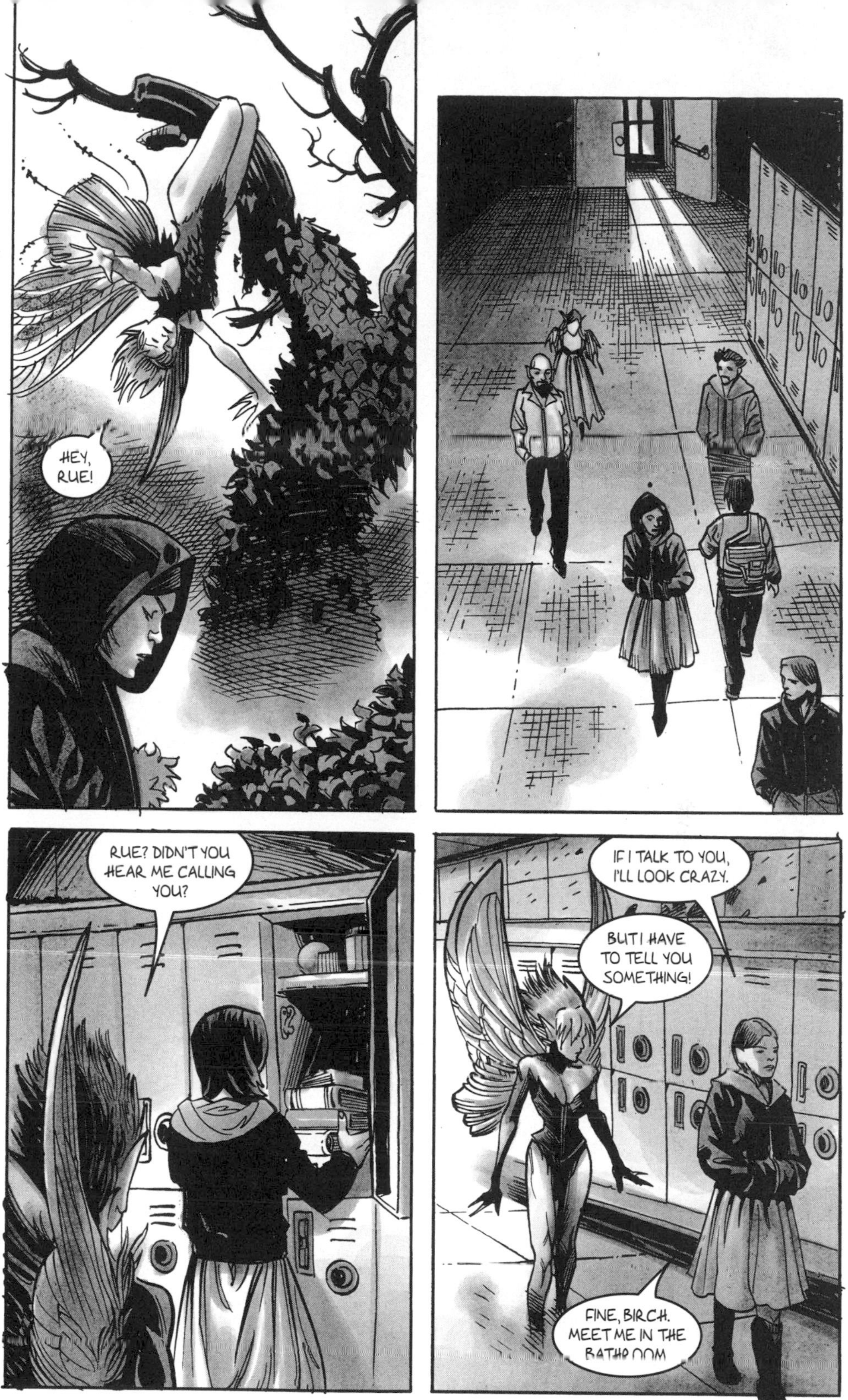
HEY, RUE!
RUE? DIDN'T YOU HEAR ME CALLING YOU?
IF I TALK TO YOU, I'LL LOOK CRAZY.
BUT I HAVE TO TELL YOU SOMETHING!
FINE, BIRCH. MEET ME IN THE BATHROOM.

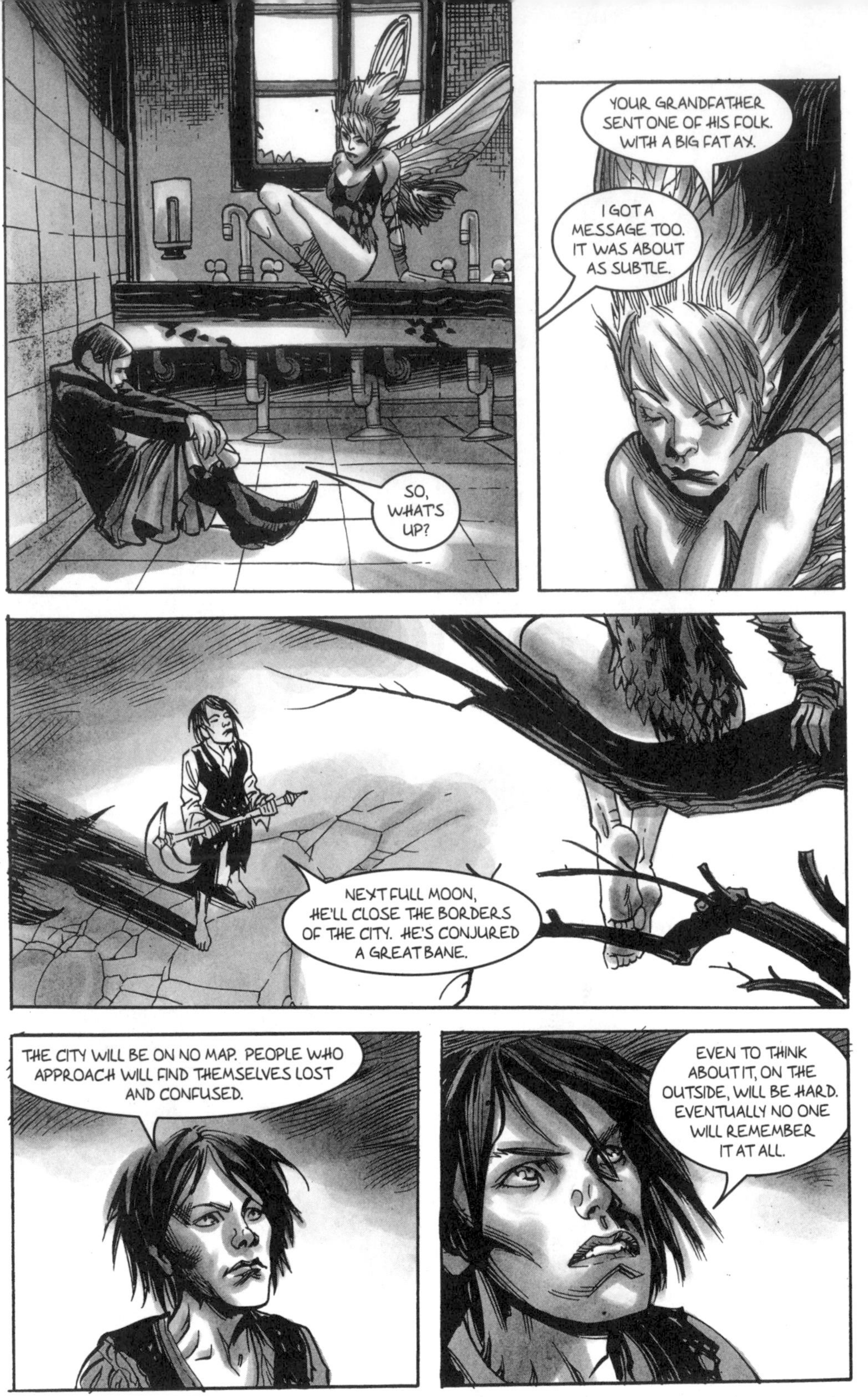
SO, WHAT'S UP?
YOUR GRANDFATHER SENT ONE OF HIS FOLK. WITH A BIG FAT AX.
I GOT A MESSAGE TOO. IT WAS ABOUT AS SUBTLE.
NEXT FULL MOON, HE'LL CLOSE THE BORDERS OF THE CITY. HE'S CONJURED A GREAT BANE.
THE CITY WILL BE ON NO MAP. PEOPLE WHO APPROACH WILL FIND THEMSELVES LOST AND CONFUSED.
EVEN TO THINK ABOUT IT, ON THE OUTSIDE, WILL BE HARD. EVENTUALLY NO ONE WILL REMEMBER IT AT ALL.

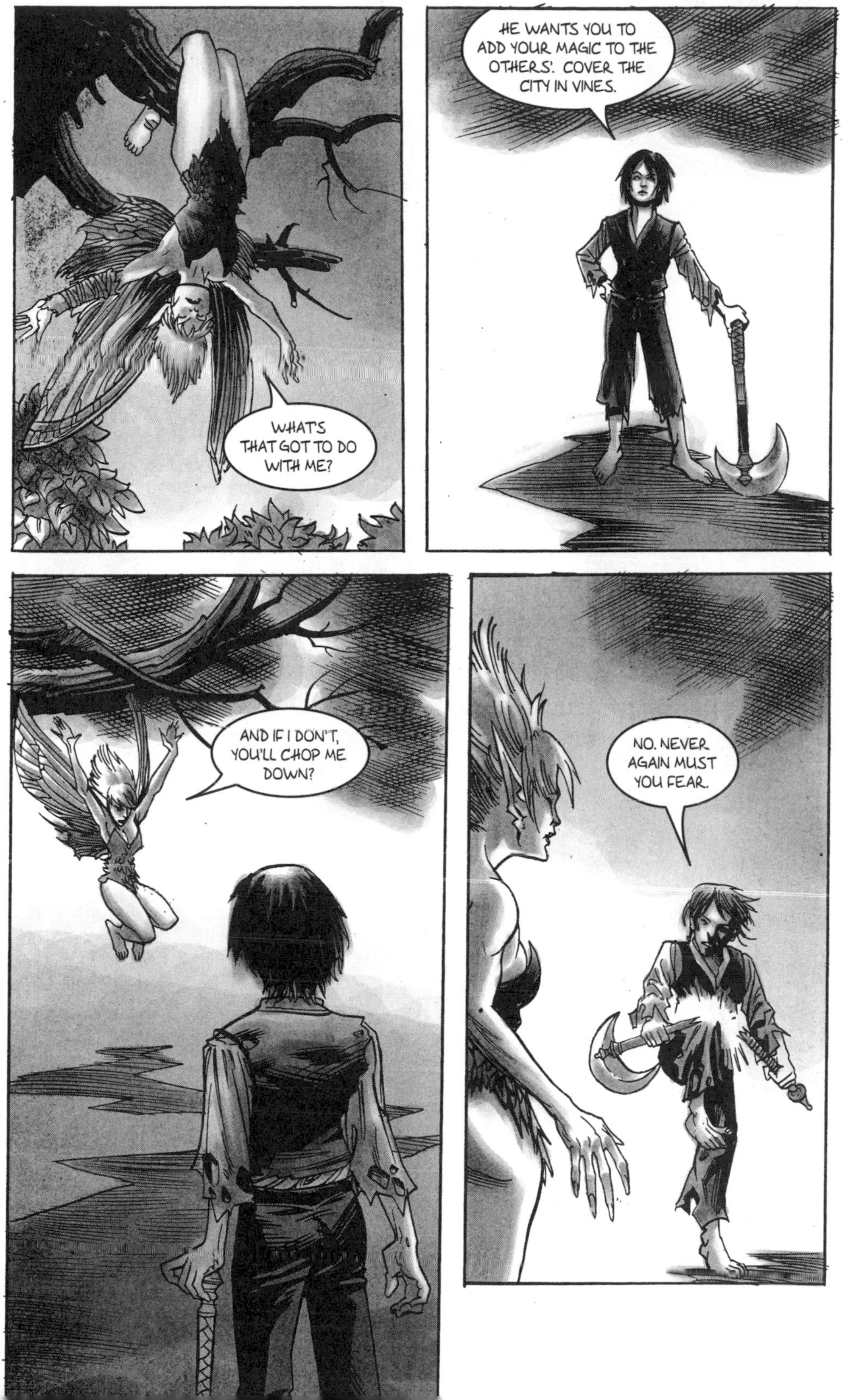
WHAT'S THAT GOT TO DO WITH ME?
HE WANTS YOU TO ADD YOUR MAGIC TO THE OTHERS'. COVER THE CITY IN VINES.
AND IF I DON'T, YOU'LL CHOP ME DOWN?
NO. NEVER AGAIN MUST YOU FEAR.

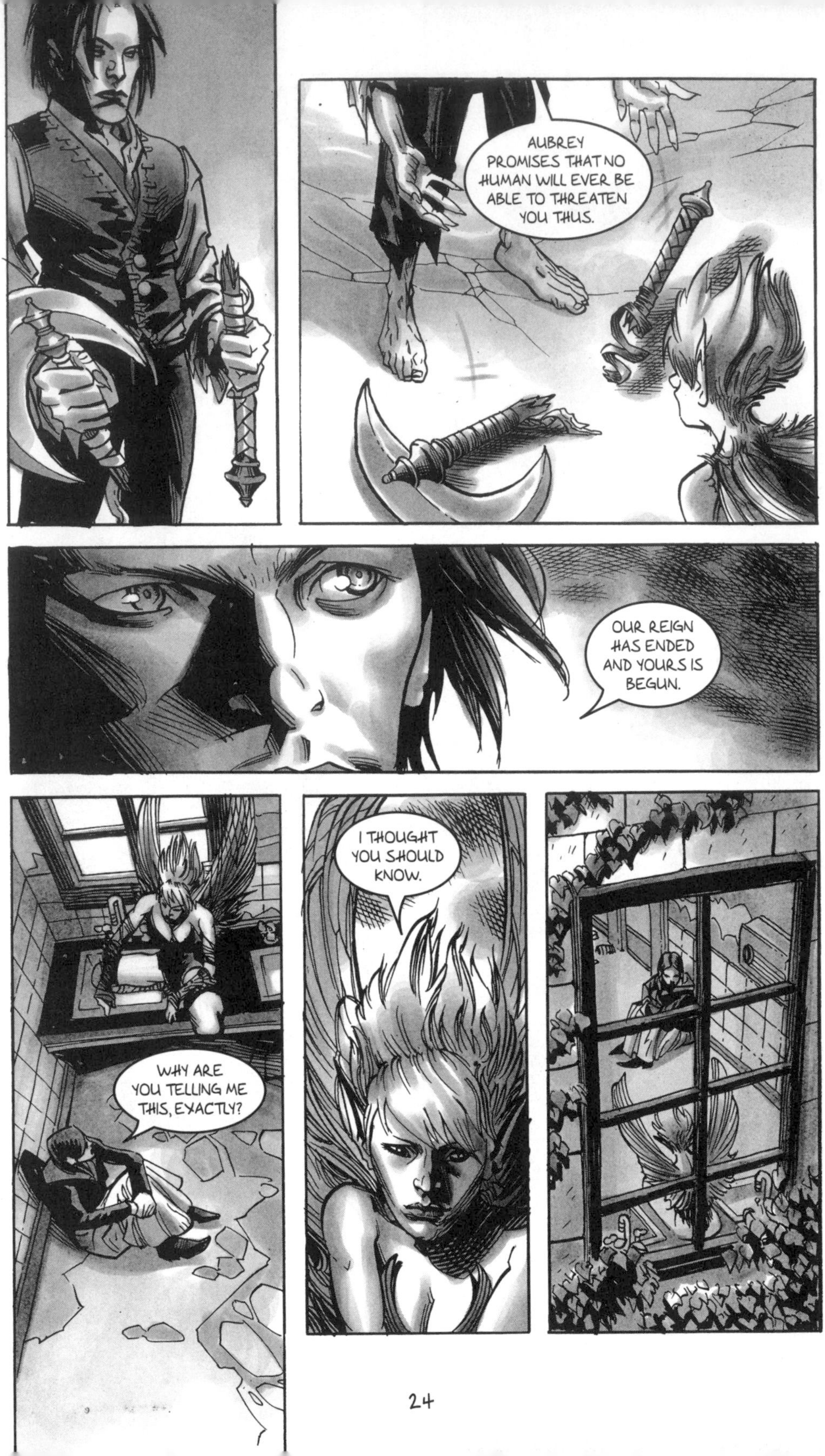
AUBREY PROMISES THAT NO HUMAN WILL EVER BE ABLE TO THREATEN YOU THUS.
OUR REIGN HAS ENDED AND YOURS IS BEGUN.
WHY ARE YOU TELLING ME THIS, EXACTLY?
I THOUGHT YOU SHOULD KNOW.

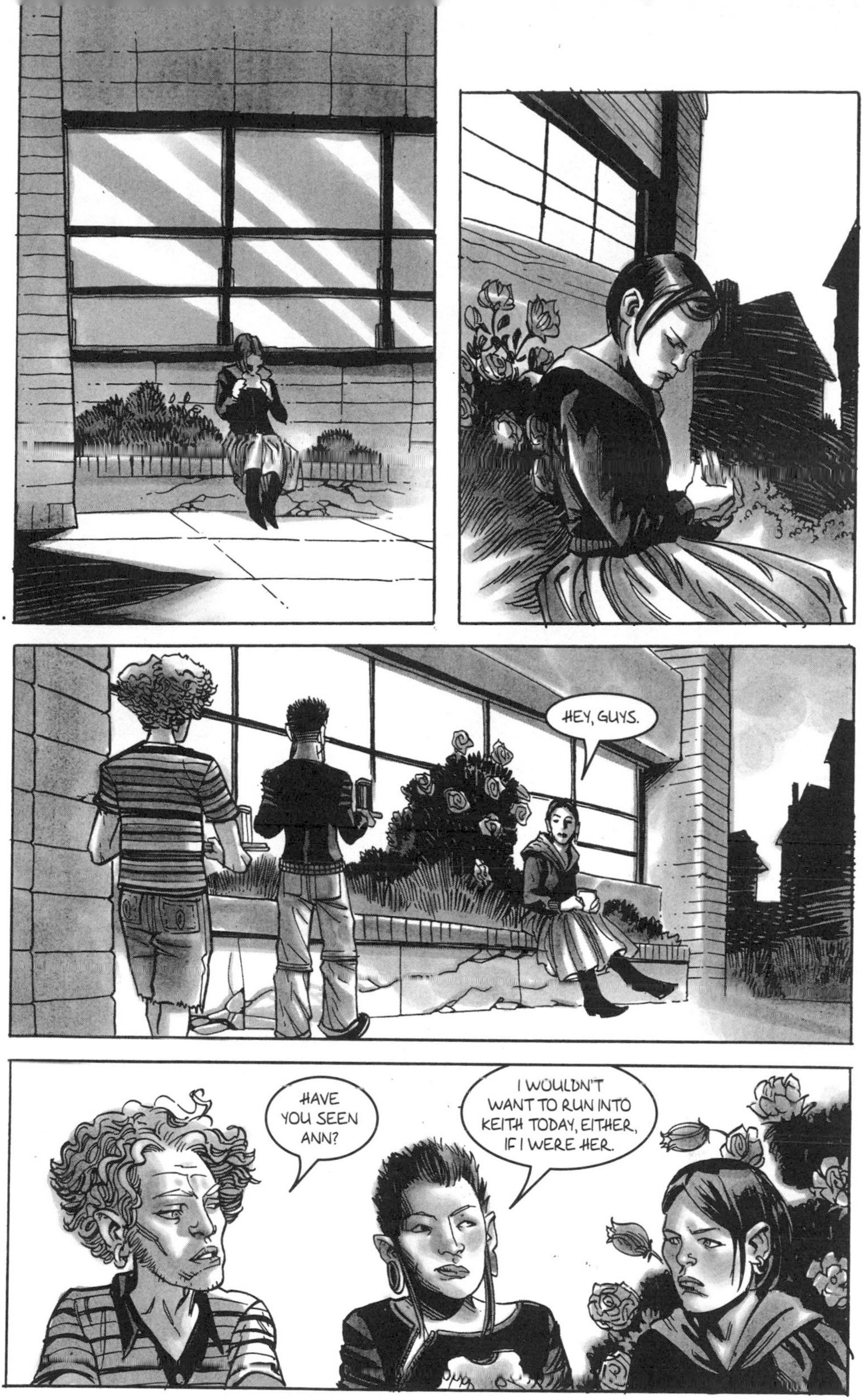
HEY, GUYS.
HAVE YOU SEEN ANN?
I WOULDN'T WANT TO RUN INTO KEITH TODAY, EITHER, IF I WERE HER.

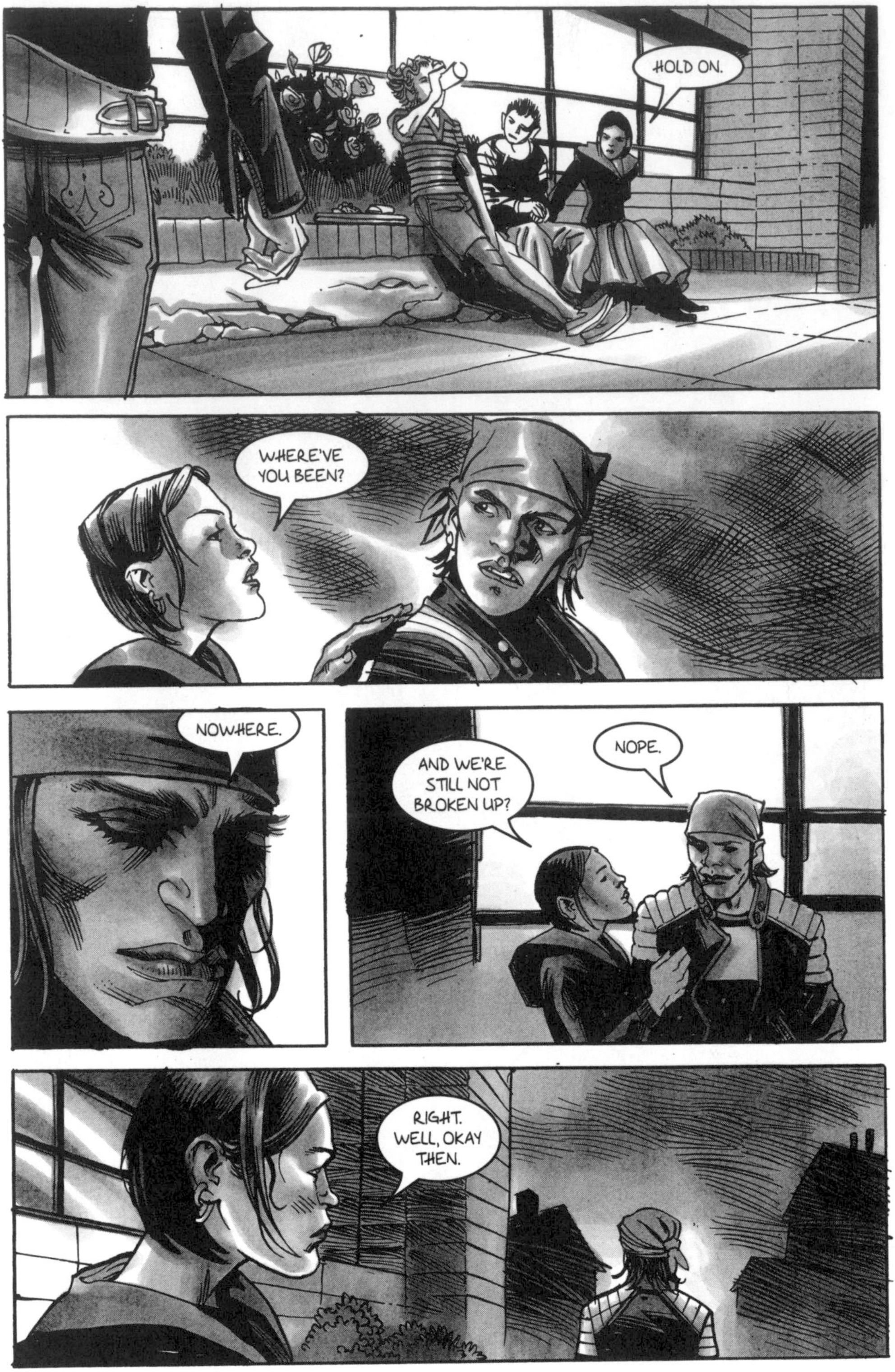
HOLD ON.
WHERE'VE YOU BEEN?
NOWHERE.
AND WE'RE STILL NOT BROKEN UP?
NOPE.
RIGHT. WELL, OKAY THEN.

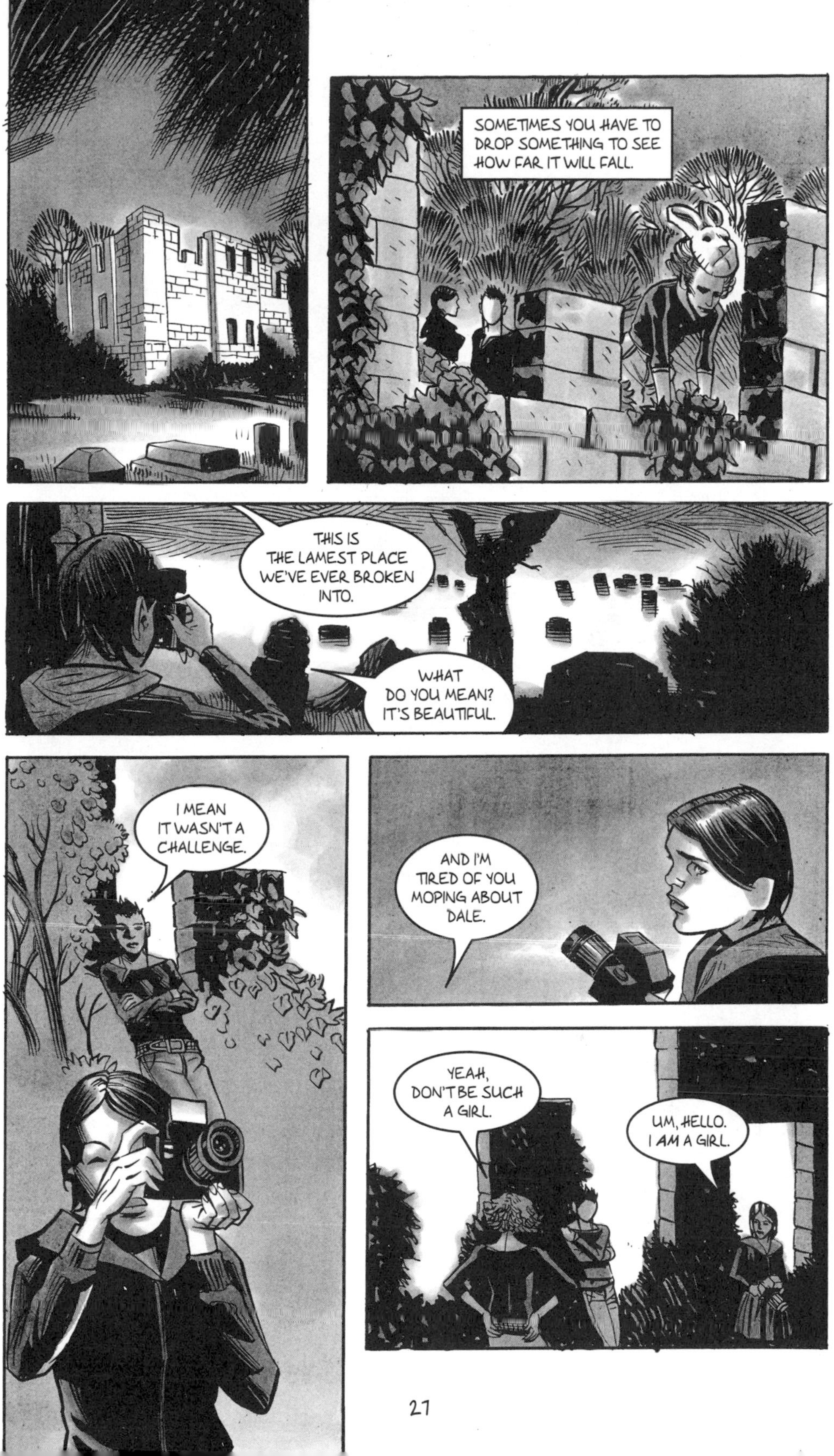
SOMETIMES YOU HAVE TO DROP SOMETHING TO SEE HOW FAR IT WILL FALL.
THIS IS THE LAMEST PLACE WE'VE EVER BROKEN INTO.
WHAT DO YOU MEAN? IT'S BEAUTIFUL.
I MEAN IT WASN'T A CHALLENGE.
AND I'M TIRED OF YOU MOPING ABOUT DALE.
YEAH, DON'T BE SUCH A GIRL.
UM, HELLO. I AM A GIRL.

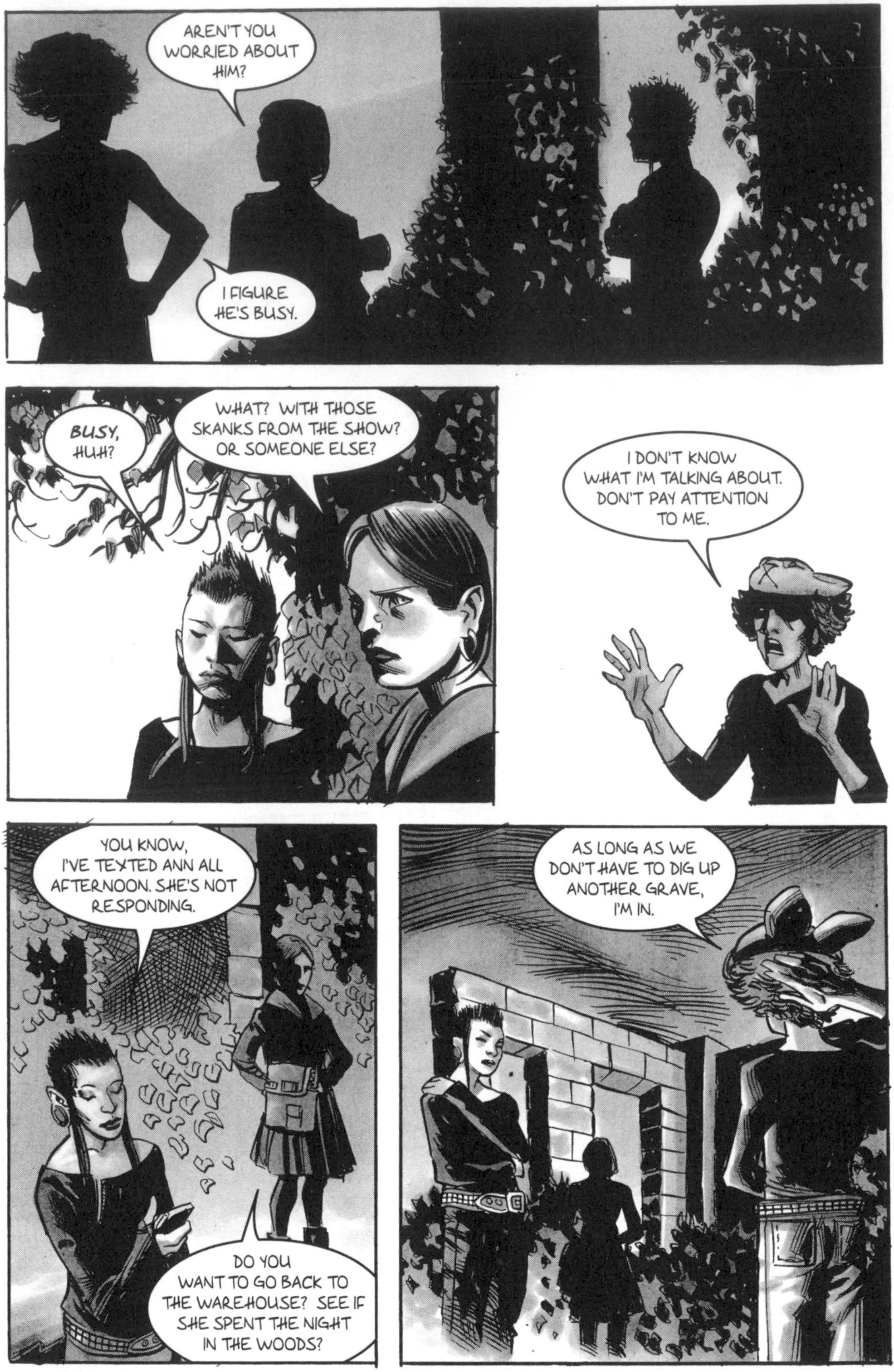
AREN'T YOU WORRIED ABOUT HIM?
I FIGURE HE'S BUSY.
BUSY, HUH?
WHAT? WITH THOSE SKANKS FROM THE SHOW? OR SOMEONE ELSE?
I DON'T KNOW WHAT I'M TALKING ABOUT. DON'T PAY ATTENTION TO ME.
YOU KNOW, I'VE TEXTED ANN ALL AFTERNOON. SHE'S NOT RESPONDING.
DO YOU WANT TO GO BACK TO THE WAREHOUSE? SEE IF SHE SPENT THE NIGHT IN THE WOODS?
AS LONG AS WE DON'T HAVE TO DIG UP ANOTHER GRAVE, I'M IN.

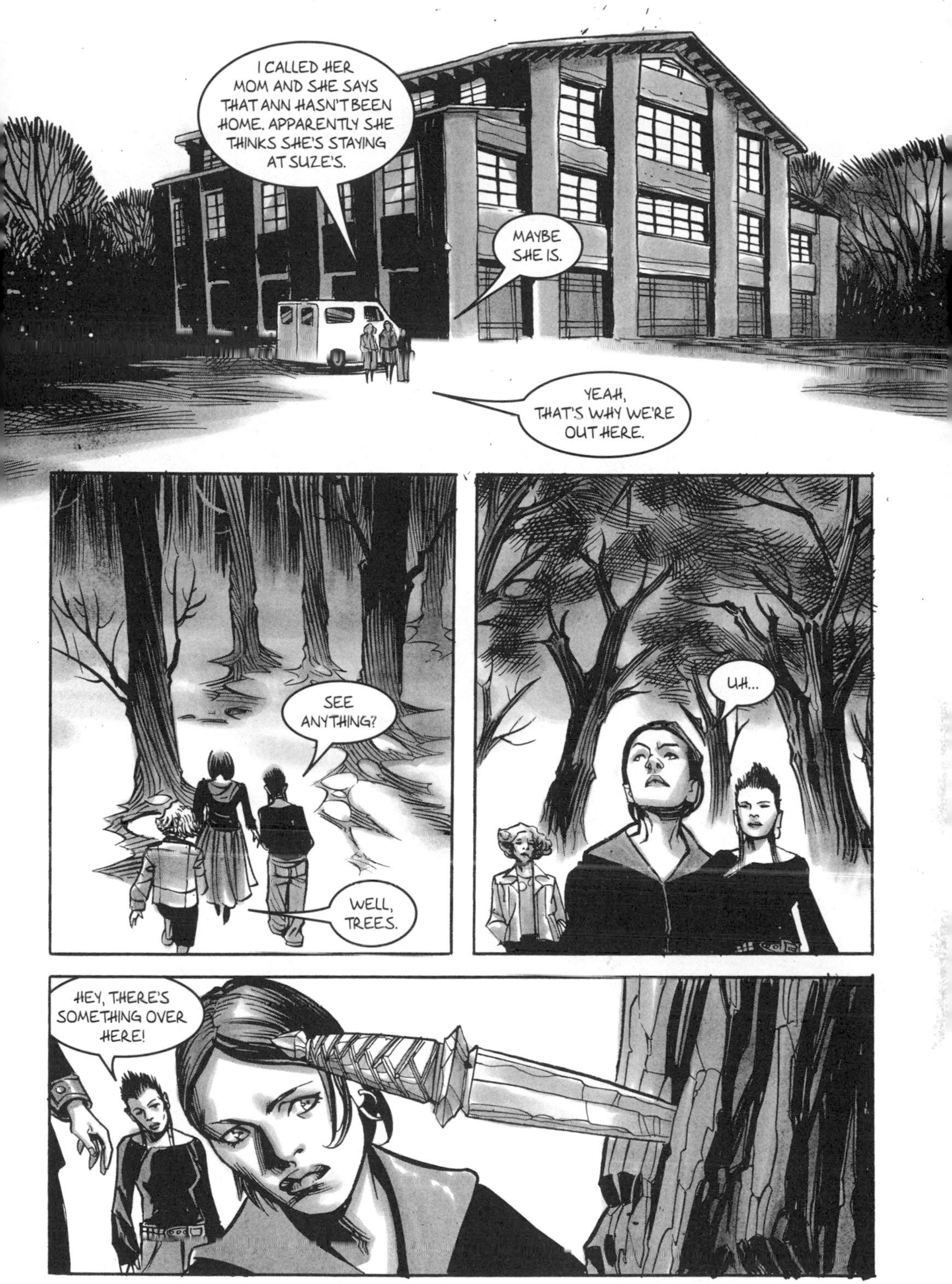
I CALLED HER MOM AND SHE SAYS THAT ANN HASN'T BEEN HOME. APPARENTLY SHE THINKS SHE'S STAYING AT SUZE'S.
MAYBE SHE IS.
YEAH, THAT'S WHY WE'RE OUT HERE.
SEE ANYTHING?
WELL, TREES.
UH...
HEY, THERE'S SOMETHING OVER HERE!

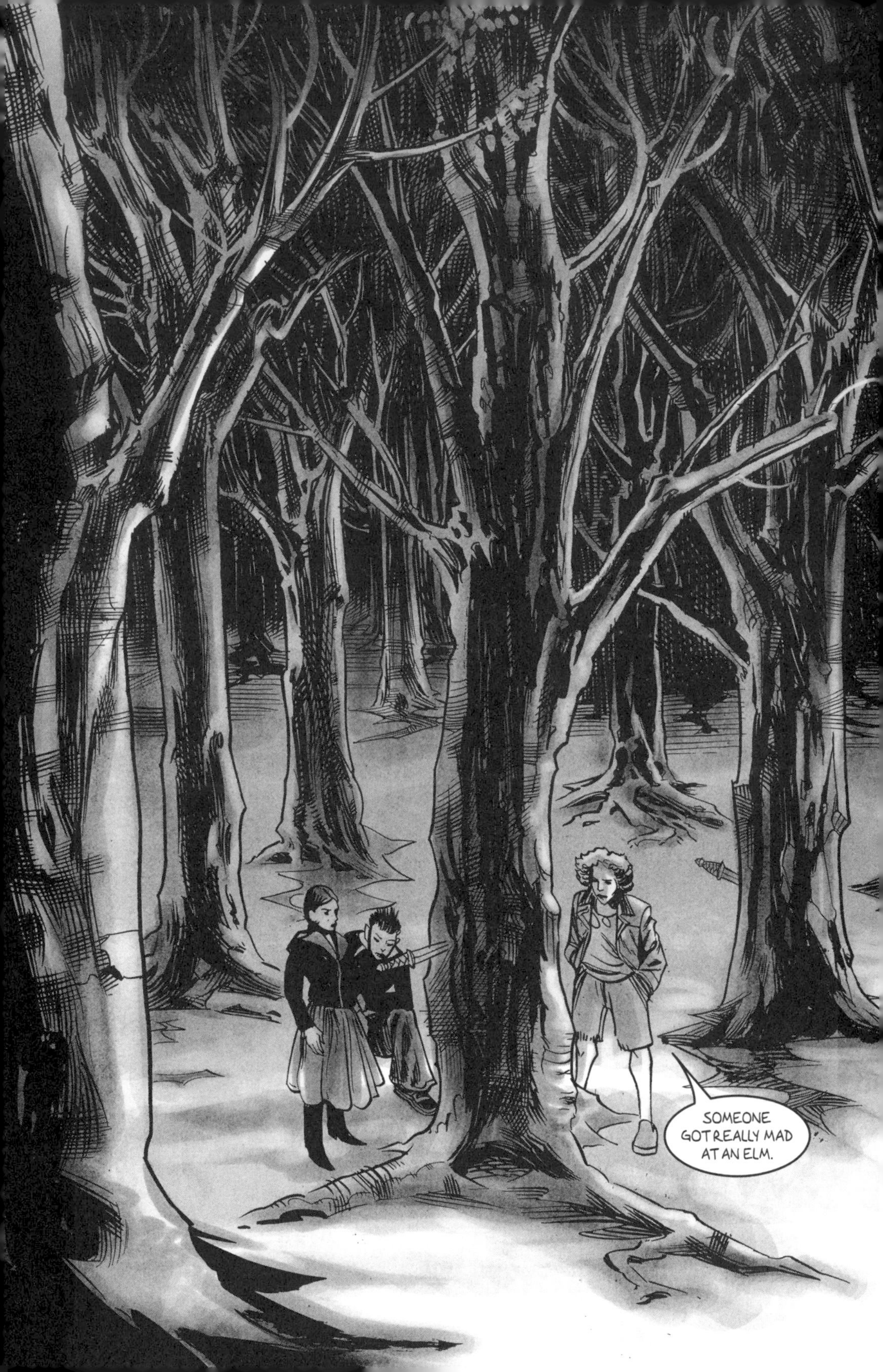
SOMEONE GOT REALLY MAD AT AN ELM.

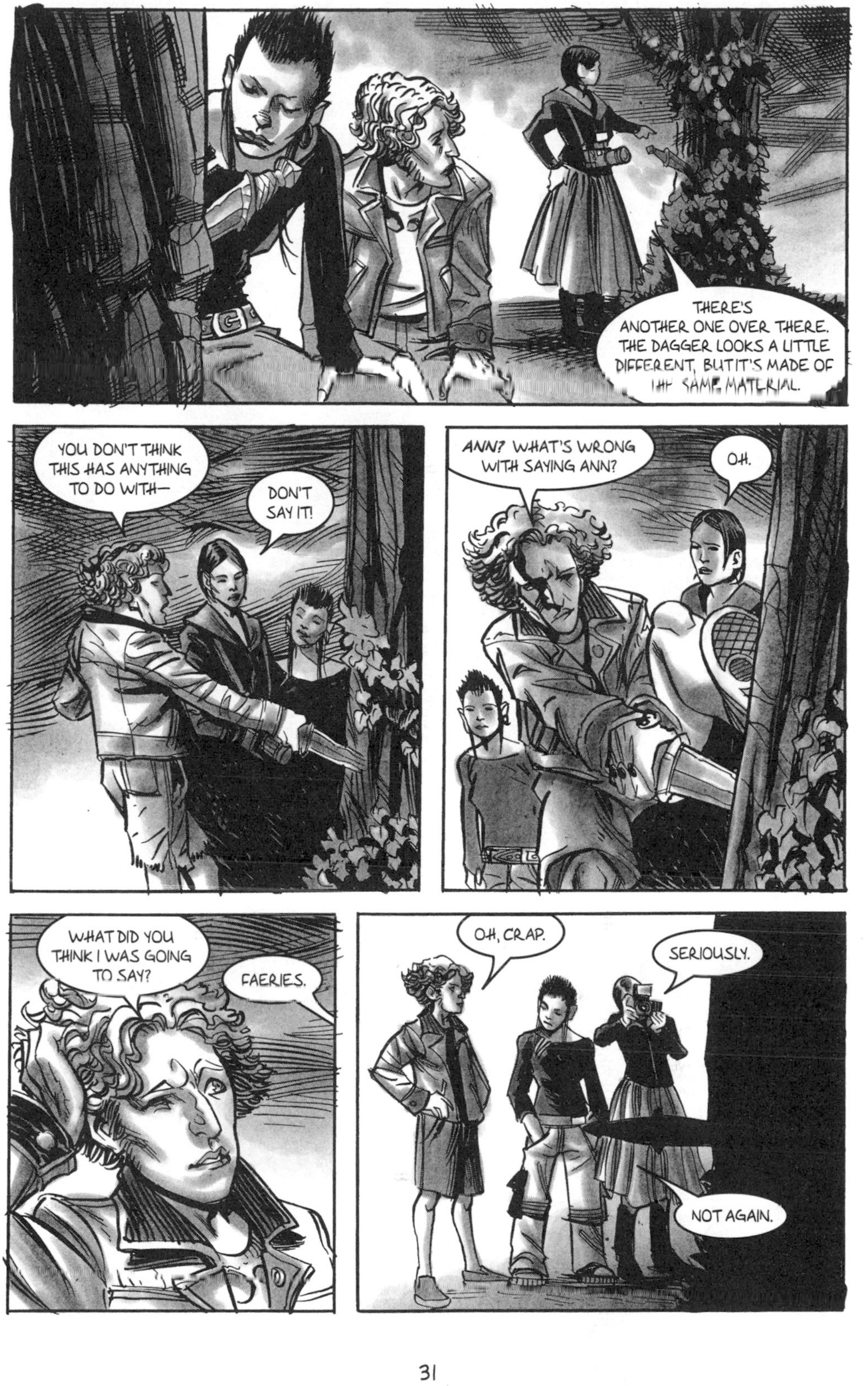
THERE'S ANOTHER ONE OVER THERE. THE DAGGER LOOKS A LITTLE DIFFERENT, BUT IT'S MADE OF THE SAME MATERIAL.
YOU DON'T THINK THIS HAS ANYTHING TO DO WITH—
DON'T SAY IT!
ANN? WHAT'S WRONG WITH SAYING ANN?
OH.
WHAT DID YOU THINK I WAS GOING TO SAY?
FAERIES.
OH, CRAP.
SERIOUSLY.
NOT AGAIN.

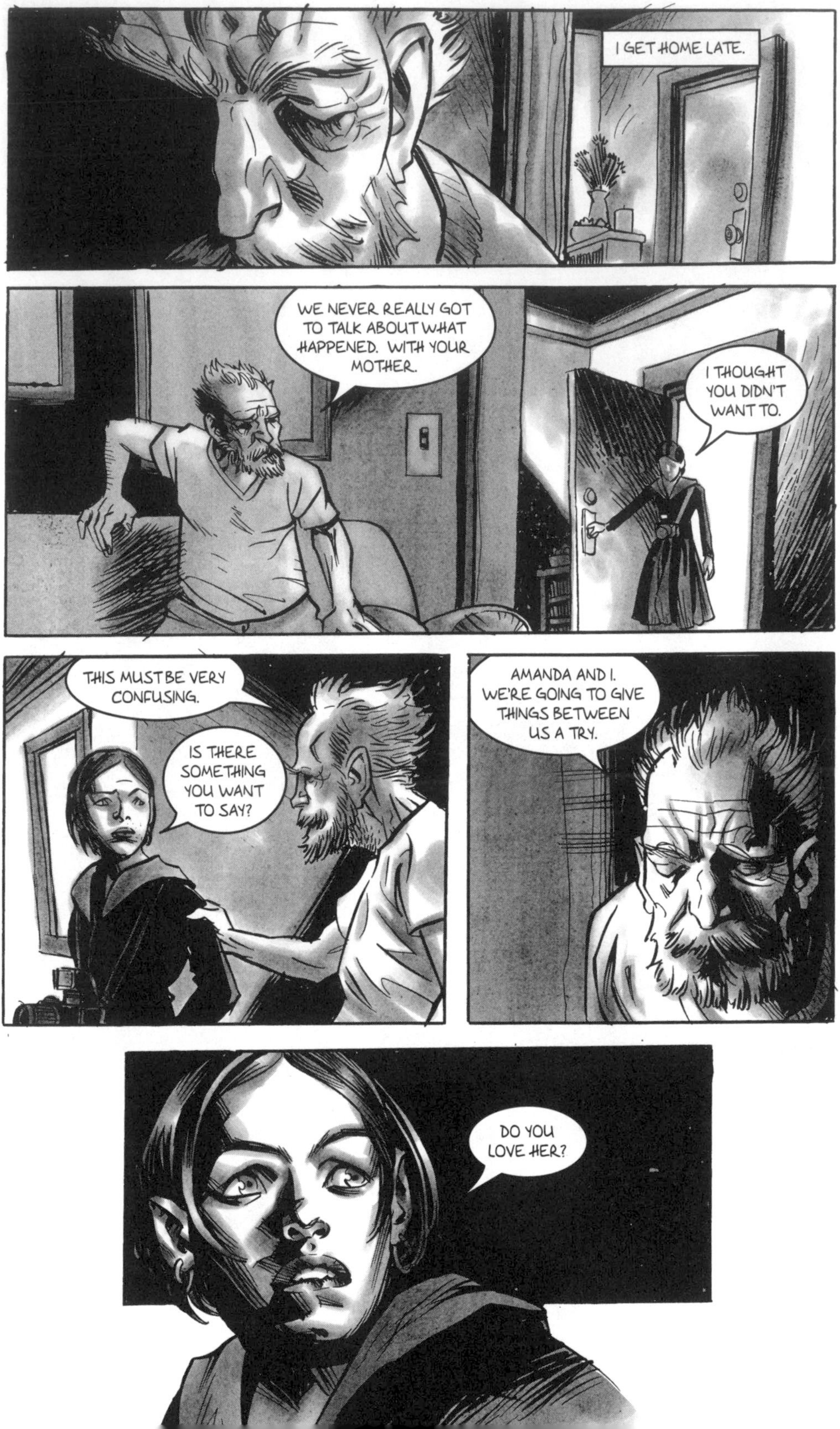
I GET HOME LATE.
WE NEVER REALLY GOT TO TALK ABOUT WHAT HAPPENED. WITH YOUR MOTHER.
I THOUGHT YOU DIDN'T WANT TO.
THIS MUST BE VERY CONFUSING.
IS THERE SOMETHING YOU WANT TO SAY?
AMANDA AND I. WE'RE GOING TO GIVE THINGS BETWEEN US A TRY.
DO YOU LOVE HER?

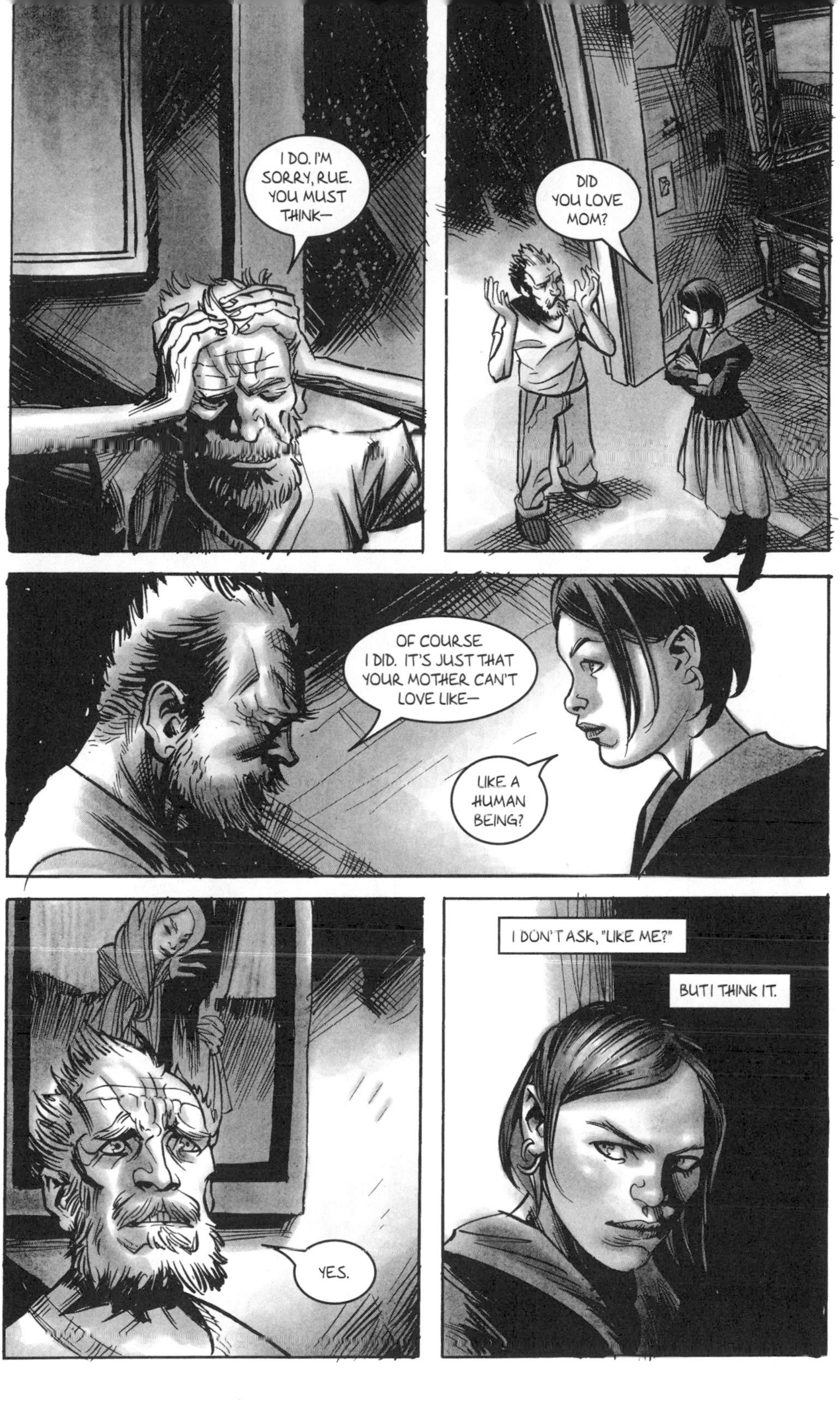
I DO. I'M SORRY, RUE. YOU MUST THINK—
DID YOU LOVE MOM?
OF COURSE I DID. IT'S JUST THAT YOUR MOTHER CAN'T LOVE LIKE—
LIKE A HUMAN BEING?
YES.
I DON'T ASK, "LIKE ME?"
BUT I THINK IT.

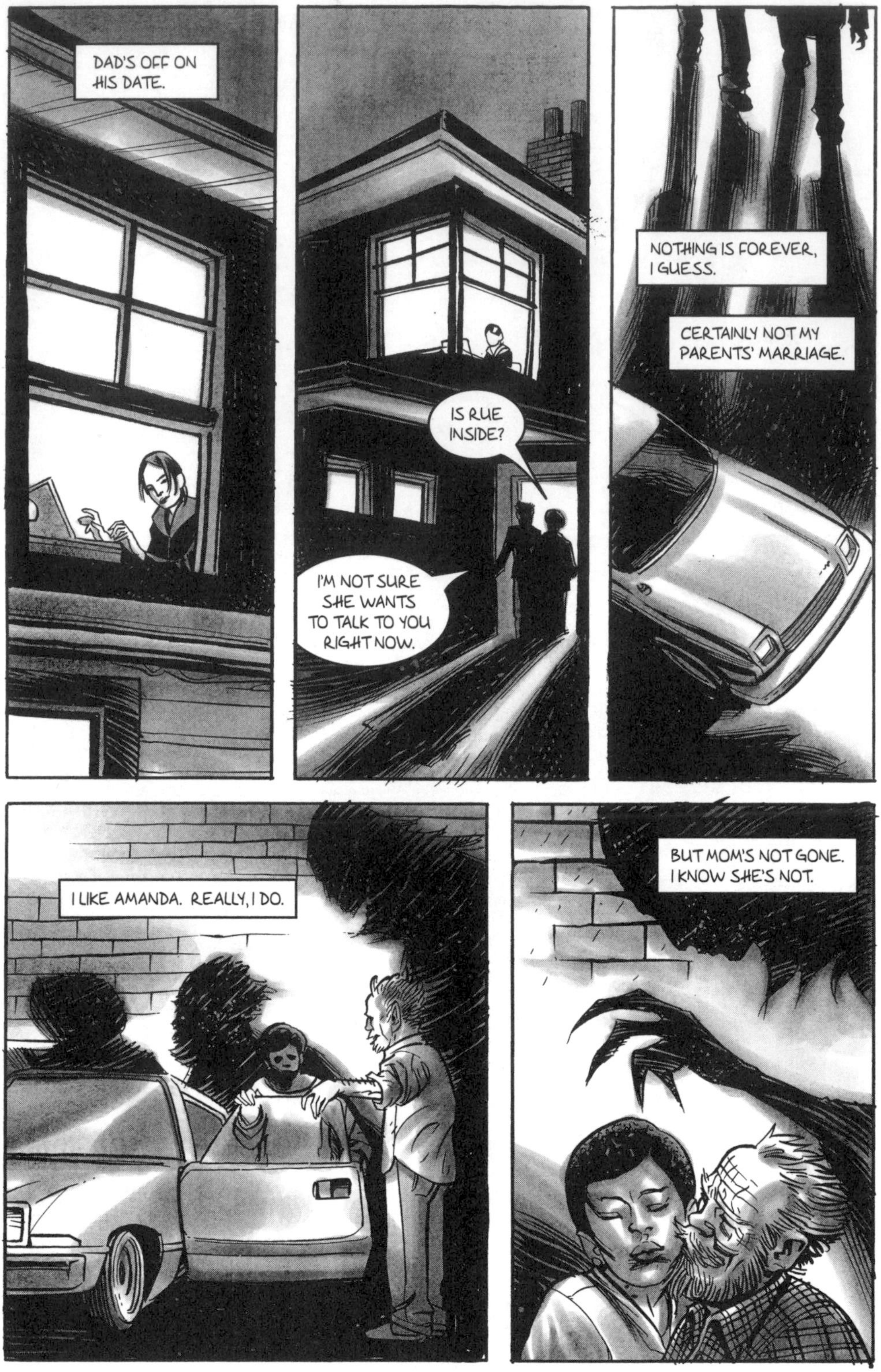
DAD'S OFF ON HIS DATE.
IS RUE INSIDE?
I'M NOT SURE SHE WANTS TO TALK TO YOU RIGHT NOW.
NOTHING IS FOREVER, I GUESS.
CERTAINLY NOT MY PARENTS' MARRIAGE.
I LIKE AMANDA. REALLY, I DO.
BUT MOM'S NOT GONE. I KNOW SHE'S NOT.

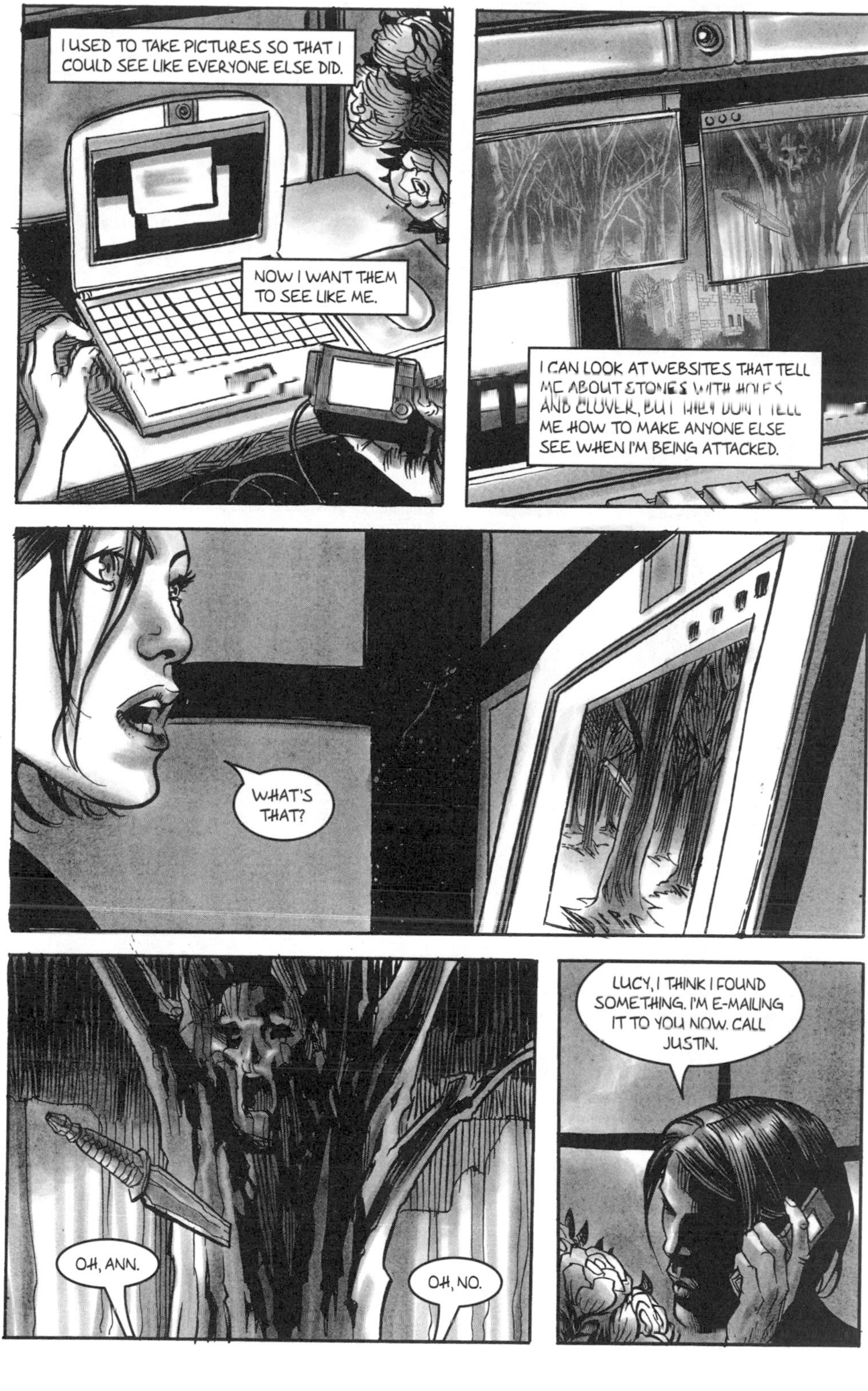
I USED TO TAKE PICTURES SO THAT I COULD SEE LIKE EVERYONE ELSE DID.
NOW I WANT THEM TO SEE LIKE ME.
I CAN LOOK AT WEBSITES THAT TELL ME ABOUT STONES WITH HOLES AND CLOVER, BUT THEY DON'T TELL ME HOW TO MAKE ANYONE ELSE SEE WHEN I'M BEING ATTACKED.
WHAT'S THAT?
OH, ANN.
OH, NO.
LUCY, I THINK I FOUND SOMETHING. I'M E-MAILING IT TO YOU NOW. CALL JUSTIN.

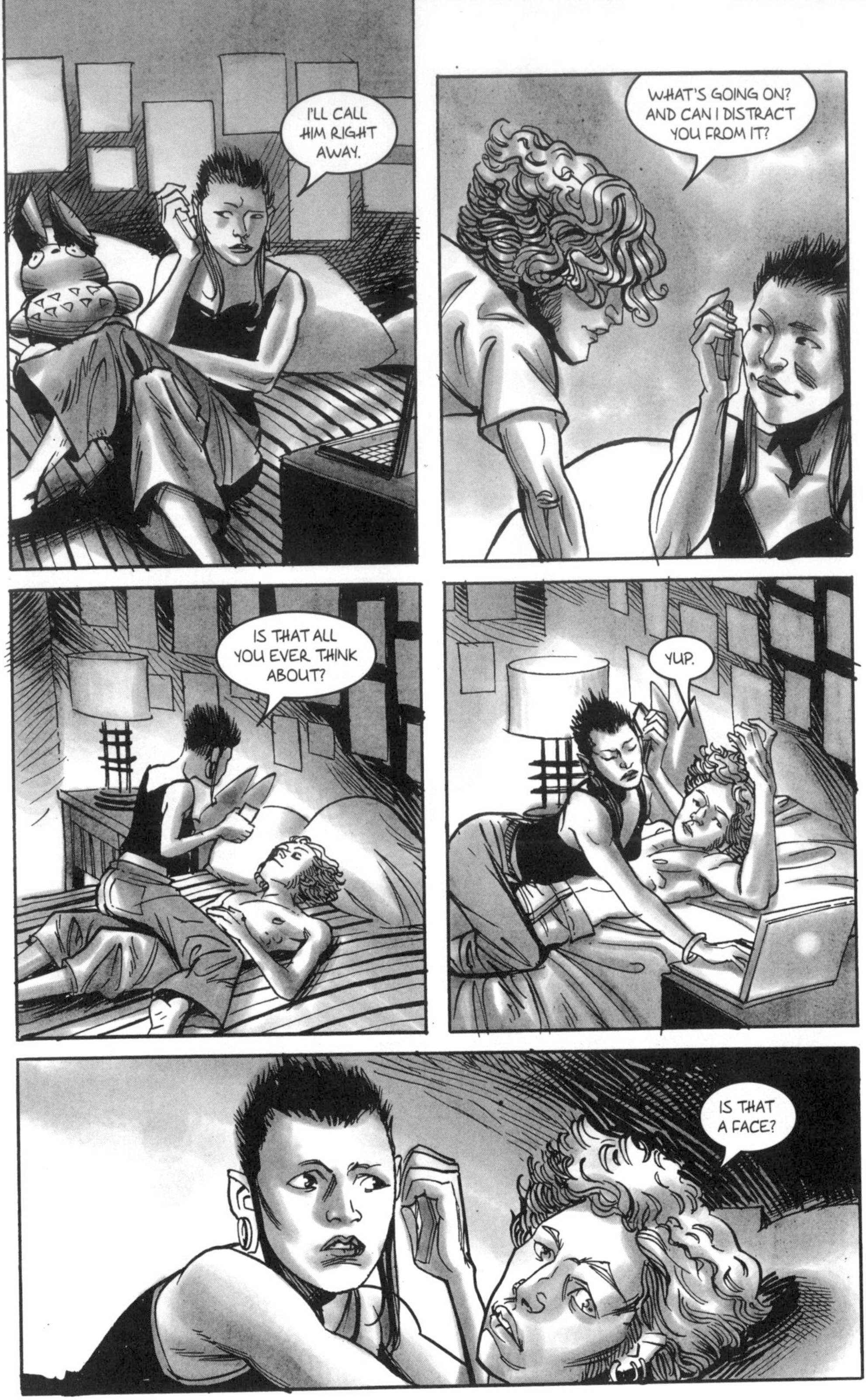
I'LL CALL HIM RIGHT AWAY.
WHAT'S GOING ON? AND CAN I DISTRACT YOU FROM IT?
IS THAT ALL YOU EVER THINK ABOUT?
YUP.
IS THAT A FACE?

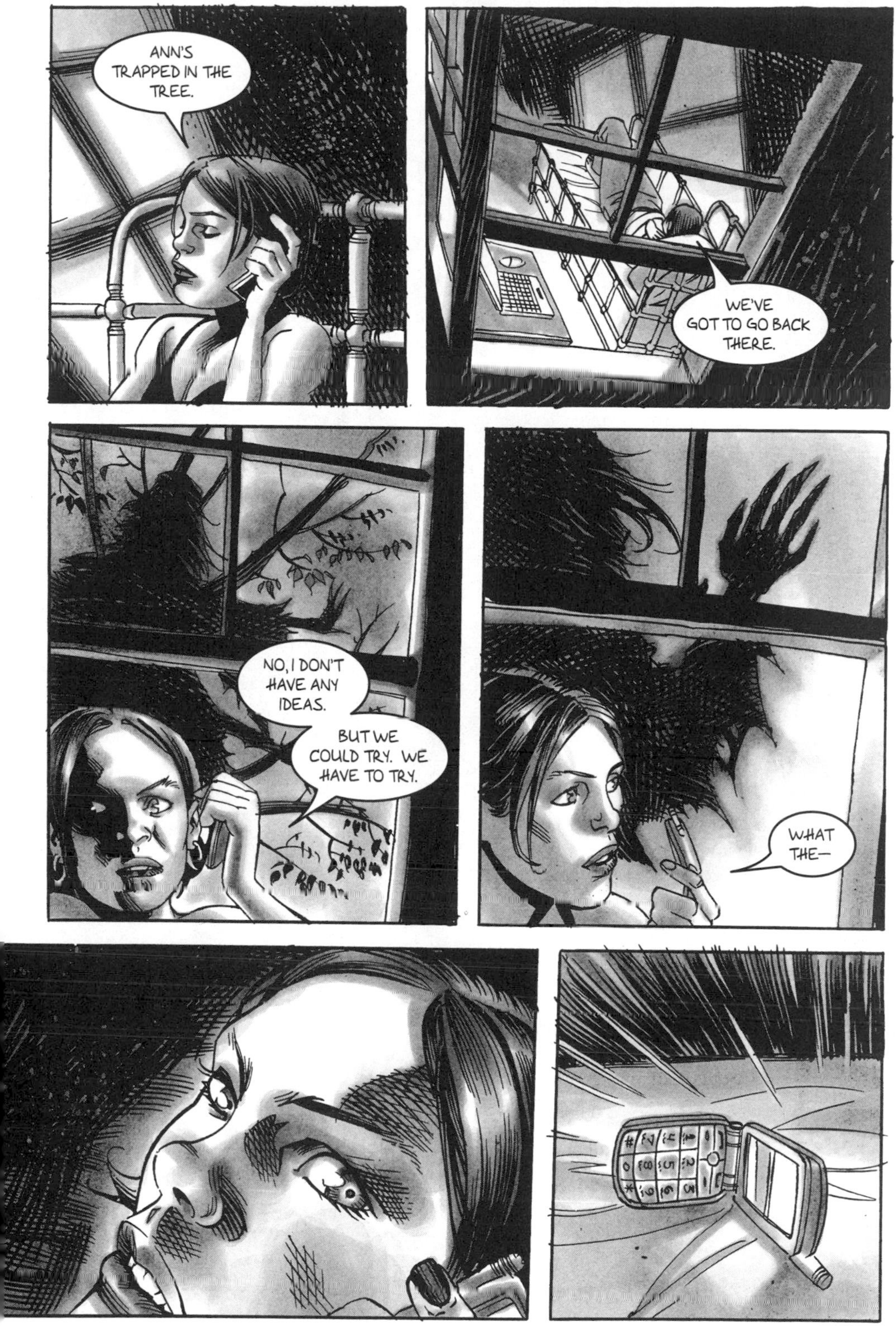
ANN'S TRAPPED IN THE TREE.
WE'VE GOT TO GO BACK THERE.
NO, I DON'T HAVE ANY IDEAS.
BUT WE COULD TRY. WE HAVE TO TRY.
WHAT THE—

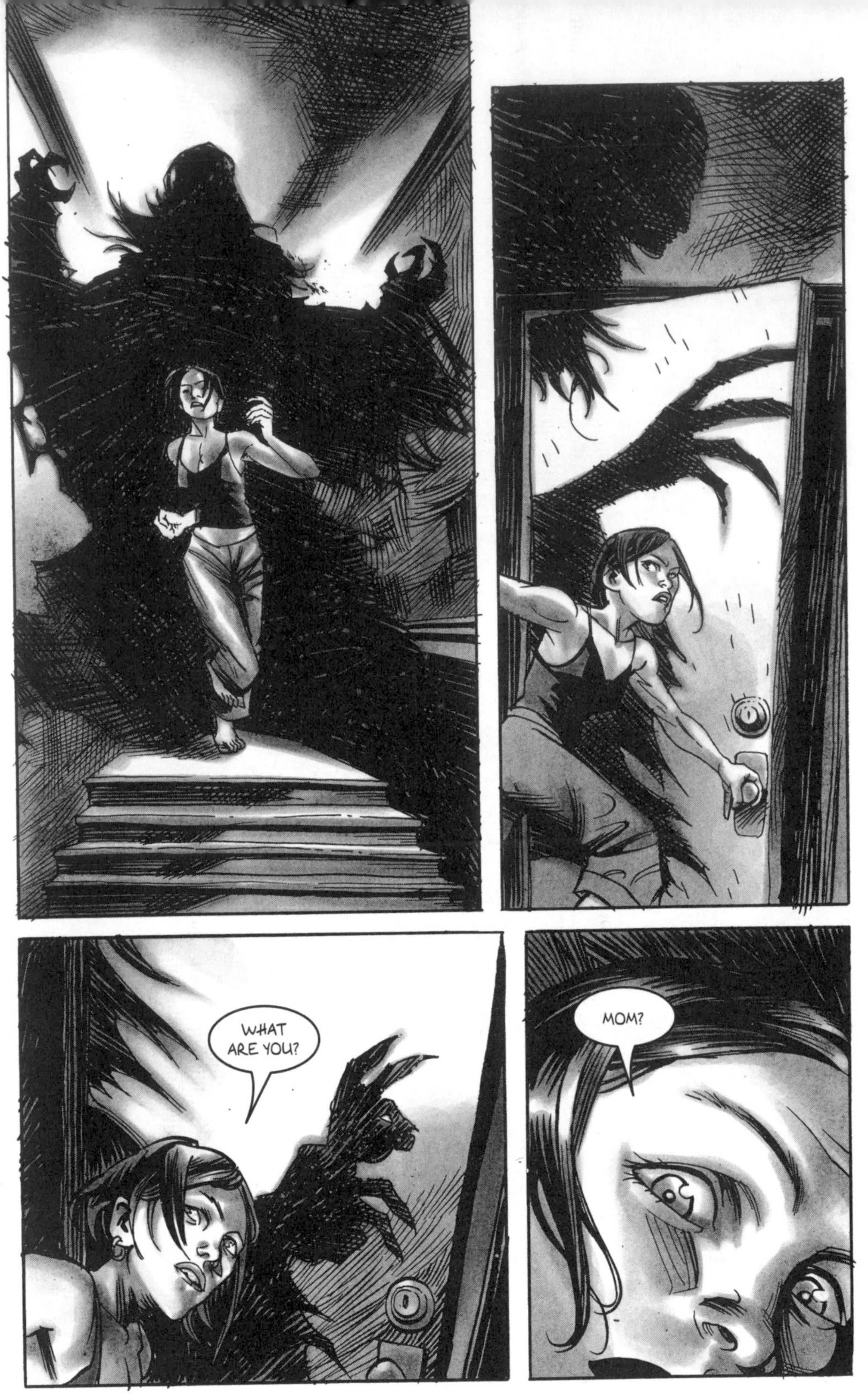
WHAT ARE YOU?
MOM?

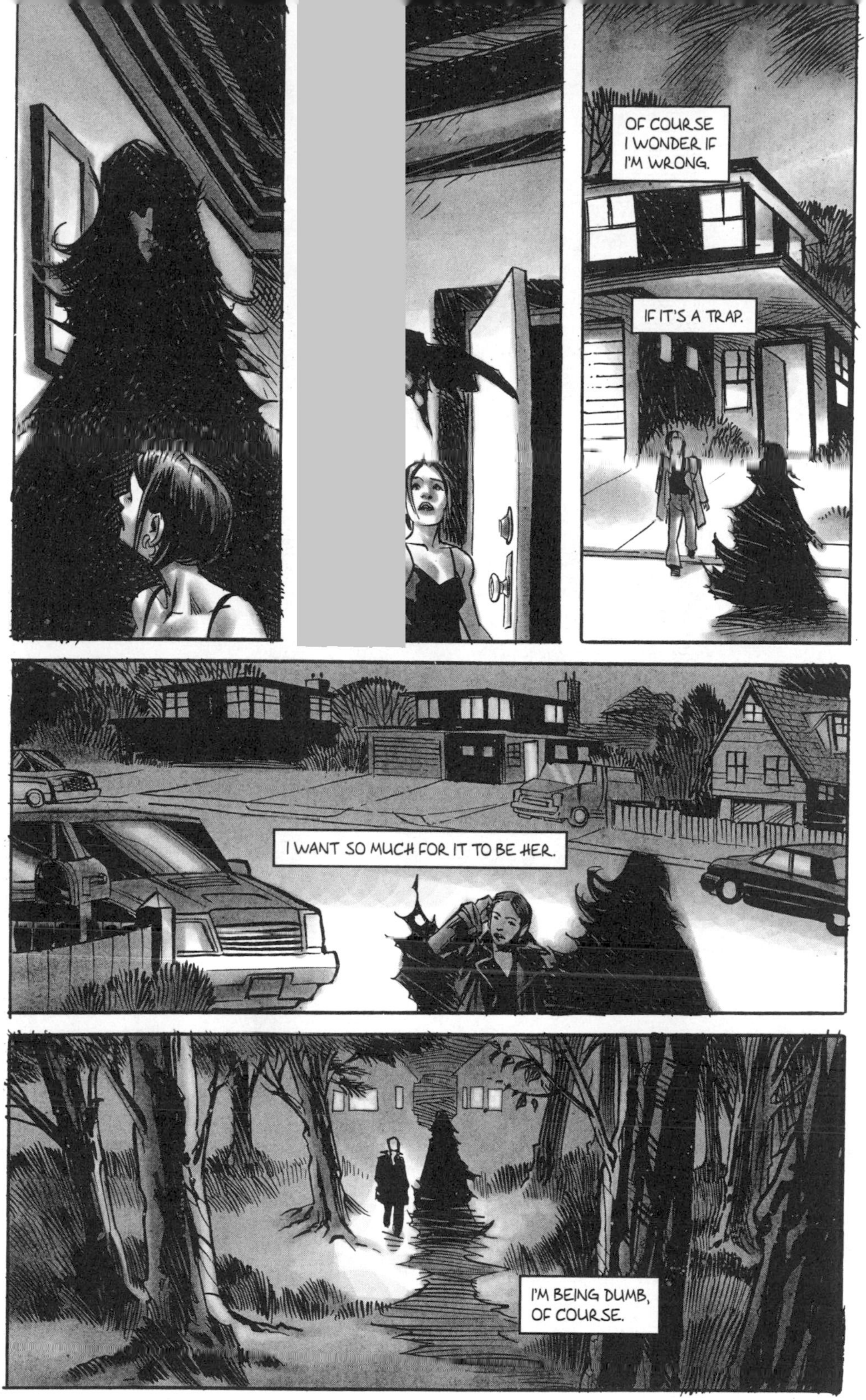
OF COURSE I WONDER IF I'M WRONG.
IF IT'S A TRAP.
I WANT SO MUCH FOR IT TO BE HER.
I'M BEING DUMB, OF COURSE.

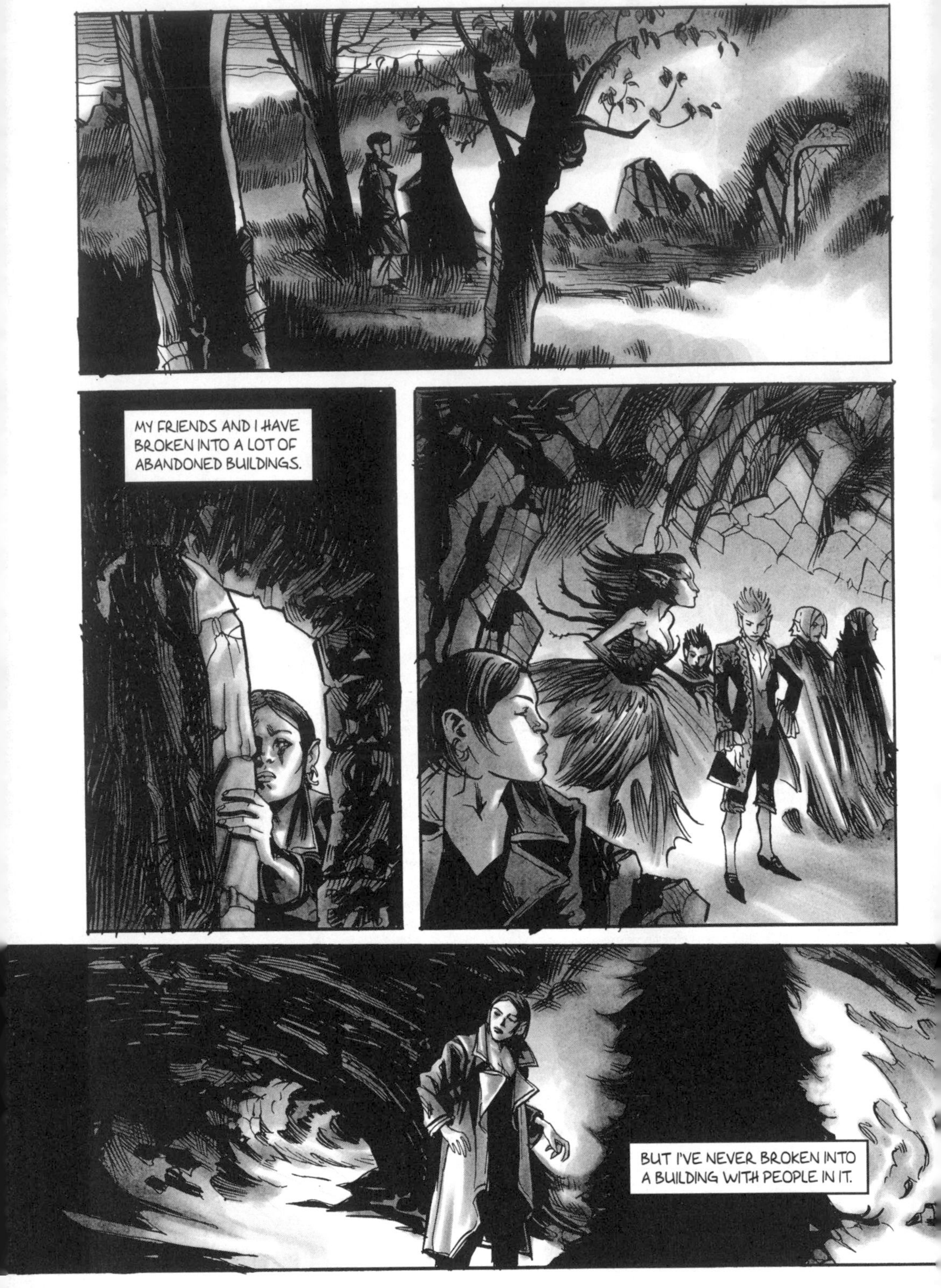
MY FRIENDS AND I HAVE BROKEN INTO A LOT OF ABANDONED BUILDINGS.
BUT I'VE NEVER BROKEN INTO A BUILDING WITH PEOPLE IN IT.

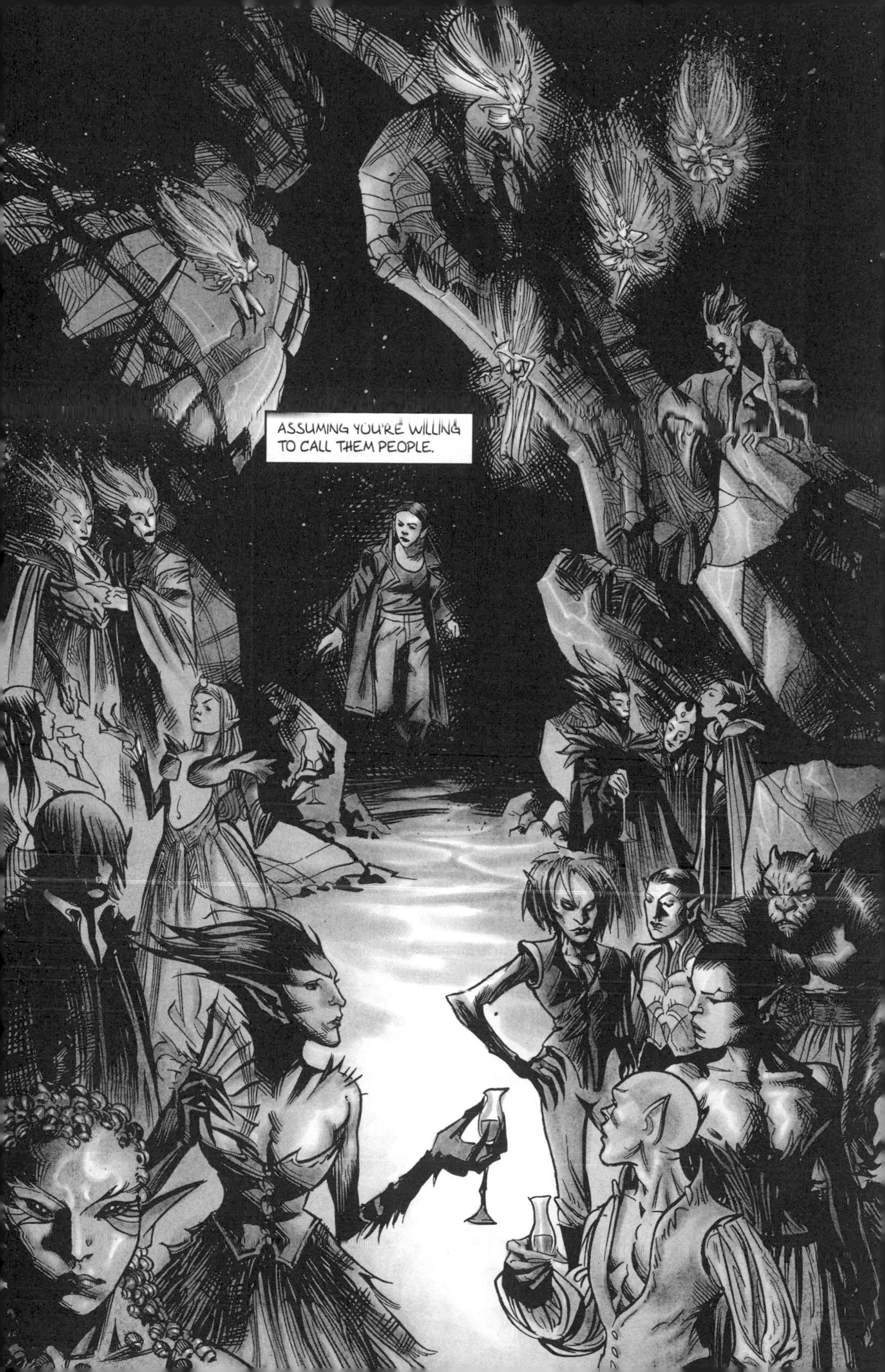
ASSUMING YOU'RE WILLING TO CALL THEM PEOPLE.

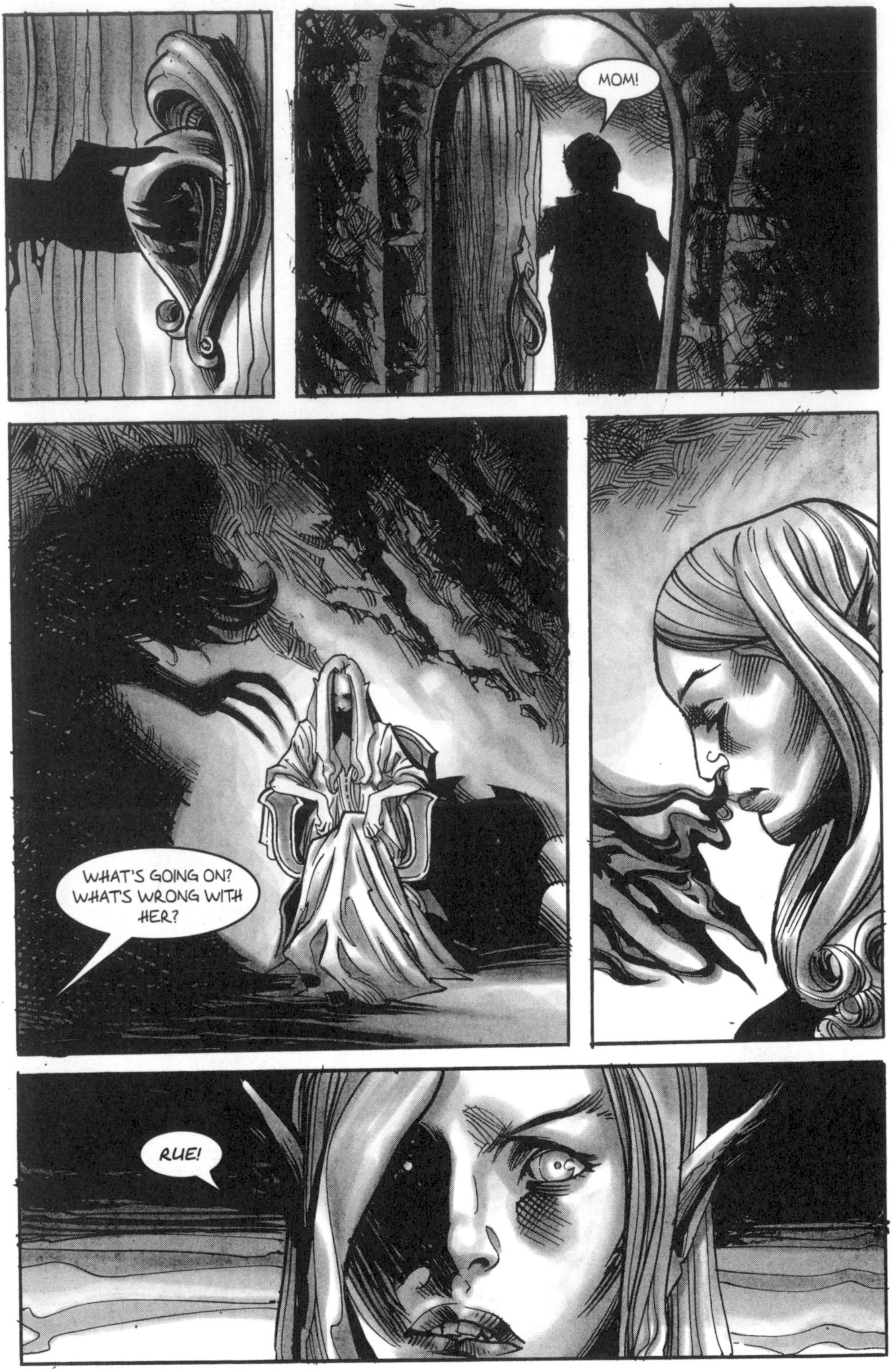
MOM!
WHAT'S GOING ON? WHAT'S WRONG WITH HER?
RUE!

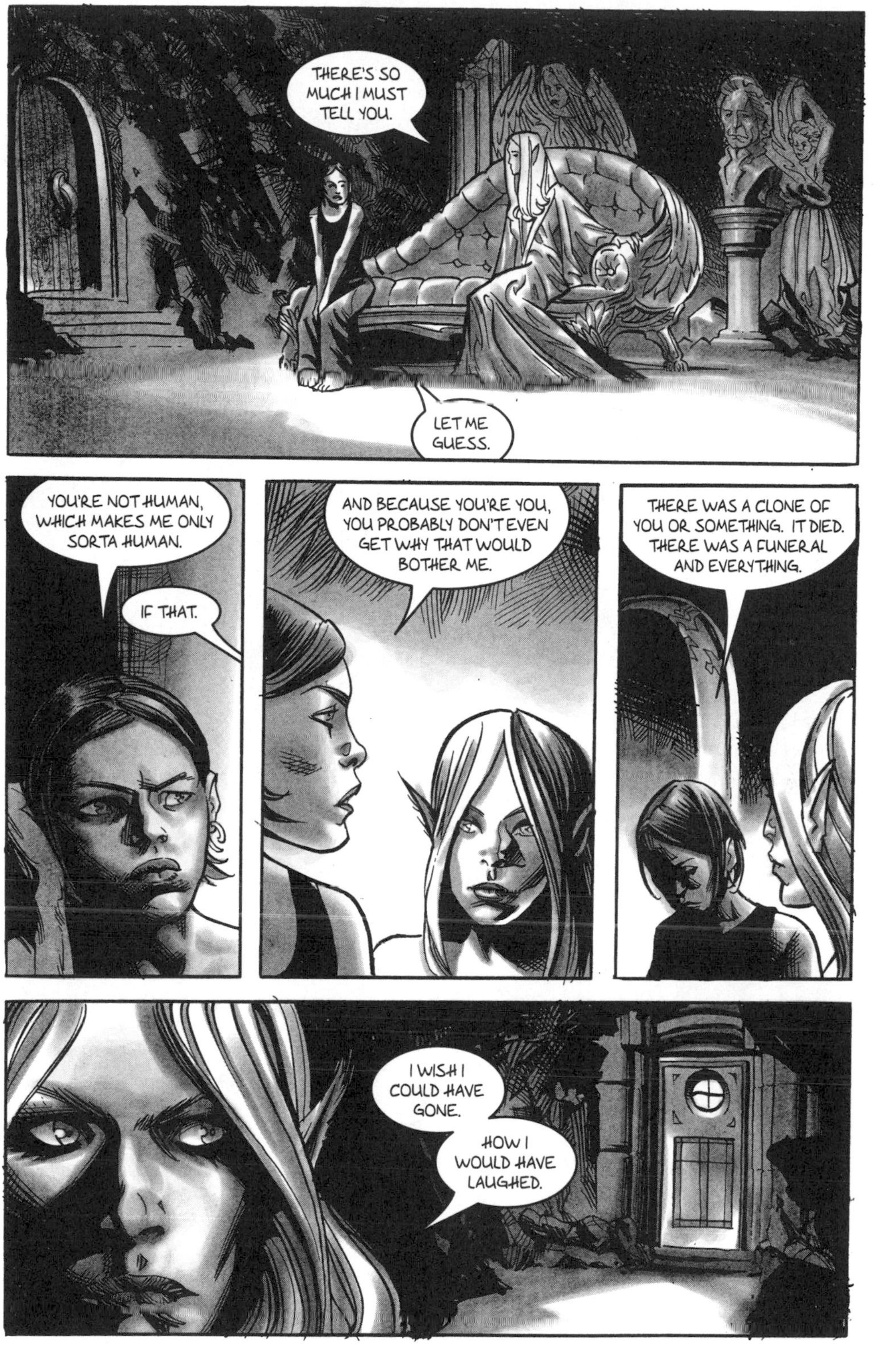
THERE'S SO MUCH I MUST TELL YOU.
LET ME GUESS.
YOU'RE NOT HUMAN, WHICH MAKES ME ONLY SORTA HUMAN.
IF THAT.
AND BECAUSE YOU'RE YOU, YOU PROBABLY DON'T EVEN GET WHY THAT WOULD BOTHER ME.
THERE WAS A CLONE OF YOU OR SOMETHING. IT DIED. THERE WAS A FUNERAL AND EVERYTHING.
I WISH I COULD HAVE GONE.
HOW I WOULD HAVE LAUGHED.

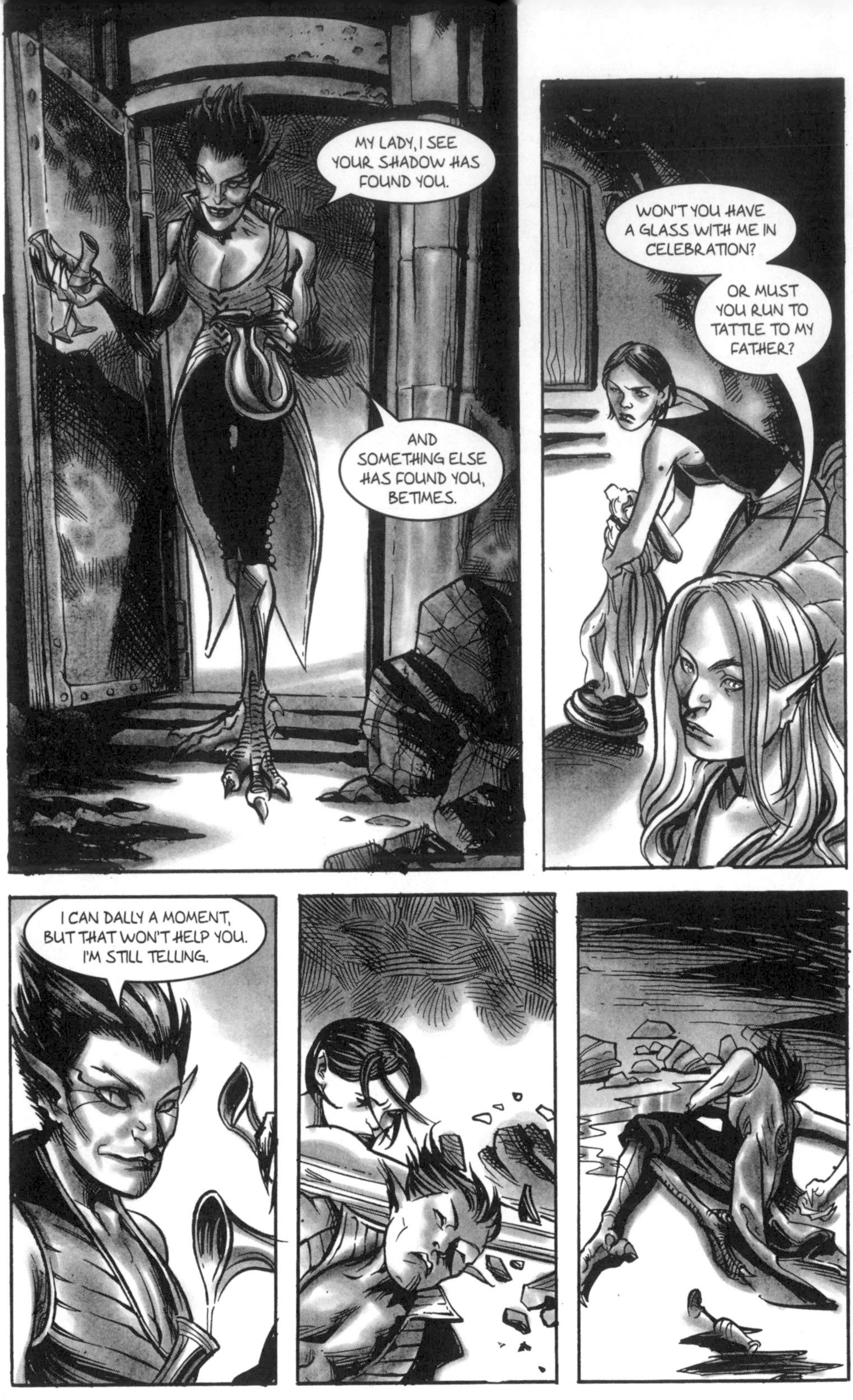
MY LADY, I SEE YOUR SHADOW HAS FOUND YOU.
AND SOMETHING ELSE HAS FOUND YOU, BETIMES.
WON'T YOU HAVE A GLASS WITH ME IN CELEBRATION?
OR MUST YOU RUN TO TATTLE TO MY FATHER?
I CAN DALLY A MOMENT, BUT THAT WON'T HELP YOU. I'M STILL TELLING.

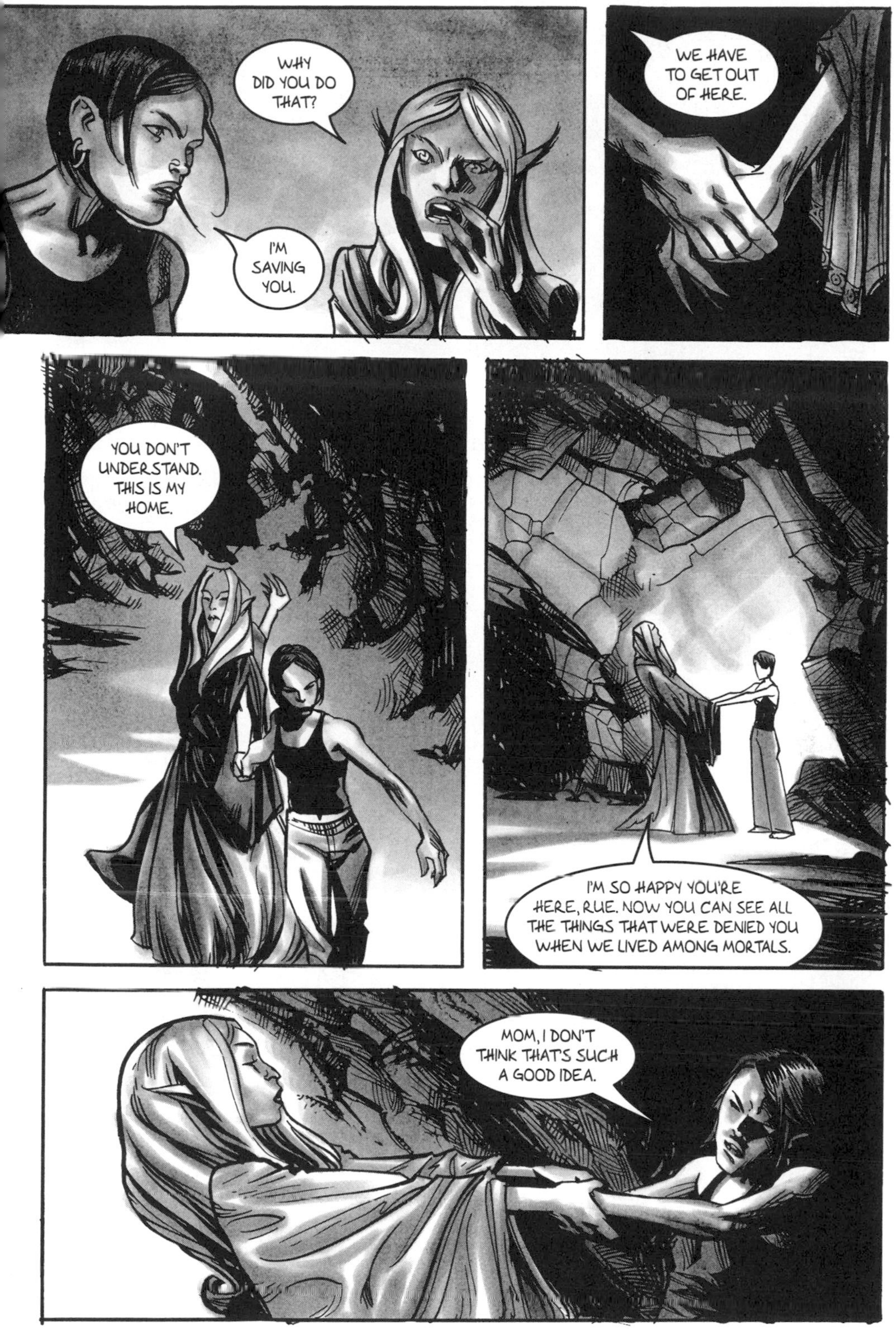
WHY DID YOU DO THAT?
I'M SAVING YOU.
WE HAVE TO GET OUT OF HERE.
YOU DON'T UNDERSTAND. THIS IS MY HOME.
I'M SO HAPPY YOU'RE HERE, RUE. NOW YOU CAN SEE ALL THE THINGS THAT WERE DENIED YOU WHEN WE LIVED AMONG MORTALS.
MOM, I DON'T THINK THAT'S SUCH A GOOD IDEA.

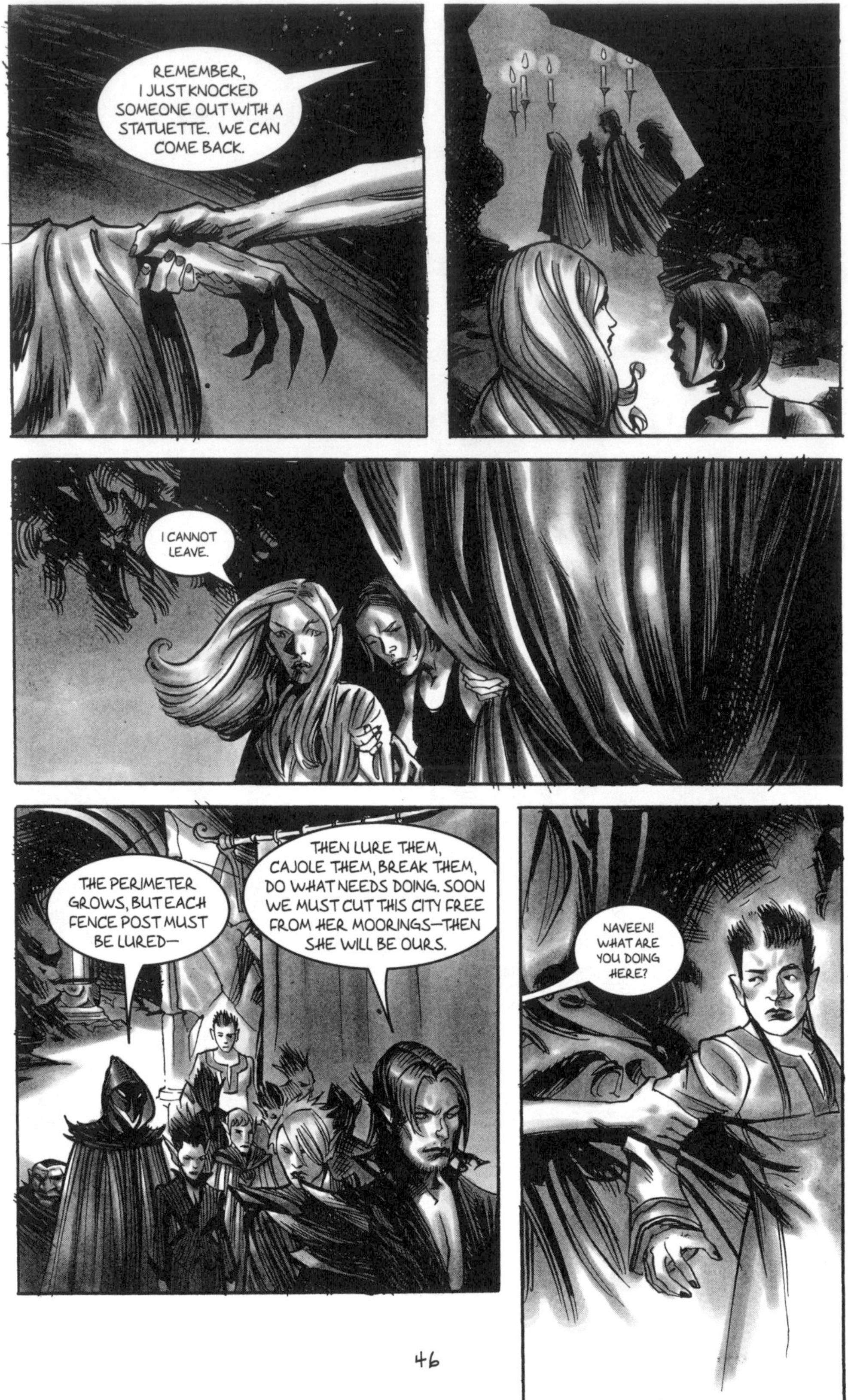
REMEMBER, I JUST KNOCKED SOMEONE OUT WITH A STATUETTE. WE CAN COME BACK.
I CANNOT LEAVE.
THE PERIMETER GROWS, BUT EACH FENCE POST MUST BE LURED—
THEN LURE THEM, CAJOLE THEM, BREAK THEM, DO WHAT NEEDS DOING. SOON WE MUST CUT THIS CITY FREE FROM HER MOORINGS—THEN SHE WILL BE OURS.
NAVEEN! WHAT ARE YOU DOING HERE?

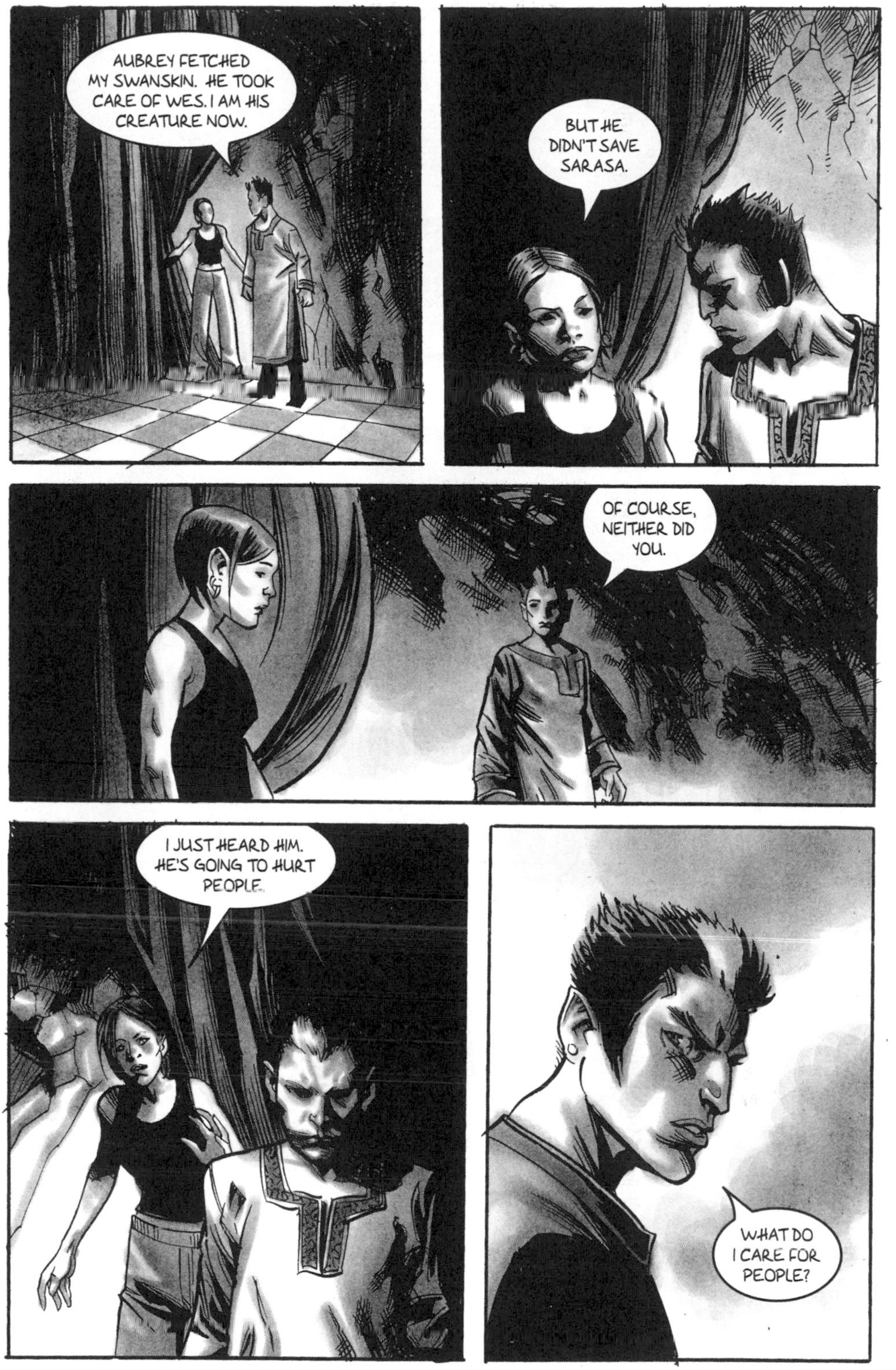
AUBREY FETCHED MY SWANSKIN. HE TOOK CARE OF WES. I AM HIS CREATURE NOW.
BUT HE DIDN'T SAVE SARASA.
OF COURSE, NEITHER DID YOU.
I JUST HEARD HIM. HE'S GOING TO HURT PEOPLE.
WHAT DO I CARE FOR PEOPLE?

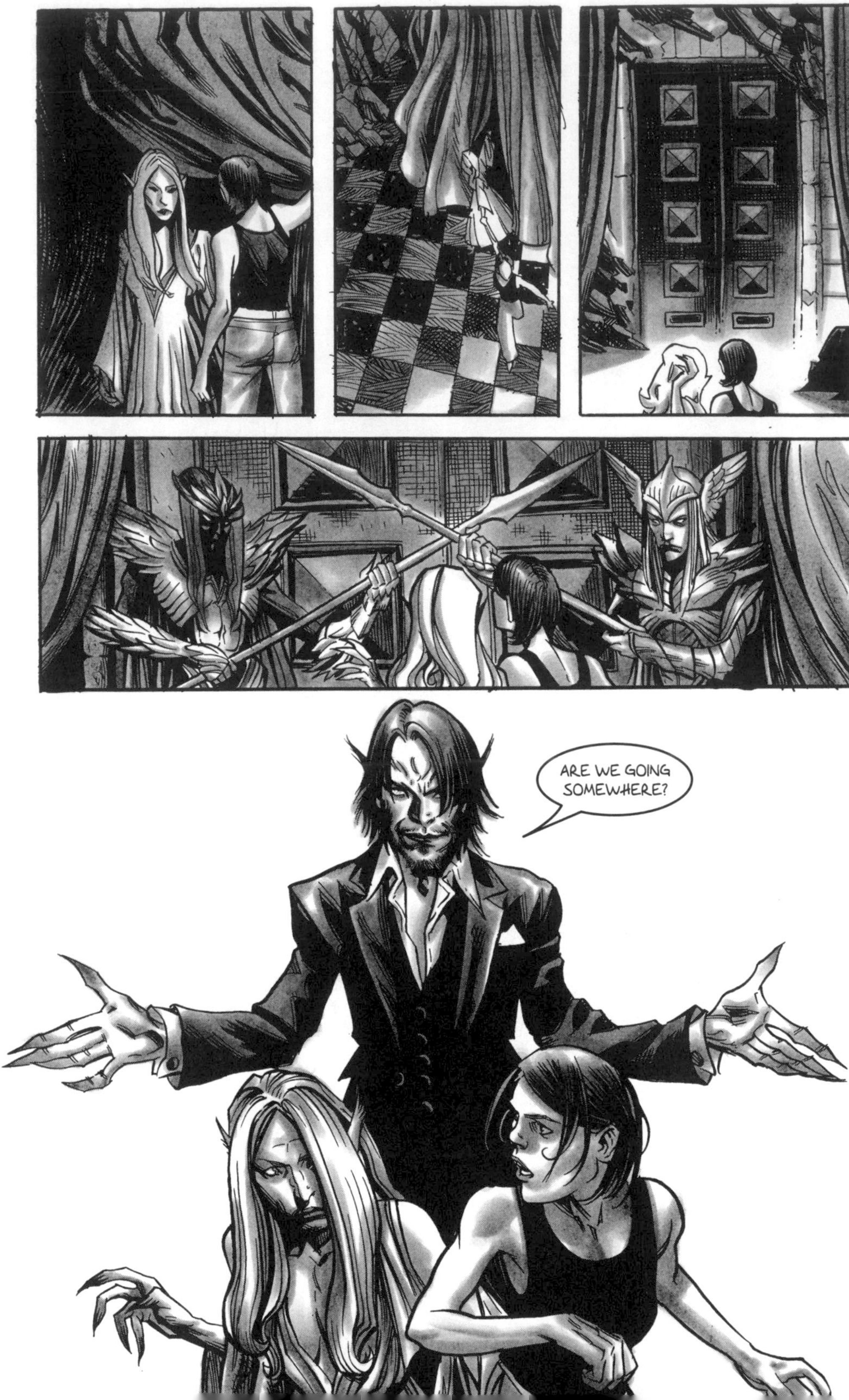
ARE WE GOING SOMEWHERE?

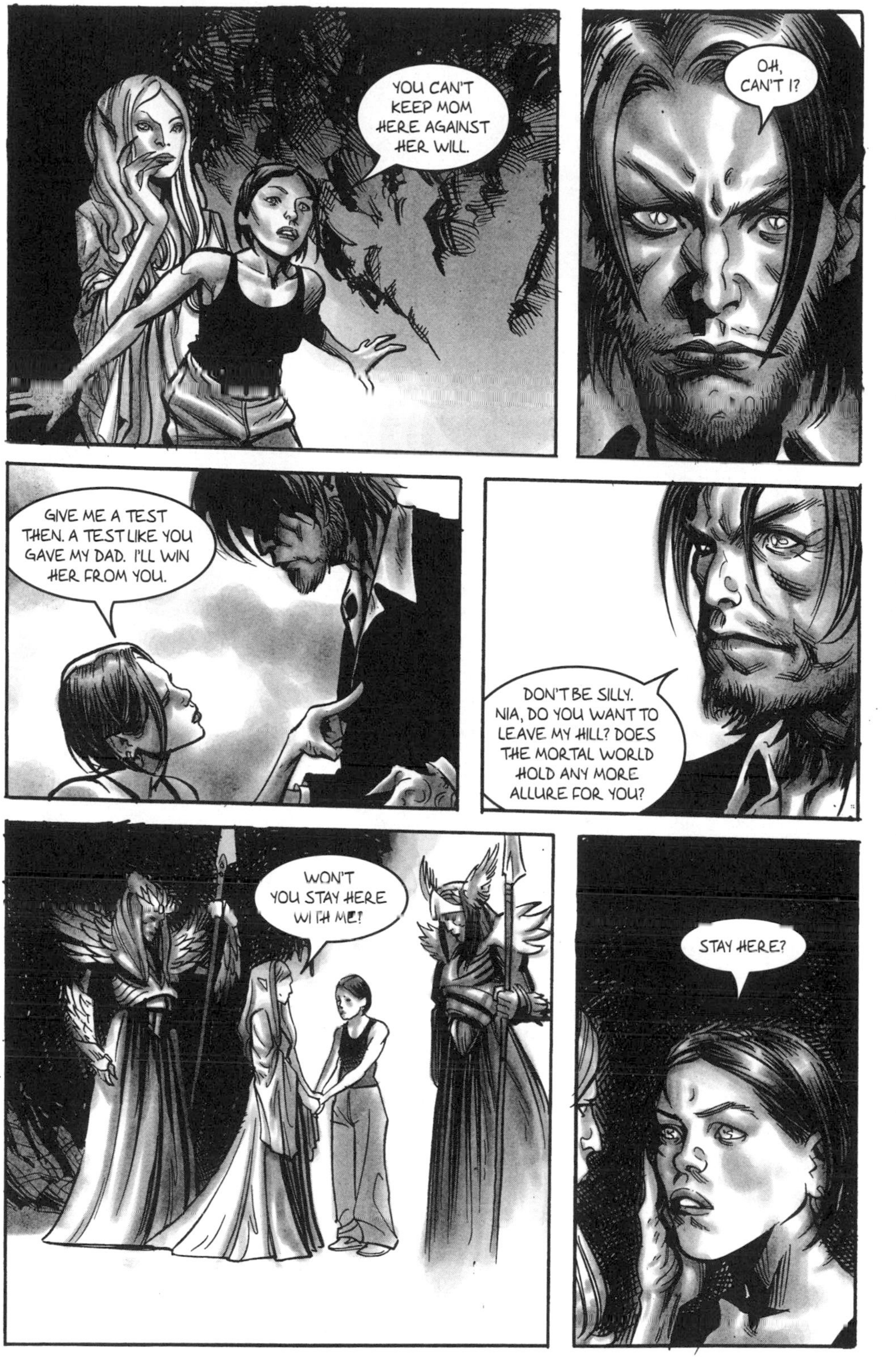
YOU CAN'T KEEP MOM HERE AGAINST HER WILL.
OH, CAN'T I?
GIVE ME A TEST THEN. A TEST LIKE YOU GAVE MY DAD. I'LL WIN HER FROM YOU.
DON'T BE SILLY. NIA, DO YOU WANT TO LEAVE MY HILL? DOES THE MORTAL WORLD HOLD ANY MORE ALLURE FOR YOU?
WON'T YOU STAY HERE WITH ME?
STAY HERE?

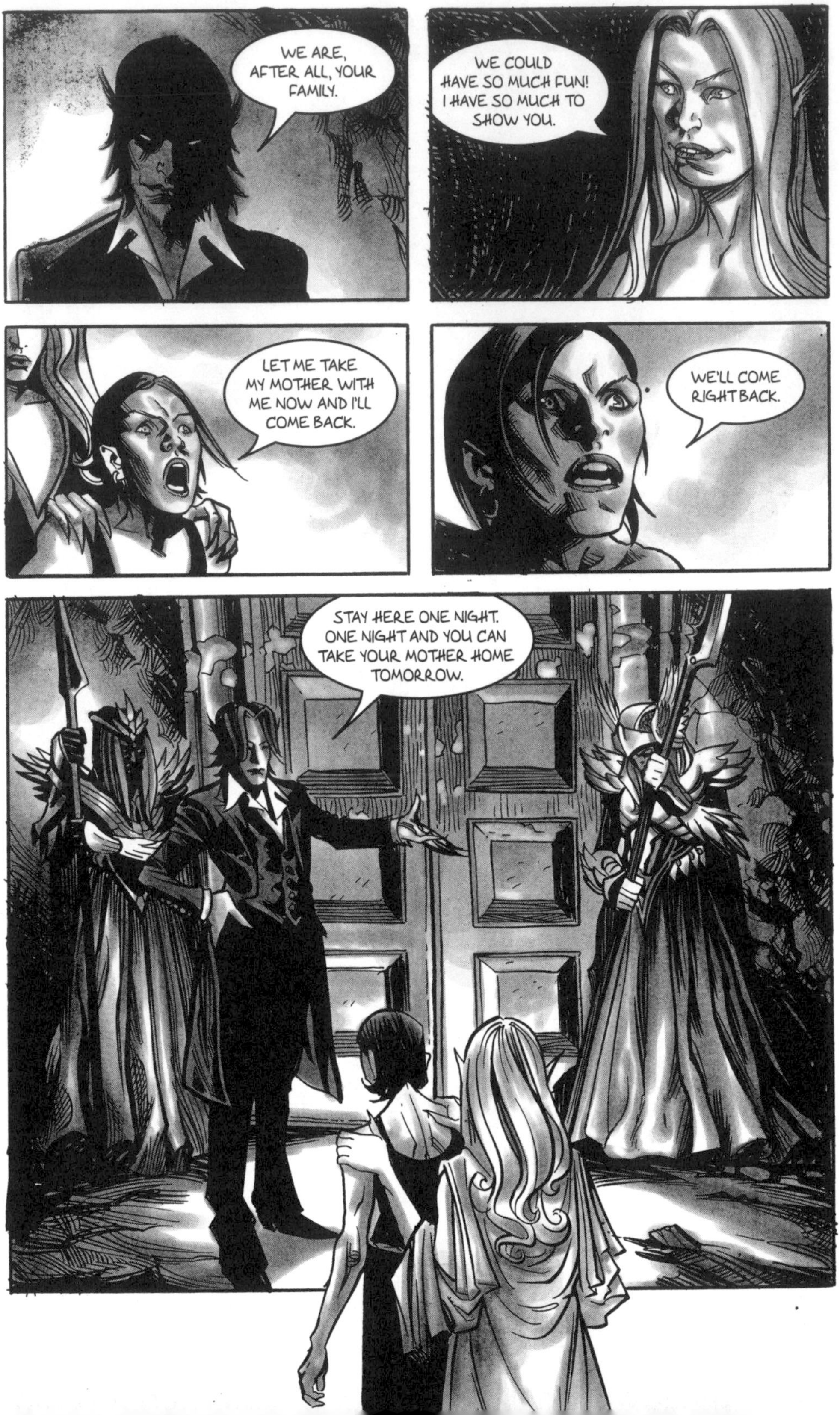
WE ARE, AFTER ALL, YOUR FAMILY.
WE COULD HAVE SO MUCH FUN! I HAVE SO MUCH TO SHOW YOU.
LET ME TAKE MY MOTHER WITH ME NOW AND I'LL COME BACK.
WE'LL COME RIGHT BACK.
STAY HERE ONE NIGHT. ONE NIGHT AND YOU CAN TAKE YOUR MOTHER HOME TOMORROW.

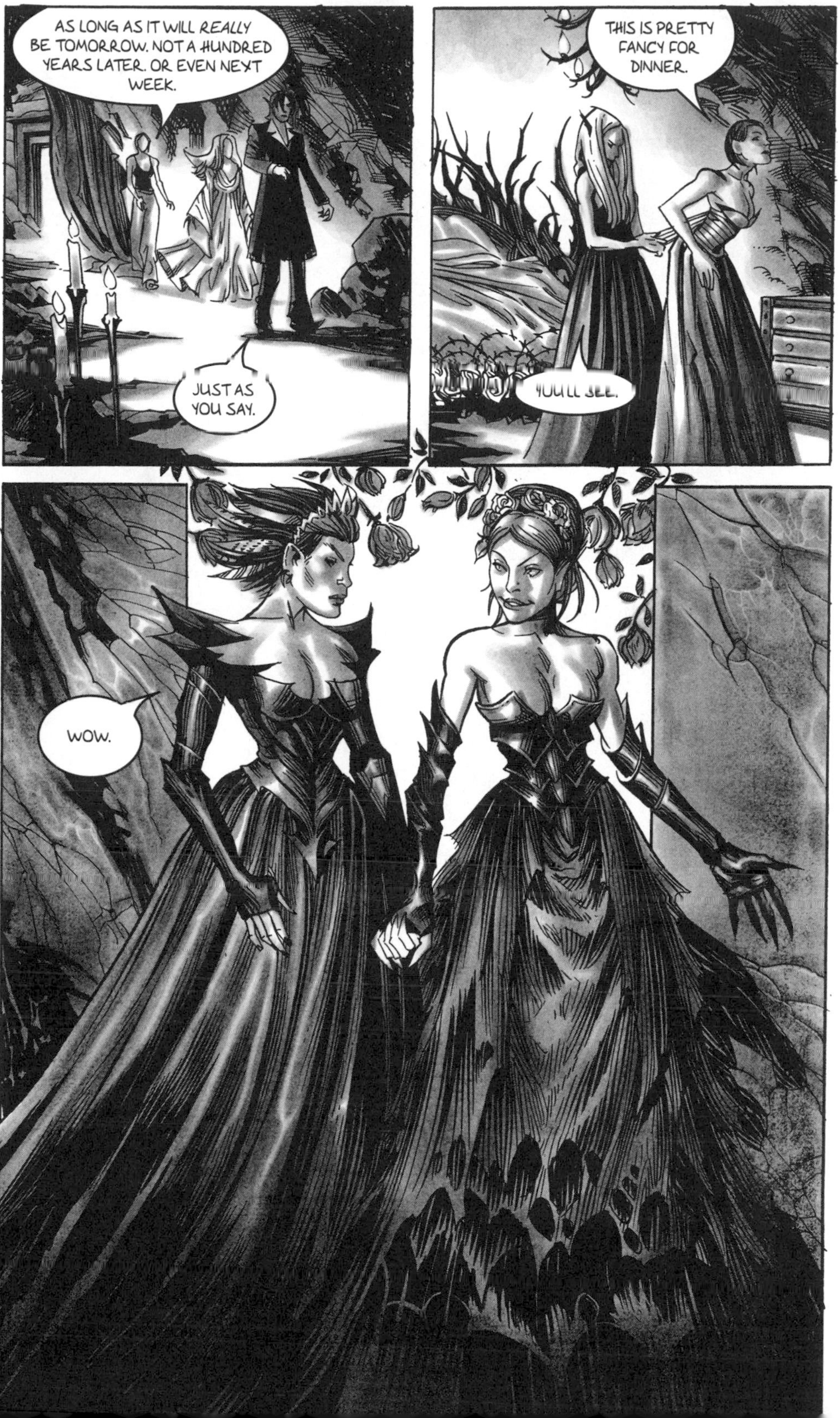
AS LONG AS IT WILL *REALLY* BE TOMORROW. NOT A HUNDRED YEARS LATER. OR EVEN NEXT WEEK.
JUST AS YOU SAY.
THIS IS PRETTY FANCY FOR DINNER.
YOU'LL SEE.
WOW.

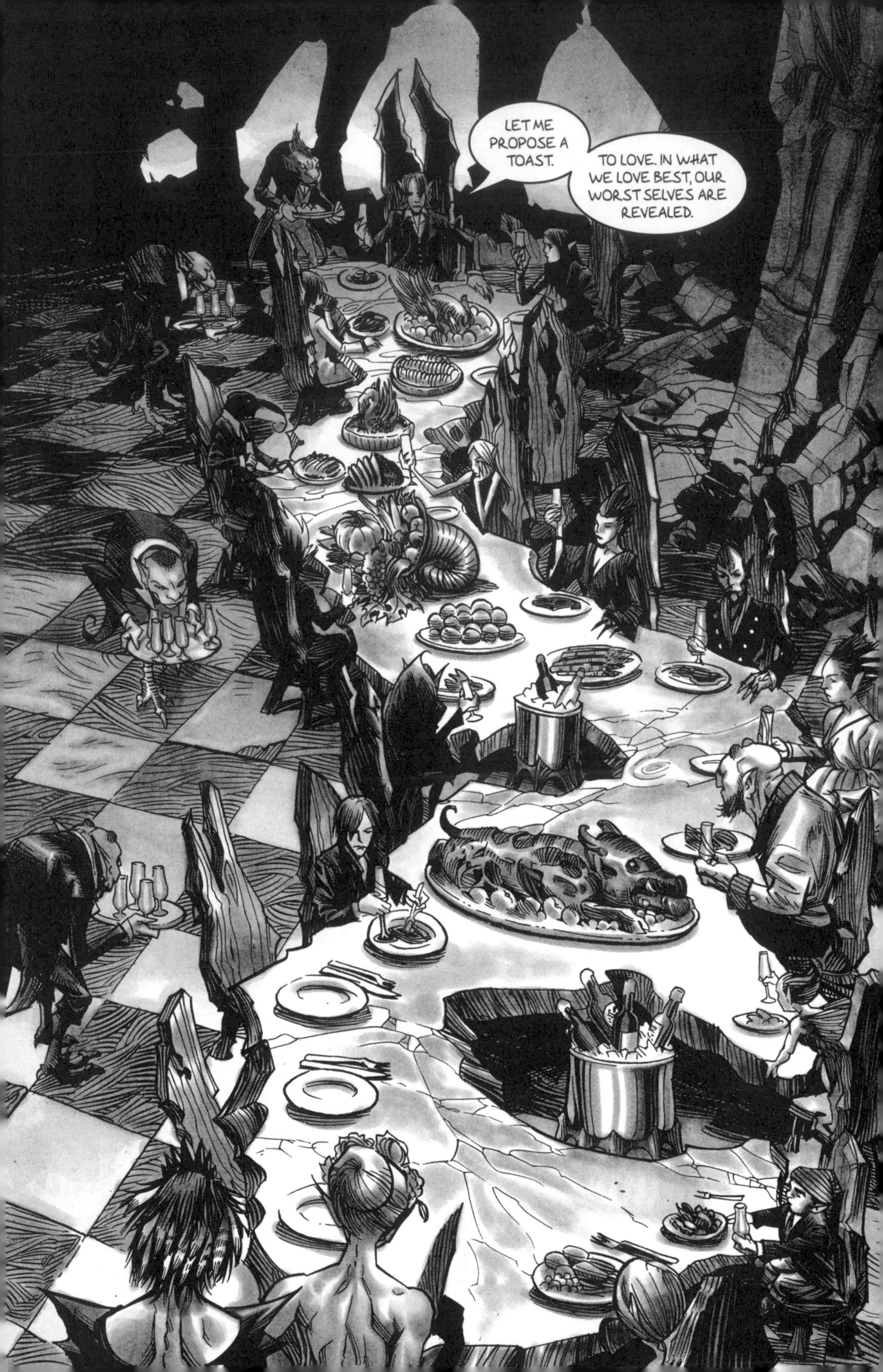
LET ME PROPOSE A TOAST.
TO LOVE. IN WHAT WE LOVE BEST, OUR WORST SELVES ARE REVEALED.

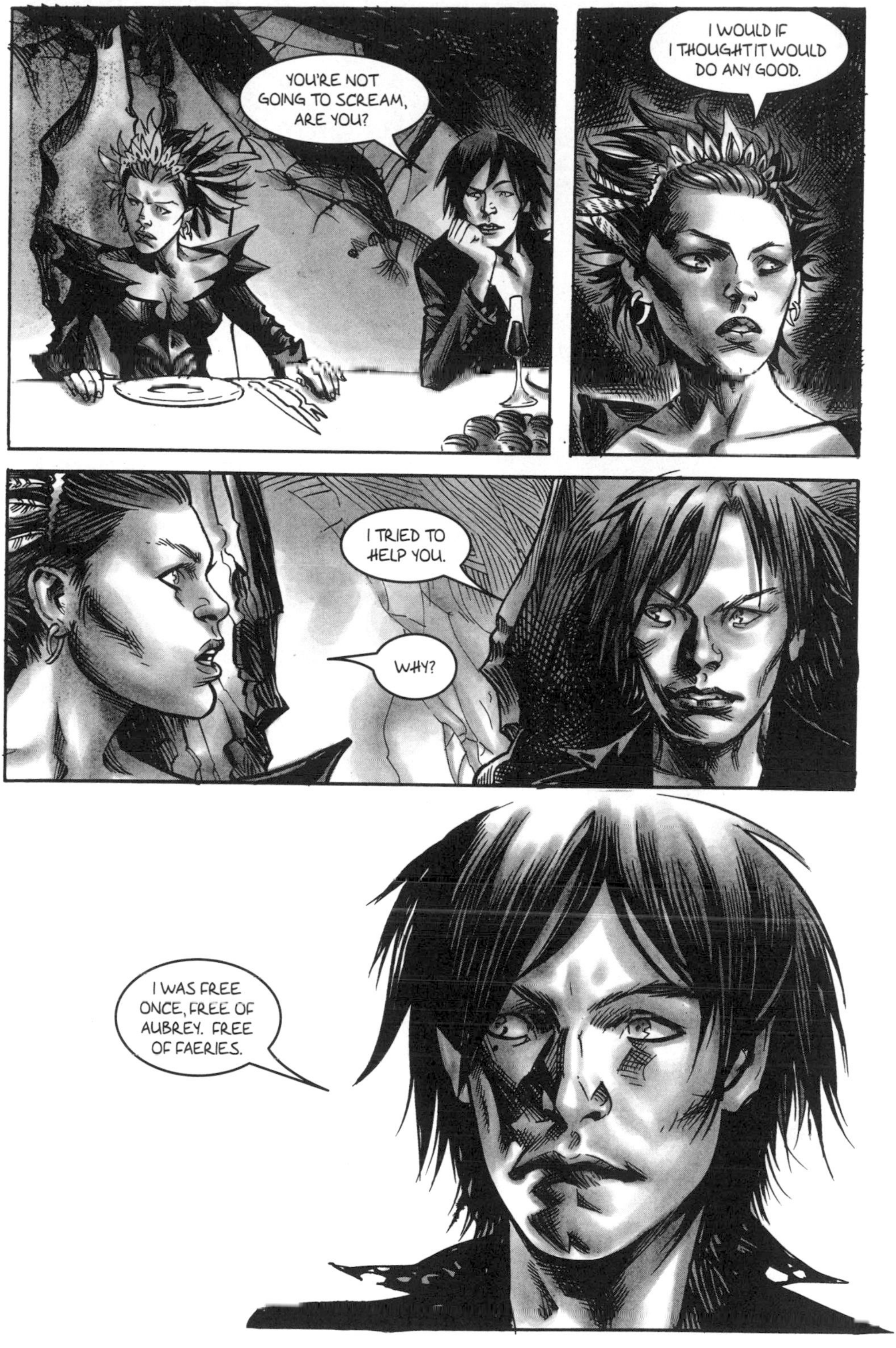
YOU'RE NOT GOING TO SCREAM, ARE YOU?
I WOULD IF I THOUGHT IT WOULD DO ANY GOOD.
I TRIED TO HELP YOU.
WHY?
I WAS FREE ONCE, FREE OF AUBREY. FREE OF FAERIES.

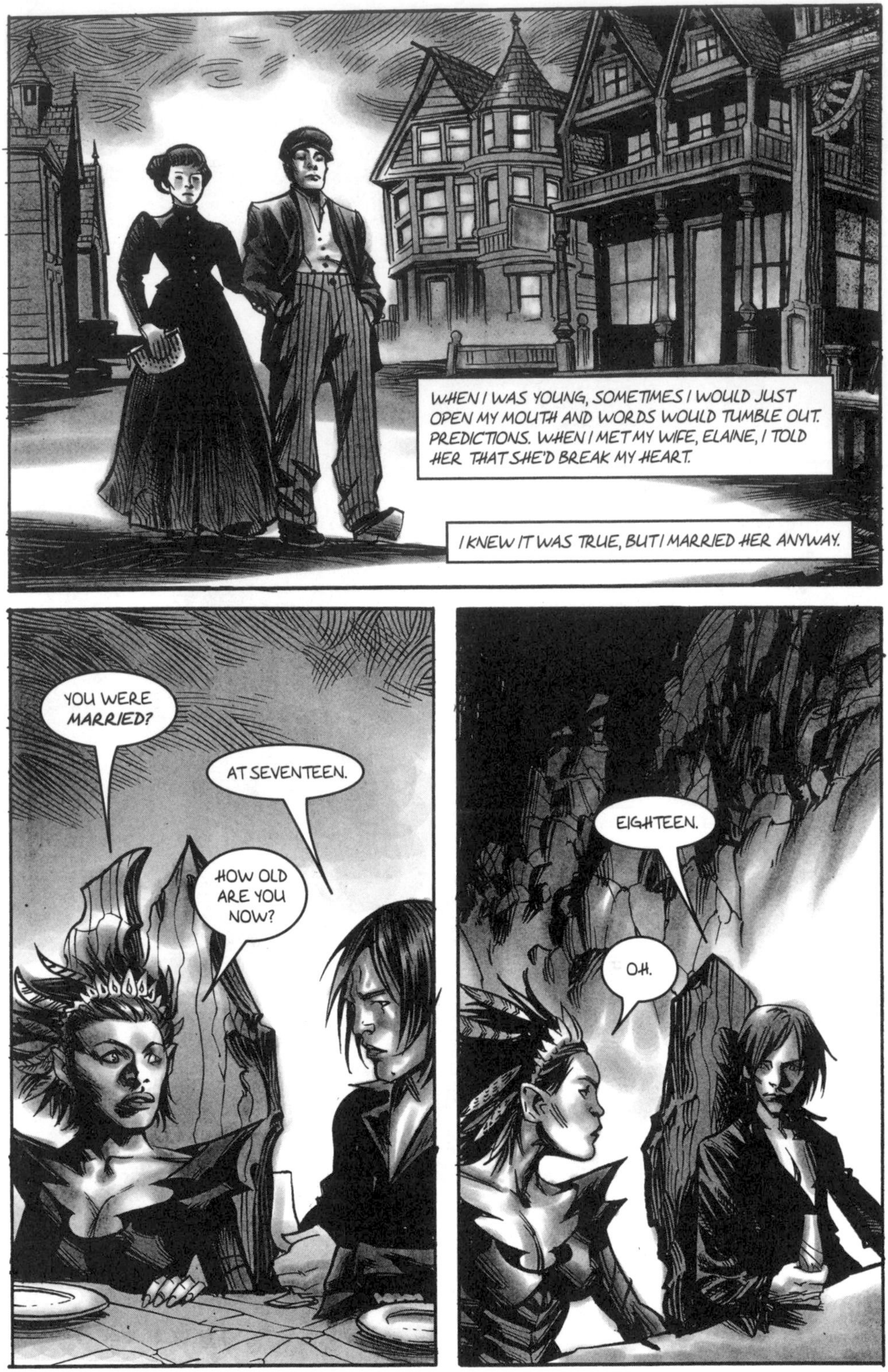
WHEN I WAS YOUNG, SOMETIMES I WOULD JUST OPEN MY MOUTH AND WORDS WOULD TUMBLE OUT. PREDICTIONS. WHEN I MET MY WIFE, ELAINE, I TOLD HER THAT SHE'D BREAK MY HEART.
I KNEW IT WAS TRUE, BUT I MARRIED HER ANYWAY.
YOU WERE MARRIED?
AT SEVENTEEN.
HOW OLD ARE YOU NOW?
EIGHTEEN.
OH.

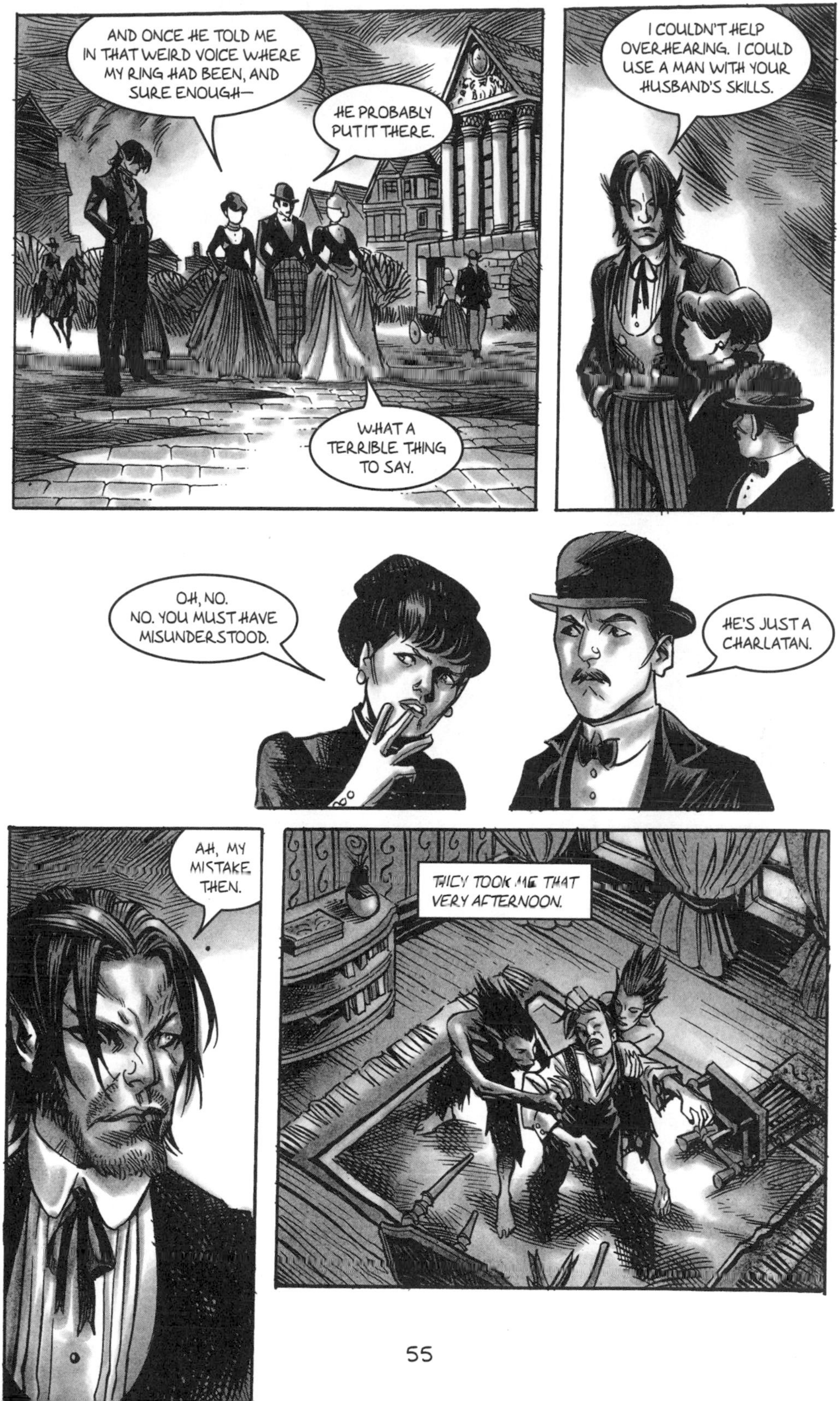
AND ONCE HE TOLD ME IN THAT WEIRD VOICE WHERE MY RING HAD BEEN, AND SURE ENOUGH—
HE PROBABLY PUT IT THERE.
WHAT A TERRIBLE THING TO SAY.
I COULDN'T HELP OVERHEARING. I COULD USE A MAN WITH YOUR HUSBAND'S SKILLS.
OH, NO. NO. YOU MUST HAVE MISUNDERSTOOD.
HE'S JUST A CHARLATAN.
AH, MY MISTAKE THEN.
THEY TOOK ME THAT VERY AFTERNOON.

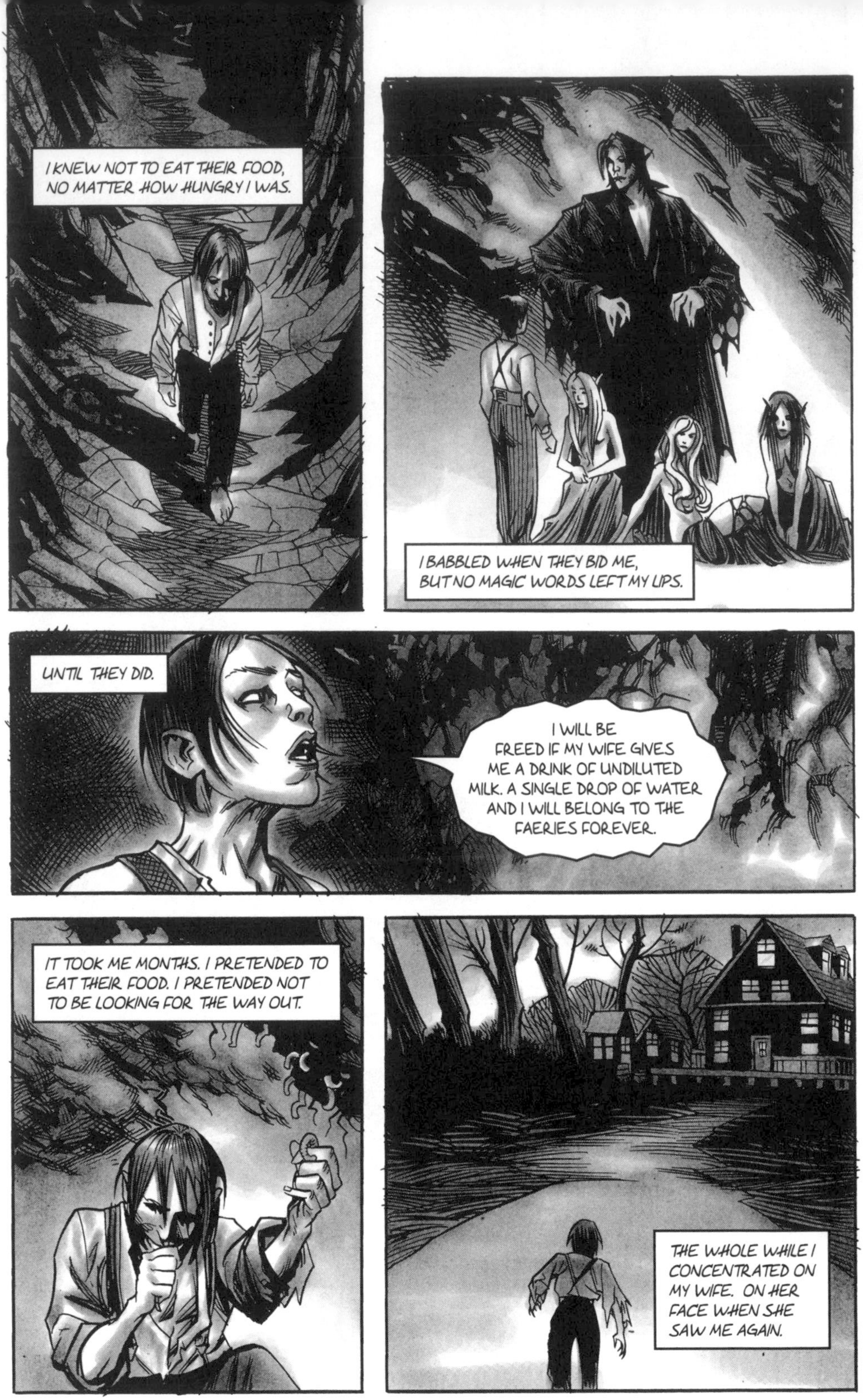
I KNEW NOT TO EAT THEIR FOOD, NO MATTER HOW HUNGRY I WAS.
I BABBLED WHEN THEY BID ME, BUT NO MAGIC WORDS LEFT MY LIPS.
UNTIL THEY DID.
I WILL BE FREED IF MY WIFE GIVES ME A DRINK OF UNDILUTED MILK. A SINGLE DROP OF WATER AND I WILL BELONG TO THE FAERIES FOREVER.
IT TOOK ME MONTHS. I PRETENDED TO EAT THEIR FOOD. I PRETENDED NOT TO BE LOOKING FOR THE WAY OUT.
THE WHOLE WHILE I CONCENTRATED ON MY WIFE. ON HER FACE WHEN SHE SAW ME AGAIN.

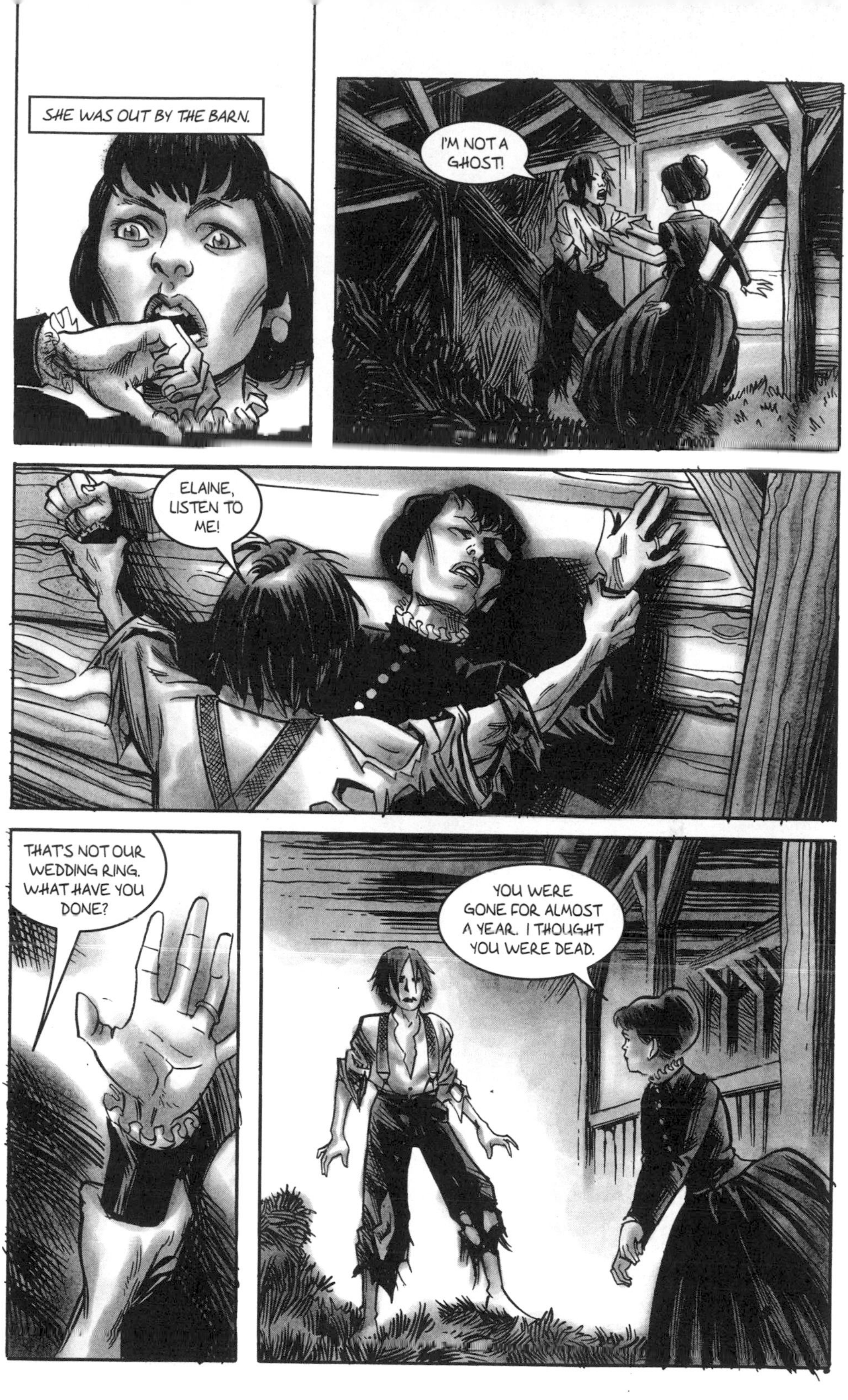
SHE WAS OUT BY THE BARN.
I'M NOT A GHOST!
ELAINE, LISTEN TO ME!
THAT'S NOT OUR WEDDING RING. WHAT HAVE YOU DONE?
YOU WERE GONE FOR ALMOST A YEAR. I THOUGHT YOU WERE DEAD.

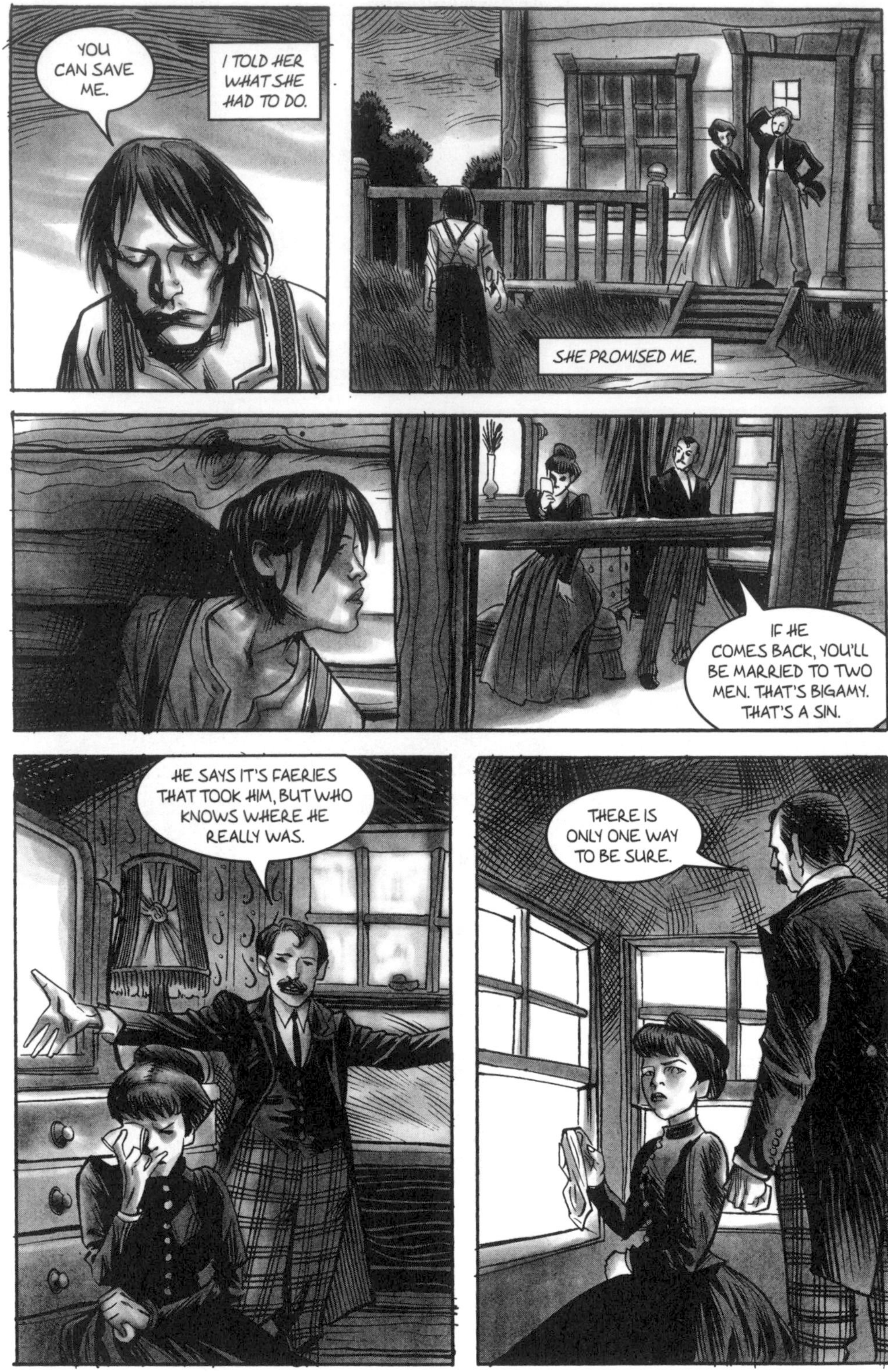
YOU CAN SAVE ME.
I TOLD HER WHAT SHE HAD TO DO.
SHE PROMISED ME.
IF HE COMES BACK, YOU'LL BE MARRIED TO TWO MEN. THAT'S BIGAMY. THAT'S A SIN.
HE SAYS IT'S FAERIES THAT TOOK HIM, BUT WHO KNOWS WHERE HE REALLY WAS.
THERE IS ONLY ONE WAY TO BE SURE.

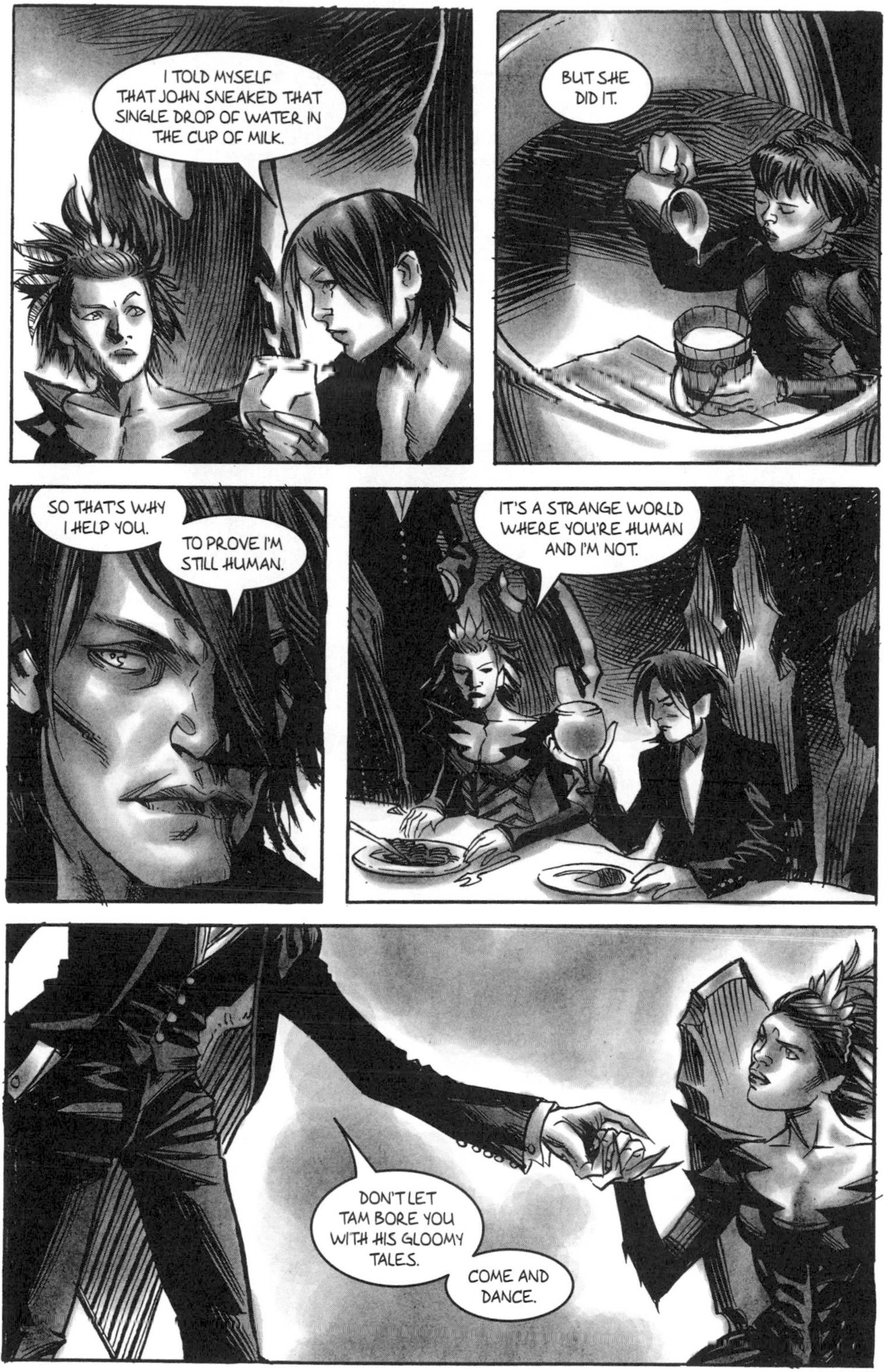
I TOLD MYSELF THAT JOHN SNEAKED THAT SINGLE DROP OF WATER IN THE CUP OF MILK.
BUT SHE DID IT.
SO THAT'S WHY I HELP YOU.
TO PROVE I'M STILL HUMAN.
IT'S A STRANGE WORLD WHERE YOU'RE HUMAN AND I'M NOT.
DON'T LET TAM BORE YOU WITH HIS GLOOMY TALES.
COME AND DANCE.

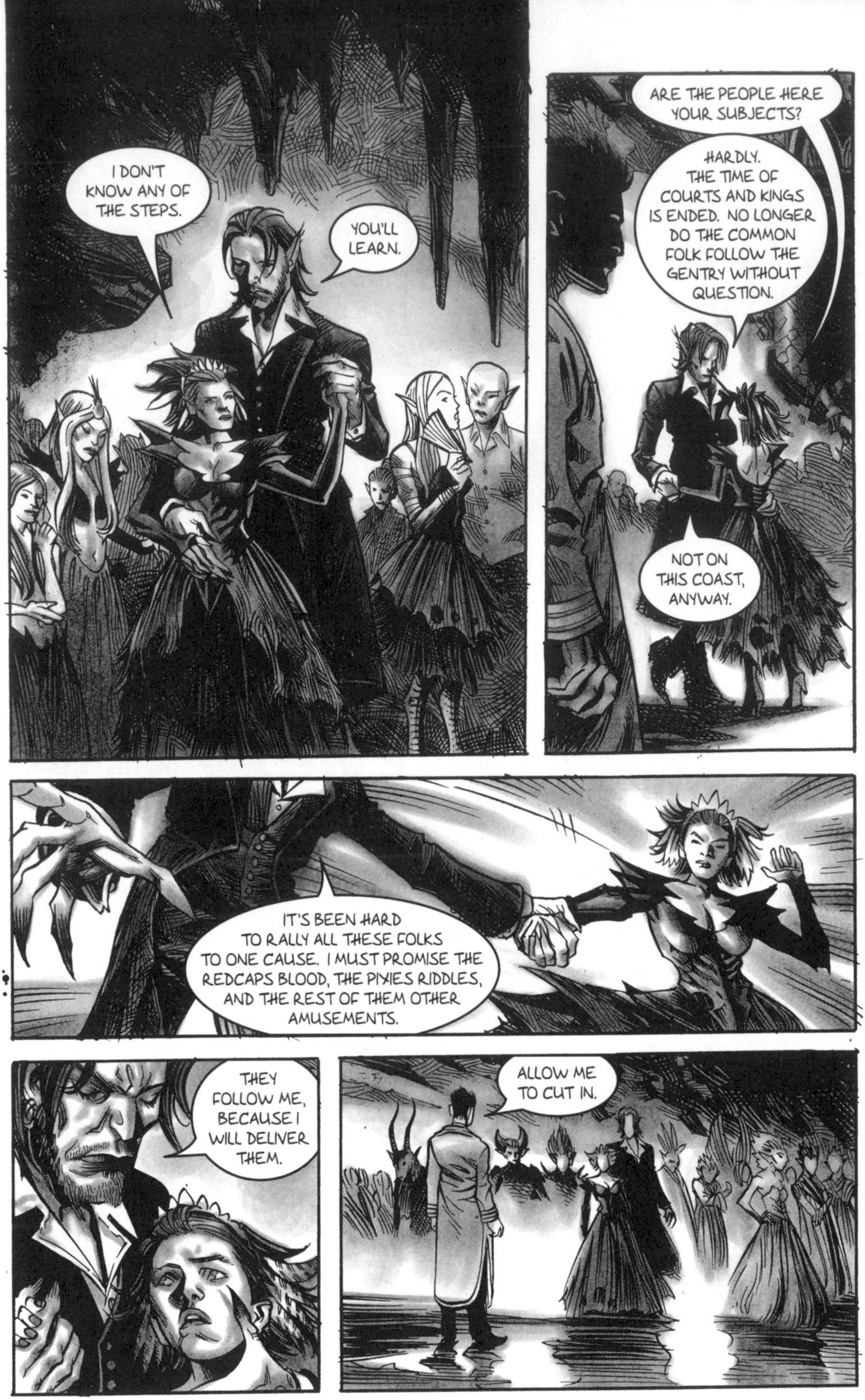
I DON'T KNOW ANY OF THE STEPS.
YOU'LL LEARN.
ARE THE PEOPLE HERE YOUR SUBJECTS?
HARDLY. THE TIME OF COURTS AND KINGS IS ENDED. NO LONGER DO THE COMMON FOLK FOLLOW THE GENTRY WITHOUT QUESTION.
NOT ON THIS COAST, ANYWAY.
IT'S BEEN HARD TO RALLY ALL THESE FOLKS TO ONE CAUSE. I MUST PROMISE THE REDCAPS BLOOD, THE PIXIES RIDDLES, AND THE REST OF THEM OTHER AMUSEMENTS.
THEY FOLLOW ME, BECAUSE I WILL DELIVER THEM.
ALLOW ME TO CUT IN.

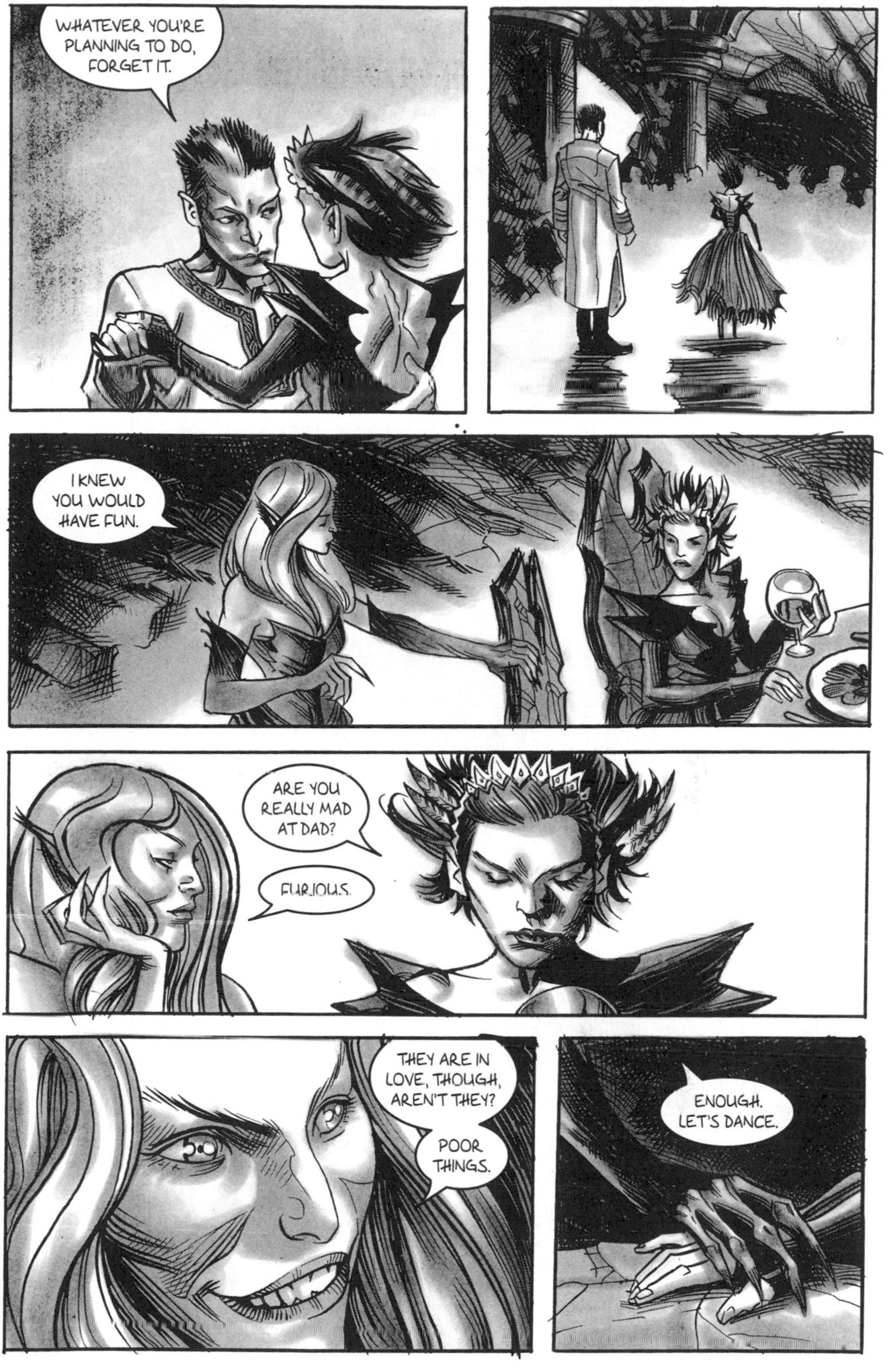
WHATEVER YOU'RE PLANNING TO DO, FORGET IT.
I KNEW YOU WOULD HAVE FUN.
ARE YOU REALLY MAD AT DAD?
FURIOUS.
THEY ARE IN LOVE, THOUGH, AREN'T THEY?
POOR THINGS.
ENOUGH. LET'S DANCE.

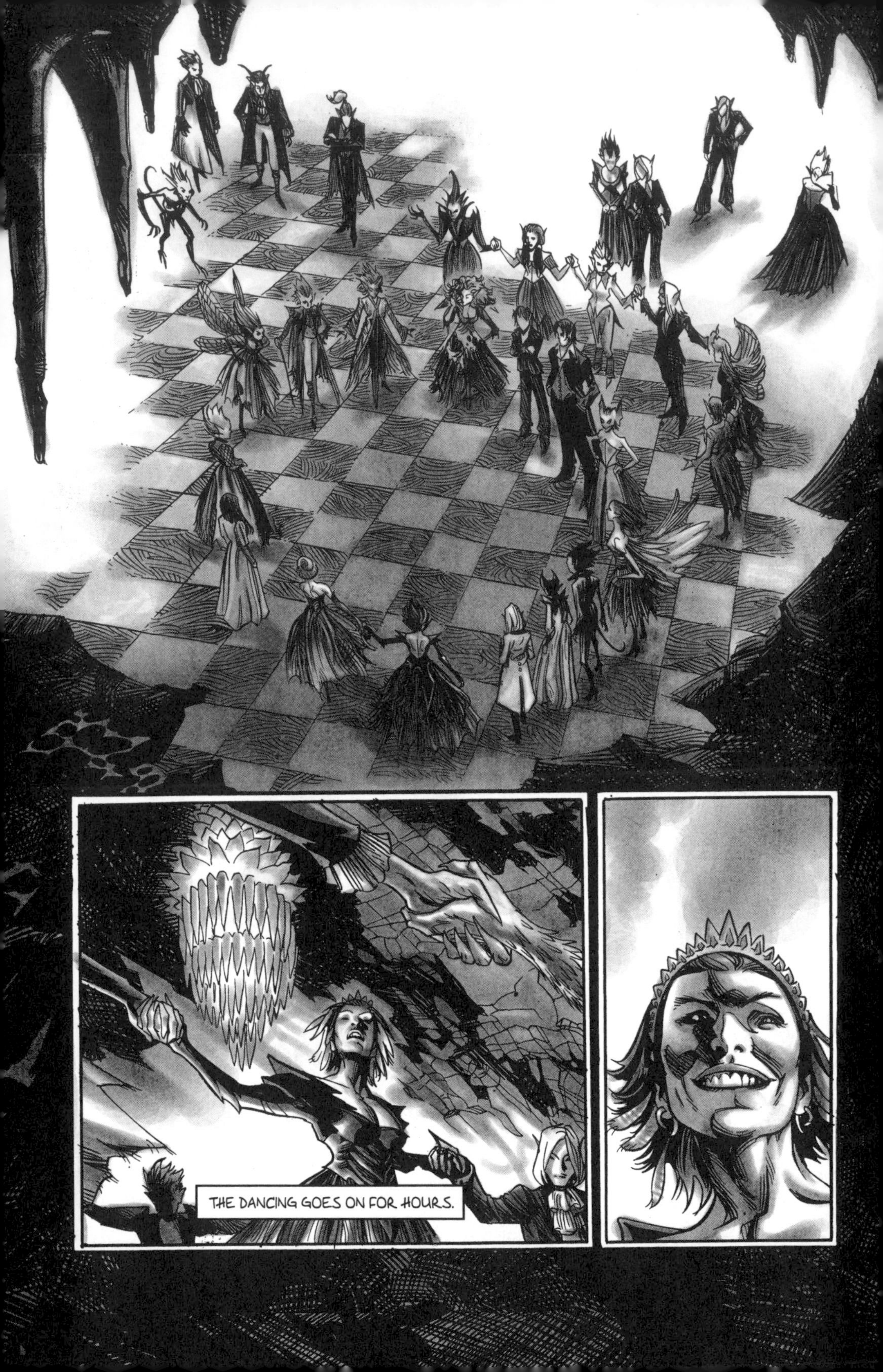
THE DANCING GOES ON FOR HOURS.

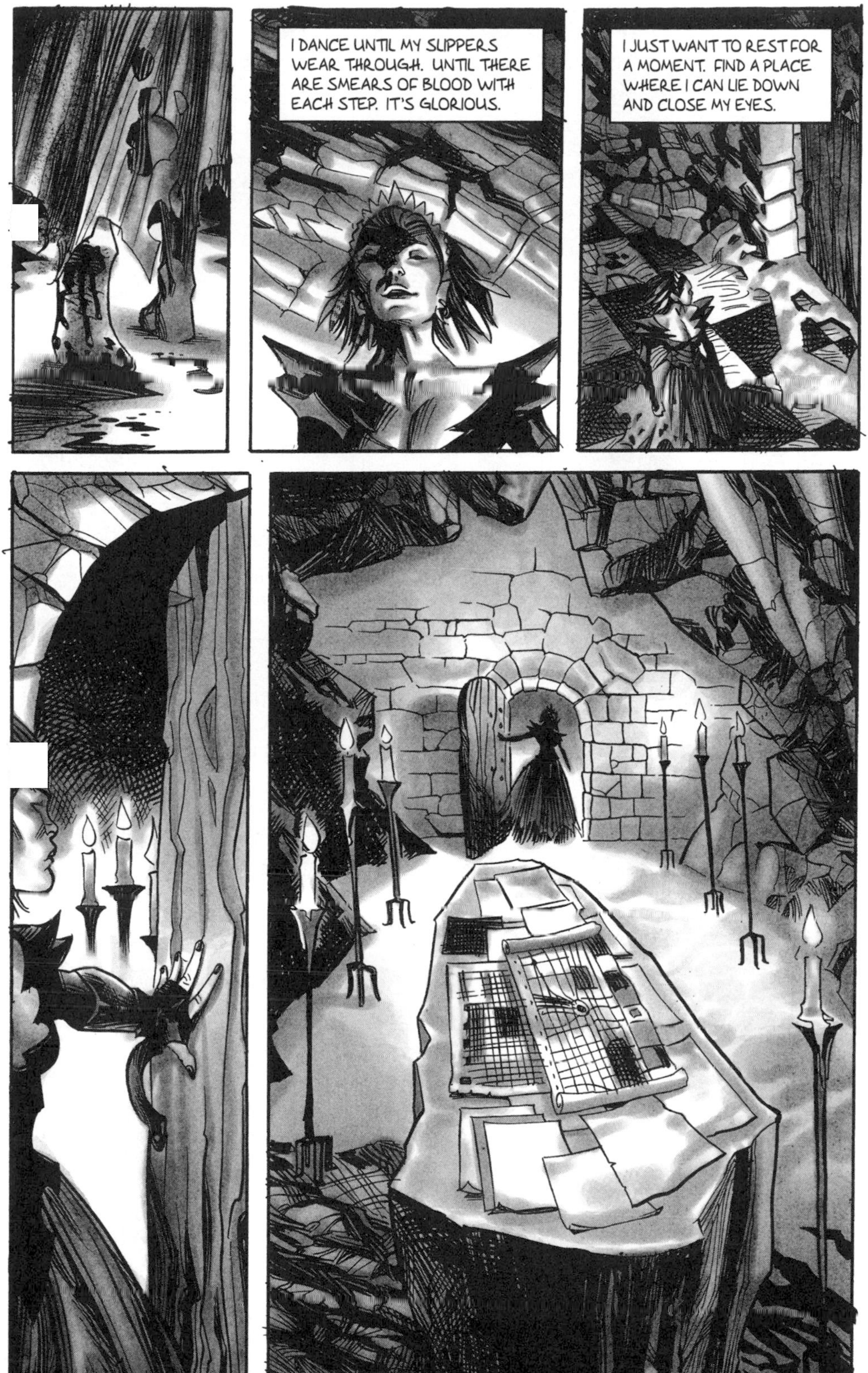
I DANCE UNTIL MY SLIPPERS WEAR THROUGH. UNTIL THERE ARE SMEARS OF BLOOD WITH EACH STEP. IT'S GLORIOUS.
I JUST WANT TO REST FOR A MOMENT. FIND A PLACE WHERE I CAN LIE DOWN AND CLOSE MY EYES.

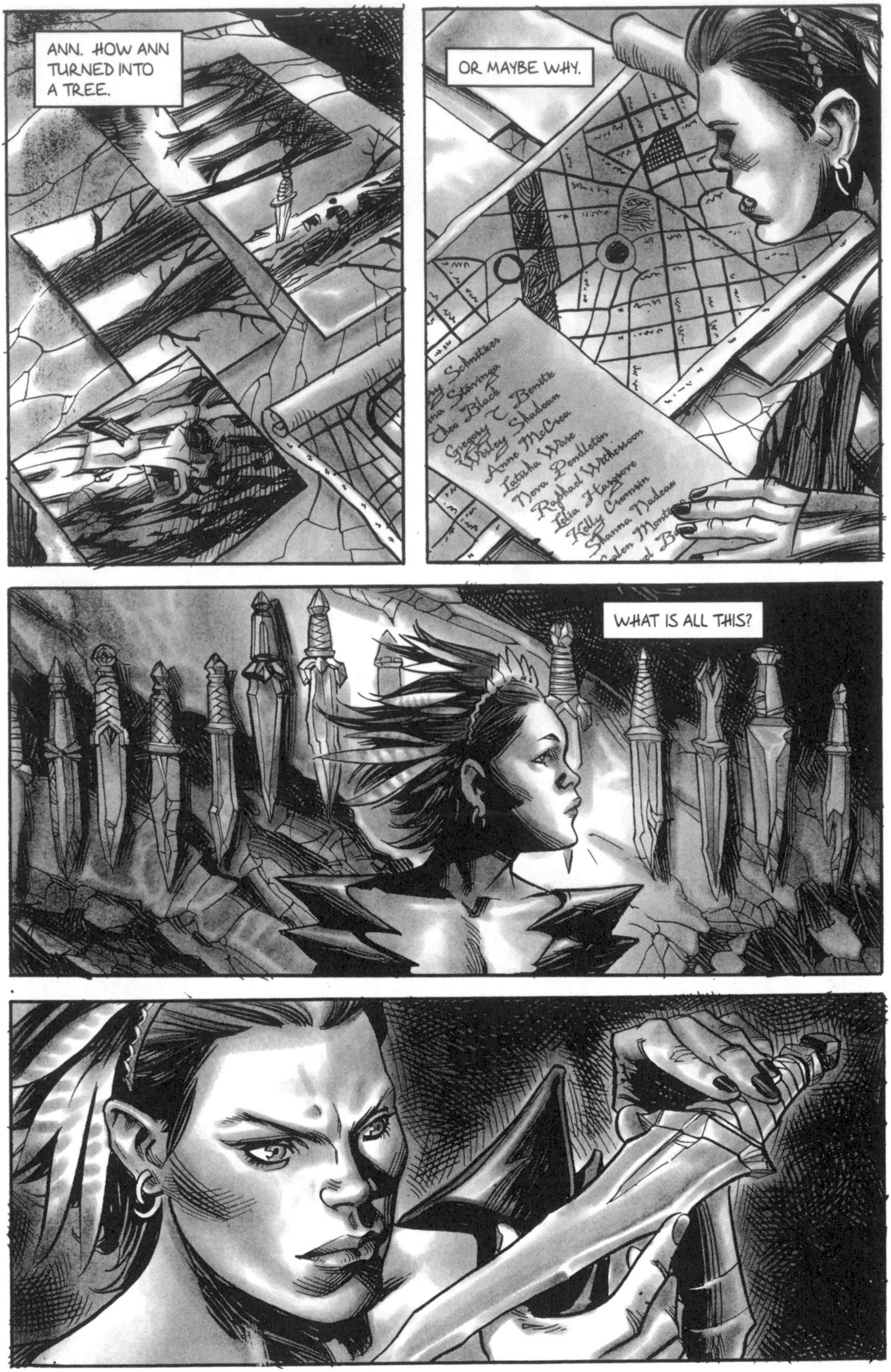
ANN. HOW ANN TURNED INTO A TREE.
OR MAYBE WHY.
WHAT IS ALL THIS?

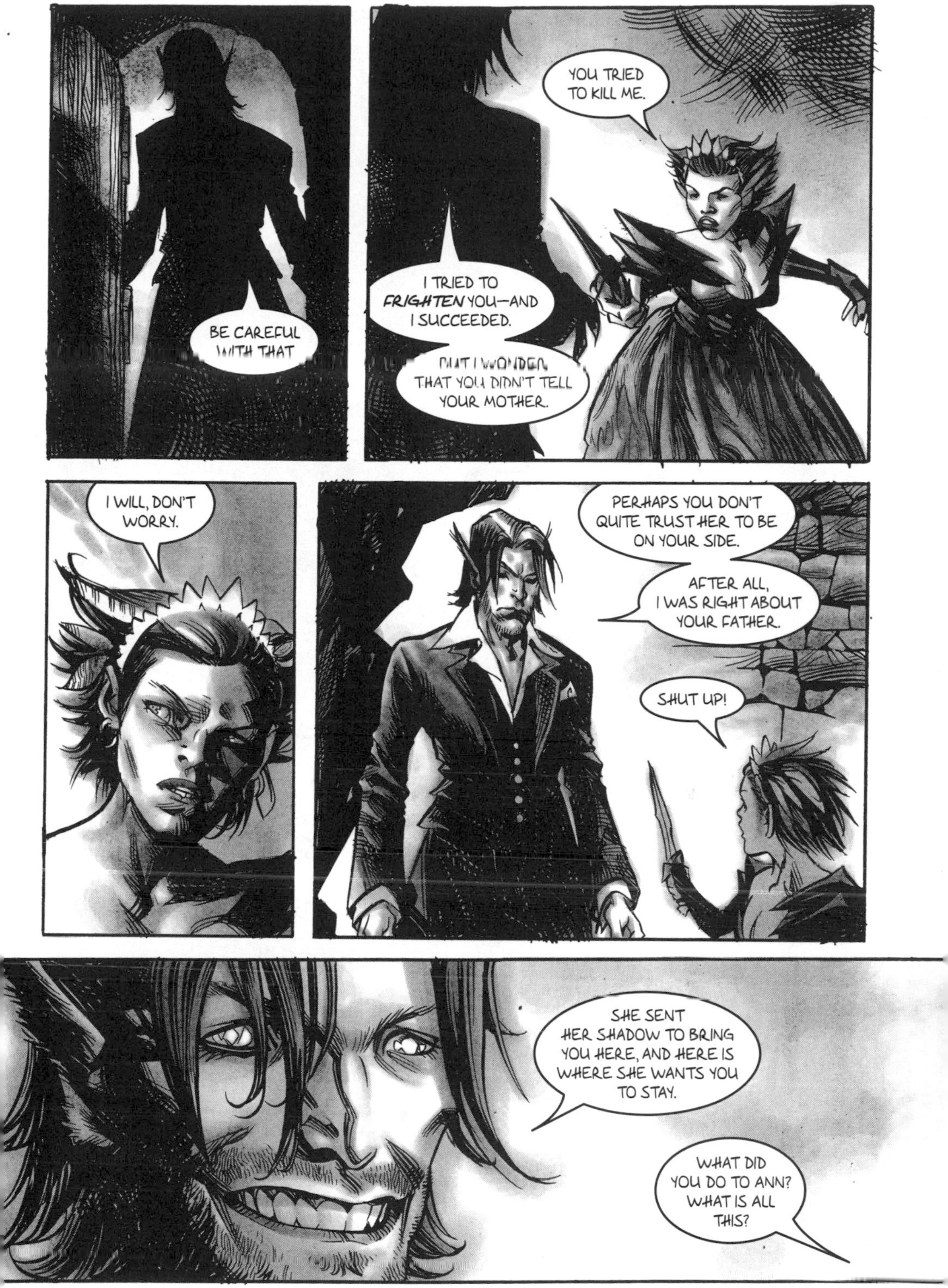

BE CAREFUL WITH THAT
YOU TRIED TO KILL ME.
I TRIED TO FRIGHTEN YOU—AND I SUCCEEDED.
BUT I WONDER THAT YOU DIDN'T TELL YOUR MOTHER.
I WILL, DON'T WORRY.
PERHAPS YOU DON'T QUITE TRUST HER TO BE ON YOUR SIDE.
AFTER ALL, I WAS RIGHT ABOUT YOUR FATHER.
SHUT UP!
SHE SENT HER SHADOW TO BRING YOU HERE, AND HERE IS WHERE SHE WANTS YOU TO STAY.
WHAT DID YOU DO TO ANN? WHAT IS ALL THIS?

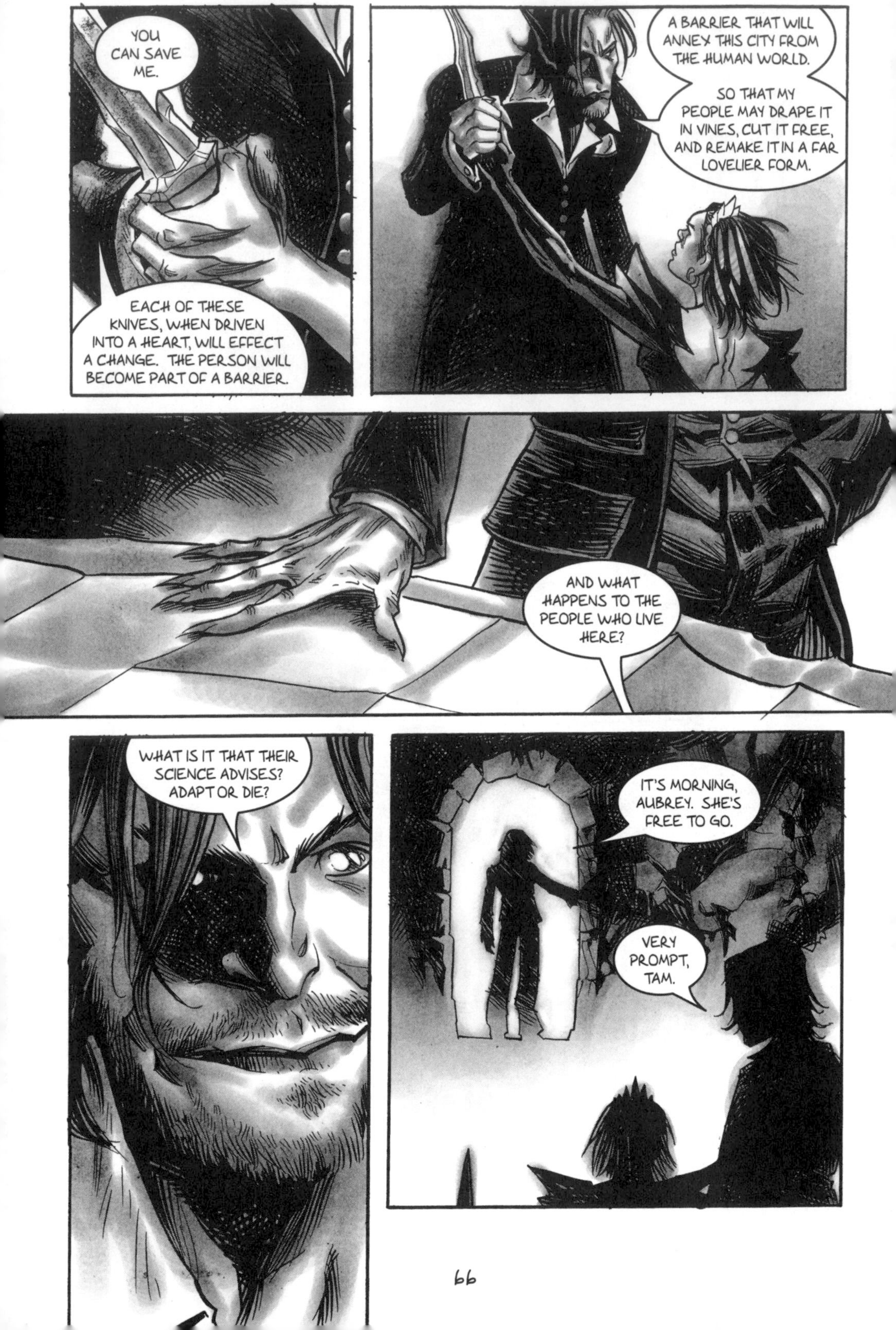
YOU CAN SAVE ME.
EACH OF THESE KNIVES, WHEN DRIVEN INTO A HEART, WILL EFFECT A CHANGE. THE PERSON WILL BECOME PART OF A BARRIER.
A BARRIER THAT WILL ANNEX THIS CITY FROM THE HUMAN WORLD.
SO THAT MY PEOPLE MAY DRAPE IT IN VINES, CUT IT FREE, AND REMAKE IT IN A FAR LOVELIER FORM.
AND WHAT HAPPENS TO THE PEOPLE WHO LIVE HERE?
WHAT IS IT THAT THEIR SCIENCE ADVISES? ADAPT OR DIE?
IT'S MORNING, AUBREY. SHE'S FREE TO GO.
VERY PROMPT, TAM.

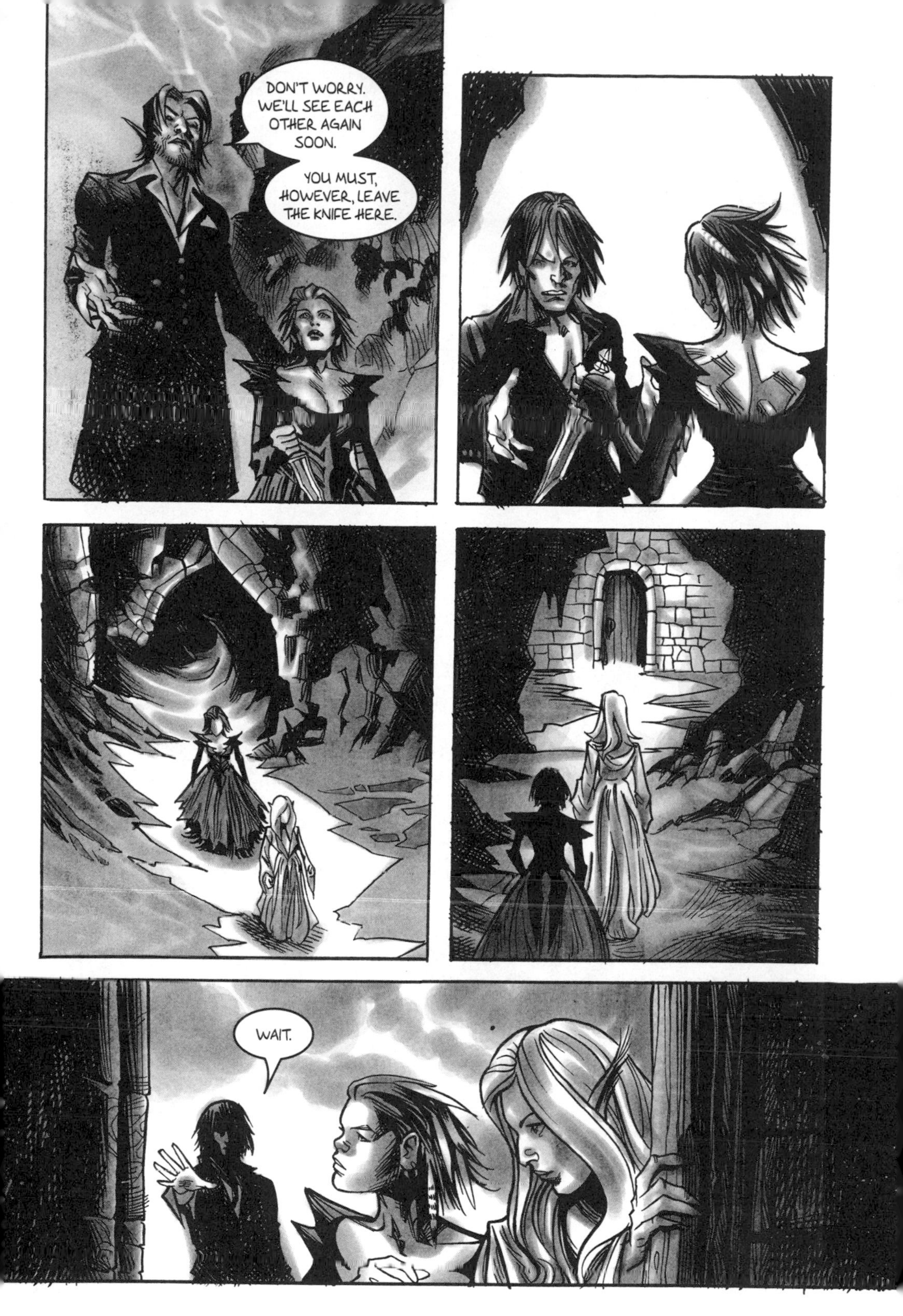
DON'T WORRY. WE'LL SEE EACH OTHER AGAIN SOON.
YOU MUST, HOWEVER, LEAVE THE KNIFE HERE.
WAIT.

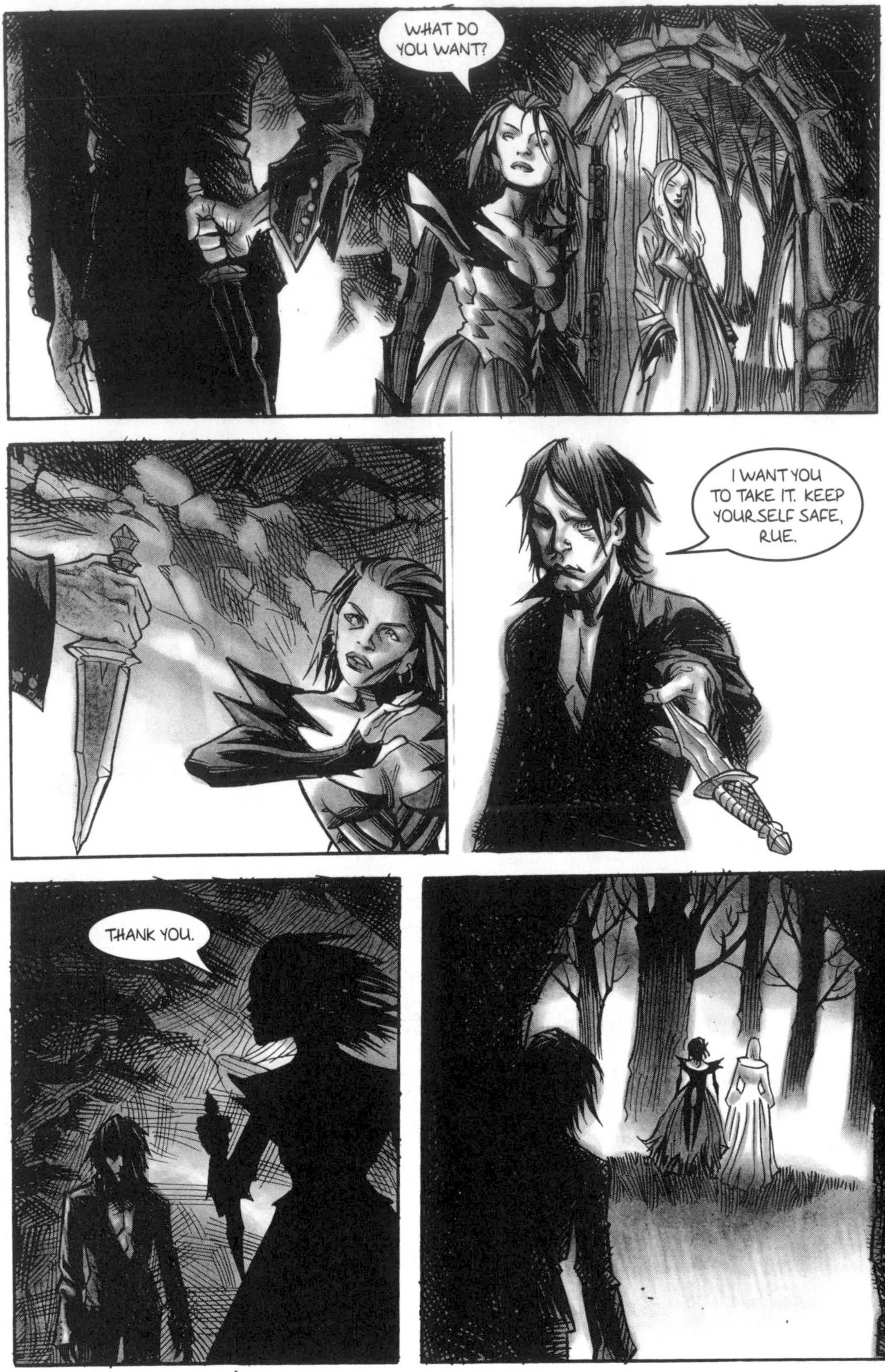
WHAT DO YOU WANT?
I WANT YOU TO TAKE IT. KEEP YOURSELF SAFE, RUE.
THANK YOU.

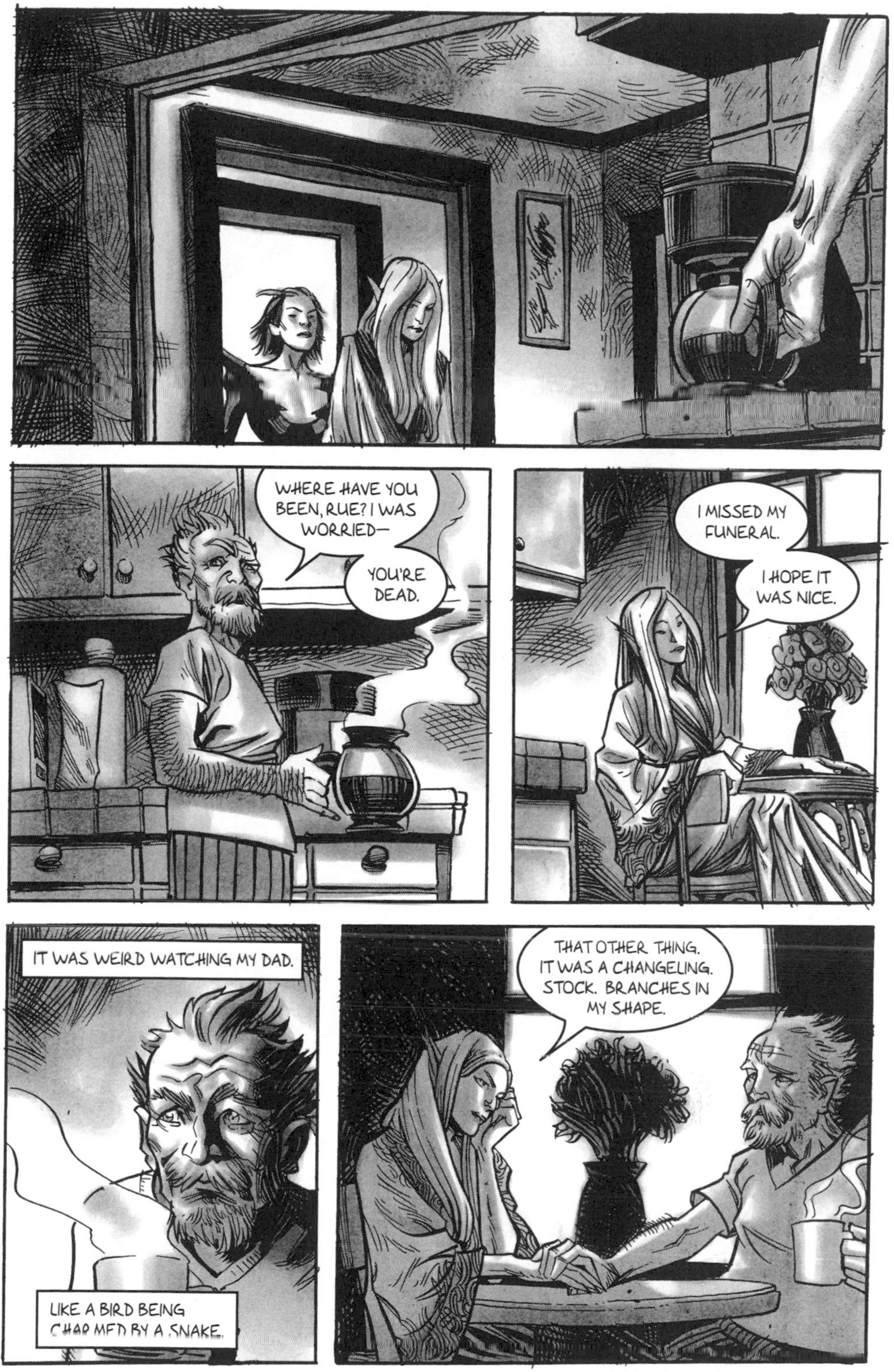
WHERE HAVE YOU BEEN, RUE? I WAS WORRIED—
YOU'RE DEAD.
I MISSED MY FUNERAL.
I HOPE IT WAS NICE.
IT WAS WEIRD WATCHING MY DAD.
LIKE A BIRD BEING CHARMED BY A SNAKE.
THAT OTHER THING. IT WAS A CHANGELING. STOCK. BRANCHES IN MY SHAPE.

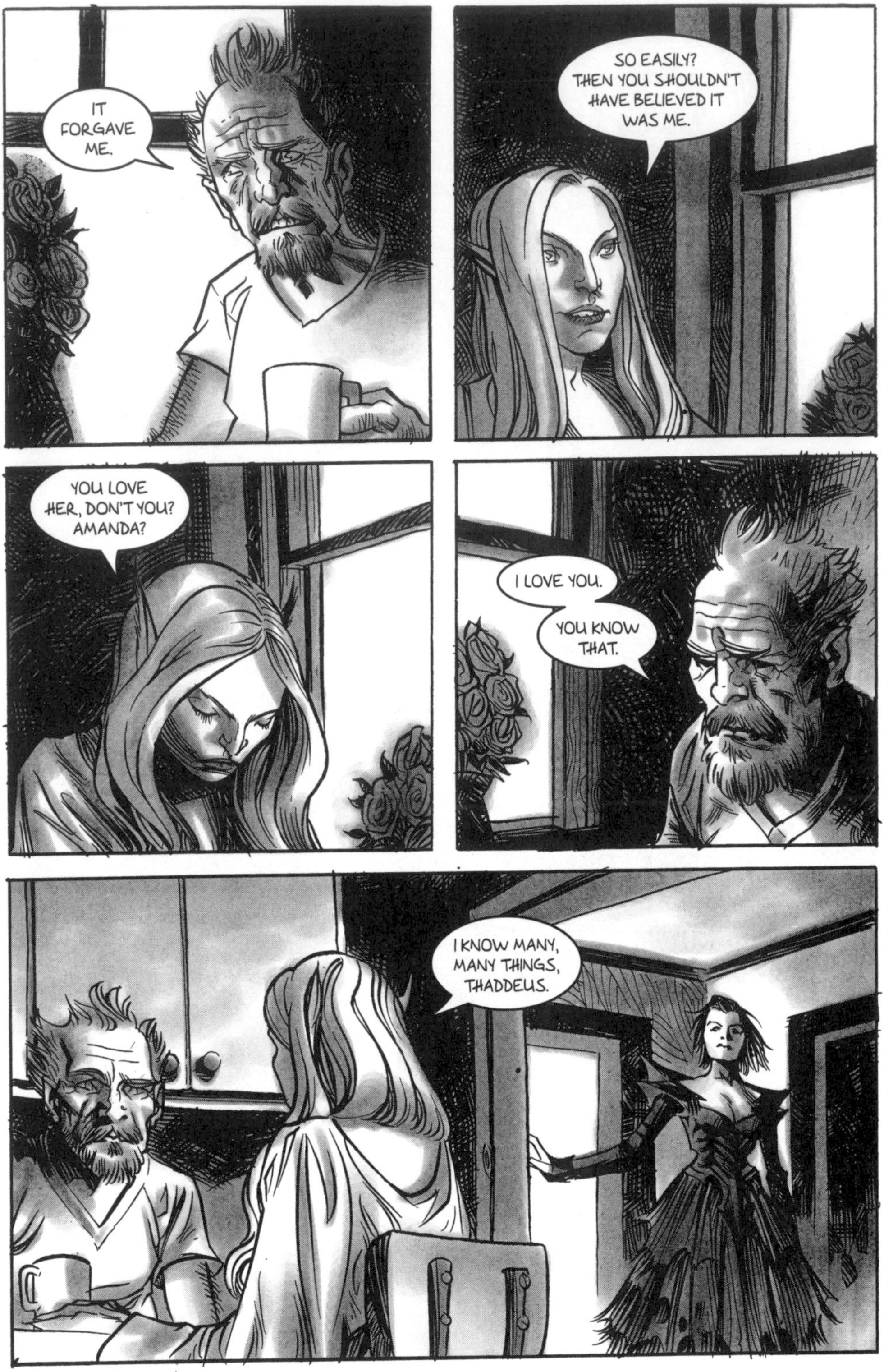
IT FORGAVE ME.
SO EASILY? THEN YOU SHOULDN'T HAVE BELIEVED IT WAS ME.
YOU LOVE HER, DON'T YOU? AMANDA?
I LOVE YOU.
YOU KNOW THAT.
I KNOW MANY, MANY THINGS, THADDEUS.

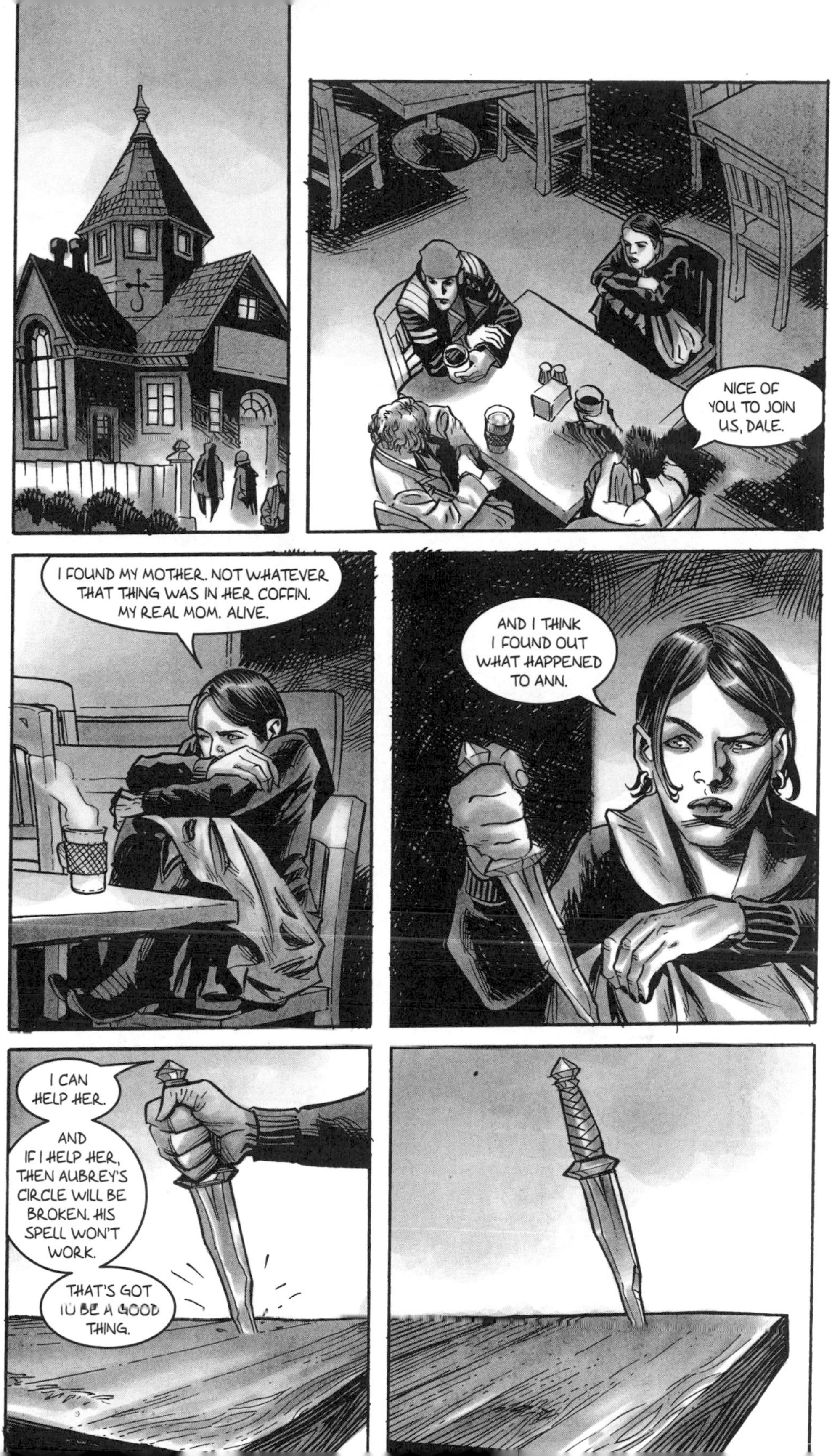
NICE OF YOU TO JOIN US, DALE.
I FOUND MY MOTHER. NOT WHATEVER THAT THING WAS IN HER COFFIN. MY REAL MOM. ALIVE.
AND I THINK I FOUND OUT WHAT HAPPENED TO ANN.
I CAN HELP HER.
AND IF I HELP HER, THEN AUBREY'S CIRCLE WILL BE BROKEN. HIS SPELL WON'T WORK.
THAT'S GOT TO BE A GOOD THING.

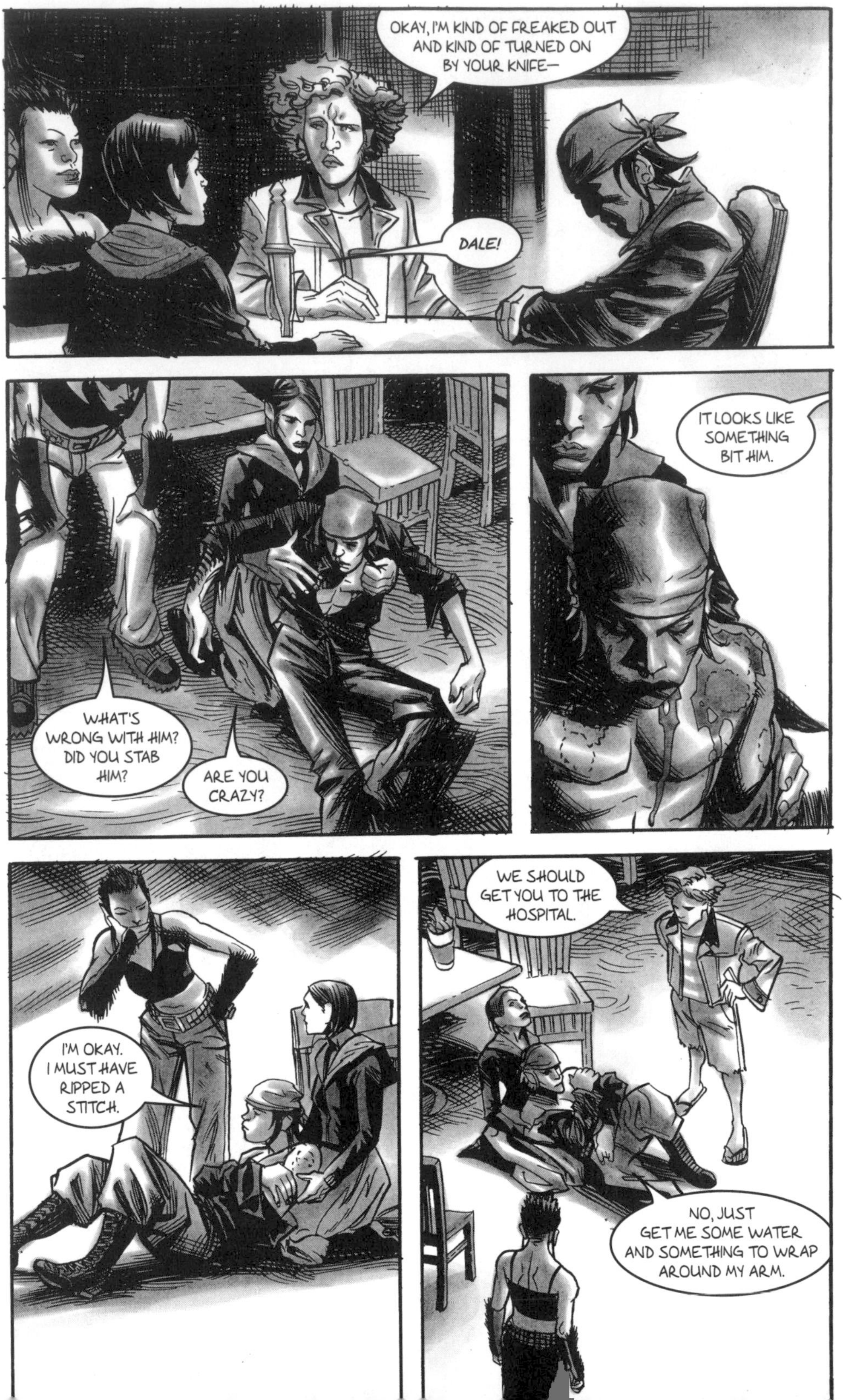
OKAY, I'M KIND OF FREAKED OUT AND KIND OF TURNED ON BY YOUR KNIFE—
DALE!
WHAT'S WRONG WITH HIM? DID YOU STAB HIM?
ARE YOU CRAZY?
IT LOOKS LIKE SOMETHING BIT HIM.
I'M OKAY. I MUST HAVE RIPPED A STITCH.
WE SHOULD GET YOU TO THE HOSPITAL.
NO, JUST GET ME SOME WATER AND SOMETHING TO WRAP AROUND MY ARM.

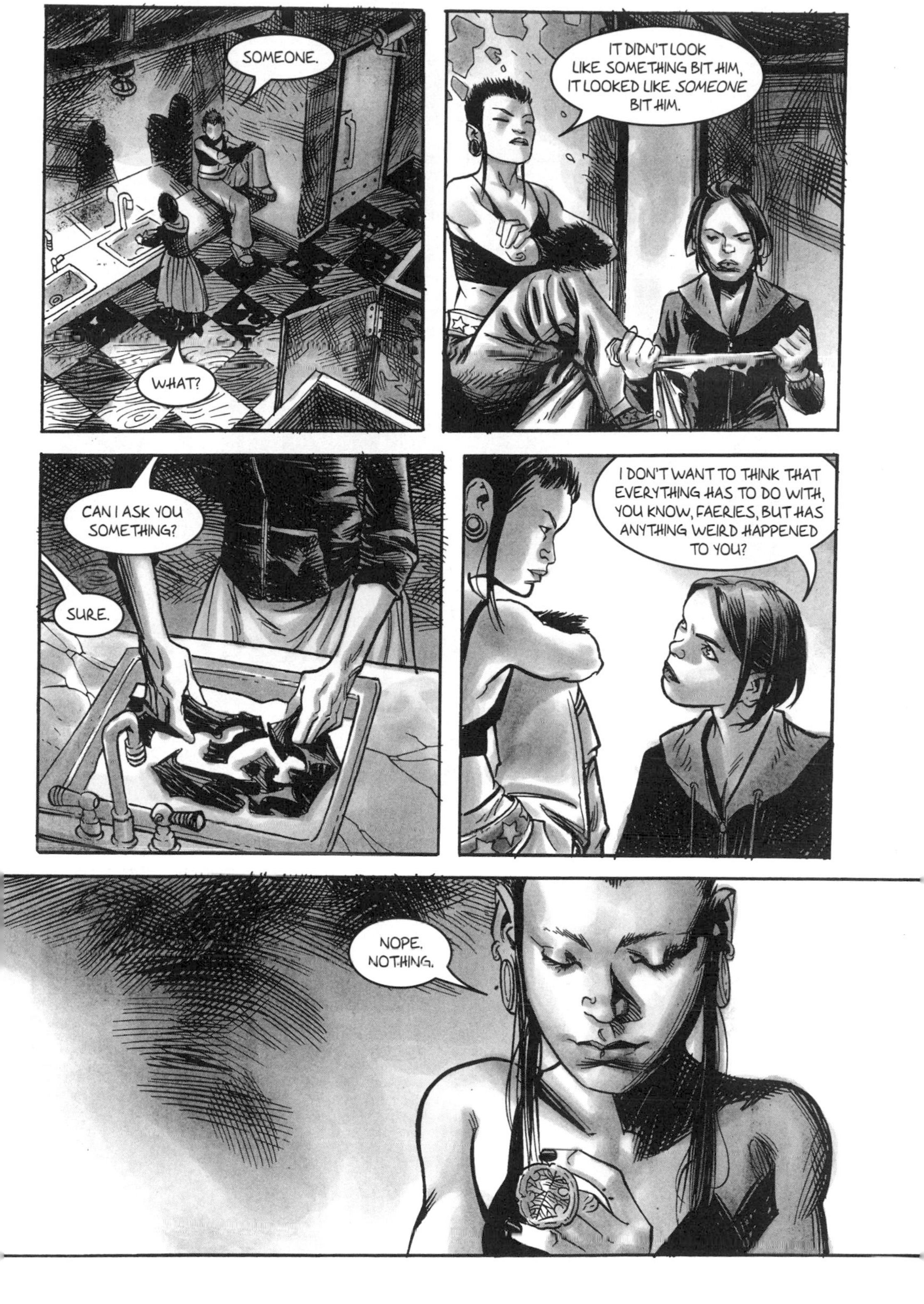
SOMEONE.
WHAT?
IT DIDN'T LOOK LIKE SOMETHING BIT HIM, IT LOOKED LIKE *SOMEONE* BIT HIM.
CAN I ASK YOU SOMETHING?
SURE.
I DON'T WANT TO THINK THAT EVERYTHING HAS TO DO WITH, YOU KNOW, FAERIES, BUT HAS ANYTHING WEIRD HAPPENED TO YOU?
NOPE. NOTHING.

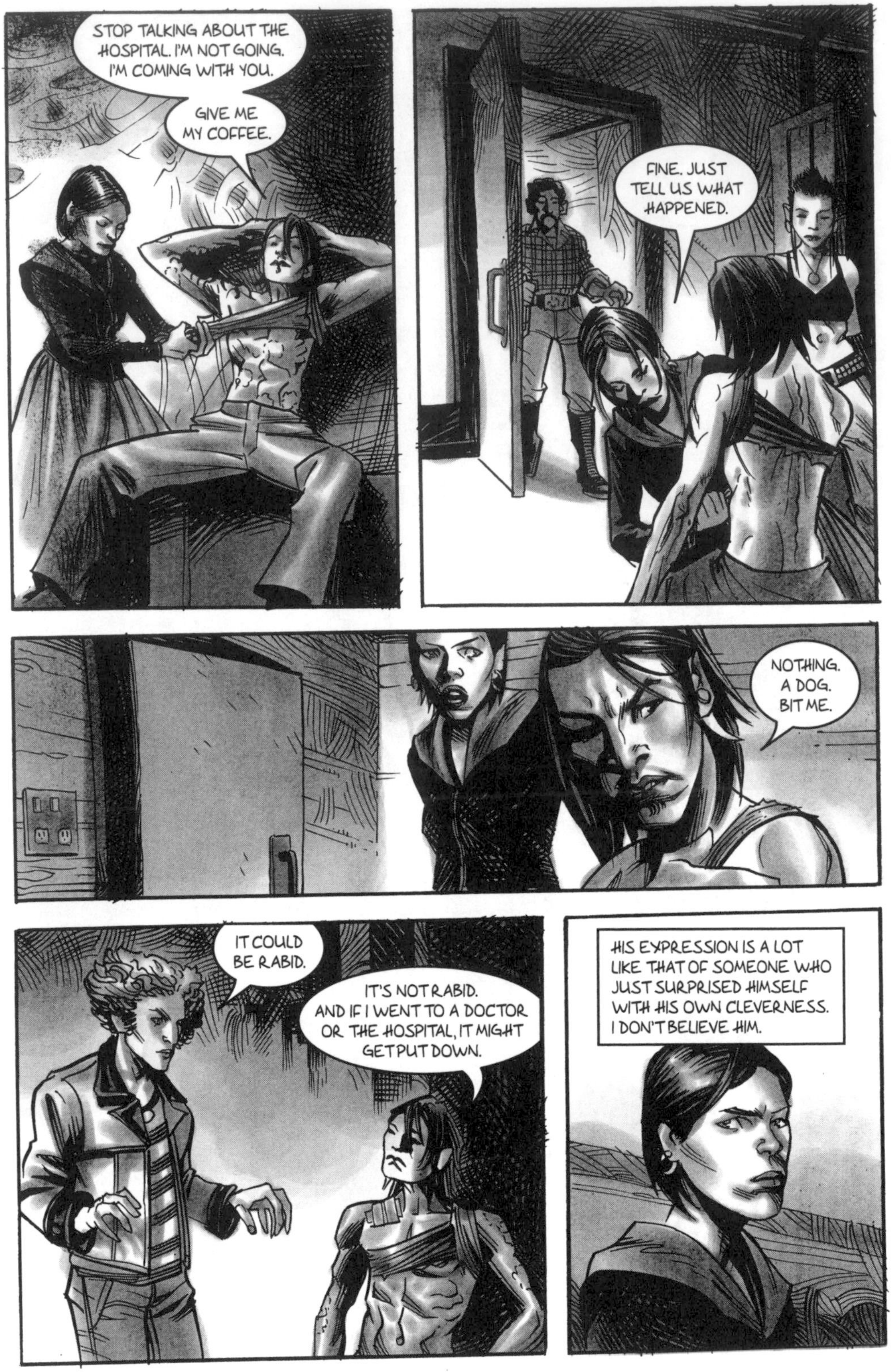
STOP TALKING ABOUT THE HOSPITAL. I'M NOT GOING. I'M COMING WITH YOU.
GIVE ME MY COFFEE.
FINE. JUST TELL US WHAT HAPPENED.
NOTHING. A DOG. BIT ME.
IT COULD BE RABID.
IT'S NOT RABID. AND IF I WENT TO A DOCTOR OR THE HOSPITAL, IT MIGHT GET PUT DOWN.
HIS EXPRESSION IS A LOT LIKE THAT OF SOMEONE WHO JUST SURPRISED HIMSELF WITH HIS OWN CLEVERNESS. I DON'T BELIEVE HIM.

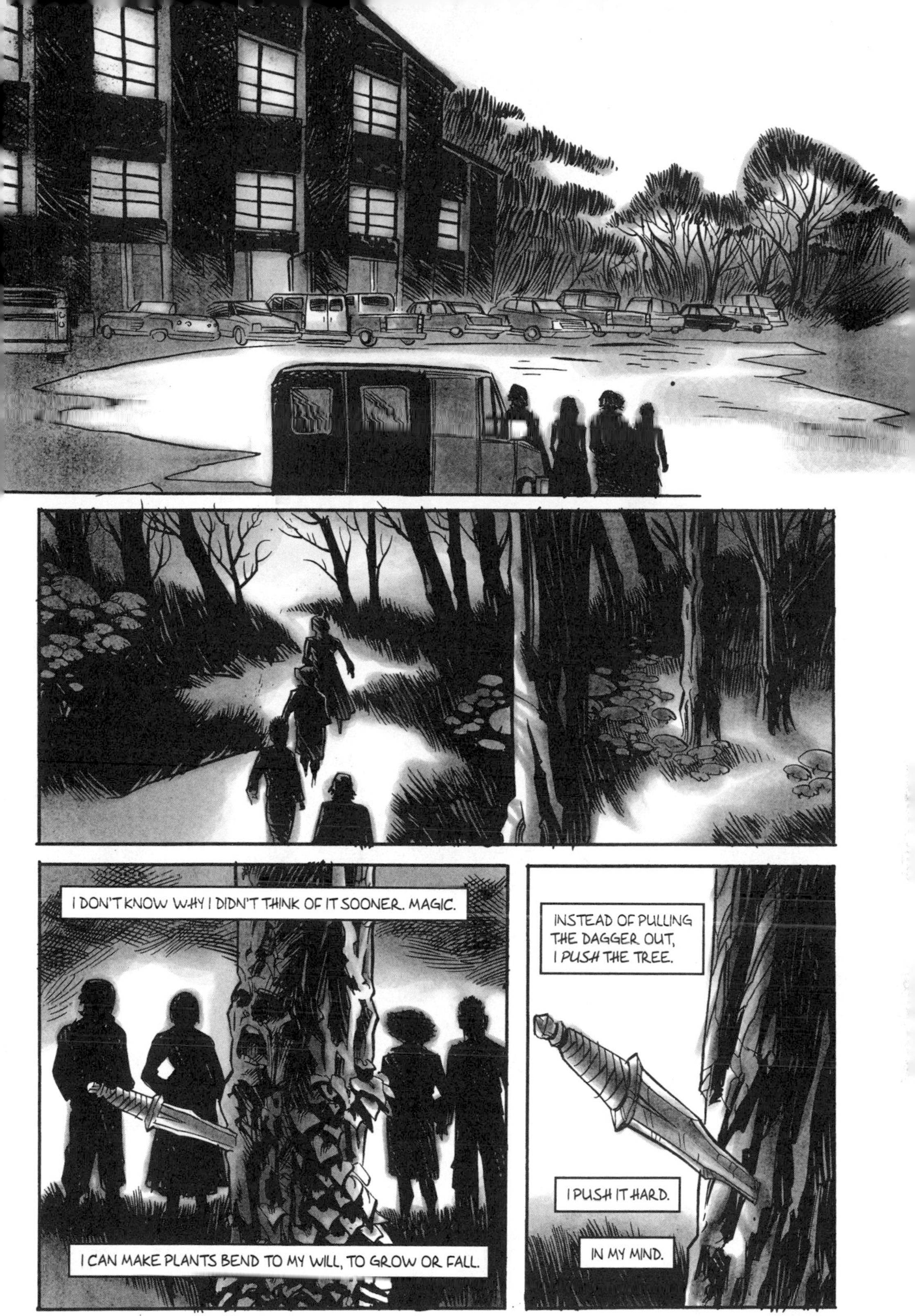
I DON'T KNOW WHY I DIDN'T THINK OF IT SOONER. MAGIC.
I CAN MAKE PLANTS BEND TO MY WILL, TO GROW OR FALL.
INSTEAD OF PULLING THE DAGGER OUT, I *PUSH* THE TREE.
I PUSH IT HARD.
IN MY MIND.

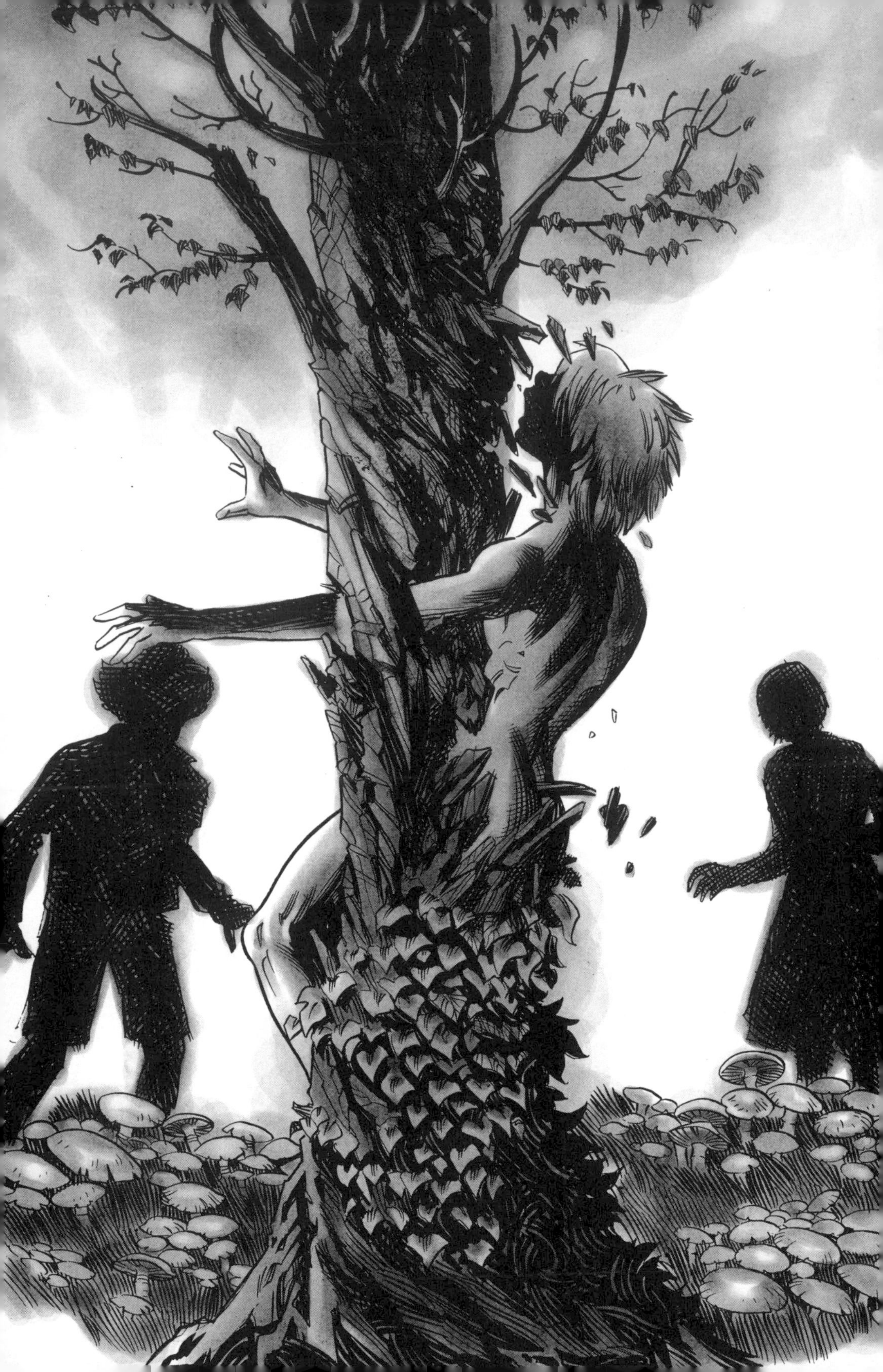

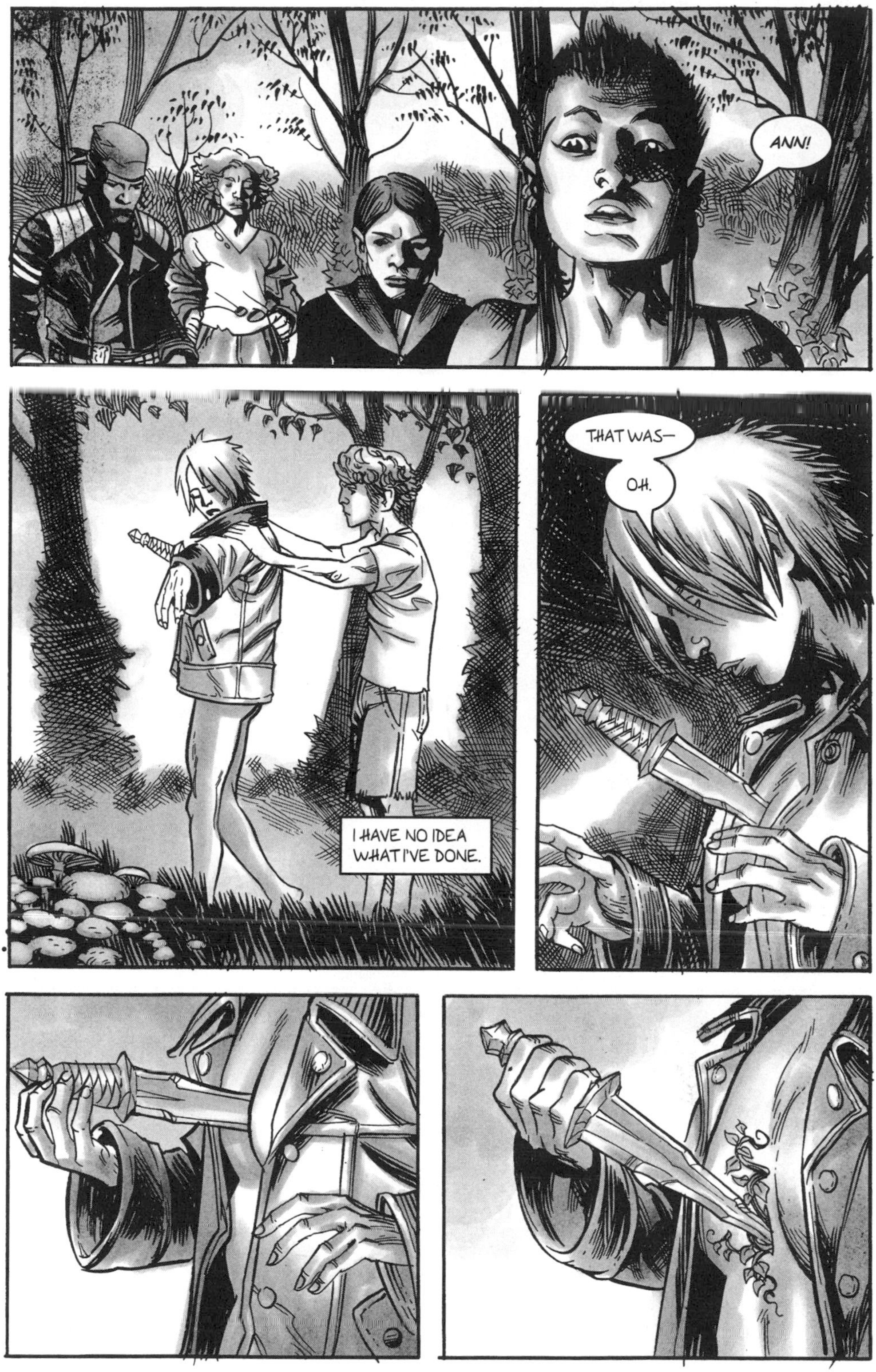
ANN!
THAT WAS—
OH.
I HAVE NO IDEA WHAT I'VE DONE.

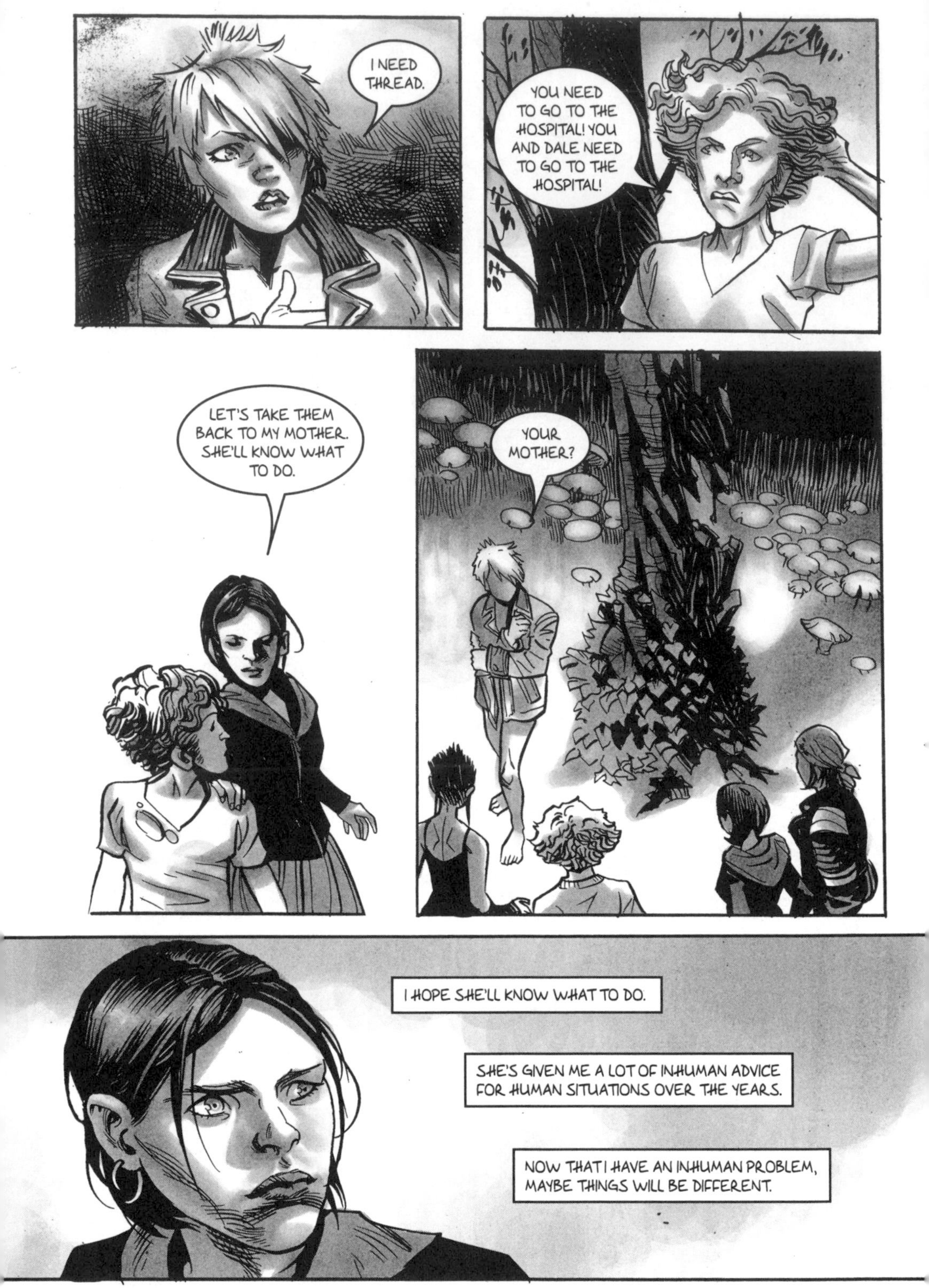
I NEED THREAD.
YOU NEED TO GO TO THE HOSPITAL! YOU AND DALE NEED TO GO TO THE HOSPITAL!
LET'S TAKE THEM BACK TO MY MOTHER. SHE'LL KNOW WHAT TO DO.
YOUR MOTHER?
I HOPE SHE'LL KNOW WHAT TO DO.
SHE'S GIVEN ME A LOT OF INHUMAN ADVICE FOR HUMAN SITUATIONS OVER THE YEARS.
NOW THAT I HAVE AN INHUMAN PROBLEM, MAYBE THINGS WILL BE DIFFERENT.

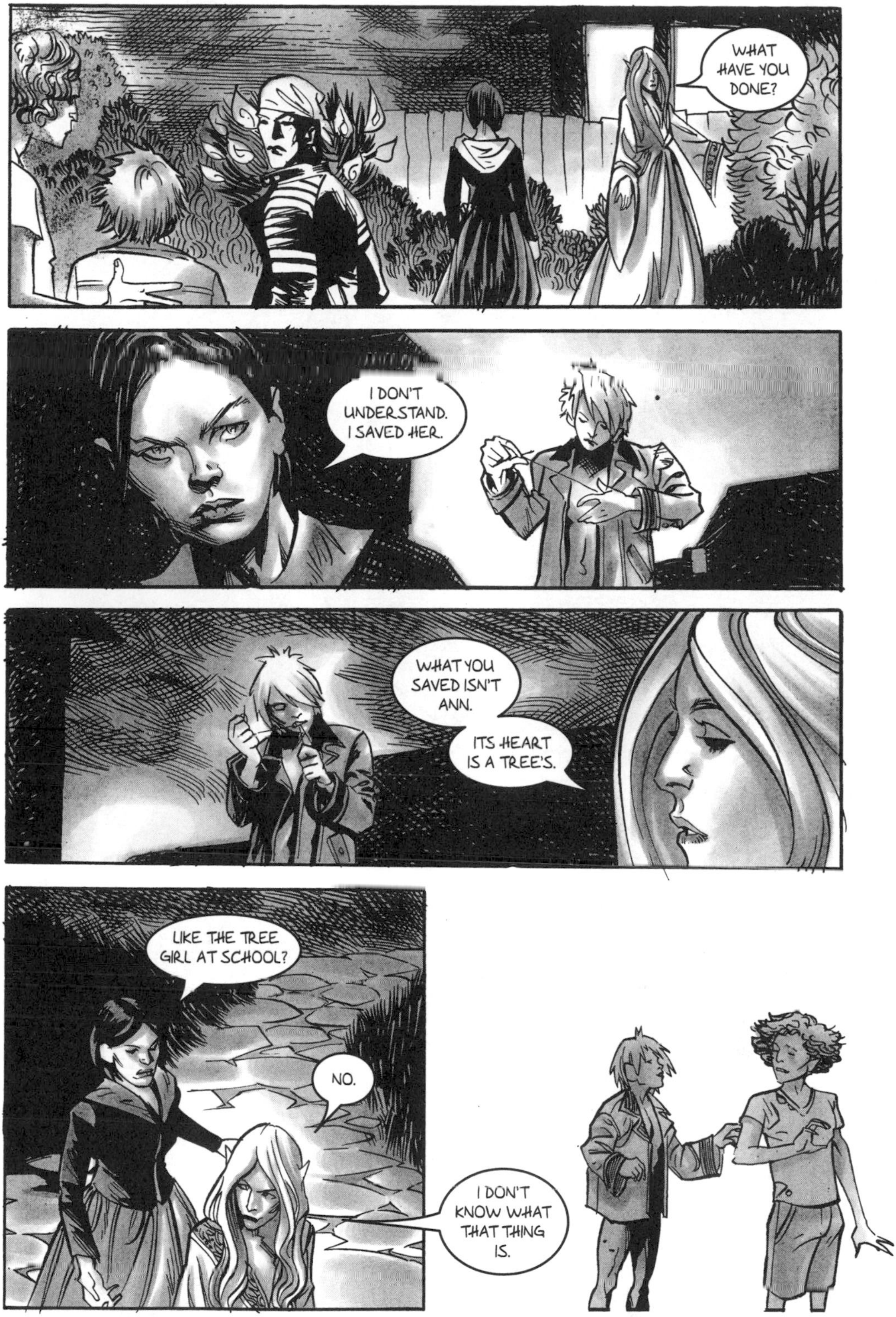
WHAT HAVE YOU DONE?
I DON'T UNDERSTAND. I SAVED HER.
WHAT YOU SAVED ISN'T ANN.
ITS HEART IS A TREE'S.
LIKE THE TREE GIRL AT SCHOOL?
NO.
I DON'T KNOW WHAT THAT THING IS.

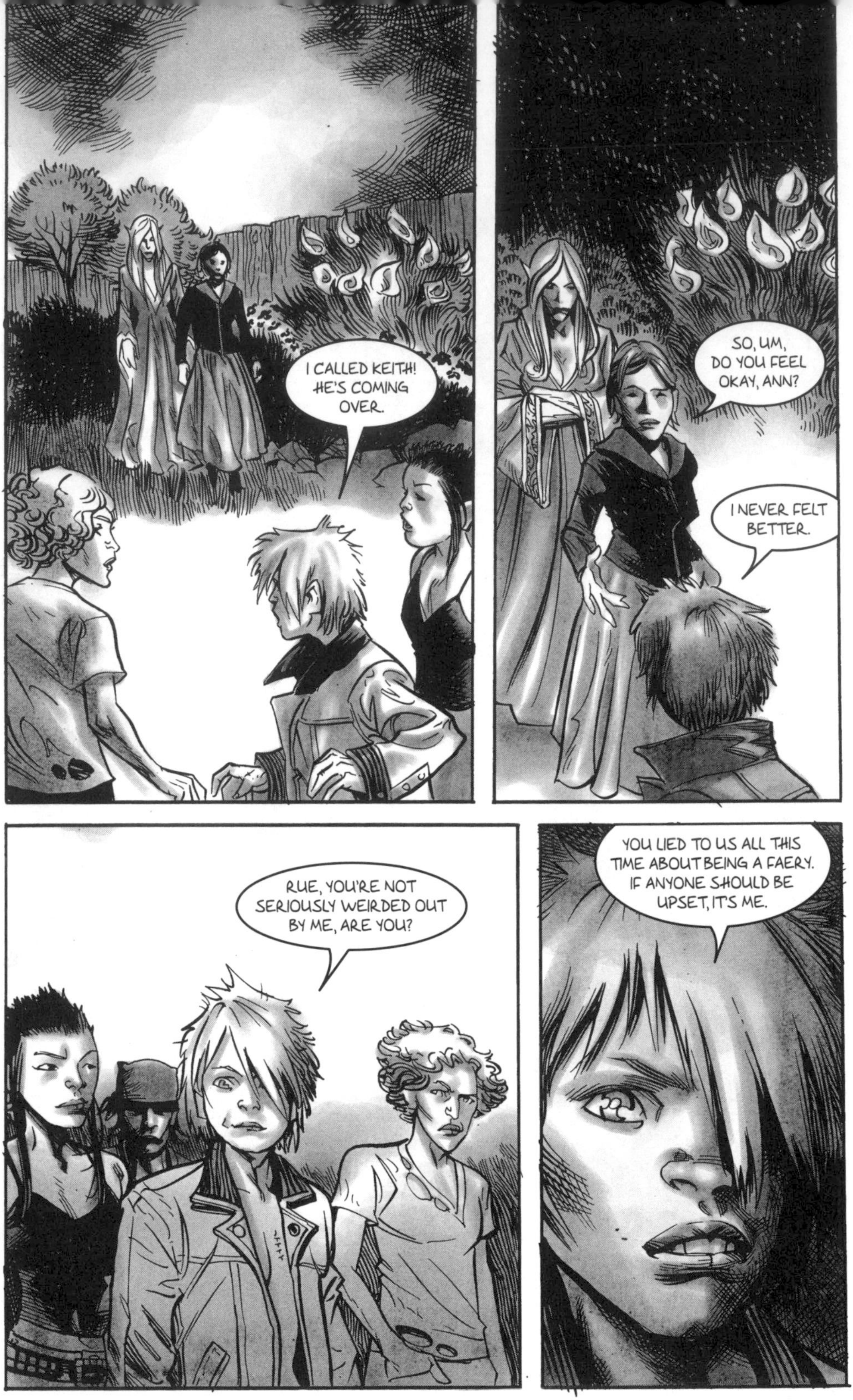
I CALLED KEITH! HE'S COMING OVER.
SO, UM, DO YOU FEEL OKAY, ANN?
I NEVER FELT BETTER.
RUE, YOU'RE NOT SERIOUSLY WEIRDED OUT BY ME, ARE YOU?
YOU LIED TO US ALL THIS TIME ABOUT BEING A FAERY. IF ANYONE SHOULD BE UPSET, IT'S ME.

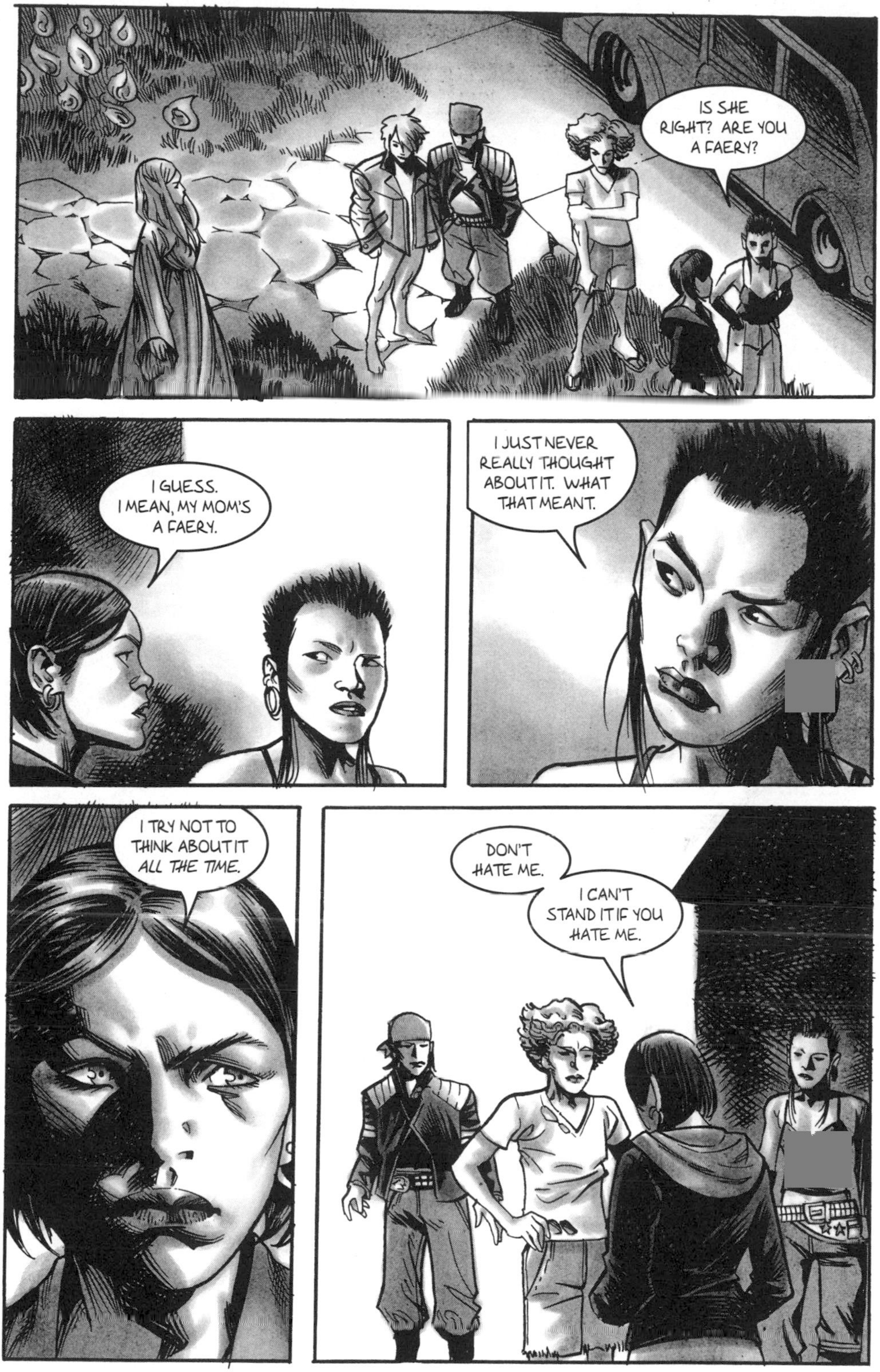
IS SHE RIGHT? ARE YOU A FAERY?
I GUESS. I MEAN, MY MOM'S A FAERY.
I JUST NEVER REALLY THOUGHT ABOUT IT. WHAT THAT MEANT.
I TRY NOT TO THINK ABOUT IT ALL THE TIME.
DON'T HATE ME.
I CAN'T STAND IT IF YOU HATE ME.

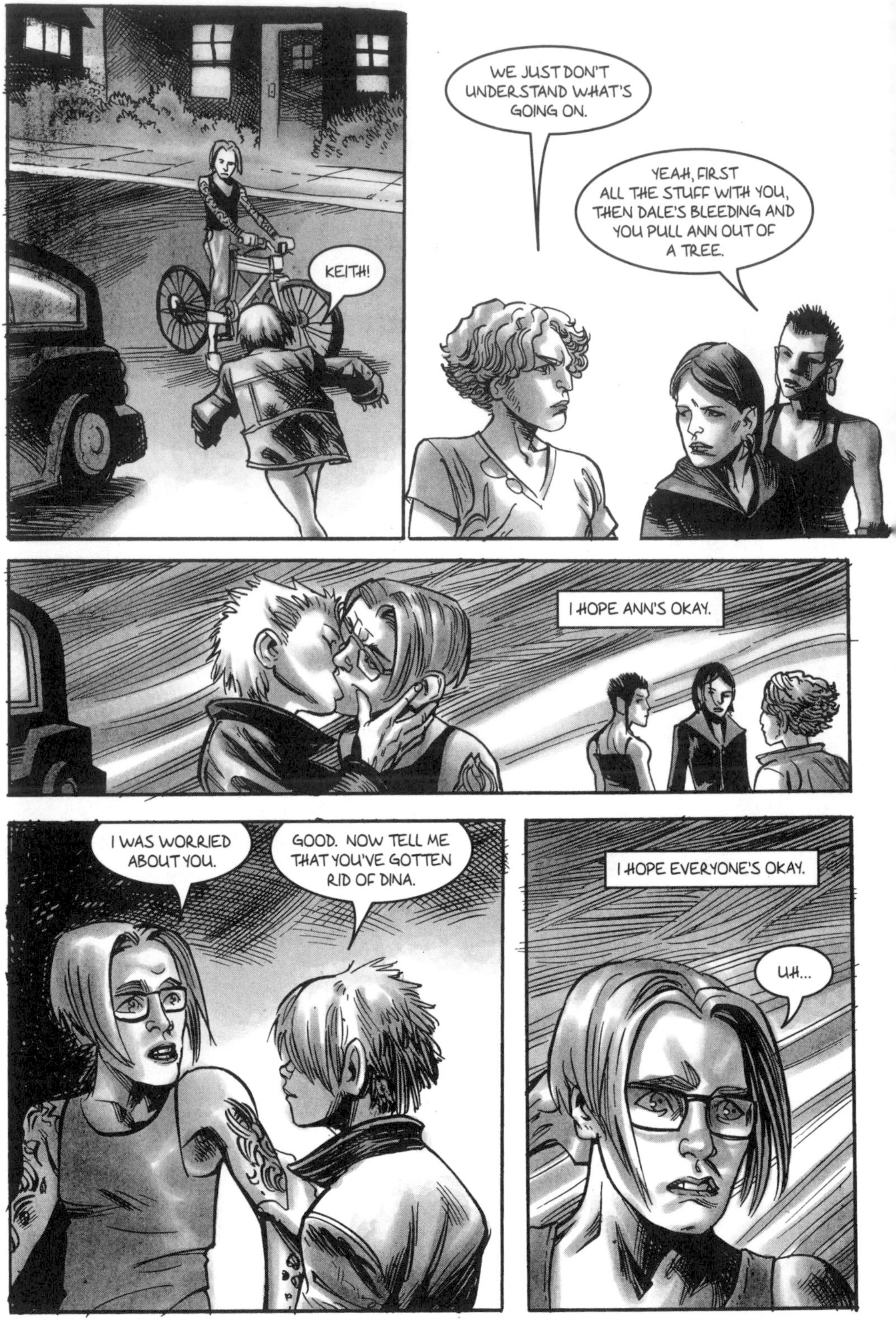
KEITH!
WE JUST DON'T UNDERSTAND WHAT'S GOING ON.
YEAH, FIRST ALL THE STUFF WITH YOU, THEN DALE'S BLEEDING AND YOU PULL ANN OUT OF A TREE.
I HOPE ANN'S OKAY.
I WAS WORRIED ABOUT YOU.
GOOD. NOW TELL ME THAT YOU'VE GOTTEN RID OF DINA.
I HOPE EVERYONE'S OKAY.
UH...

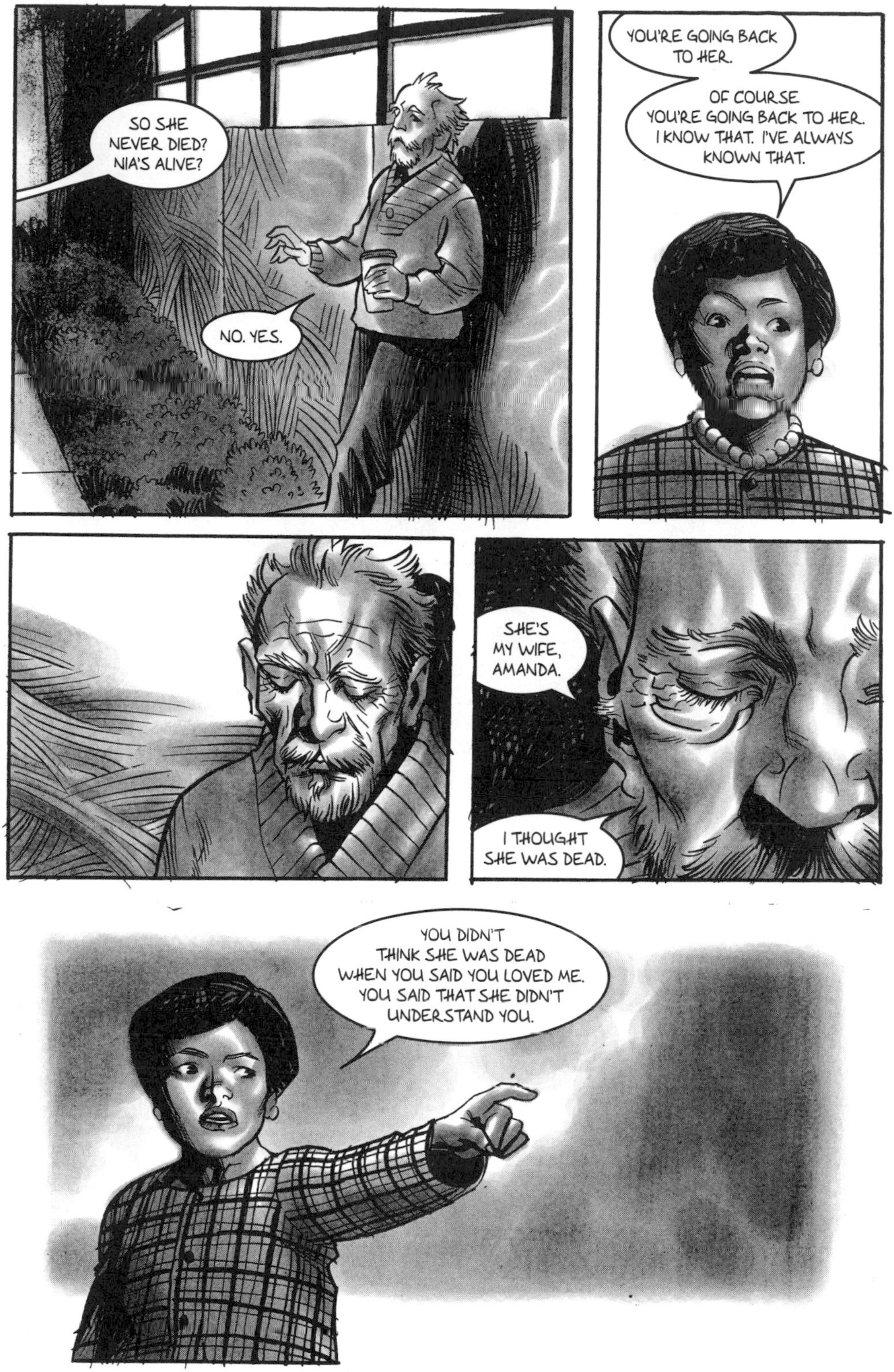
SO SHE NEVER DIED? NIA'S ALIVE?
NO. YES.
YOU'RE GOING BACK TO HER.
OF COURSE YOU'RE GOING BACK TO HER. I KNOW THAT. I'VE ALWAYS KNOWN THAT.
SHE'S MY WIFE, AMANDA.
I THOUGHT SHE WAS DEAD.
YOU DIDN'T THINK SHE WAS DEAD WHEN YOU SAID YOU LOVED ME. YOU SAID THAT SHE DIDN'T UNDERSTAND YOU.

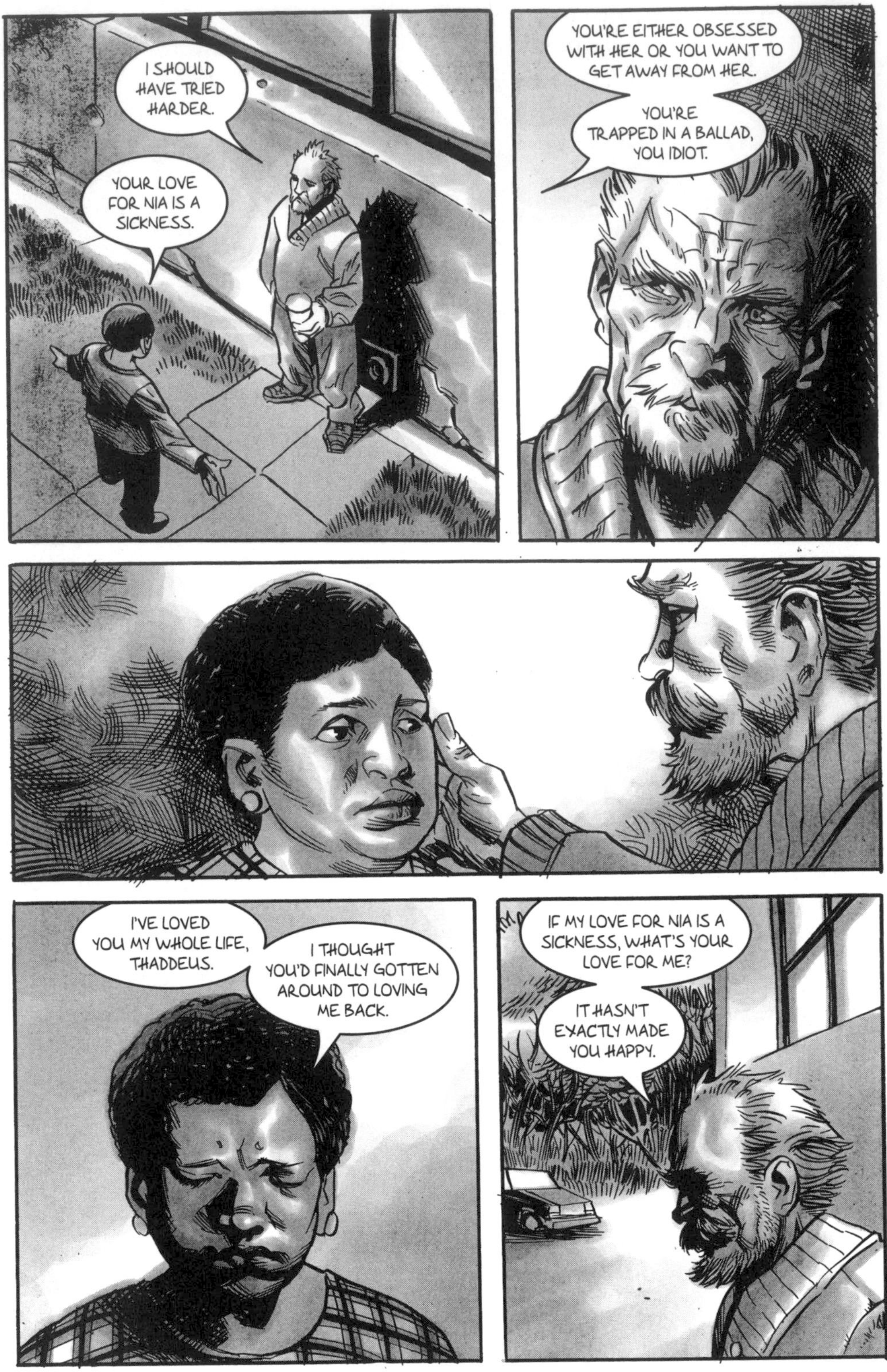
I SHOULD HAVE TRIED HARDER.
YOUR LOVE FOR NIA IS A SICKNESS.
YOU'RE EITHER OBSESSED WITH HER OR YOU WANT TO GET AWAY FROM HER.
YOU'RE TRAPPED IN A BALLAD, YOU IDIOT.
I'VE LOVED YOU MY WHOLE LIFE, THADDEUS.
I THOUGHT YOU'D FINALLY GOTTEN AROUND TO LOVING ME BACK.
IF MY LOVE FOR NIA IS A SICKNESS, WHAT'S YOUR LOVE FOR ME?
IT HASN'T EXACTLY MADE YOU HAPPY.

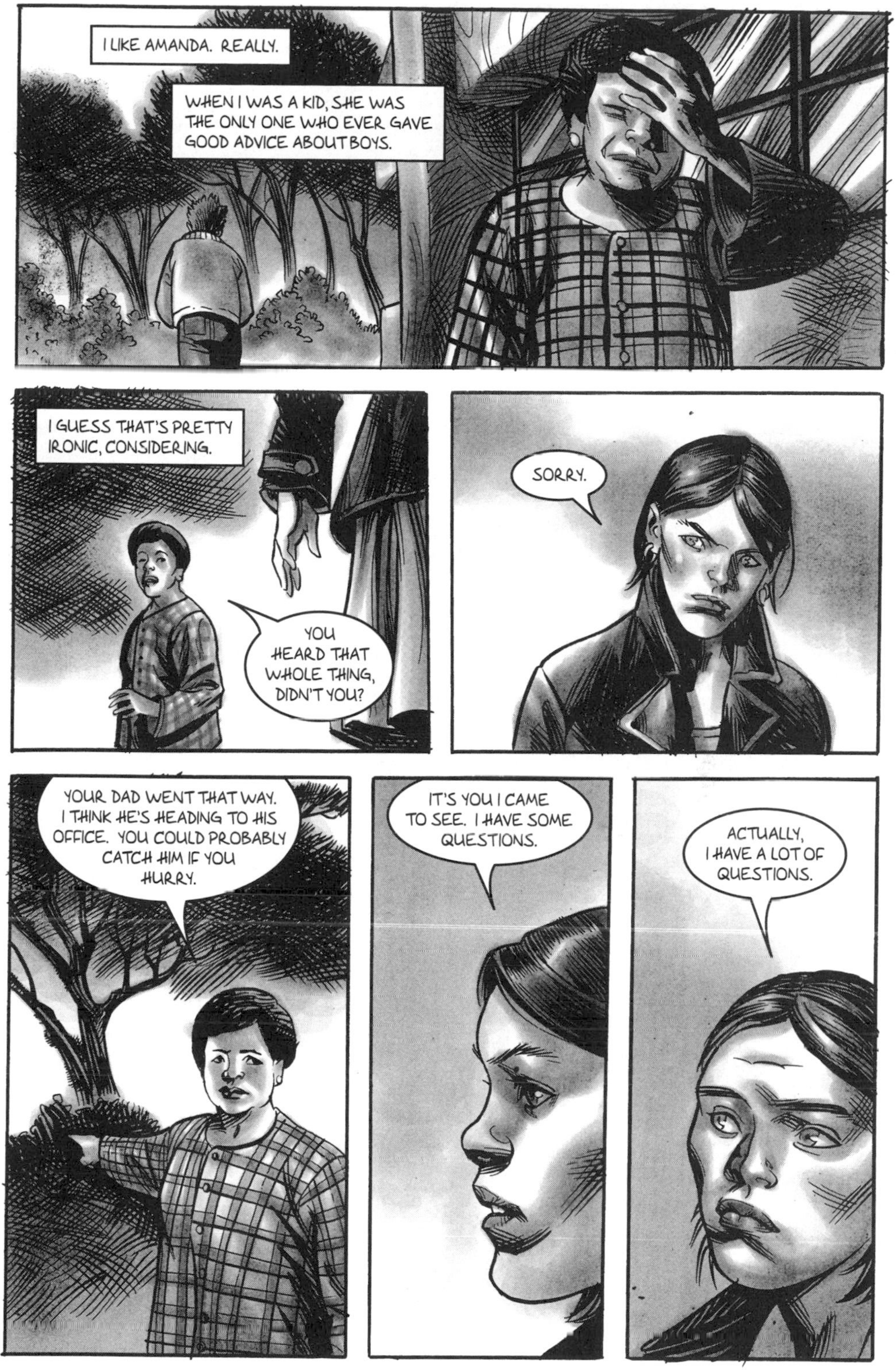
I LIKE AMANDA. REALLY.
WHEN I WAS A KID, SHE WAS THE ONLY ONE WHO EVER GAVE GOOD ADVICE ABOUT BOYS.
I GUESS THAT'S PRETTY IRONIC, CONSIDERING.
YOU HEARD THAT WHOLE THING, DIDN'T YOU?
SORRY.
YOUR DAD WENT THAT WAY. I THINK HE'S HEADING TO HIS OFFICE. YOU COULD PROBABLY CATCH HIM IF YOU HURRY.
IT'S YOU I CAME TO SEE. I HAVE SOME QUESTIONS.
ACTUALLY, I HAVE A LOT OF QUESTIONS.

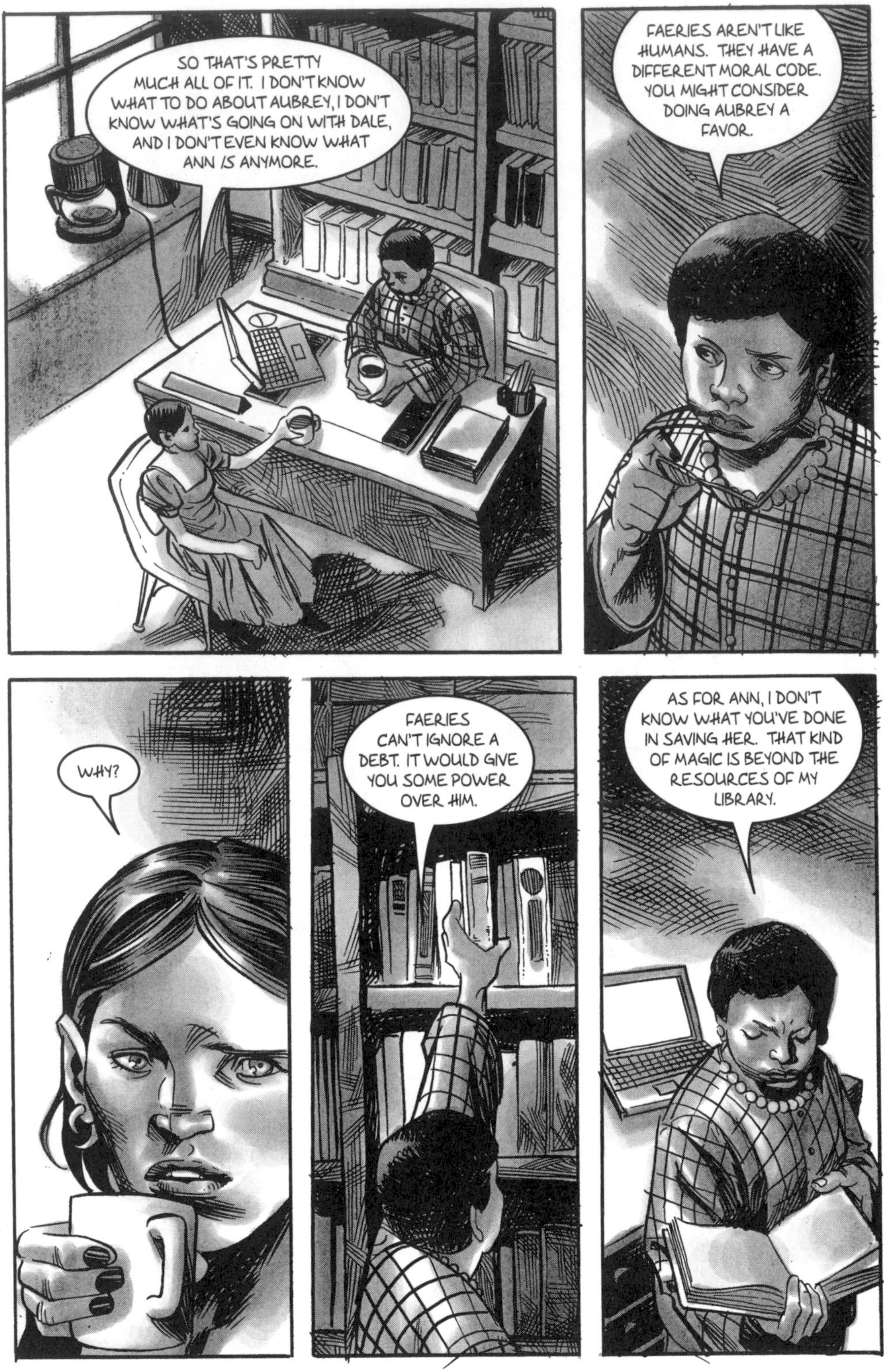
SO THAT'S PRETTY MUCH ALL OF IT. I DON'T KNOW WHAT TO DO ABOUT AUBREY, I DON'T KNOW WHAT'S GOING ON WITH DALE, AND I DON'T EVEN KNOW WHAT ANN IS ANYMORE.
FAERIES AREN'T LIKE HUMANS. THEY HAVE A DIFFERENT MORAL CODE. YOU MIGHT CONSIDER DOING AUBREY A FAVOR.
WHY?
FAERIES CAN'T IGNORE A DEBT. IT WOULD GIVE YOU SOME POWER OVER HIM.
AS FOR ANN, I DON'T KNOW WHAT YOU'VE DONE IN SAVING HER. THAT KIND OF MAGIC IS BEYOND THE RESOURCES OF MY LIBRARY.

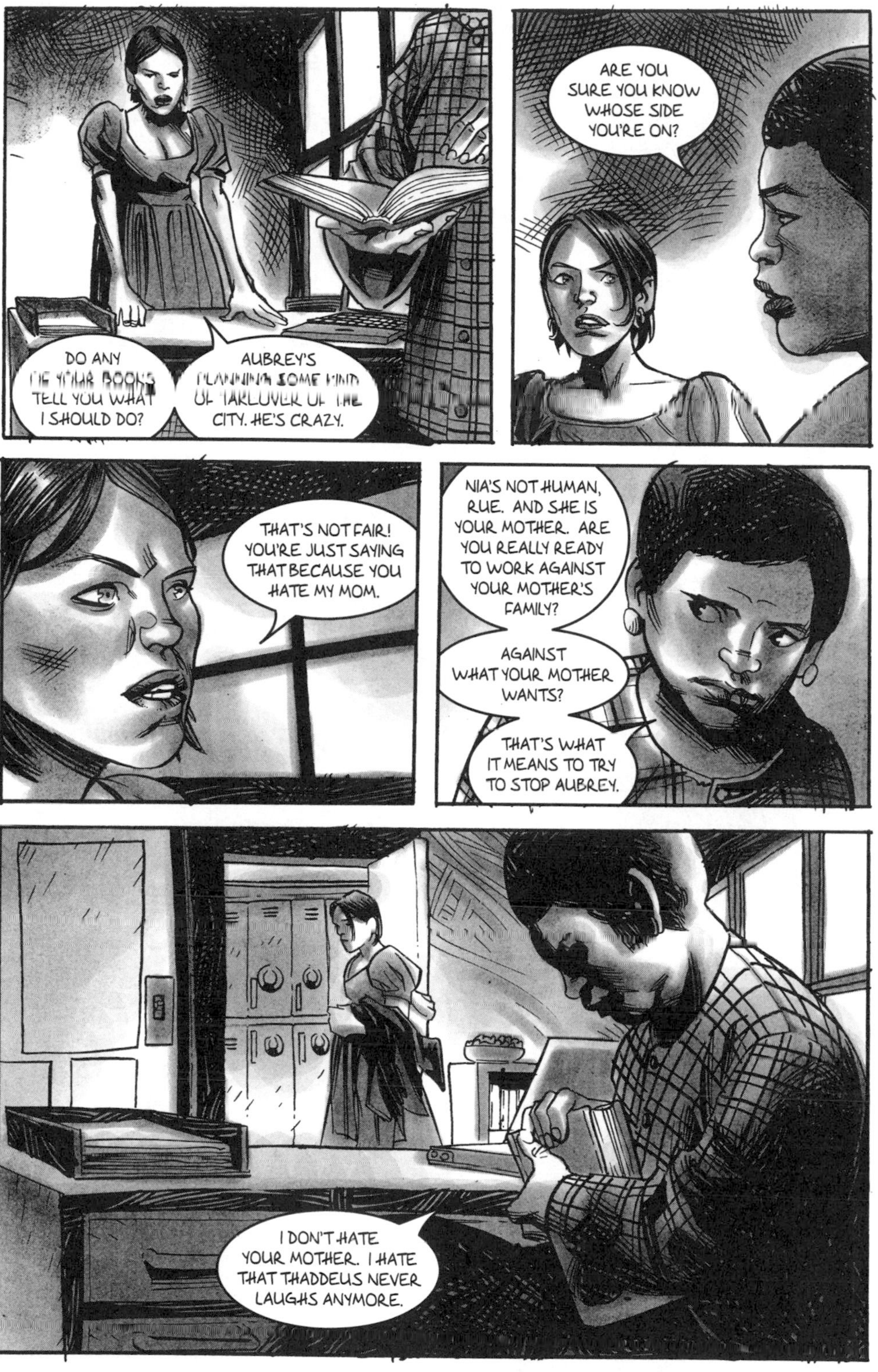
DO ANY OF YOUR BOOKS TELL YOU WHAT I SHOULD DO?
AUBREY'S PLANNING SOME KIND OF TAKEOVER OF THE CITY. HE'S CRAZY.
ARE YOU SURE YOU KNOW WHOSE SIDE YOU'RE ON?
THAT'S NOT FAIR! YOU'RE JUST SAYING THAT BECAUSE YOU HATE MY MOM.
NIA'S NOT HUMAN, RUE. AND SHE IS YOUR MOTHER. ARE YOU REALLY READY TO WORK AGAINST YOUR MOTHER'S FAMILY?
AGAINST WHAT YOUR MOTHER WANTS?
THAT'S WHAT IT MEANS TO TRY TO STOP AUBREY.
I DON'T HATE YOUR MOTHER. I HATE THAT THADDEUS NEVER LAUGHS ANYMORE.

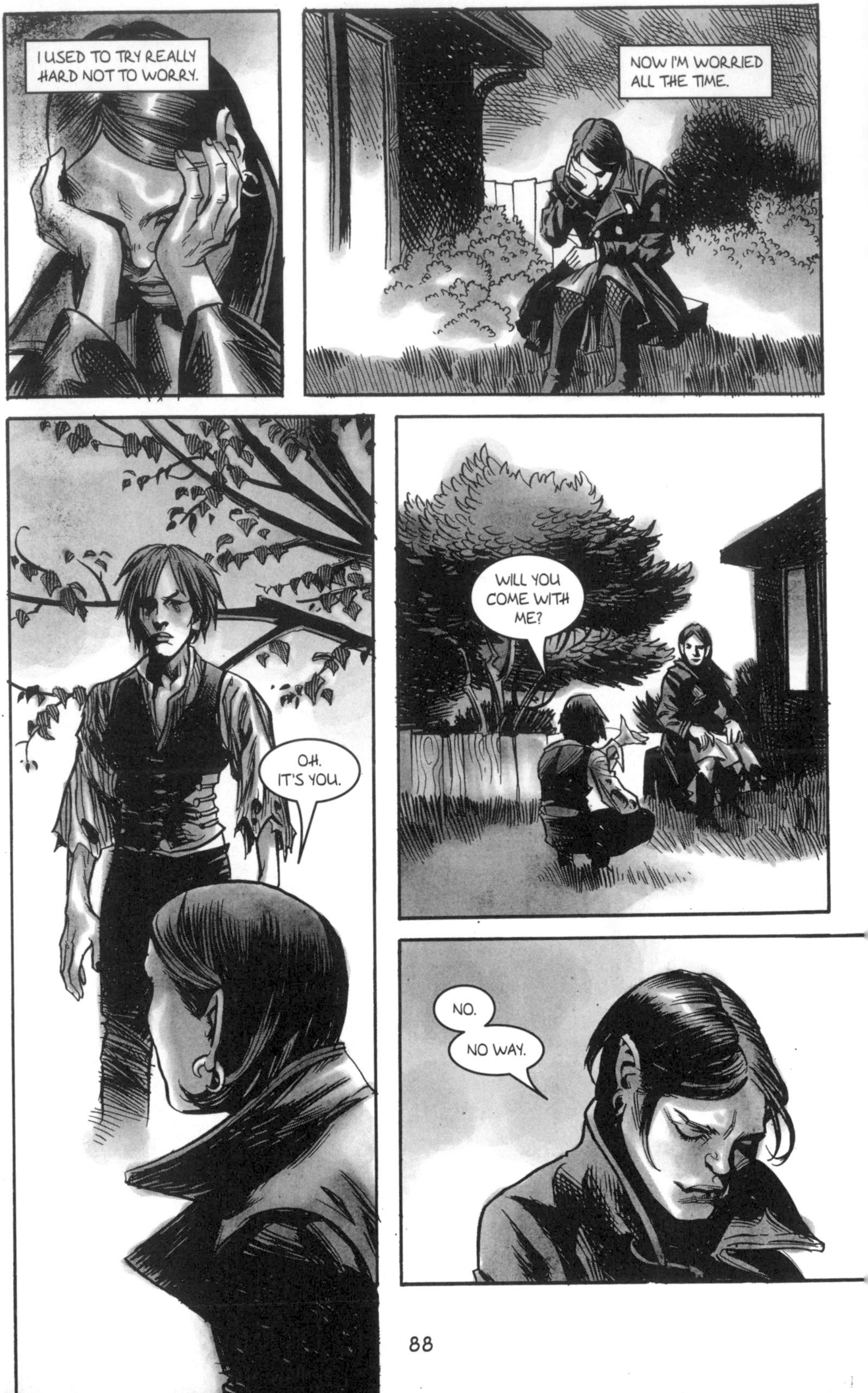
I USED TO TRY REALLY HARD NOT TO WORRY.
NOW I'M WORRIED ALL THE TIME.
OH. IT'S YOU.
WILL YOU COME WITH ME?
NO.
NO WAY.

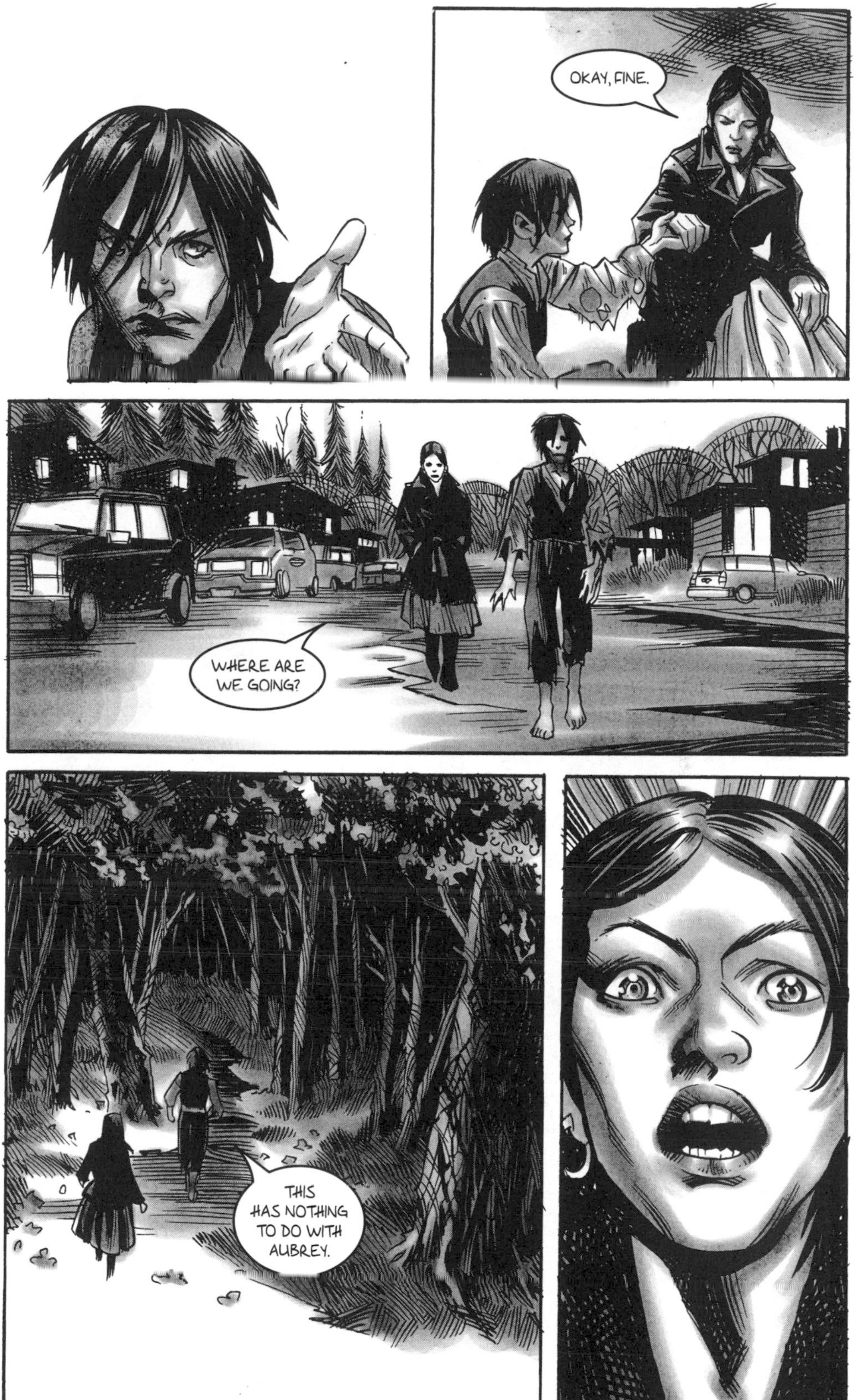
OKAY, FINE.
WHERE ARE WE GOING?
THIS HAS NOTHING TO DO WITH AUBREY.

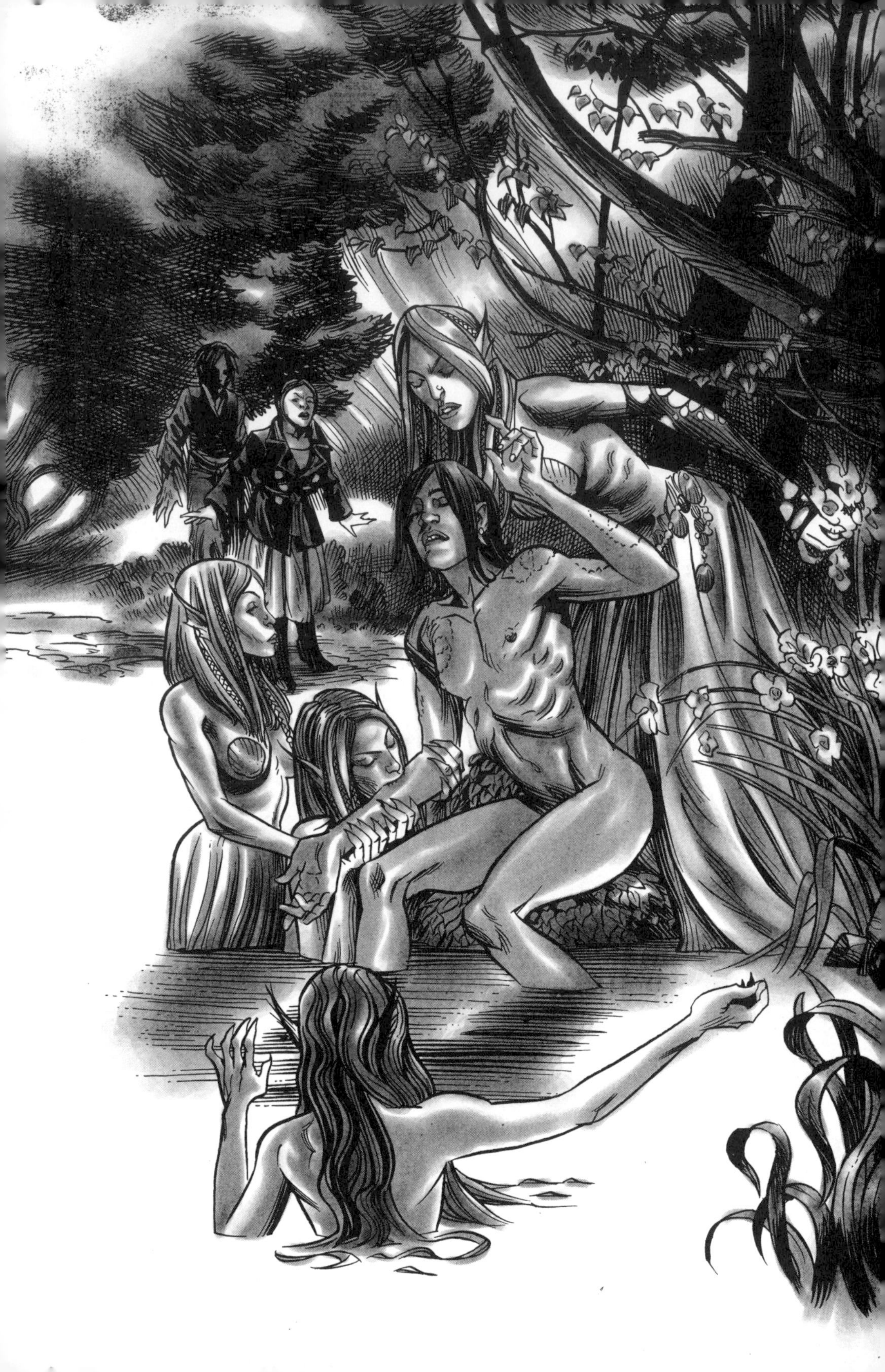

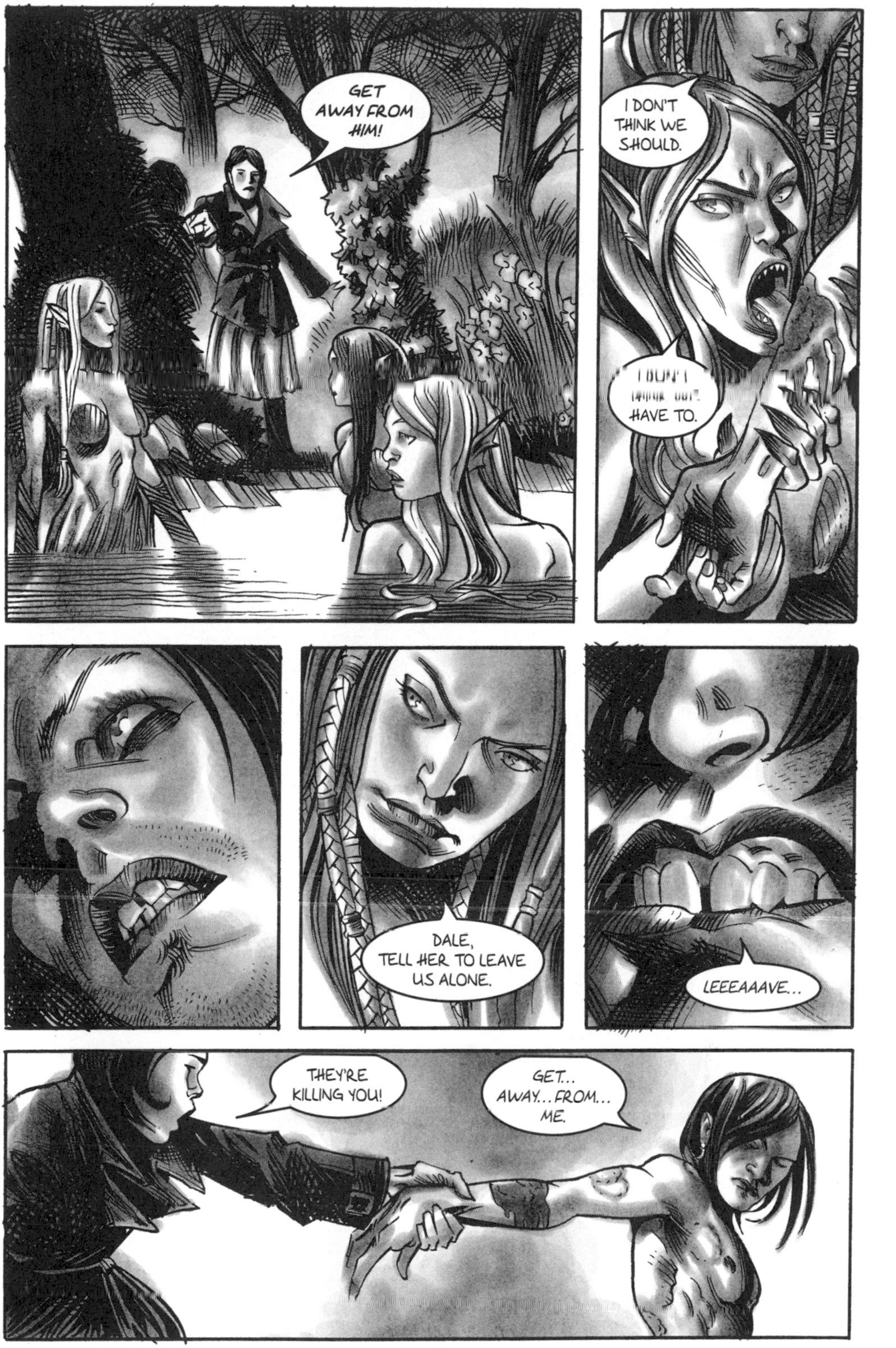
GET AWAY FROM HIM!
I DON'T THINK WE SHOULD.
HAVE TO.
DALE, TELL HER TO LEAVE US ALONE.
LEEEAAAVE...
THEY'RE KILLING YOU!
GET... AWAY... FROM... ME.

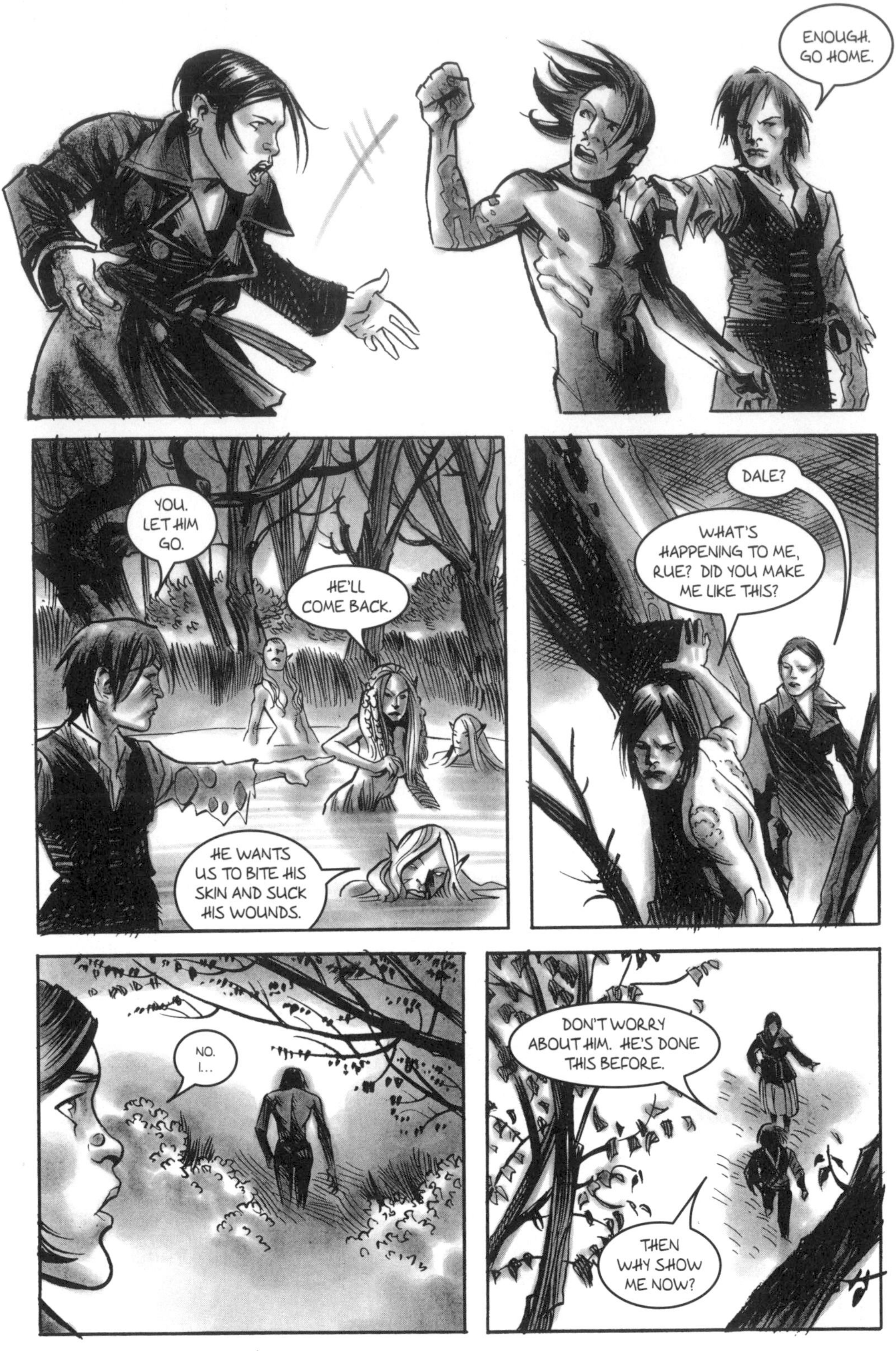
ENOUGH. GO HOME.
YOU. LET HIM GO.
HE'LL COME BACK.
HE WANTS US TO BITE HIS SKIN AND SUCK HIS WOUNDS.
DALE?
WHAT'S HAPPENING TO ME, RUE? DID YOU MAKE ME LIKE THIS?
NO. I...
DON'T WORRY ABOUT HIM. HE'S DONE THIS BEFORE.
THEN WHY SHOW ME NOW?

I DIDN'T WANT TO TELL YOU, BUT AUBREY KNOWS WHAT YOU DID.

YOU SAID IT WASN'T ABOUT HIM, BUT IT ALWAYS IS, ISN'T IT?

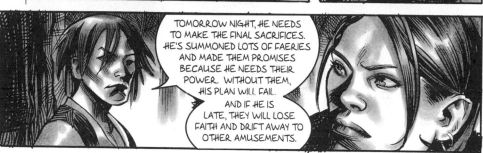

TOMORROW NIGHT, HE NEEDS TO MAKE THE FINAL SACRIFICES. HE'S SUMMONED LOTS OF FAERIES AND MADE THEM PROMISES BECAUSE HE NEEDS THEIR POWER. WITHOUT THEM, HIS PLAN WILL FAIL.

AND IF HE IS LATE, THEY WILL LOSE FAITH AND DRIFT AWAY TO OTHER AMUSEMENTS.

I DON'T UNDERSTAND. WHAT IS IT THAT HE WANTS?

HE'S GOING TO CLOSE OFF THE CITY AND REMAKE IT INTO A FAERY CITY, ONE THAT HE CALLS NEW AVALON. ONCE THE LAST LIVING TREE IS IN PLACE, HE WILL CLOSE THE BORDERS.

NO ONE WILL FIND NEW AVALON. IT WILL APPEAR ON NO MAP. THOSE WHO WANDER TOO CLOSE WILL BECOME CONFUSED AND RETRACE THEIR STEPS WITHOUT EVER KNOWING WHY.

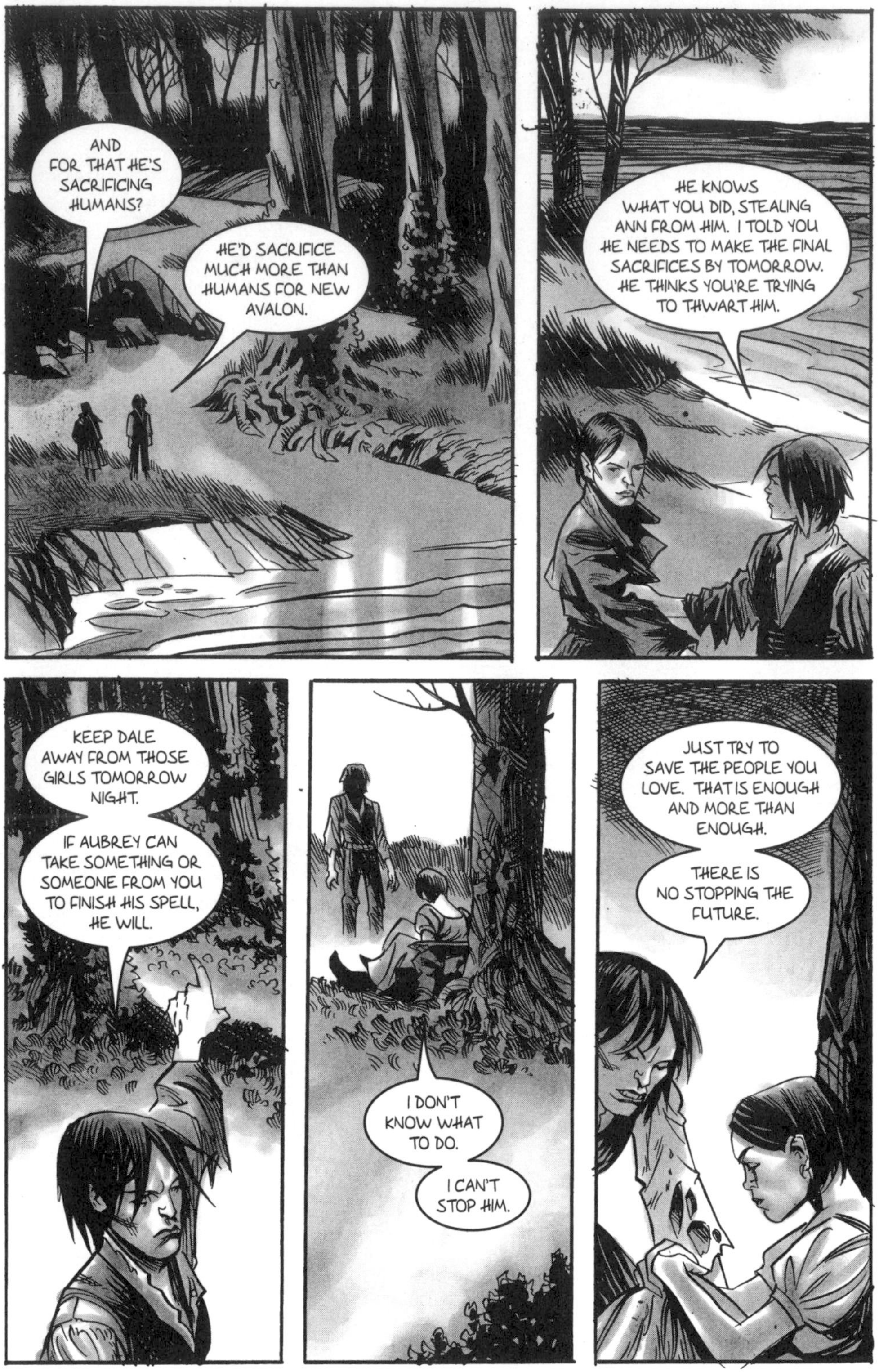
AND FOR THAT HE'S SACRIFICING HUMANS?
HE'D SACRIFICE MUCH MORE THAN HUMANS FOR NEW AVALON.
HE KNOWS WHAT YOU DID, STEALING ANN FROM HIM. I TOLD YOU HE NEEDS TO MAKE THE FINAL SACRIFICES BY TOMORROW. HE THINKS YOU'RE TRYING TO THWART HIM.
KEEP DALE AWAY FROM THOSE GIRLS TOMORROW NIGHT.
IF AUBREY CAN TAKE SOMETHING OR SOMEONE FROM YOU TO FINISH HIS SPELL, HE WILL.
I DON'T KNOW WHAT TO DO.
I CAN'T STOP HIM.
JUST TRY TO SAVE THE PEOPLE YOU LOVE. THAT IS ENOUGH AND MORE THAN ENOUGH.
THERE IS NO STOPPING THE FUTURE.

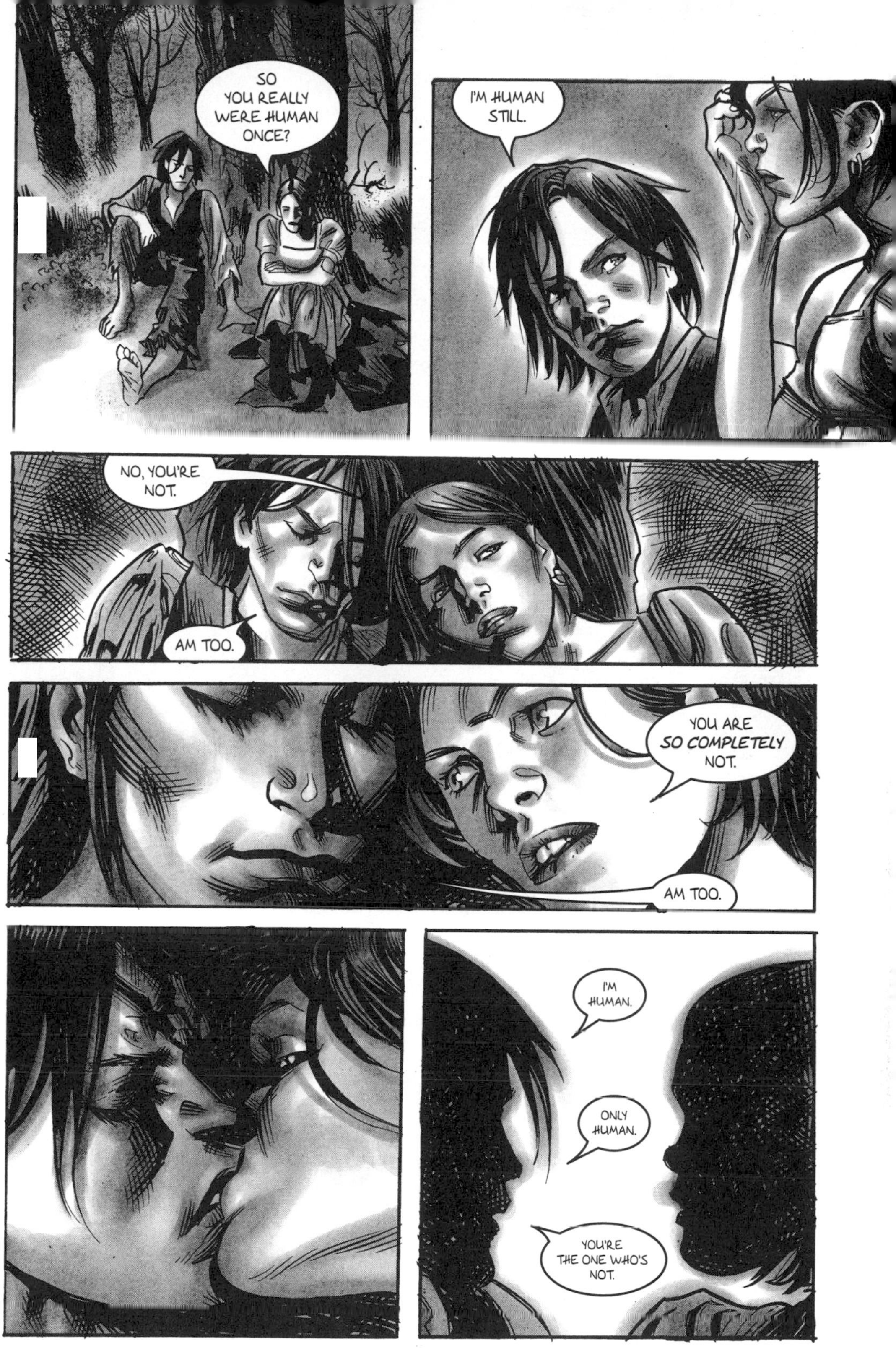
SO YOU REALLY WERE HUMAN ONCE?
I'M HUMAN STILL.
NO, YOU'RE NOT.
AM TOO.
YOU ARE *SO COMPLETELY* NOT.
AM TOO.
I'M HUMAN.
ONLY HUMAN.
YOU'RE THE ONE WHO'S NOT.

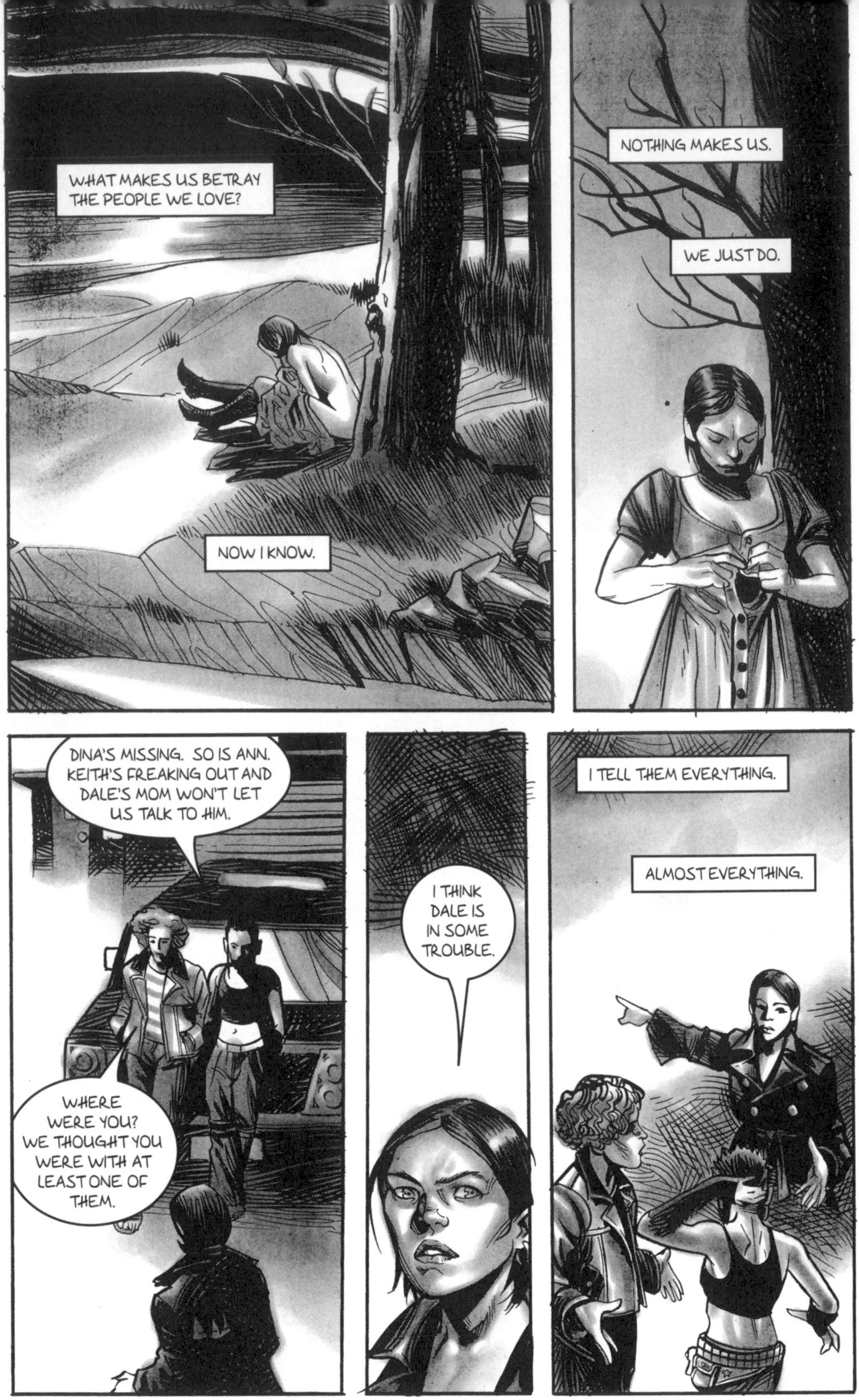
WHAT MAKES US BETRAY THE PEOPLE WE LOVE?
NOW I KNOW.
NOTHING MAKES US.
WE JUST DO.
DINA'S MISSING. SO IS ANN. KEITH'S FREAKING OUT AND DALE'S MOM WON'T LET US TALK TO HIM.
WHERE WERE YOU? WE THOUGHT YOU WERE WITH AT LEAST ONE OF THEM.
I THINK DALE IS IN SOME TROUBLE.
I TELL THEM EVERYTHING.
ALMOST EVERYTHING.

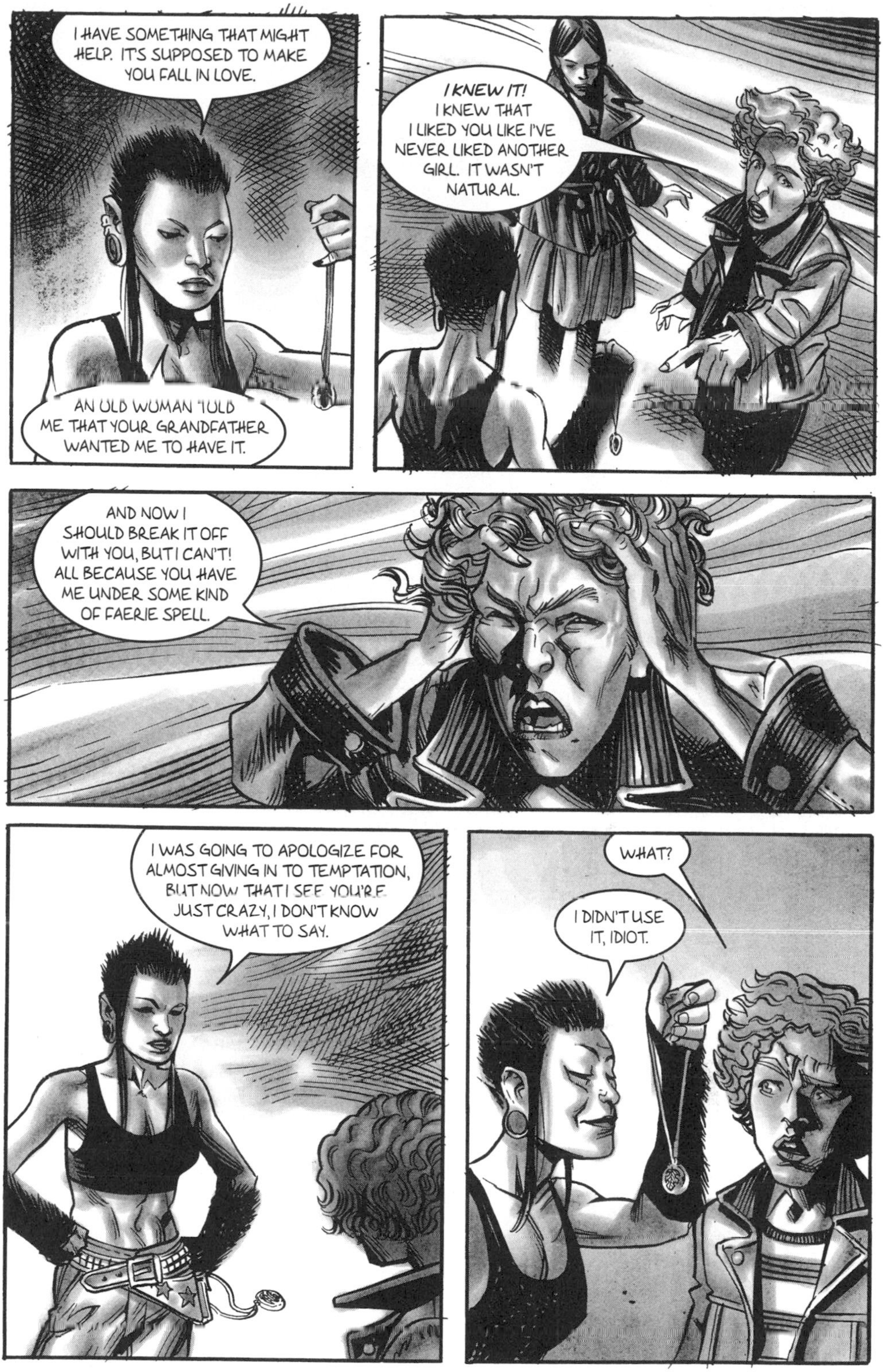
I HAVE SOMETHING THAT MIGHT HELP. IT'S SUPPOSED TO MAKE YOU FALL IN LOVE.
AN OLD WOMAN TOLD ME THAT YOUR GRANDFATHER WANTED ME TO HAVE IT.
I KNEW IT! I KNEW THAT I LIKED YOU LIKE I'VE NEVER LIKED ANOTHER GIRL. IT WASN'T NATURAL.
AND NOW I SHOULD BREAK IT OFF WITH YOU, BUT I CAN'T! ALL BECAUSE YOU HAVE ME UNDER SOME KIND OF FAERIE SPELL.
I WAS GOING TO APOLOGIZE FOR ALMOST GIVING IN TO TEMPTATION, BUT NOW THAT I SEE YOU'RE JUST CRAZY, I DON'T KNOW WHAT TO SAY.
WHAT?
I DIDN'T USE IT, IDIOT.

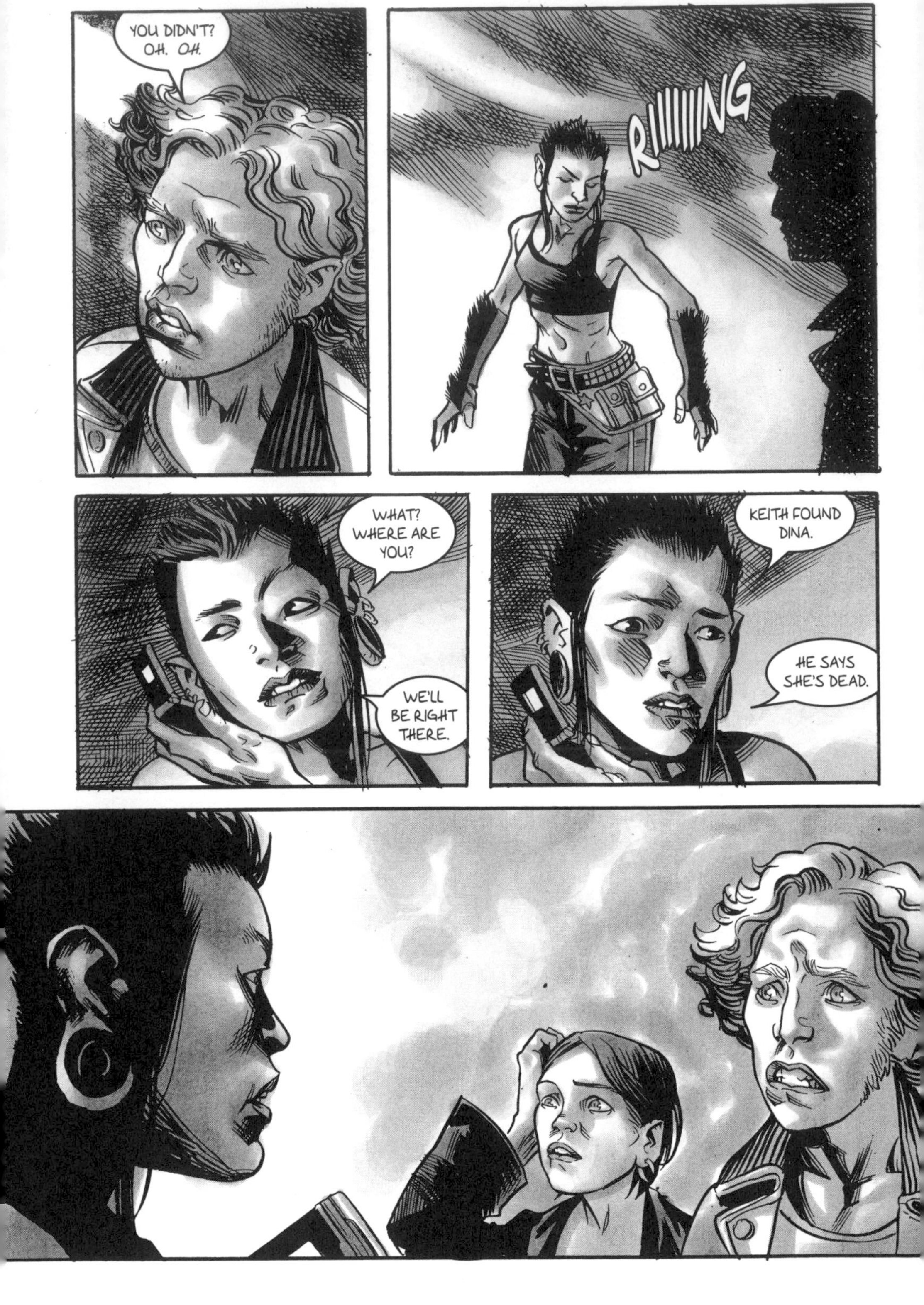
YOU DIDN'T? OH. OH.
RIIIIIING
WHAT? WHERE ARE YOU?
WE'LL BE RIGHT THERE.
KEITH FOUND DINA.
HE SAYS SHE'S DEAD.

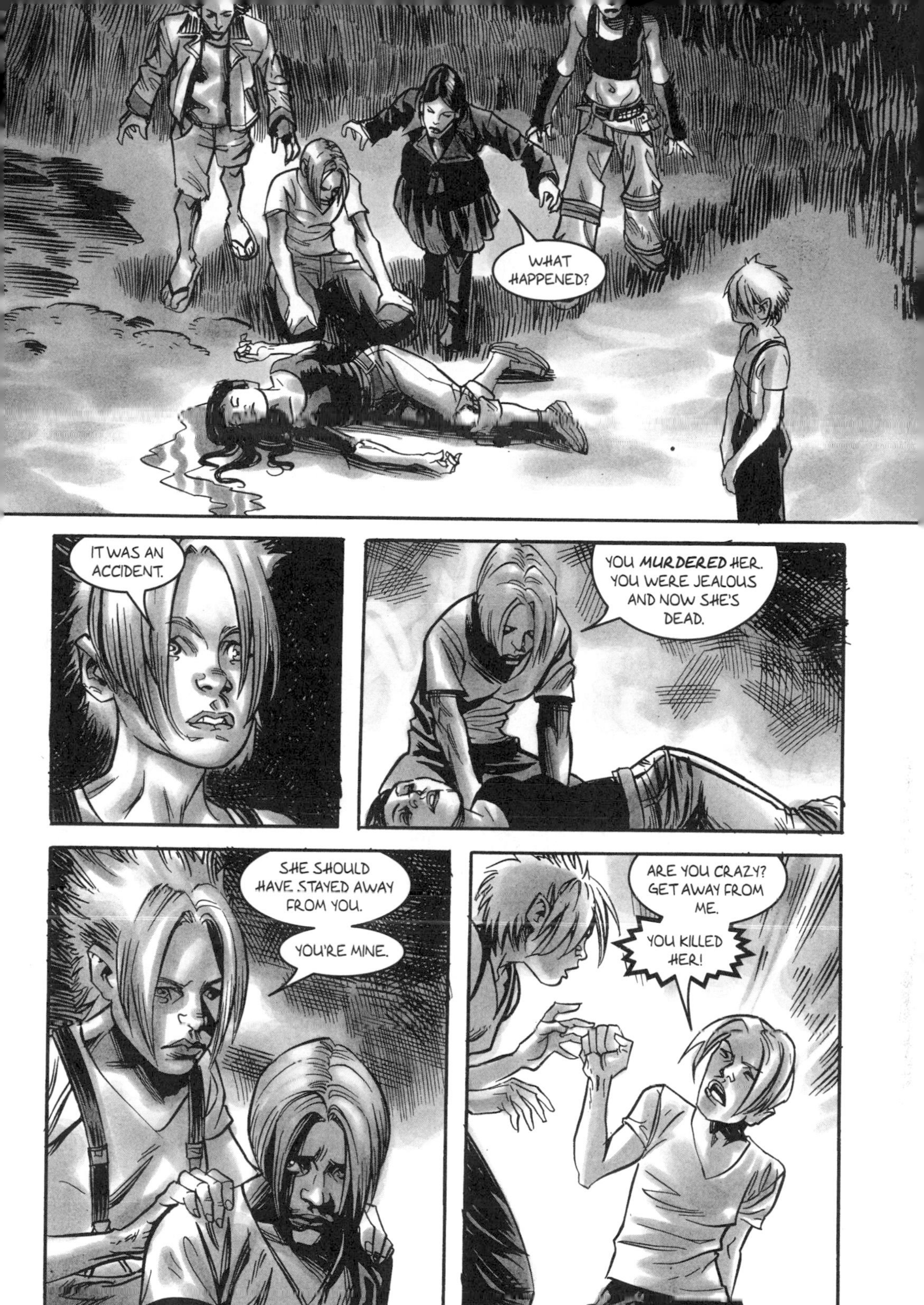
WHAT HAPPENED?
IT WAS AN ACCIDENT.
YOU **MURDERED** HER. YOU WERE JEALOUS AND NOW SHE'S DEAD.
SHE SHOULD HAVE STAYED AWAY FROM YOU.
YOU'RE MINE.
ARE YOU CRAZY? GET AWAY FROM ME.
YOU KILLED HER!

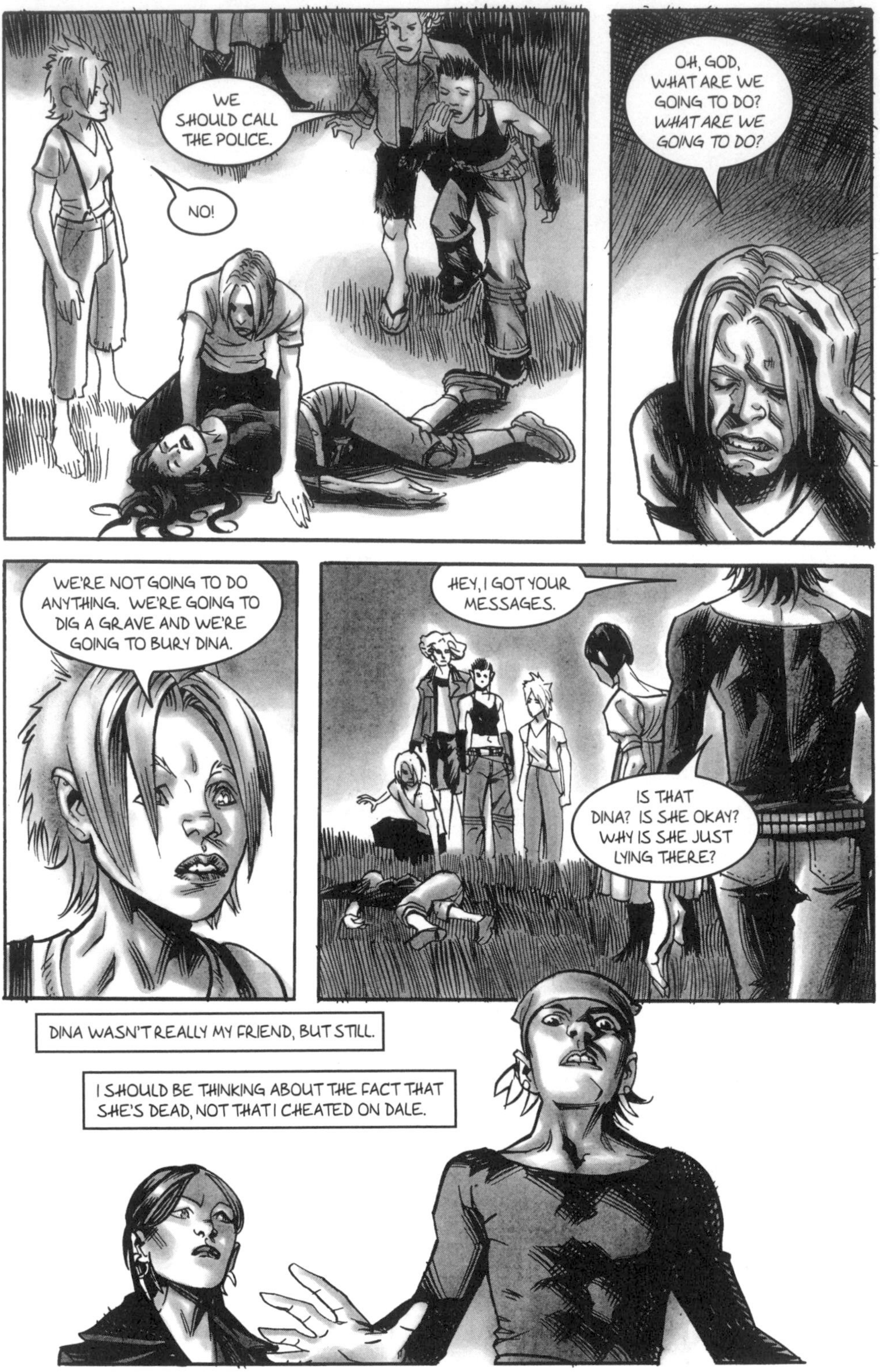
WE SHOULD CALL THE POLICE.
NO!
OH, GOD, WHAT ARE WE GOING TO DO? WHAT ARE WE GOING TO DO?
WE'RE NOT GOING TO DO ANYTHING. WE'RE GOING TO DIG A GRAVE AND WE'RE GOING TO BURY DINA.
HEY, I GOT YOUR MESSAGES.
IS THAT DINA? IS SHE OKAY? WHY IS SHE JUST LYING THERE?
DINA WASN'T REALLY MY FRIEND, BUT STILL.
I SHOULD BE THINKING ABOUT THE FACT THAT SHE'S DEAD, NOT THAT I CHEATED ON DALE.

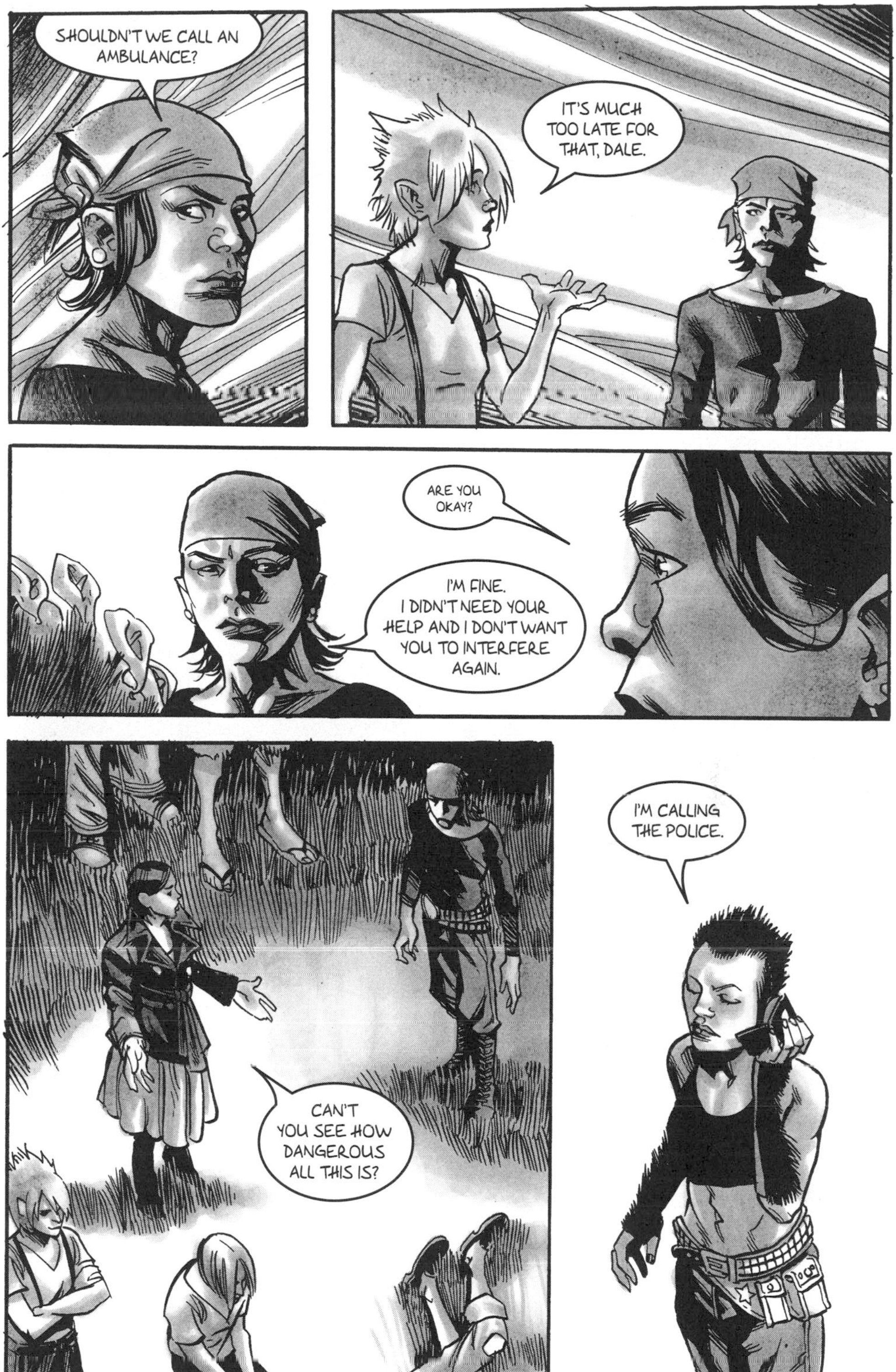
SHOULDN'T WE CALL AN AMBULANCE?
IT'S MUCH TOO LATE FOR THAT, DALE.
ARE YOU OKAY?
I'M FINE. I DIDN'T NEED YOUR HELP AND I DON'T WANT YOU TO INTERFERE AGAIN.
CAN'T YOU SEE HOW DANGEROUS ALL THIS IS?
I'M CALLING THE POLICE.

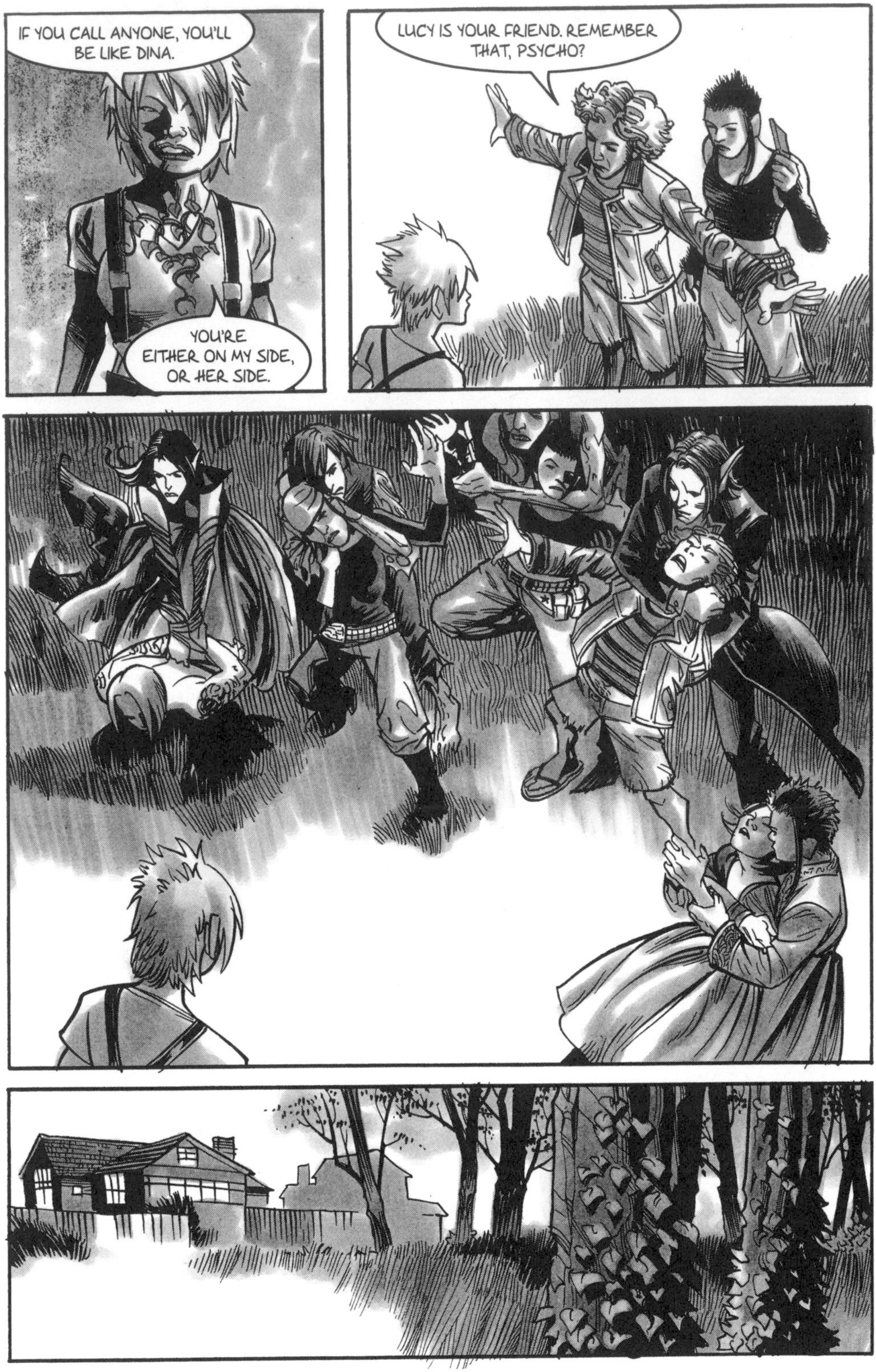
IF YOU CALL ANYONE, YOU'LL BE LIKE DINA.
YOU'RE EITHER ON MY SIDE, OR HER SIDE.
LUCY IS YOUR FRIEND. REMEMBER THAT, PSYCHO?

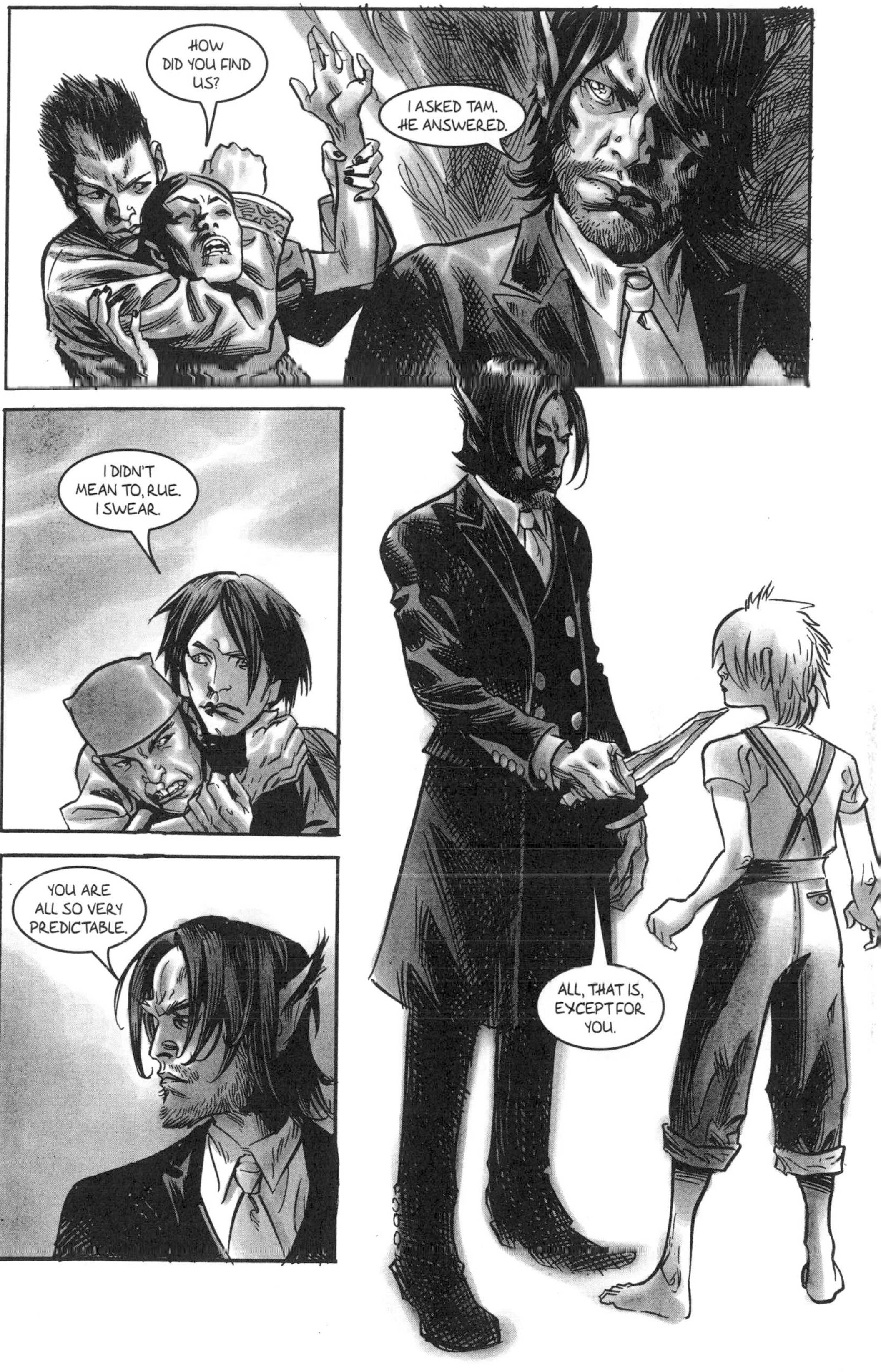
HOW DID YOU FIND US?
I ASKED TAM. HE ANSWERED.
I DIDN'T MEAN TO, RUE. I SWEAR.
YOU ARE ALL SO VERY PREDICTABLE.
ALL, THAT IS, EXCEPT FOR YOU.

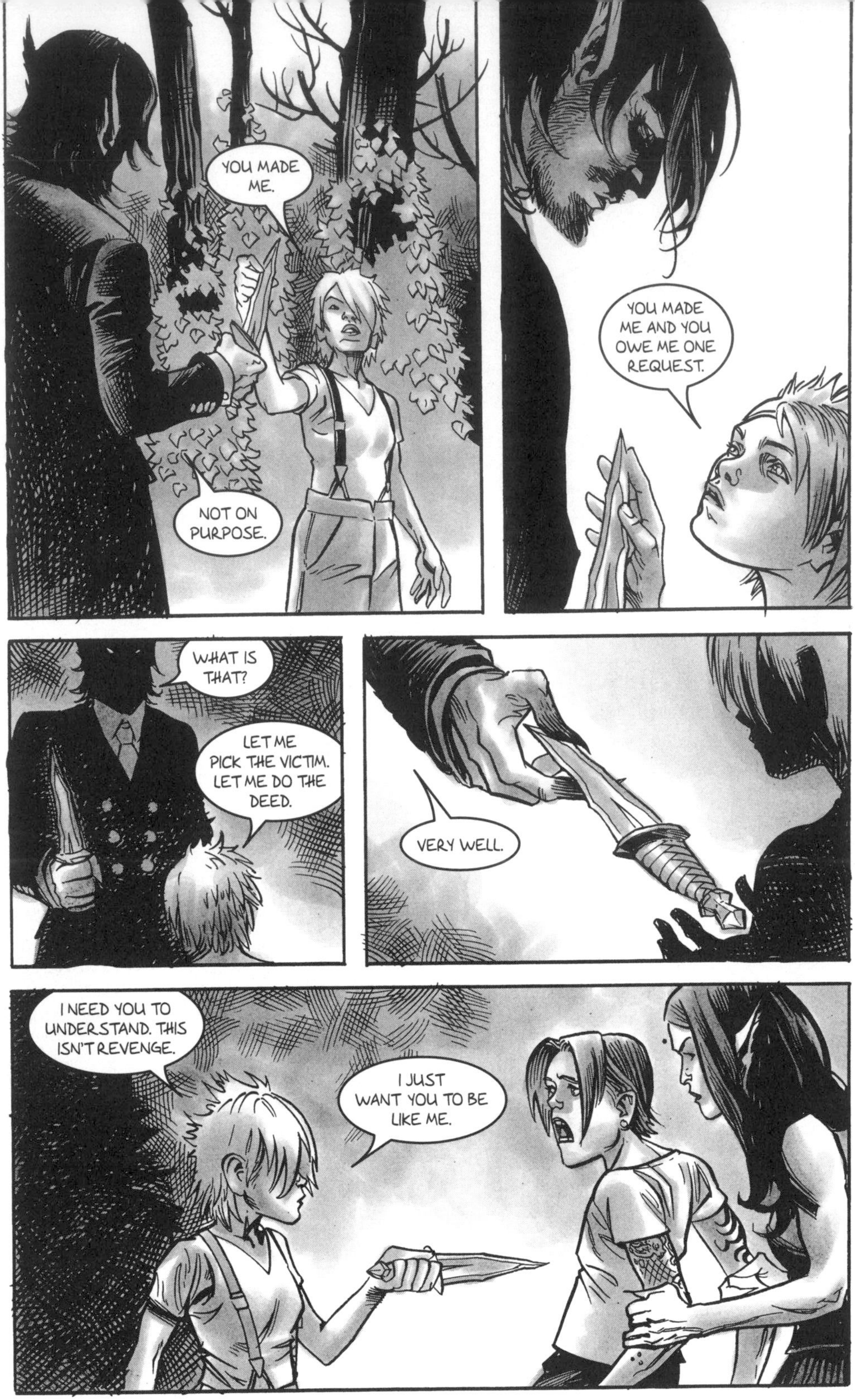
YOU MADE ME.
NOT ON PURPOSE.
YOU MADE ME AND YOU OWE ME ONE REQUEST.
WHAT IS THAT?
LET ME PICK THE VICTIM. LET ME DO THE DEED.
VERY WELL.
I NEED YOU TO UNDERSTAND. THIS ISN'T REVENGE.
I JUST WANT YOU TO BE LIKE ME.

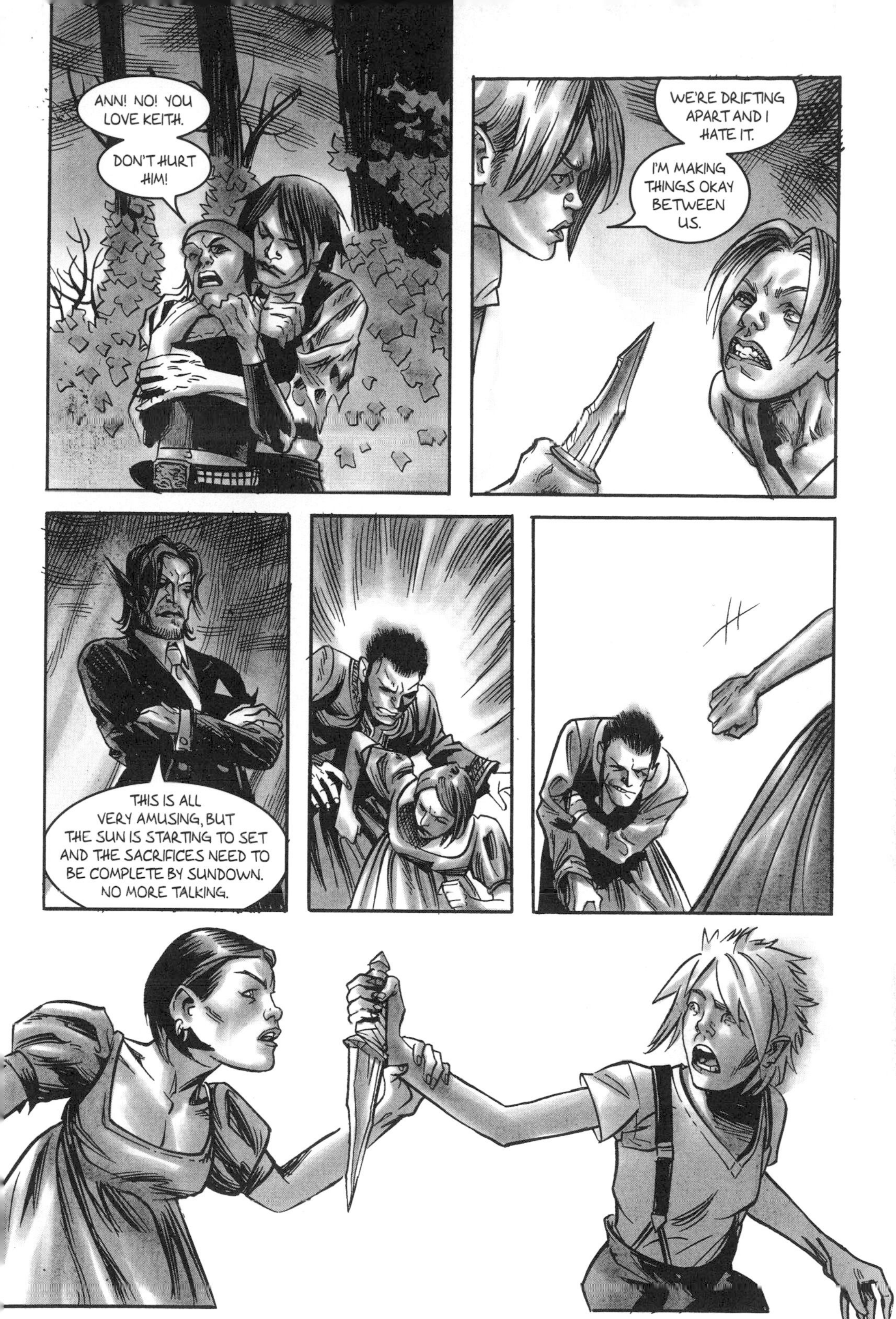
ANN! NO! YOU LOVE KEITH.
DON'T HURT HIM!
WE'RE DRIFTING APART AND I HATE IT.
I'M MAKING THINGS OKAY BETWEEN US.
THIS IS ALL VERY AMUSING, BUT THE SUN IS STARTING TO SET AND THE SACRIFICES NEED TO BE COMPLETE BY SUNDOWN. NO MORE TALKING.

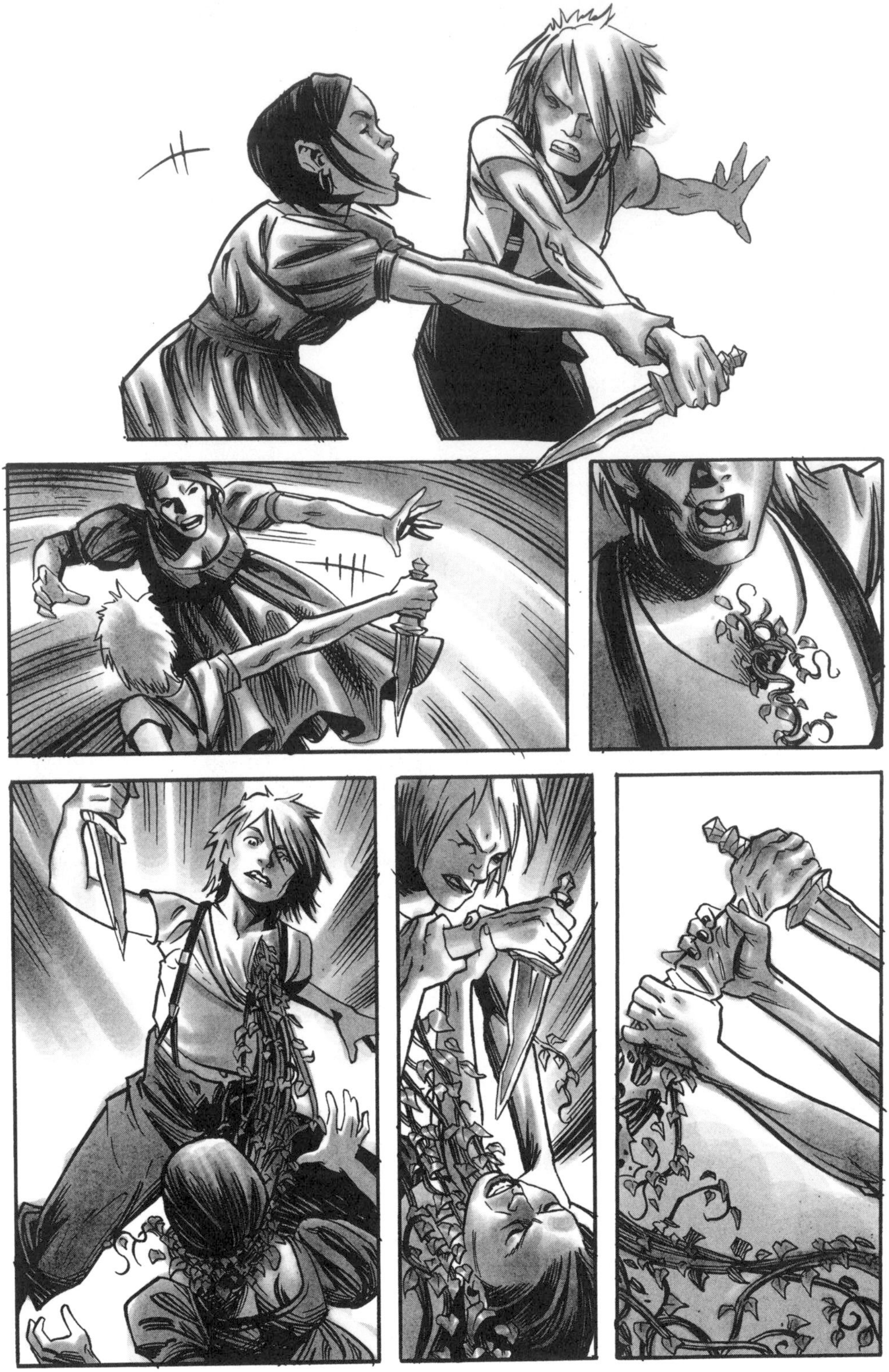

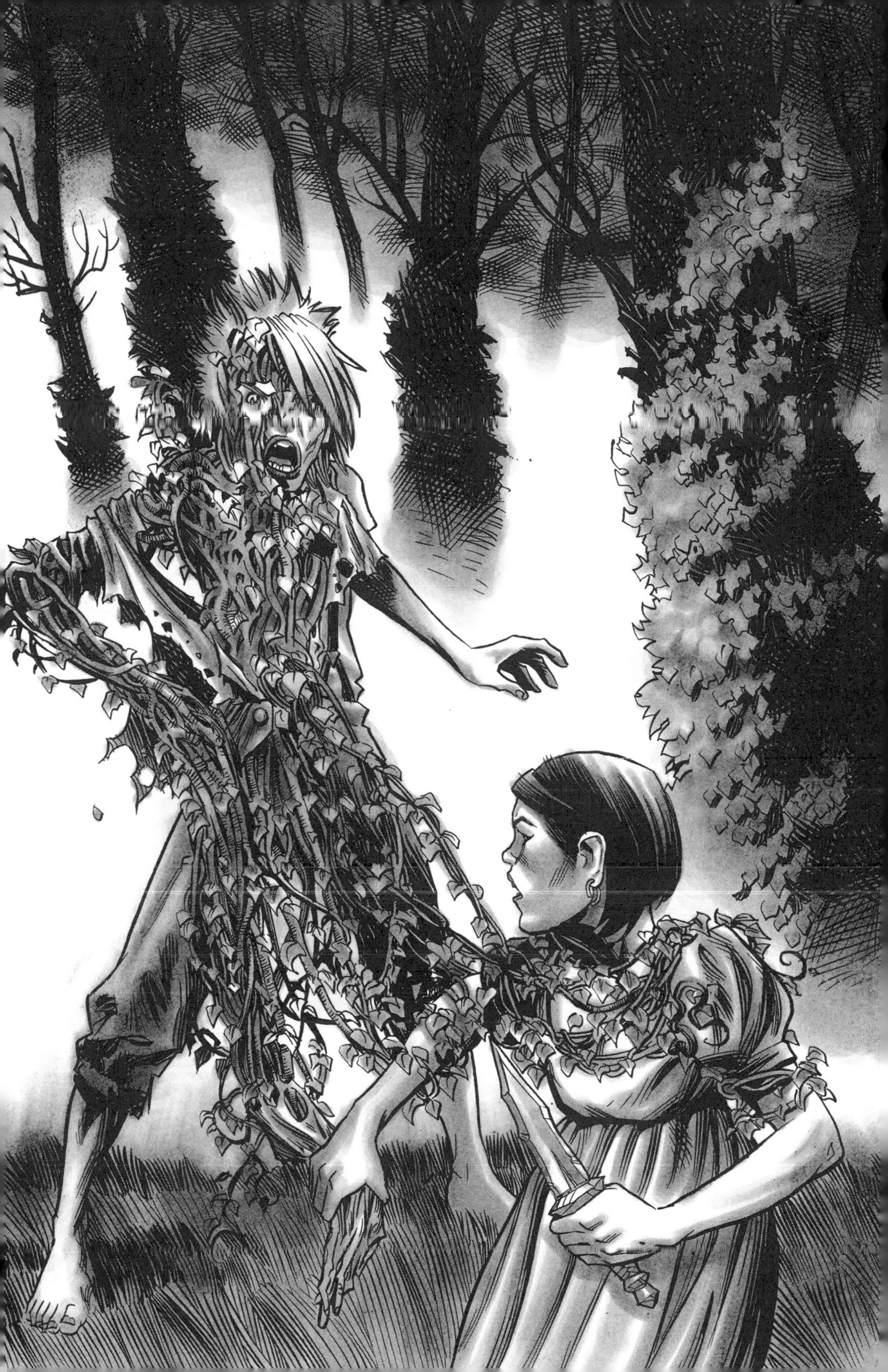

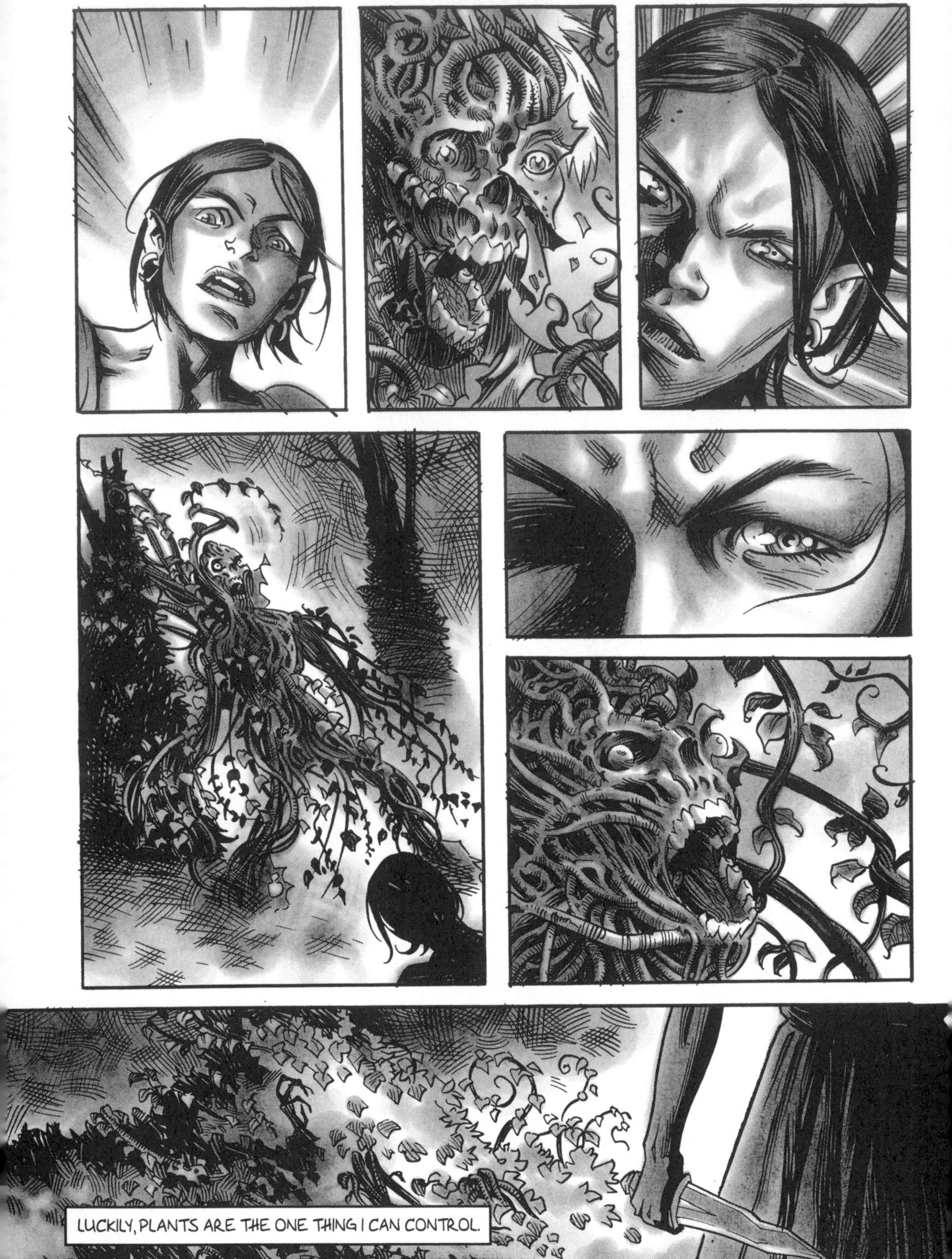
LUCKILY, PLANTS ARE THE ONE THING I CAN CONTROL.

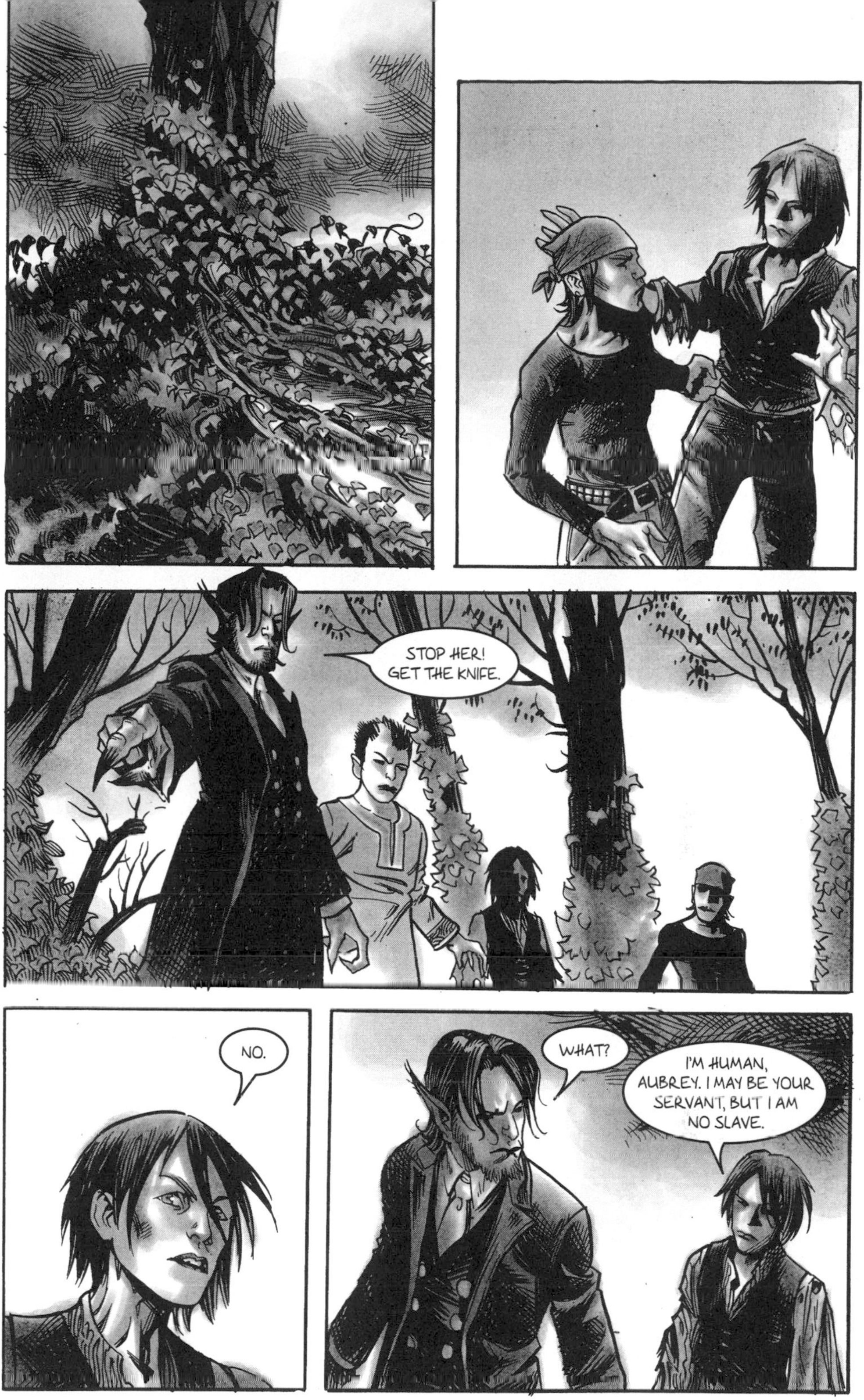
STOP HER! GET THE KNIFE.
NO.
WHAT?
I'M HUMAN, AUBREY. I MAY BE YOUR SERVANT, BUT I AM NO SLAVE.

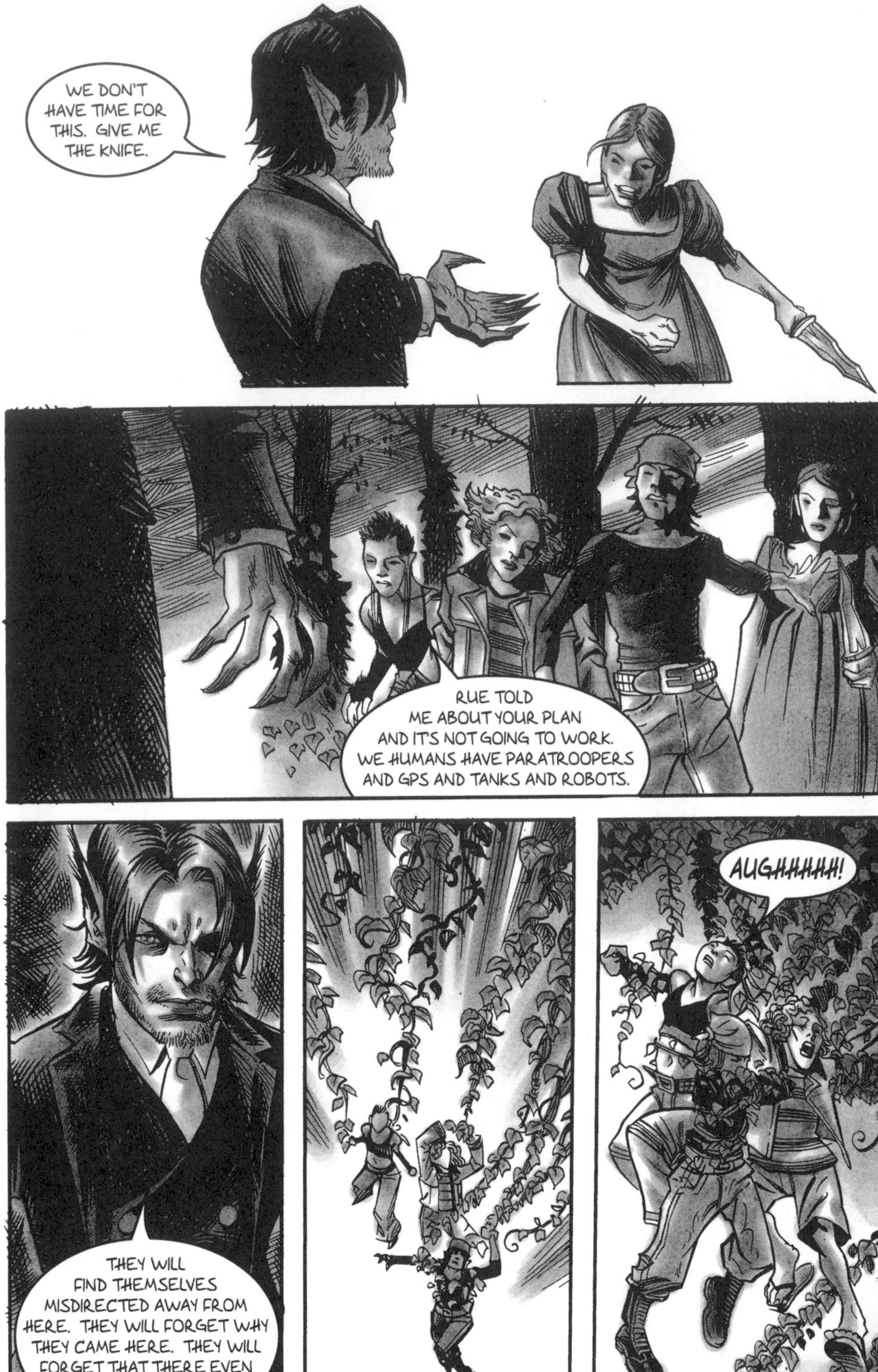
WE DON'T HAVE TIME FOR THIS. GIVE ME THE KNIFE.
RUE TOLD ME ABOUT YOUR PLAN AND IT'S NOT GOING TO WORK. WE HUMANS HAVE PARATROOPERS AND GPS AND TANKS AND ROBOTS.
THEY WILL FIND THEMSELVES MISDIRECTED AWAY FROM HERE. THEY WILL FORGET WHY THEY CAME HERE. THEY WILL FORGET THAT THERE EVEN WAS SUCH A CITY.
AUGHHHHH!

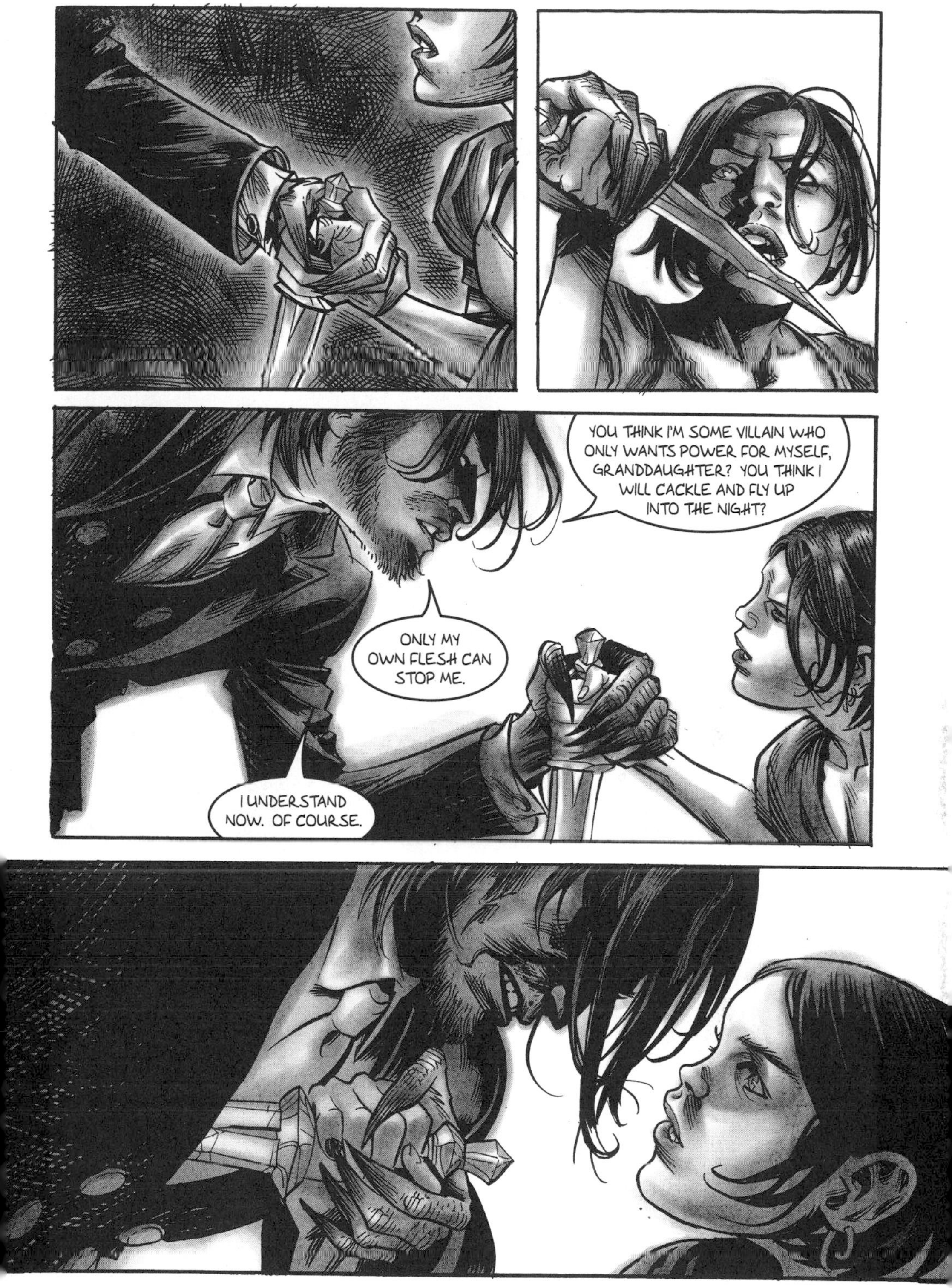
YOU THINK I'M SOME VILLAIN WHO ONLY WANTS POWER FOR MYSELF, GRANDDAUGHTER? YOU THINK I WILL CACKLE AND FLY UP INTO THE NIGHT?
ONLY MY OWN FLESH CAN STOP ME.
I UNDERSTAND NOW. OF COURSE.

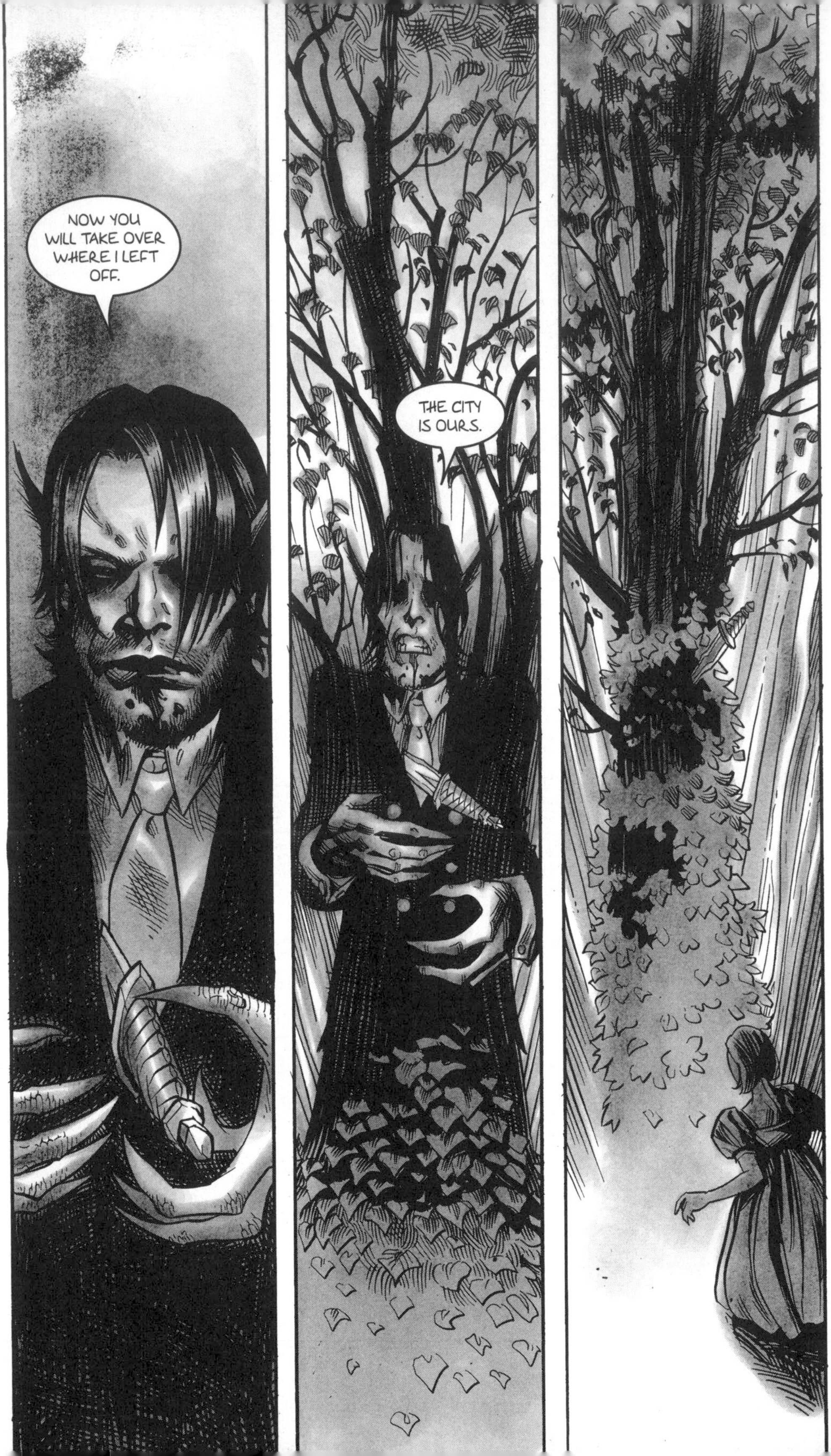
NOW YOU WILL TAKE OVER WHERE I LEFT OFF.
THE CITY IS OURS.

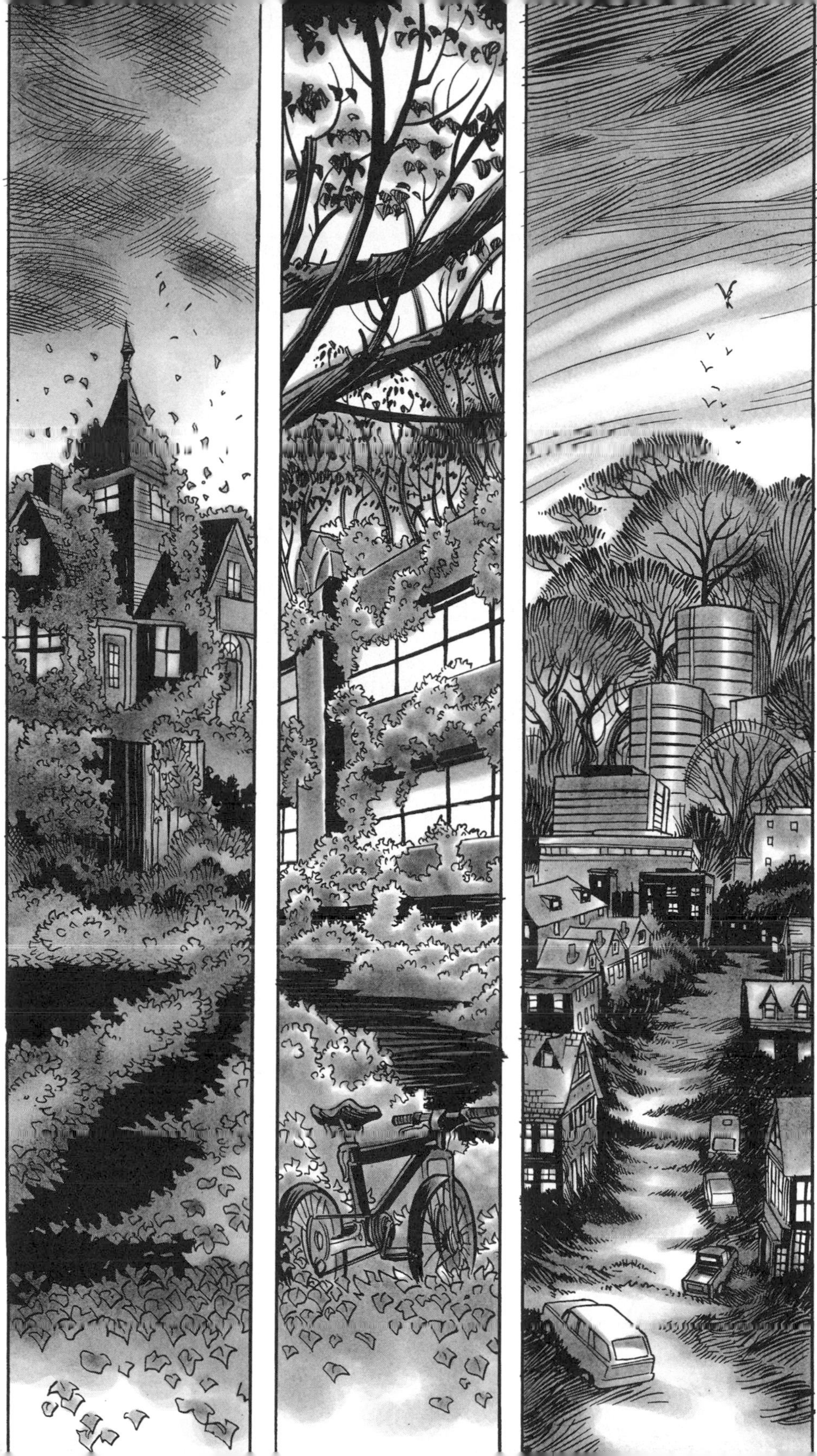

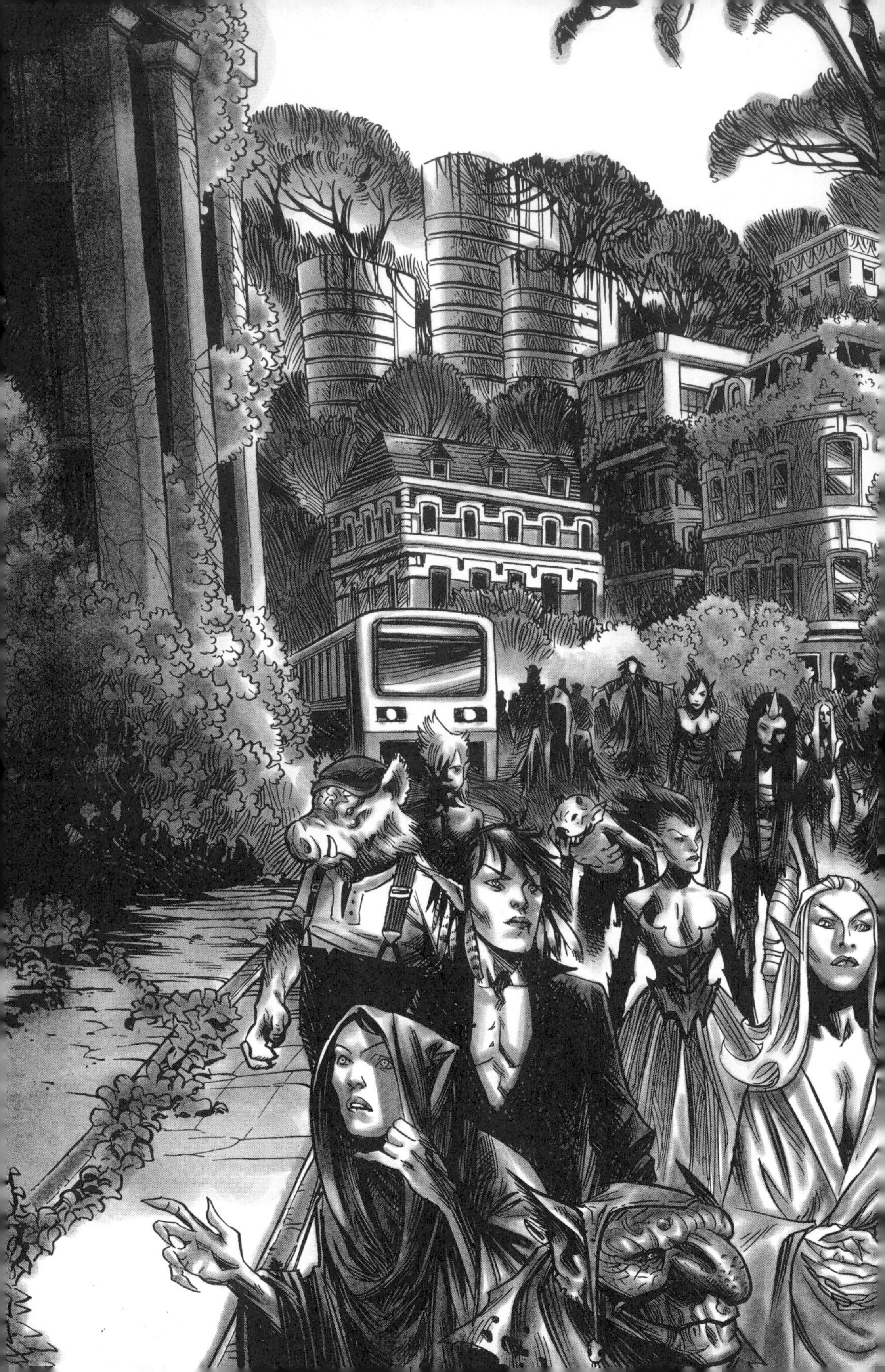

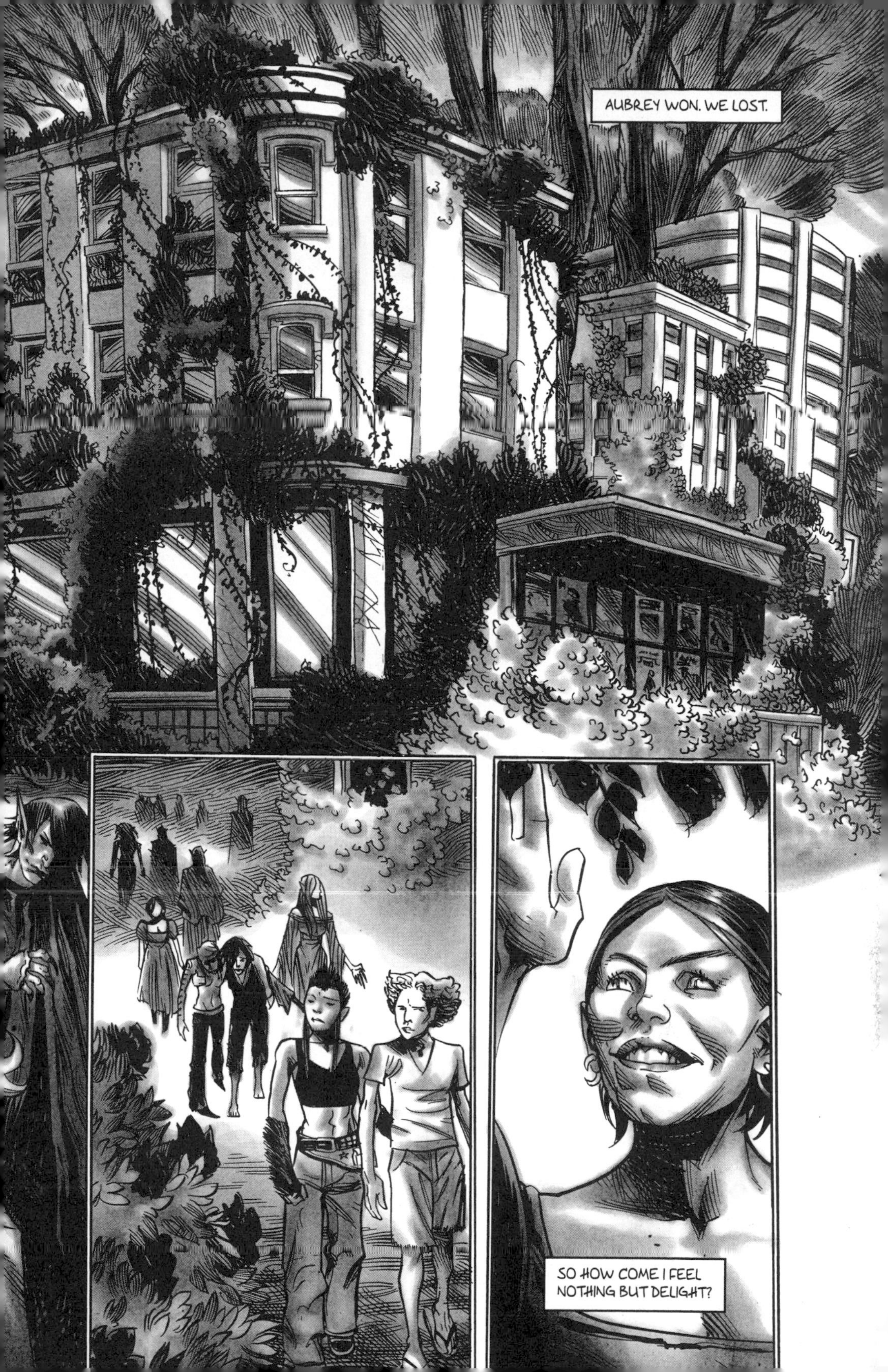
AUBREY WON. WE LOST.
SO HOW COME I FEEL NOTHING BUT DELIGHT?

end of book two

ABOUT THE AUTHOR

Holly Black is the author of contemporary fantasy novels for teens and children. Born in New Jersey, Holly grew up in a decrepit Victorian house piled with books and oddments. She never quite recovered.

Her first book, *Tithe: A Modern Faerie Tale*, was called "dark, edgy, beautifully written and compulsively readable" by *Booklist*, received starred reviews from *Publisher's Weekly* and *Kirkus*, and was included in the American Library Association's Best Books for Young Adults. Holly has since written two other books in the same universe: *Valiant*, a recipient of the Andre Norton Award for Excellence in Young Adult Literature, and *Ironside*.

Holly collaborated with her long-time friend, Caldecott Honor–winning artist Tony DiTerlizzi, to create the best-selling Spiderwick Chronicles. The serial has been called "vintage Victorian fantasy" by the *New York Post*, and *Time* reported that "the books wallow in their dusty Olde Worlde charm." The Spiderwick Chronicles were adapted into a film in 2008.

Holly is currently working on a curse magic caper novel called *The White Cat*.

She lives in Massachusetts with her husband, Theo, and an ever-expanding collection of books. She spends a lot of her time in cafes, glaring at her laptop and drinking endless cups of coffee.

ABOUT THE ARTIST

Ted Naifeh swooped onto the comics and goth culture scene as the co-creator of *Gloomcookie* with Serena Valentino in 1998. Ted illustrated the first volume of the gothic romance hit before departing to pursue his own projects.

In 2002, he introduced us to the world of Courtney Crumrin, a young loner girl who learns magic from her mysterious and curmudgeonly Uncle Aloysius and uses it to navigate her world of school bullies and bloodthirsty goblins, adolescent peer pressure and deadly coven politics. Courtney's adventures have been published in five volumes: *Courtney Crumrin and the Night Things*, *Courtney Crumrin and the Coven of Mystics*, *Courtney Crumrin in the Twilight Kingdom*, *Courtney Crumrin and the Fire-Thief's Tale*, and *Courtney Crumrin and the Prince of Nowhere*.

Ted's next creation was *Polly and the Pirates*, also published through Oni Press, a swashbuckling tale of proper, rule-abiding young Polly Pringle, who is spirited away from her comfortable boarding school existence by pirates who insist that she is their rightful queen and captain. *Polly and the Pirates* was nominated for a Harvey Award.

Ted has also illustrated six volumes featuring video game character Death Jr. for Image Comics, and is the co-creator of *How Loathsome*, strictly for the 18-and-up crowd.

Ted lives in San Francisco, which influenced his aesthetic from a young age with its magnificently spooky Victorian houses, romantic foggy nights, and significant population of Night Things and other fantastic beings.

ACKNOWLEDGMENTS

A lot of people had a hand in pushing me to try writing a graphic novel and helping me along the way. Thanks to Jon Shestack and Ellen Goldsmith-Vein in particular, for asking me about another faery story and liking the one that I told them. Thanks to Steve Burkow for his calm counsel. I am indebted to my literary agent, Barry Goldblatt, and to my editor, the ever-encouraging and amazing David Levithan. And to Ted Naifeh, who brought these characters to life.

I am grateful to Cecil Castellucci, Kelly Link, Justine Larbalestier, Steve Berman, and Cassandra Clare for pushing me to write better and more cleverly. Thanks to Theo for letting me know when things made sense. And thanks to all of you for putting up with my whingeing.

I was greatly inspired by two books, *The Cooper's Wife Is Missing* by Joan Hoff and Marian Yeates and *The Burning of Bridget Cleary* by Angela Bourke. This book was written with the program Scrivener.

— **Holly Black**

I'd like to thank my girlfriend, Kelly, for pestering Cassie Clare into friendship, and Cassie for suggesting me to Holly. Thanks to both Cassie and Holly for not freaking out at us weird San Francisco kids. I'd also like to thank Phil Falco for the gentle, cheerful nudging, and for being a friendly voice getting me out of bed before the day was completely wasted. Sorry it ran so late.

— **Ted Naifeh**